Killing Cold

This is a work of fiction. Names, characters, and incidents are either the product of the author's imagination or are used fictitiously, and any resemblance to actual persons living or dead, business establishments, events, or locales, is entirely coincidental.

Hushion House Publishing Limited
36 Northline Road
Toronto, Ontario
Canada M4B 3E2

Wickes, David

Killing Cold/by David Wickes

Canadian Cataloguing in Publication Data
Wickes, David, 1934–
Killing Cold

ISBN 0-9687968-1-8

Printed and bound by University of Toronto Press Inc.

Toronto, Canada

10 9 8 7 6 5 4 3 2 1

Acknowledgements

As always, many people helped in producing this novel. Endearing thanks to the following:

Karen Parlette and Rick Sirisko, for again enduring the time consuming process of proofing the manuscript.

Chief Rod Freeman, Orangeville Police Service, for answering endless questions on police work and criminality. And for opening doors to other police departments.

Constable Wendy Walker, for enlightening me on sulphur tracing.

Constable Mike Bowman, Police Dog Services with Peel Regional Police, for explaining the roles provided by man's best friends.

Dr Jim Swann, McNeil Products, for taking me through hospital procedures and trauma units.

Michael Tieber, for coordinating the printing and jacket design.

Typography and proofreading by Dane Wong and Oscar Flores.

Jacket design and creative by Boris Folkenfolk.

All the Garveys, for their constant encouragement.

My son Stephen and daughter Lara, for their love and support.

To Bill Hushion, for his insight and knowledge of the publishing industry.

Especially to Michael Crawley, for proofreading, critiquing, and continually sharing his wisdom and vast knowledge of writing and publishing.

And to my wife, Maureen, for her patience and love.

Also by David Wickes

Killing Time

*Killing Time is the debut novel of a major new talent in crime fiction.
Plotted with the precision of a Remington bolt-action, written in prose that
sings like a Samurai sword drawn from its scabbard, this tour-de-force
from David Wickes hurls its reader through countless twists and turns
from the high speed opening to the satisfying crunch in the final pages.
This reviewer looks forward to Wickes' next with considerable relish.*
—Michael Crawley, *Author/critic*

Fast action. Chapter ending 'cliffs' keep you on edge till the end.
—Maurice Doucet, *President Maritime Beauty Supply*

*Great suspense. Don't take this to bed if you have to get up early in the
morning.*
—Daniel Alfredsson, *Captain Ottawa Senators, NHL*

A flat out thriller. Couldn't put it down.
—Kenny Jonsson, *New York Islanders, NHL*

Killing Cold

A NOVEL BY
David Wickes

HUSHION HOUSE

PUBLISHING LIMITED
Hushion House Publishing Limited
TORONTO   NEW YORK

Chapter 1

THE KILLER TURNED OFF THE LIGHTS on his snowmobile. Halfway across the frozen lake the cabin he was headed for was obvious. It was the only one with lights showing. They were controlled by a timer, set to turn on an hour before her arrival. That would give him time to get settled. The woman had planned to come up a day ahead of her husband. Finally his opportunity was here.

The headaches had started again. He'd been thinking about this moment for a long time. Everything was coming together.

He eased his machine onto the shore at a point where it was hidden from the cabin. Most people here had one thousand feet of lake frontage, a commodity rarely found these days on any Minnesota lake.

How many times had he been here to help with their boat, skidoo, or any one of their other fancy machines? This was all familiar ground. It was a nervous time, but exciting as well. Hard to believe he was actually going through with this, but he had to.

His planning had been meticulous. There would be no way anyone could connect him. The wind had picked up and more snow was forecast. Perfect. It would obscure any trace of his visit. It had to be an omen.

When she arrived, he would disconnect the electricity and phone. He'd unlocked the back door earlier. It lead into a utility room off the kitchen where the fuse box and phone cables were.

He slipped the latch and eased inside. After a few minutes he removed his jacket and boots, while keeping the gloves and toque on to avoid leaving any prints or hair at the scene.

He waited for his eyes to adjust to the darker interior. His eyes. Dark brooding eyes. Eyes that never betrayed him, not like...other betrayals. Well, no more.

Now, only to wait. It shouldn't be long.

Chapter 2

ERICA HAD STOPPED at the local store to pick up provisions. As she strode to her Land Rover, her boots crunched the hardened snow. It was a sound she loved. Cold air prickled her nostrils. Pure and fresh. It was glorious to be in the midst of a Minnesota winter, especially at their country retreat. Another weekend in heaven.

Her four-wheel drive easily negotiated the wintry roads, which today were blanketed from the recent snowfall. Over a foot and a half had fallen in the last twenty-four hours. Although the main highway had been cleared, the final three miles to their cabin was over a secondary road which hadn't yet been plowed. Erica slowed to a safe speed.

The late afternoon sun was low on the horizon but still dazzled off the pure, white snow. The countryside sparkled from the sun's rays, like thousands of miniature lights blinking off and on in the pristine fields. She squinted. She felt a stinging sensation as her eyes watered from the glare of the sun.

Her husband, Dan, had suggested she wait till Saturday morning when they could come up together, but Erica was anxious to get an early start to the weekend. She'd driven the route so often in the last eight years she could make the trip blindfolded. The anticipation of an early supper and settling down with a good book before a roaring fire, excited her.

She was looking forward to this weekend. Dan was taking Monday off, a rarity, which would give them three whole days together. She'd ordered a prime rib for tomorrow's supper — Dan's favorite. A 1988 Barolo Enrico VI was in her overnight bag. She could taste the wine and the beef already. Their first evening alone for some time. What a delicious thought. There'd also be time for some cross-country skiing in the morning before he arrived. Erica could feel the fresh air and hear the swish of her skis as she imagined the outing.

There was more snow than she'd anticipated. Still, she was confident of arriving before dark. The final mile and a half was a stretch of rough driving on an old trail, followed by three hundred feet down a private drive to their cabin. It was the only way into their isolated retreat, one of the reasons they'd bought it. After eleven years of marriage and no hope for any children, they had filled their lives with a variety of pursuits.

Erica turned onto the trail leading to the cabin. It was almost dark. There were many turns and although they'd marked much of the route, it would be tricky staying on the narrow path in the dark with this much snow. Some of the drifts were two or three feet high.

She easily handled the conditions, thanks to the Land Rover. The soft voice of John Denver filled the interior. Erica felt the calming effect of his music as she eased forward, concentrating on the twisting path. There were a few small hills coming up, and for the first time she wondered if this had been a good idea. There wasn't enough room to turn around and if she got stuck here, it would be a long walk to the cabin. The outside temperature was minus eighteen degrees. She felt an involuntary shudder at the thought of finishing the trip on foot.

The first few inclines presented little difficulty but the final hill would offer a challenge to driver and vehicle. Dusk disappeared and darkness fell without warning. She started as her headlights picked up an enormous drift halfway up the rise. Erica accelerated.

She crashed into the snow. It flew wildly. The Rover skidded a bit from the impact but Erica made the correction to stay on the path. Snow blanketed the windshield. She turned on the wipers. Now, just one more drift to get through before cresting the hill.

Erica selected low gear in the four-wheel mode to get more traction. 'Crump,' the Rover hit the next snow drift. For a second she didn't move. Then the vehicle began to inch forward. Slowly, yet steadily, the Rover reached the top of the hill.

She breathed a sigh of relief as she coasted down the path, with the cabin now in sight. Having a timer on the lights had been wise. The driveway was well lit. Erica opened the garage door with her remote then stopped well short to leave enough room to plow through the snow and glide into the garage.

The few incidentals she had picked up at McCord's were quickly stored. A phone call to Dan let him know the trip had been slower than usual, but basically no problem. The snow was forecast to stop soon, so conditions would be even better for him in the morning. She hinted at the surprises awaiting his arrival. They chuckled.

Next the fireplace. They always left essentials in the grate, kindling and large oak logs, making it easy to get a fire going. Erica merely had to open the damper, get the chimney drawing, and a crackling fire was underway.

She'd just begun to read when it happened. The lights went out and the furnace clanked to a stop. The only sound was the gentle sizzle of the fire and the occasional hiss and snap as a log erupted. Power failures were not uncommon so there was no need to panic. Electricity was normally back on in no time. She'd call the local store to find out when power would be restored.

There were flashlights throughout the cabin for emergencies such as this. One was on the table beside her reading chair. She found it easily but its light was quite dim — it obviously needed a new battery. There was barely enough light to get to the kitchen phone. After she'd light a few candles.

She picked up the receiver. No dial tone. Nothing.

The phone was dead.

Chapter 3

THE KILLER OPENED THE DOOR to the kitchen and strolled in. Erica Martin, who was looking for the candles when she heard the noise, turned and screamed.

"What the hell? Jesus, it's you! What are you doing coming in our back door unannounced?"

"That's what you're about to find out."

She stared in disbelief. "What's that supposed to mean? Did you come to fix the electricity or what?"

"I'm responsible for both problems. They're not going to be — 'fixed.' I just need some time with you."

"I don't believe this. You need some time with me?"

"You know, some friendly time. I want you." He moved toward her.

Erica backed away. Her defiant attitude changed. There was a puzzled look on her face, mixed with fear.

"Why are you here?"

"I thought I'd made that obvious. I'm going to have you, one way or another. You going to cooperate?"

"Look. This just isn't you. You — you're not yourself. I've never seen you this way."

"Do you like the new me?"

"No. You're beginning to scare me."

"Don't be afraid. Just play along and enjoy." He advanced again.

She turned and ran, but he was on her immediately. He tackled her and they both fell. He began kissing her. He kissed her hair, her shoulder, her face, anywhere he could reach as she wriggled to free herself. She wouldn't stay still.

"Stop moving," he said.

"You stop. I don't want this, or you. Stop it." She rained punches on him.

"Don't do that," he said. "I'll have to hurt you."

"What do you think you're doing now?"

He tried to kiss her again. She flailed at him.

He struck her so hard, her head snapped to the side as if her neck had been broken.

"Now, be still. Don't move."

He shoved her skirt up over her hips, then tore off her underpants. He was quiet now, but deliberate. For a few minutes he was transformed and actually enjoyed the experience. However, the moment he'd finished and pulled on his pants, he glared at her. He was furious that she had given in, allowed him to enter her. She was stunned, barely conscious.

"Why did you do that?" he screamed at her. "What made you do that?"

She was unable to move. "Do what?" she mumbled.

"You opened your legs for me."

He moved around the room hurriedly. The pacing continued as he became more agitated. He roared into the kitchen. There was a large, iron frying pan hanging over the butcher block. He grabbed it and returned to the living room.

Erica was trying to stand up. With a violent swing, he knocked her over. The blow landed high on her head and cracked her skull open.

Erica Martin died from the first contact, but it wasn't enough for the killer. He continued with the beating. Only sheer fatigue made him stop. He stood over the misshapen form that had been battered beyond recognition. He was panting and covered with sweat. Why had she provoked him so? That wasn't necessary. He hated her for what she'd done.

He turned and went to the utility room where he put on his jacket and boots. The snowmobile started easily and soon he was crossing the lake, again with the lights off.

There was a single machine working its way along the far shore on the west side of the lake. It was heading south so he'd have little trouble making his crossing unnoticed. He altered his course slightly to a northwesterly heading. The lights wouldn't be turned on till the other snowmobile was a safe distance away.

The wind had picked up and was now whipping the snow into carved drifts. All the snowmobile tracks were erased instantly. He huddled behind the windshield as the shore neared.

Chapter 4

JACK FELT HER STIR. He curled his arms around his wife, enjoying the smell and feel of her. They hadn't slept in pajamas since the day they married, twenty-three years before. Jennifer snuggled against him, turned, and they kissed. They loved the taste of each other.

He felt her long fingers gently stroking him. It was uncanny how she barely touched him yet there was no doubt she was. Fully aroused now, he watched as she rolled over and descended on him. The movements were tantalizingly slow. She held that pace for several minutes till they both sensed their climaxes were imminent. Not a word had been spoken; there was no need.

She held him inside her as they looked at each other lovingly. Gradually he felt her easing downward, resting her head in the crook of his neck. "It's always so good, Jack."

"I know. The quality is great, it just the lack of frequency that bothers me."

"Me too. Heh, I have to get to my class."

Jack reached out to stop her. "Why not be late? Tell the teacher you had to have one more go with your best friend."

"You are funny," said Jennifer. "Tell you what though, I'll be back by eleven. Think you'll be up to some more?"

"Afternoon delight? Can't wait."

Jennifer wriggled free.

"I'll get your breakfast," said Jack. "What would you like?"

"Cereal and toast will be fine."

Lieutenant Jack Petersen was enjoying this, a rare Saturday off. As a homicide detective with the Bureau of Criminal Apprehension, he seldom knew when time would be his own, but he and Jennifer accepted that as a fact of life. They did have a trip planned in February, only a month from now. It would be their first holiday in three years.

He set the table and organized the breakfast, before watching her finish applying what little make-up she wore. He loved the way she looked, now clad in only her bra and panties, as she moved to get dressed.

"Are you sure you have to go to that class this morning?" asked Jack.

"Don't tempt me. We'll just have to wait till noon. Okay?"

"If you say so." He held her. "That was a hell of a way to start the day."

"Thanks. I believe I do agree with you. Now get out of here before I change my mind." They had one last squeeze, then she gently pushed him away.

She joined him at the kitchen table. "It's so good having you home."

"Maybe the day's not too far off when I'll move up to a desk job. We'd have more time together."

"The sooner the better," said Jennifer. "Just having juice?"

"Yeah. Going for a run."

"Look at this, eight-thirty already. I should be out the door by now."

"Want a coffee to go?" asked Jack.

"Please," said Jennifer as she headed for the bathroom.

Jack pored the coffee, added cream, then zapped it as she liked it extra hot.

One last hug and kiss and Jennifer was out the door. Jack went through his pre-run exercise routine then headed out into a typical Minnesota winter morning. The sun was bright, fortunately no wind as the temperature was five below, which made the day ideal for a run. One didn't have to worry about the cold with all the new running gear — insulated gloves and socks, special wick-out under garments to keep you dry, and a wool toque for the head.

He was through the first mile when the pain came on. Several times during the last couple of months he had experienced minor chest pain when running or swimming. It was never severe, but enough discomfort to make him slow down. The pattern was always the same. Pain early in the run, he'd slow down, it would go away, and he'd finish without any further problems.

He decided it should be looked at. There had been enough incidents to indicate it was time to take some action, much as he disliked doctors. Not really disliked them, just didn't want to hear any bad news. He'd discuss it with David Folk, a brilliant forensic scientist who had worked many cases with him. They were close friends so David's input would be welcome.

He completed the run, cleaned up, then went out to get a couple of hamburgers from a fast food outlet. They were not on a par with the burgers from his favorite, Pete's in St Cloud where his office was, but that was half an hour away. He'd settle for local fare today. Besides, in Jack's mind, there was no such thing as a bad hamburger, just that some were better than others. Jennifer would be home by noon for an ice-skating excursion along with their other planned activities.

The message light was flashing when he returned. There was one call, from Sheriff Sven Larsen. Jack had recently worked with the likeable Sheriff from Brainerd and they'd got along well. He dialed his number.

"Crow Wing County Sheriff's Department, Julie speaking."

"Good morning, Julie, it's Lieutenant Petersen returning the Sheriff's call."

"Right, Lieutenant, I'll get him for you." He heard the call being transferred to Sven's line.

"Jack, how are you?"

"Couldn't be better, Sven. What's happening?"

"Not good news I'm afraid. We had a brutal killing here last night. A young woman, most likely raped, then bludgeoned to death."

"Where did it happen?"

"One of the cabins on Wilton Lake. It's a secluded area, very private. Victim has been identified as a Mrs Erica Martin."

"Who found the body?"

"Special Agent Al Welsh from the B.C.A. The victim's husband had called our office at eight-thirty this morning when he couldn't reach his wife. He was still in the Cities, had planned on coming up this morning. After trying to call his wife but only getting a busy signal, he called the local store, McCord's, to find out what was going on. They hadn't heard of any other phone problems."

"Have you checked out the husband's story?"

"We're working on that. So far he looks okay. The call we received this morning was from the Cities. He claimed his wife called last night around eleven. If that's true, it'd be unlikely he could have driven up here after eleven, committed the crime, then made it back to the Cities. Not with the weather we've had. Also, Mrs Martin had stopped at McCord's around five o'clock last night on her way to the cabin. Told the young girl who served her that her husband would be arriving tomorrow."

"That doesn't mean he didn't surprise her," said Jack.

"I know," said Sven. "We had two detectives from Mulholland's division sent over to give him the news and they claim he was genuinely devastated. His brother is driving him up here now. Forensics have been at the scene for a couple of hours and the body has been sent to St Paul. We're going to need you on this case, Jack. You're the closest to us and the best."

"Thanks. I've worked with Mulholland. I'll have him send that detective's report to both of us. How do I get there, Sven?"

"Come up to Little Falls. I'll have someone meet you at that burger joint you like. They'll have a four wheel drive to take you to the site. Can't make it with anything else. When can you get there?"

"In half an hour."

"Thanks, Jack."

He left a note for Jennifer. Just when they'd found time for each other. Hopefully, the afternoon frolic would only be postponed. He hoped to make it home in time for supper.

Chapter 5

BILLY M^CCORD SHOOK HIS HEAD and trembled. Mrs Martin dead? A regular customer for eight years, she'd been so polite and friendly. Why would anyone want to kill her?

He stumbled in the dark. Where is that darn light switch? He always forgot stuff when things bothered him. Like now, with this killing right here on Wilton Lake. Why was he down here anyway? Oh, yes, the salt. Had to bring out bags of salt for those water softeners. They were heavy too, forty pounds each. No problem for him really, but he'd only be able to manage four at a time, because they were awkward to carry.

He found the light switch. That's better. How many times had he come down here and forgot to turn on the lights? That's why there was a switch at the top of the stairs. He smacked one of the support beams in frustration.

"Billy, where's that salt?" asked Frank. "We have a customer waiting." The tone of voice was polite. Thank goodness Frank was patient with him, even when he was mixed up, which was often.

"I've got it right here, Frank. Won't be long," said Billy. He hoisted the four bags, one hundred and sixty pounds of salt, balanced the load carefully, and climbed the stairs. They were so short of space, a lot of the stock had to be stored in the basement. It was quite a chore bringing the heavier stock back up but that was okay. Billy didn't mind, or didn't think he minded.

The store had been their parent's idea. With more and more people buying property on Wilton Lake, they'd decided to quit working in the Cities and move up to the area. They'd open a store and have their boys work with them. Frank had finished high school and didn't have any serious plans for his future. And Billy, well Billy was struggling in school. Had been all his life. Maybe a move to the country and running their own business would be the answer.

When their parents were killed in a car crash, the two brothers were on their own running the family store, now in its twelfth year. Frank took care of the business while Billy did whatever Frank told him to do. Not that Frank was mean or unreasonable. On the contrary, he continually tried to help Billy. He was always understanding with his younger brother's mental lapses.

Billy arrived with the four bags. He stood there waiting for Frank to tell him where to take the salt. Frank was commiserating with Mrs Cooper, who was a close friend of the Martin's. The load was getting heavier so Billy cleared his throat, carefully. He didn't want to seem rude.

Frank looked over at him. "Oh, sorry, Billy. You can leave two by the front door and take the others to the Cooper's Range Rover."

"Morning, Mrs Cooper," said Billy. "Want me to put these in the back for you?"

"Yes, Billy. The tailgate's open."

He moved to the front of the store before lowering half the load on the floor. Parked right next to the entrance was a shiny, new Range Rover. There were many things Billy didn't understand, but cars were not one of them. He knew all about the luxury four-wheel drive and its off-road capability. Most of the lake people had four-by-fours, all of them in the high-priced bracket. Billy knew them all by heart.

He thought of the late Mrs Martin who had owned a Land Rover, a more reasonable version of the Cooper's Range Rover. He hoisted the salt into the rear and gently closed the tailgate. Poor Mrs Martin. Hard to believe she was gone.

When he reentered the store, Frank was still with Mrs Cooper. It amazed him the way Frank could talk to the customers. Mrs Cooper was a stunning woman, yet Frank had no problem carrying on a smooth and easy conversation. He wanted to do that, especially with someone as beautiful as Mrs Cooper. Not that he would have anything else in mind. Not at all. He was just uncomfortable when it came to talking with any woman.

What woman would be interested in hearing about car engines or motor boats or snow blowers or furnaces or any of the other things Billy knew about? He was only comfortable with one woman, the high school teacher, Ingrid Nielsen. She'd always been kind, not because she felt sorry for him. He really believed she was a better person than that. Anyway, one day he was going to get up enough courage to ask her.

"Billy, Mrs Cooper's decided to take another two bags of salt. Take them out for her please."

Mrs Cooper thanked Frank and made her way to the front door. "Let me get the door for you, Billy."

As she neared, Billy was enchanted. Even with a winter jacket she was so attractive, physically. It didn't take much imagination to know there was a shapely body underneath. Of course he'd seen her in the summer when she wasn't bundled up like now. And Mrs Cooper sure wore clothes designed to show off her figure. Not that he would have any designs on a married woman. However, he was not blind and could appreciate beauty when he saw it.

As she held the door open he was careful to squeeze by, so as not to touch her. That would be improper, even though it seemed Mrs Cooper might want some contact. He couldn't quite understand that but could sense it.

"I can't believe how easily you move those heavy bags around, Billy."

Billy could feel himself start to blush. "No problem when you do it all the time, Mrs. Cooper."

"Here, let me open the back for you."

"Thank you." Billy deposited the bags alongside the others. He could smell her perfume even out here in the cold. It made his head swim. He turned quickly to head for the store.

"Thanks, Billy," said Mrs Cooper.

Billy didn't break stride but nodded and waved in recognition. He'd have been embarrassed to linger and try to say something intelligent. He didn't think he could do that.

Chapter 6

JACK PULLED INTO BERT'S BURGERS at one-thirty. He saw the Jeep with the 'Sheriff' plate but the driver wasn't in the vehicle. Must have good taste if he's in Bert's trying one of the house specials. They were known to use pure sirloin which made for a great burger.

"Are you Lieutenant Petersen?" asked a young officer standing by the entrance.

Jack nodded while shaking his hand. "Jack Petersen."

"I'm Sergeant Matt Erickson."

"Hi," said Jack. "I'm going to grab a burger to go. You interested?"

"No thanks, I'm dieting." He smiled. "Sven told me you'd probably want one of Bert's finest. I'll just wait here."

Jack returned in a few minutes with his burger.

"You can follow me to McCord's where we'll park your car. The road from there to the lake properties is fairly rough and a four-by-four is a must."

"See you there," said Jack.

It took only twenty minutes to reach the store. Jack parked his car and joined Matt in his Jeep. They turned onto the trail to the lake which was narrow and filled with snow.

"I see why you need a four-wheel drive for this road," said Jack as they cut through the heavy snow. "How do you know about Bert's burgers?"

"I was born and raised in Little Falls. Went to the school right across the street. It seems Bert's has been there forever. At least ever since I was born."

"What do you know about this case?"

"Not much more than you do, I expect. Wilton Lake is just inside our jurisdiction and I've followed its development during the last fifteen years. There was nothing out there when I was a kid. It's really something now."

"Did you know Mrs Martin or her husband?"

"No. Actually I don't know any of the 'lake people,' as the locals call them."

"How many are there?" asked Jack.

"There must be over a hundred by now. The McCords would know."

"Are they the family that has the store?"

"Yeah. Two brothers run it. I hear it's a little gold mine. This is the only way into the lake properties and you saw their store right at the head of this road. You have to go by there to get to the cabins, or I should say, estates. These places are really mansions."

"Sven told me about that. I understand there's money on the lake."

"Lots of money," said Matt. "You can see it's a tricky drive with all this snow."

"Obviously the killer made it in and out," said Jack.

"He'd have to know his way to tackle this road at night. Either that or he got there by snowmobile. There wasn't much moving last night."

"Why do you say 'he'?"

"Sheriff heard she was probably raped. They should know that by the time we get there. Al Welsh is at the scene. Heard he's really good."

"Is he new?"

"Yeah. He just got here this month. Came up from the Cities. Eighteen years experience with the B.C.A."

"Sven said Mrs Martin stopped at McCord's last night."

"Wouldn't be surprised. Practically all of them stop there on the way to the lake. Guess you'll want to see the store later," said Matt.

"Yeah. We'll do that on the way back. How far to the Martin's?"

"I think it's a couple of miles, not much more."

"And this is the only way you can get to their place?"

"By road, yes. Unless you go by snowmobile."

Matt handled the Jeep expertly as they fought the heavy snow on the deserted, twisting road. It couldn't be classified as a road, more like an old trail.

"With all the money around, why haven't these people got together to build a decent road to their properties?" asked Jack.

"Don't know. Guess they like the privacy. Sort of discourages any kind of traffic."

It took fifteen minutes to reach the Martin's driveway. They could make out the tracks left by the other police vehicles. Jack had a better understanding of how difficult the trip would be if made in the dark. Anyone undertaking this at night in these conditions would certainly have had to know their way, and know it well.

Matt just managed the last hill before the path crested and gently descended toward the Martin's. He'd been right. This wasn't just a cabin. It was a handsome flagstone, split-level house, perched high above the lake. The shore line was easy to spot, despite the accumulation of snow and drifting that had occurred overnight. There must have been a forty foot difference in elevation from the house to the lake. Snowmobiles were scooting along the middle of the frozen lake. Three police vehicles were parked out front and the crime scene tape was already in place.

An officer waved them over, giving them the all clear to enter the house. The interior was an open concept with the kitchen, dining room, and great room all visible from the front hall. Jack thought the area was large enough for a Vikes practice. Sven spotted him immediately.

"Jack, thanks for coming. This is Special Agent Welsh from the B.C.A. He found the body."

Al Welsh was on the small side, but Jack could tell he was in great shape and probably deceptively strong. He had a winning smile and seemed unaffected by the work he'd just completed.

"I've heard good things about you," said Jack. "It's 'Al' isn't it?"

"That's right and thanks. Heard the same about you."

"Looks like you're just about done. What've you got so far?"

"The victim was raped first. There's proof of intercourse and from the torn panties and skirt, I'd say it wasn't consensual. He then beat her to death with a frying pan. The coroner listed the cause of death as severe brain damage, probably from the first blow. He didn't stop hitting her. Body was covered with bruises and cuts. Guy's a sicko."

"Got the murder weapon?" asked Jack.

"Yeah, he left it right beside the body." Al indicated a sealed plastic bag containing a large frying pan.

Jack grimaced. "That would certainly do it. Any prints?"

"Yeah, probably from her and the husband but you never know."

"Any samples for DNA testing?"

"Not yet. No semen, he probably used a condom. The beating was so brutal there was blood spattered everywhere. He must've had a lot of her blood on his clothing 'cause we found traces throughout the utility room at the back door. It was definitely her blood and she sure didn't leave this room."

"You figure he came and left through the back door?"

"Yeah. It had to be unlocked when he arrived, no sign of any damage, and it was still open when I got here. Don't know if they always left the doors open, or if the killer had a key. Have to wait for the husband, who should be here soon."

"How'd the killer get here?" asked Jack.

"That'll be tough to determine. We had all that snow during the night, and as you can see by the drifting, a lot of wind. Any tracks are long gone. He could've come by road, or across the lake, most likely by snowmobile. We won't be able to tell. When I drove here this morning, it was all fresh snow. There were no tracks left on the road or path coming down to the cabin."

"Anything taken from here?"

"Not that we can tell. Looks like straight up rape and murder. He's a mean bastard, Lieutenant. And strong. Wait till we get the P.M. on her. I think he broke every bone in her body."

"Any ideas, Sven?"

"Not yet. Maybe the husband will help."

"Any local weirdos you know of that might be capable of this?"

"No. There's only seven hundred people in the area, including Wilton itself, which is about four miles from here."

"Only takes one, Sven."

"Yeah, but why a local?"

"This looks personal to me. Somebody she knew. There's no evidence of an extended struggle. The place looks pretty orderly other than the actual spot where it happened. Whoever came in here most likely wasn't a stranger. If that's the case, it should be someone who either lives in the area, or comes up here a lot. Then, if the guy was from the Cities, why would he come all the way to Wilton Lake? He could take her down there."

"It's not that far, Jack."

"True. But a stranger in this place would be spotted right away, wouldn't he?"

"Maybe," said Sven. A vehicle arrived. "That should be the husband."

A visibly shaken Dan Martin came in with his brother Wally. Introductions were made all around, then Dan spotted the chalk mark on the carpet, outlining where his wife had been. Along with all the blood, it was too much for him. Dan Martin headed for the nearest bathroom and promptly threw up his breakfast.

If this was an act, it was a very convincing performance. The man looked like he had been struck down. They still had to ask some questions. Not the easiest part of the job. The guy's just lost his wife, but they don't know where he was last night, so that needs clarifying.

Dan came out looking miserable and Wally led him to a chair in the living room. He wasn't crying but he looked distraught. Although not a big man, he seemed fit. A little less than six feet and about a hundred and eighty.

"Mr Martin, I'm Lieutenant Jack Petersen. We're sorry about your wife."

Dan looked at him blankly and nodded.

"There's a few things I'd like to go over if you feel up to it. It could help us."

Wally glared at Petersen.

"It's okay. I understand," said Dan.

"We'd like you to look around, check if anything's missing. If you see anything at all out of the ordinary, we want to know."

"I'll do that."

"Does you know of anyone who might be a suspect?" asked Jack.

"I don't know what you mean."

"Does either of you have any enemies? Something related through your work, or your wife's perhaps?"

"Not anyone capable of murder, for Christ's sake," said Dan.

"What time did your wife call you last night?"

"It was a little after eleven. Why?"

"It'll help establish the time of death. We can't overlook anything, Mr Martin. What happened after your call?"

"What the hell is this, Lieutenant?" asked Wally. "Is Dan a suspect?"

"The more information we have, the better our chances are of finding the killer. That's not only important in solving this case, but maybe in preventing another crime."

"The timing's sure rotten," said Wally.

"We don't have a choice," said Sven. "We need everything we can get — now."

"We want him too," said Dan. "I'll do my best to help you, but make it short. I'd just like to be alone with my brother."

"We won't be long. The last time you talked to your wife was sometime after eleven?"

"Right. I organized a few things and was in bed at a quarter of twelve. I remember the exact time because I set the alarm for the morning. I was awake at seven-thirty, cleaned up, and phoned Erica. There was a busy signal. I tried again, about five minutes later. Same thing. I..." Dan broke down.

Wally was at his side. "I think you know the rest, Lieutenant."

"That's fine, Mr Martin. I'm sorry about this. Here's a number where you can reach us. Call anytime."

The four officers left.

"What's your take on him, Sven?"

"I think he's okay."

"So do I, but you never know. Let's go to McCord's. I'd like to talk to the girl who served Mrs Martin last night. Ed, have you gone over the back area thoroughly? If he came that way, it would have to be by snowmobile, right?"

"Or on skis. The snow and wind did us in. If there were any tracks, they're gone. We'll give it another look just in case."

Jack glanced back at the lake which was dotted with snowmobiles. "Does everybody up here own one of those, Sven?"

"Just about. There're clubs up here. Members get togther, ride for a couple of hours, stop for lunch, then trek back. It'll take the whole day."

"Matt, look into that for us. Check out every club, everyone who was out on that lake yesterday. We'll set up a command post here. Are there any vacant buildings that would be suitable, Sven?"

"I don't know about that but there is the Wilton Lake Motel. It's just past McCord's."

"How many rooms?"

"Maybe twelve," said Sven.

"That's the right size. See if we can close the motel. We'll need all their rooms."

"I'll call them on the way to McCord's."

"You two check in there when you're finished this afternoon," said Jack. Al and Matt left on their assignments while Jack drove off with Sven. The motel had only one room occupied which would be vacant by late afternoon. Occupancy was down this time of year so they'd welcome the business. Jack called St Cloud Division. He had one of his Sergeants organize a B.C.A. team of twelve agents to meet at the Wilton Lake Motel.

They pulled into the parking lot at McCord's. It had been neatly plowed and there was a vast assortment of four wheel drive vehicles, anything from Toyota 4 Runners to Lexus, Range Rovers, and Mercedes. The place was hopping. Sven said that Saturday was their busiest day with the weekenders and lake people stocking up.

McCord's was a huge log cabin with more character than any general store Jack had ever seen. The floors were rough hardwood which blended well with the massive logs that made up the interior. There was a second level accessed by a wide set of wooden stairs.

You could tell it was well run. The staff were efficient and courteous. Despite the throng of people and brisk business, there was a relaxed atmosphere with customers being tended to with little fuss. A food bar served snacks which smelled and looked homemade. The aroma of fresh baked goods and brewed coffee had its effect and Jack was tempted. Where did he put it all? He had an enormous appetite, yet his hundred and ninety-five pounds were evenly distributed over a muscular six foot frame. And the cholesterol level? What were those pains about anyway? Definitely going to talk to David even though he didn't relish the idea of having to see a doctor.

Sven pointed out a smart looking guy who was one of the brothers. He was talking to a younger couple and showed a kind, friendly manner toward them. Probably commiserating with friends of the Martins. He noticed Sven and excused himself.

"Sheriff, good to see you, but not under these circumstances," said Frank McCord, "And this is?"

"Lieutenant Jack Petersen," said Sven, "Homicide Detective with the B.C.A. He'll be heading up this investigation."

Jack shook his hand. The guy was strong and very good looking. You'd think he was a model, the kind you see in men's clothing ads. Hell, he could probably pose in swim wear by the looks of his frame. The natty sports shirt clung to his broad shoulders and full chest, which tapered to a tiny waist. His smart, casual trousers fit snugly and you had the sense he was aware of his attractive looks. Over dressed for the store?

"We understand that the victim, Mrs Martin, stopped here last night," said Jack. "We want to talk with anyone who saw her."

"Well that would be me and Cheryl Dean. Billy, that's my younger brother, and I take turns closing up on Friday, and it was my turn. This time of year we get by with only two helpers on Friday nights."

"Who was the other helper?"

"Jim Bradford. He'd stepped out for a minute when Mrs Martin was here, so he missed seeing her."

"We'd still like to talk to him," said Jack.

"He's off today, but I can give you his home number if you want to go over there."

"Yeah, we'll do that. Let's start with Cheryl, then we'll talk to you."

"We're kinda busy right now Lieutenant, but if you insist..."

"Yes," said Jack.

Frank used an intercom phone. "Billy, is Cheryl upstairs?"

In short order they heard the reply. "Yes, Frank. There's a lot of customers up here."

"Billy, there's a policeman here, wants to talk to Cheryl. Bring her down and take them back to my office will you?"

"Police? Right away, Frank."

"I'll have to take care of business, Lieutenant. Call me when you're finished with Cheryl."

Moments later Billy McCord came down the stairs with Cheryl Dean. He was a bigger version of Frank. Jack kept himself in pretty good shape, running, swimming, and working out with weights, but he wouldn't want to tangle with either of the McCord brothers.

Cheryl was a petite redhead with a saucy look. She wore a tight fitting blouse, unbuttoned to show some cleavage which was quite ample for such a young girl. Jack guessed she couldn't be more than sixteen or seventeen. She must have poured herself into her slacks which clung to a shapely rear end. She came right up to Sven and Jack and introduced herself, full of confidence and sex appeal. "And this is one of my bosses, Mr Billy McCord."

Billy seemed shy and awkward, but courteous. "Pleased to meet you, Lieutenant. Afternoon, Sheriff. If you'll come this way, I'll show you to Frank's office."

Billy bumped into a display, scattering a few batteries that were featured there. He was obviously embarrassed as he hurriedly picked up the odd battery and replaced them. Cheryl smiled in a knowing way and helped put the display back in order. They continued to Frank's office where Billy opened the door and showed them inside.

"Just let us know if you need anything."

The office was small, with a single desk, two filing cabinets, and two chairs. On the far wall was a well-worn sofa.

"Am I in trouble, officer?"

Jack wasn't impressed. He and Sven were old enough to be her father, and here she was coming on like a sex kitten.

"Sit down," said Jack. He took out his note pad, looked right through her, and started writing. "Your name is Cheryl Dean?"

The saucy smile faded slightly. She nodded.

"Your address and phone number?"

She gave them the details.

"Live with your parents?"

"Yeah. I'm still in school."

"We're investigating the death of Mrs Martin. You saw her last night here in the store, didn't you?"

"Yeah, well I..."

"What time was that?"

"Not long after five. I'd just started work and she was my first customer. It wasn't quite dark yet and..."

"Tell us what happened?"

Cheryl shifted a little uneasily. Most of the cockiness had disappeared. "She'd picked up some milk, bread, lettuce, maybe a few other things, I don't really remember. She brought them to the cash and I checked her out."

"What conversation was there?"

"Nothing too much. Mrs Martin never said a lot. She was a little, you know..."

"No, I don't know."

"Sort of hoity-toity. Don't get me wrong, she was nice. I don't mean to say anything bad about her. I feel terrible about this. I really liked Mrs Martin."

"What did she say?" asked Jack.

"Just like — 'well I guess that's all I'll need tonight.' She did mention that Mr Martin would be coming up today. That's about all."

"And she seemed to behave normally?"

"Yeah. I mean, she was just her cool self."

"Cool?"

"Yeah. She's okay you know. Rich, but okay."

"Did you see anybody else here last night?"

"We weren't that busy. Mrs Cooper was here earlier and a few of the local kids. They're usually around here Friday night for treats and stuff."

"No strangers?"

"Nope."

"What time did you leave the store, Cheryl?"

"I was here till closing with Mr McCord. Nine o'clock."

"You live close by?"

"We live in Wilton."

"Did you see anything unusual when you left — like a vehicle you've never seen?"

"No. There wasn't much happening with the weather we had last night."

"I want a list of everyone you saw in the store yesterday. You think of anything at all, you let us know, okay?"

"Sure, officer." Some of the cockiness returned.

"We'll want to talk to Mr McCord now."

"I'll get him for you. See you." She swung out of the office.

Sven shook his head. Jack nodded. "Bet she's a handful for her folks."

Frank was right outside the office when Cheryl left. He sauntered in, all full of himself. Jack had been using his chair and got up to offer it to Frank. "Not at all, Lieutenant, you stay right there. I'll just sit here on the sofa. Don't get to do that very often."

"Jack, I'll go over to the motel and get things arranged. Be back in a while."

"Thanks, Sven. Mr McCord, you were here last night when Mrs Martin came in. Were you here all day?"

"No, Billy opened up. I started about noon, took off for about half an hour around six for a bite, then came back till closing."

"And did you talk to Mrs Martin when she was here?"

"Yeah. Just the usual greeting. Welcome back to the lake, sort of thing. Chatted about the weather and the roads. Told her if she had any trouble getting to the cabin, just call us. That road doesn't get too much service and it wouldn't have been the first time Billy or I had to go out and help someone."

"You didn't hear from her again?" asked Jack.

"No. Mr Martin called sometime after eight o'clock this morning asking about the phones up here. Said he couldn't get through to his house. We tried too and got a busy signal. Next thing I know the police are out there and we get the terrible news. First time we've had a murder here."

"Who said it was murder?"

"The Sheriff's department. She didn't die of natural causes, they said."

"Did you see anybody around here yesterday who didn't belong? Or any vehicles that you didn't recognize?"

"No. None that I can think of right now."

"Then you stayed till closing?"

"Yeah. I closed up and did the paper work. I always like to balance before the next day. Took about an hour before I got out of here."

"Put together a list of all the people who worked here yesterday, with their phone numbers. Also include anyone you can remember being here. We'll want to talk to all of them. While you're at it we'll see your brother. Thanks for your help."

Jack met with Billy who also hadn't seen any strangers during the day. He did learn that Billy had left the store just before Mrs Martin had arrived. He'd gone straight home, had supper by himself, and watched TV till about ten when he turned in. He knew Saturday was a busy day so he always made sure he got to bed early on Fridays. Jack thought he was nervous and definitely upset with the Friday night killing. Although a little slow and flustered at times, he came across as sincere.

He lived in a small cabin his parents had bought when they first moved away from the Cities. It was on a river that fed into Wilton Lake.

He liked the water but couldn't afford lake front property. In winter he traveled to and from the store on his snowmobile. He did have a pickup truck but seldom used it to go to work.

Sven had returned when Jack and Billy came out of the office. They said good night to the McCords and headed for the motel. The command post was ready. Half the team had arrived and they'd cleared out a room to be used as the statement room. The walls would be stripped bare of any pictures, no furniture except a desk, chairs, and a video camera. They didn't want any distractions when they were interviewing.

Another room was set up as the command center. The bedroom furniture was replaced with desks, computers, conference tables, telephones, fax machines, and other assorted necessities for carrying out the investigation. All motel locks were redone and an alarm system installed to ensure the security of any evidence collected.

Jack had one of the officers call the Cities for two specialists, a polygraph technician and a profiler. The technician would bring the necessary equipment to perform lie detector tests. Although this type of evidence was still not admissible in court, it did serve as a valuable aid during investigations. If they did get a confession, they wanted to be ready.

The profiler would go over all the evidence from the crime scene and autopsy to establish a profile of the killer. Any suspect being interviewed would be taped and the profiler could then analyze them on video to see if they fit the 'profile.'

The first call from the press came in. Jack gave a brief overview, always careful to hold back information that could jeopardize their investigation. More queries would certainly come in as the evening progressed. Jack set up a team meeting for seven o'clock before calling Jennifer.

"Sorry, honey. It's happened again. There's been a murder up here and I'll have to stay for a few hours."

"That desk job can't come soon enough, Jack."

"I know. At least the holiday plans shouldn't be affected by this. We still have three weeks before the trip. Miss you."

"And I, you. I'll be awake when you get here, Jack."

"Thanks. I'll make sure it's worth your while."

Soft chuckles from both.

Chapter 7

INGRID NIELSEN HEARD THE NEWS while grocery shopping late Saturday morning. Like all Wilton residents, she was shocked. In the habit of sleeping in Saturday mornings, she didn't get to the supermarket until noon. This was her first year teaching seniors, and while she thoroughly enjoyed it, the work load was heavier than she'd experienced thus far in her career. Friday evenings were spent organizing next week's lessons and she often didn't get to bed till well after midnight. This left the rest of the weekend open for sports and relaxation, though not always if the work wasn't completed to her satisfaction.

She spotted Ken and Nancy Rowland in the store and approached them to discuss the plans for the ski meet scheduled for Sunday. The Rowlands, in their sixties, still organized many of the winter sports activities in Wilton. Ingrid loved cross-country skiing and competed regularly in fun events as well as organized races. Her Swedish ancestry undoubtedly had a role in her passion for this activity, not to mention her incredible talent.

"Morning Nancy, Ken. Looks like the weather is going to cooperate with you for the race tomorrow." There was a soft, throaty quality to her voice that captivated most men.

"I just love hearing you speak, Ingrid."

Nancy elbowed her husband, playfully. "Yes, we hope the race will be a go. I guess you haven't heard about the murder."

"The...what?"

"Yeah, last night," said Ken. "Erica Martin was killed in her cabin on Wilton Lake. She used to ski with us occasionally."

Ingrid fell against her shopping cart. Her chin dropped. "Good God. I remember her. Murdered? That's impossible."

"I know," said Nancy. "But it did happen."

"I — I can't believe this. Do they know who did it?"

"Don't think so," said Ken. "There's a Sheriff from Brainerd out there now and we hear more police officers are on the way."

"This will shake the community," said Ingrid. "Murder is never good news, but in a small place like this, it'll be even more traumatic. I've lived here all my life except for my university years in the Cities, and this is a first. Come to think of it, Dad was born in Wilton and I've never heard him mention a major crime taking place here."

"Same for us and we've been here, what, twenty-two years now, Nancy?"

"More like twenty-four. Do you think we should cancel the meet, Ingrid?"

"That's a tough one, Nancy. I certainly understand why you'd want to. It's a way of showing your respect I guess. I just don't know. Maybe you should discuss it with others in town, try to get a consensus. Or, if you do go ahead, dedicate the meet to the memory of Erica Martin."

"That might be a good idea," said Nancy.

"Maybe that's what we'll do," said Ken. "Will you be racing tomorrow, Ingrid?"

"Yes. My timing's off a little this year, but I'll give it a go."

"You always say that, then go out and clean everybody's clock," said Ken. "Are you still living with your folks?"

"No, I moved into my own place, but I do look after their house in the winter. Since Dad retired, they go south from October to March."

"Well, take care, Ingrid. See you tomorrow morning. Ten o'clock start."

"Look forward to it." Ingrid moved off to finish her shopping. She normally enjoyed taking her time, buying carefully, and greeting friends. Not today. She settled on a few necessities, checked through the cashier, and headed home.

Ingrid was stunned. She was thinking of Billy and how he would react to this tragedy. He knew all the lake people who shopped at their store regularly. He would certainly have known Erica Martin and would be deeply troubled.

There was no one he could confide with but her. She respected and liked Billy, believed he was a principled and decent human being. Yes, he was slow mentally and a little unpredictable, but overall a good person. She knew how frustrated he became when he was confused and her heart went out to him.

Ingrid entered her small home and after putting away the few groceries, called Billy at the store. She would have lunch or dinner with him, knowing he would appreciate talking to her.

Frank answered the phone. She had never really cottoned to Billy's brother. It was not in her nature to think badly of people as she believed there was good in everyone, it's just that sometimes it takes more digging to find that goodness in some. Frank was such an individual. Occasionally he had slyly attempted to 'come on' to her, yet he was married with two young children. That, she didn't like. He was careful though not to make it too obvious.

"Hi, Frank. It's Ingrid..."

"I'd recognize that voice anywhere, Ingrid. You looking for Billy?" asked Frank in a conciliatory tone that suggested she might have better options.

"Yes, Frank," said Ingrid rather formally. Without another word she heard Frank call Billy to the phone. She knew he wasn't pleased. Tough. How are the wife and kids, Frank? She'd like to throttle him.

"Hullo," said Billy.

"Hi. It's me. How are you today?"

"Could be better. Have you heard the news?"

"I did. It's terrible. Guess you knew Mrs Martin."

"Sure did. She came in here two or three times every weekend. She was a fine lady, Ingrid."

"I remember her from a couple of our ski meets. Billy, would you like to have lunch today?"

"Gee, I can't, Ingrid. We're really busy. The police are here questioning everybody and it's really tough."

"Then what about supper?"

"Can't do that either. It's my turn to close tonight so I'll be late. I could meet you tomorrow though, if that's okay with you."

"Yes, let's do that. I'll be skiing in the morning but should be finished by eleven or so. What if I pick you up around twelve-thirty and we'll go over to Helen's?"

"Okay. Uh...sure you want to go that far?"

"Definitely. I'll make a reservation for us. See you tomorrow."

"Okay. Oh, Ingrid, good luck in the race."

"Thanks, Billy." She hung up.

Ingrid enjoyed her platonic relationship with Billy. Since her fiancé died in a freak accident a year ago, she just hadn't any interest in dating. However, it was easy to be with Billy who seemed indifferent to women, or maybe he was just shy. In any event it was comforting having the company of a man who was simply a friend.

Chapter 8

BILLY WAS HAVING TROUBLE concentrating again. It was ten-thirty, they'd been closed since eight o'clock and he still hadn't balanced the cash. Some nights were just more difficult than others. Today had been really busy, with lots of customers and the police around talking to everybody. He knew the police had a job to do, but did they have to be in the store all day, the busiest of the week?

Finally, he balanced. It was close to a record day, with a higher than usual take from the food bar. They split the sales into two categories, merchandise sold, and food and beverages consumed in their food court. The latter continued to grow. What had started out to be an extra service offering coffee and occasional baked goods, had grown to include hot breakfasts and lunches. Many of the lake people now came in for full meals prior to their regular shopping. It had become a meeting place. With last night's tragedy there'd been clusters of people there all day. You didn't have to guess what they were discussing. Police mingled with little groups and the number of officers grew as the day progressed.

It was past eleven when Billy left the store. His snowmobile was the only vehicle left in the parking lot. Over the years he'd experimented with different routes between the store and his cabin on the Walleye River. He could make the trip in fifteen minutes, or take any number of trails and stretch the trip into a half hour, hour, or longer. It all depended on how he felt when work was done. He'd spent many hours on his snowmobile and knew the routes by heart. Not only those from the store to his cabin, but how to get anywhere in the area.

He still hadn't developed the confidence to socialize and date. He wanted to but wasn't quite ready yet, so he spent extra time on his snowmobile when there was snow, on his bicycle when there wasn't.

Tonight, he just wanted to get home. It had been an exhausting day, mentally and physically. The snowmobile started smoothly. He eased out of the parking lot. His machine was always in good working order as he loved tinkering with it, fine tuning the engine. Fifteen minutes later he pulled into his garage, went inside the cabin and made a cup of hot chocolate. He took the steaming cup into his bedroom, undressed, and got into bed.

He couldn't resist the book, the latest erotica novel that he kept hidden in the dresser underneath his shirts. Despite being worn out he was so excited to begin reading, he shook in anticipation. He felt the usual pangs of desire in his stomach and was semi-hard just with the thought of what lay ahead in the pages of his book.

His fantasies were lived out in these novels. It was so easy to conjure up romantic thoughts and sexual exploits with women he didn't know. He could have them anyway he wanted and they loved it. He didn't have to talk to them or know them and that was the best part for Billy.

He would read as much as he could stand, getting more and more excited with each paragraph, before giving in to satisfy himself. Up to that point everything was wonderful, but once he was spent he would experience a let down, with a feeling of shame and regret. Billy couldn't understand why he felt that way, but he had no one to tell him if this was normal. The only person he could really talk to was Ingrid, and he certainly couldn't discuss that with her.

Sometimes he even thought of doing it with Ingrid but then he would feel really guilty. After all, he liked her, admired her, even...what did he feel toward Ingrid? It was so difficult to figure out.

He realized that people who were not strangers did it with each other. Married couples obviously did it together, like Frank and Jean. Then why couldn't he feel the same way?

He was going to see Ingrid tomorrow. Could he bring himself to talk to her, at least about his feelings toward her? He was nervous and started to sweat just thinking about it.

Yet he felt he would do anything for Ingrid. A single tear rolled down his cheek as Billy feel asleep.

Chapter 9

JACK HAD DECIDED to spend his nights at home and drive the thirty odd miles to Wilton Lake. It took only forty-five minutes and providing there wasn't a serious snow storm or his work days didn't exceed twelve to fourteen hours, he would continue to commute. At least he'd have some time with Jennifer.

After the last case with the crazed serial killers, he'd promised Jennifer a holiday in the Caribbean. The trip had been booked and they were to leave February 19th. They were enjoying planning the two weeks of basking in the warm sun on white sand beaches. It would be their first holiday in three years. Each had forgotten the fun of merely organizing the trip and discussing what they would do and see while away.

Jack arrived at the motel before seven Sunday morning and went directly to the command center. Several computer terminals were arranged on tables at the periphery of the room with charts and files in abundance everywhere.

He began reviewing notes from interviews and the crime scene. Nobody had noticed any strangers or new vehicles on the day of the murder. They'd interviewed the lake people who'd been here on Friday or who arrived Saturday — twenty-eight in all. Every employee from McCord's had been questioned regardless of when they'd worked the past week. Not one unknown person had been through their store during that time.

He couldn't imagine anyone arriving here unnoticed, late at night and making the trip to the Martin place by road. If they did, it had to be someone who had traveled that trail many times — the husband?

A possibility but not likely given the time frame defined by the phone calls, even though the calls didn't prove he was in the Cities.

The husband was at home for the call to McCord's on Saturday morning, but Friday night's call to their home in the Cities only suggested he was there. Mr Martin said he received the call from his wife sometime after eleven Friday night, but they had only his word for that. Yes, a call was made from the house on Wilton Lake to their residence in the Cities, but who talked to who? There was only Mr Martin's version to go on. If other parties were involved in the phone call, Mr Martin would have needed an accomplice. Not out of the question, but unlikely.

Were there others who knew the trail well enough to navigate it at night? Certainly all the lake people for starters. Most of the locals agreed that the killer probably arrived by snowmobile, which were in abundance here. As one resident had said, 'Snowmobiles are like telephones up here — two or three per family.'

What about a skier? Jack knew there was a cross-country ski meet today, one of many they had in the area. There must be a good number of people who participated in that activity. Another note.

There was a knock at the door. Jack turned to see a tall, young man dressed in a winter flying suit and sporting aviator style sun glasses. He removed the shades and came forward with a wide grin. "Hi. I'm Reg Whitby, your pilot. You're Lieutenant Petersen?"

"Yes, Jack Petersen." They shook hands. He had a strong grip, typical of pilots, and steely, crystal clear eyes that seemed to penetrate right through you. They were deep blue and contrasted with his trim, light blond hair.

Jack enjoyed flying and had it not been for his love of police work he would have chosen aviation as a career. He'd requisitioned the pilot and skiplane to get a good look at the lake and surroundings from the air. Although today would be all business, he none the less was excited to get airborne again. It had been a year since his last flight.

"How does it look for our trip this morning?" asked Jack.

"We should be all right. There's some scattered to broken cloud now with a little weather moving this way. From what you told me we'll need an hour, an hour fifteen to cover the area. By then some stratocumulus will be here, giving us overcast conditions and a ceiling of 3,000 feet. Most of our flying will be at 1,000 feet, so we'll have plenty of room. There'll be some turbulence that'll give us a bumpy ride, but nothing to worry about."

"Sounds good to me. I'd like to get it done this morning."

"Well then, are you ready to get some air under your ass, Lieutenant?"

"Definitely. Let's take a look at your maps and get an idea of what we're going to do up there."

Thirty minutes later they were in Jack's cruiser heading for the lake where Reg had left the plane. Reg went through the pre-start checks which Jack followed with interest.

They lifted off smoothly at 65 knots. Reg checked forward slightly to pick up speed, cleaned up the flaps, and climbed away. The frozen lake and snow-covered landscape quickly fell away as Jack again felt the exhilaration of flying.

They'd fly at varying altitudes, allowing Jack to get the detail he needed for his investigation. Reg suggested starting at 1,000 feet to get an initial overview of the area. He'd then make passes at 200 and 500 feet if Jack needed a closer look. They'd cruise at 120 knots but could also cut back to 80 knots to give Jack a better look at any specifics.

Despite the increasing cloud cover, they had good visibility and so far, very little turbulence. Jack wanted to start with the periphery of Wilton Lake, which had a shoreline of approximately twenty-five miles. It was a little more than nine miles long and pear shaped, being two miles across at its widest point. The length of the lake ran north-south with the only road access being the trail from McCord's.

Jack noted that the highway back to the Cities was parallel to the lake, about a mile west. The area between the lake and the highway was solid brush. The entire lake was surrounded by heavy woods although there were some cleared areas.

The highway continued to McCord's, then worked its way northeast to the town of Wilton, about four miles from the store. South of McCord's, the Walleye River entered Wilton Lake. It ran northwesterly from the lake, then turned due west as it passed under the highway, coming to within a quarter of a mile of the store. Billy McCord lived on the river, another five miles further west.

The trail, which had been unofficially named 'The McCord Trail,' ran southeast from the store following the contour of the lake, always a quarter of a mile from the shoreline and the homes of the residents. The only other way to get to any of the properties was by plane — floats in the summer, skis in the winter, or by boat.

There were now fifty-two houses on the lake, all on the north and east side. Each lot had 1,000 feet of lake frontage and was restricted to one dwelling. Some had bought two lots, with plans of building a second house later on. The lots had been numbered sequentially, with number one being closest to McCord's and the latest, number fifty-seven, at the bottom southeast corner of the lake, eleven miles from the store. The Martin's was number four.

"It looks like they're going to extend the McCord Trail around the bottom of the lake," said Jack.

"Yeah, and about time too. It'll run out to the highway giving access to the southern part of the lake. Residents there will have only a three or four mile drive to their properties. As it is now, they have to drive up the highway to McCord's and double back down the trail. That's about a twenty mile trip."

"These homes look like they've been here for a while. Why has it taken so long?"

"Rumor has it that a few parties helped delay the permit. You see that next town about six miles south on the highway? That's Maryville." Reg tilted the plane on its right wingtip and headed south down the highway.

"When you open up the south end, the residents won't have to travel up to McCord's or Wilton for their shopping."

"I get the picture," said Jack. "So McCord's and retailers in Wilton won't be thrilled at losing that business."

"That's it. They succeeded in delaying the permits until a few months back. For the developers to continue to sell lots at the south and west side of the lake they had to have better access. They put their case before the board and finally received permission to extend the trail."

"Let's travel north along the highway back to McCord's and over to Wilton," said Jack.

Reg completed a lazy turn around Maryville to a northerly heading. As they came out of the turn, the plane encountered some turbulence. The small craft shuddered and promptly lost fifty feet of altitude. Jack saw Reg looking at him and he responded by rolling his eyes.

"I think my stomach's back up there somewhere," said Jack. They both laughed.

"You're okay for a guy who doesn't fly too often."

"I wanted to be a pilot, but when the time came for me to start a career, I changed my mind and chose the police academy instead. Later I tried to transfer to the airborne division but I was over thirty, too old by their requirements."

They followed the highway past McCord's to Wilton. The highway, towns, and lake were all surrounded by dense brush although there were some swaths cut out that meandered through the woods, in and out of Wilton and the lake area.

"What're those trails?" asked Jack.

"They're old logging trails, used today by snowmobilers and cross-country skiers. There's a group of skiers now, there must be more than a hundred. Looks like some kind of meet."

"There's only 700 people in Wilton, isn't there?"

"Yeah, about that, but they'll draw from the surrounding area for these races. Besides, practically everyone up here skis or has a snowmobile or both."

They spent another fifteen minutes skirting the town with Jack making notes.

"That's good enough for here, Reg. I'd like a look at the Walleye River."

"10-4, Lieutenant." Reg cranked into a steep bank to pick up a southerly heading back to Wilton Lake and the river. A few minutes later they passed McCord's, located the Walleye River, and banked sharply to the right to follow it away from the lake.

"You'll see the odd home on the river," said Reg. "Billy McCord has a cabin here about five miles west of the highway."

Jack continued his note taking. A secondary road ran along the north side of the river. "Tell me when you see Billy's."

Less than a minute later Reg circled a cozy piece of property cut out of the woods. The cabin was on the small side, maybe 800 square feet, with an attached garage and shed. There was a small dock sitting atop the ice, one of those floating types that can withstand the winter ice and snow. Environmentally friendly, the dock doesn't have to be moored to the river bed. Wisps of smoke curled from the chimney. Billy must be home.

Jack nodded and they continued west along the river. It twisted and turned for about thirty miles before emptying into a small lake, more like a pond. Jack indicated he'd seen enough and Reg again stood the plane on its wingtip to pick up the heading back to Wilton Lake.

Halfway through the turn, the starboard engine backfired once, twice, before sheets of flame bellowed from the nacelle. The oil pressure dropped instantly. A fire or engine seizure was imminent. Reg eased out of the bank, methodically turned off the switches, feathered the prop, and corrected for the loss of power. They'd lost 500 feet during the process and were still descending.

He increased power to the port engine and leveled off. Trim was corrected to ease the pressure of applying excessive opposite rudder, necessary to offset severe yaw caused by the loss of the one engine. A spin at this low altitude would be fatal.

Throughout the entire sequence Jack, who was slightly unnerved, marveled at the composure of Reg as he handled the emergency calmly and professionally. "Are we going to be okay?"

"Yeah," said Reg. "We'll get up just below this cloud base. The extra height will come in handy if we lose the other engine. If that happens, we won't make it back to Wilton Lake. Keep your eyes out for a potential landing site just in case."

Reg radioed in his current situation and position. He estimated fifteen minutes flying time to the lake. It seemed there was nothing but forest out here. The river offered little hope for a landing strip with its continual series of turns. The small plane climbed through 2,000 feet at an agonizingly slow pace. Every foot of altitude could be important.

They continued to scour the countryside for an opening. There weren't any. Another ten minutes to Wilton Lake. Outside air temperature, minus twenty-four degrees. Jesus, that's fifty-six degrees below freezing, thought Jack.

The remaining engine surged once, suffered a slight loss of power, then returned to normal. "What's that?" asked Jack, showing his anxiety.

"Just a hiccup. Not to worry," said Reg.

The radio crackled, asking for an update. "We're at 2,700 feet, estimating Wilton Lake in seven or eight minutes," replied Reg.

The skies were now totally overcast and they were experiencing the bumpy ride that Reg had predicted.

"We won't be able to climb through this overcast," said Reg, "so this is our maximum altitude for the rest of the flight. At this height we'll have only two miles of gliding available if we lose the other engine."

"Will that be enough?" asked Jack, a little too loudly.

"Should be."

"Are you as scared as I am?" asked Jack.

"Not yet," Reg said laconically.

The partly sunny day had deteriorated and they were now surrounded by a dull grey exterior. The little plane bounced around with the increased turbulence. The port engine continued to behave.

"There's the lake," said Reg. "About five miles to go."

Jack thought he'd never seen a more glorious sight. Only ten minutes had elapsed, but it had seemed an eternity. Now they should make it to Wilton Lake.

The plane pitched violently forward and decelerated rapidly. The other engine had just failed. Reg feathered the engine, adjusted the trim, and set the plane up for its optimum speed to maximize the gliding distance.

"Christ, you make it look so simple. What now, Reg?" asked Jack, with a strangle hold on the arm rests. For the first time while flying, he was actually frightened.

"Make sure you're strapped in tightly, Lieutenant, it's going to be close. Our only hope is reaching the lake. There's no other choice."

They bored on through the turbulent skies. No sound.

"One option could be the highway this side of the lake," said Reg. "But with any traffic we couldn't risk it. We still have a good shot at the lake, just have to clear those trees."

Jack tried to remain calm. He urged the plane forward. They passed over the highway. Altitude now eleven hundred feet. Lake about half a mile. Close.

Reg selected fifteen degrees of flap. Jack looked at him.

"Decreases the stalling speed, gives max lift."

They were down to 150 feet. Continued turbulence. Both pilot and passenger were coaxing the plane past the yawning trees. The rate of descent was magnified as they neared the treetops. The forest seemed to be reaching out to the aircraft.

Jack heard a loud crack — the plane lurched as if giant hands had plucked it from the sky. The right ski had clipped the top of a towering oak. Reg jammed the control column forward to prevent a stall. They hung suspended for a few seconds, before gradually accelerating. The plane entered a steeper dive and regained some of its speed.

Jack's stomach dislodged from his throat. Then he looked around. No trees. No turbulence. Only the lake. They'd made it. Seconds later they touched down on the frozen surface of Wilton Lake. The landing was soft. They slowly came to a stop.

Jack looked over at the amazingly calm Reg Whitby who was now completing his post landing checks. "Great piece of flying, Reg. Thanks."

"No sweat. Clipped a treetop back there. Luckily just broke off a couple of twigs. I've been flying these for seven years now and have never had one engine failure, let alone two. They must have been tampered with. Somebody doesn't want you around here, Lieutenant."

Chapter 10

INGRID HAD ENJOYED THE OUTING, finishing first among the women and fourth overall. However, she felt a lack of excitement amid the general apathetic mood of her fellow competitors and friends. Everybody was discussing the Wilton Lake murder. It had captured the town and altered the normal, easy going manner of most.

Ingrid graciously accepted congratulations, saying how fortunate she'd been and encouraged those who had failed to best her time again. She was one of the more popular skiers in the group and well respected in the small town.

She didn't have a lot of time before having to leave. It was normal for Ingrid to run a little behind but it'd be rude to just up and leave without having at least one cup of hot chocolate. She visited a while with the group, everyone discussing the tragedy.

She was anxious to meet with Billy and see how he was handling this. Surely he'd be distraught.

Ingrid showered and changed and was on her way to Billy's by noon. It was only nine miles or so, but it would take about twenty minutes as the road to his cabin was narrow and twisting. Her 1998 Toyota 4 Runner was a pleasure to drive. Ingrid's parents had bought a new model last year and offered to give her their vehicle. Of course she'd refused.

"I have to give you something for your car, Dad."

"All right. You take care of our house when we're down south. In return we'd like to give you the 4 Runner."

Ingrid had insisted on paying something so they finally agreed on a price, which was less than a third of the value. That kept everyone happy.

She was an only child and had a special relationship with her parents.

She arrived at Billy's at twelve-thirty and found him outside and ready to go. He got into the Toyota and while fastening his seat belt, stole a glance at Ingrid. "Hi. Thanks for coming to get me."

"Good to see you, Billy." She gently touched his hand and he started slightly. Although they had touched before, he was always a little uneasy with any contact, especially when they first got together. He usually became more comfortable as the 'date' progressed. He was more edgy than usual so she'd take things slowly.

"Our reservation is for one-thirty. Hope you've had breakfast."

"Yeah. I helped open this morning, then came back here to eat."

"So you have the afternoon off, Billy?"

"No. I have to be back around four."

"That'll be perfect. Gives us plenty of time to get there and back."

Helen's was on the outskirts of Crosslake, an area they both liked. The hour's drive each way would give them time to talk. They drove for a while in silence and Ingrid was thankful she had turned on the CD in advance, providing some background music.

Gradually they began discussing general topics, the weather, the passing scenery, when abruptly Billy switched to the murder and its investigation. He talked non stop for longer than she'd ever heard him.

First it was the murder, then Mrs Martin, then the police at the store, and finally just this morning, the news of the incident in the airplane with the lead investigator and pilot on board.

"I didn't hear about that. What happened, Billy?"

"They lost power in both engines and were lucky to make it back to Wilton Lake. If they'd hit the trees or something, they'd have been killed."

"That's terrible. How could both engines fail at the same time?"

"The police believe someone did something to them."

"Billy, they're not suggesting this is linked to the murder, are they?"

Billy nodded. "That scares me." His face was flushed.

"Easy now. Why does that scare you, Billy?"

"Well everybody around here knows I'm good with engines and stuff. If there's a snowmobile or lawn mower that needs fixing, a lot of them call me."

"Wait a minute, Billy, you're not the only mechanic in town. Certainly one of the best, but you're not alone."

"But they say the person who killed Mrs Martin is a man. He's big and strong, and..."

"Billy, please, that's enough. I don't want to hear you talk that way. First of all it's a little far fetched to even begin to link these two events and to suggest you might be involved, is preposterous."

As quickly as the conversation had started, it ended. They drove on in silence but only for a few minutes. They'd arrived at Helen's.

"Don't worry, Billy, the police will solve this. Let's go and enjoy our lunch."

Helen's was packed as usual. The smell of home baked goods permeated the cozy, forty diner restaurant. If Billy was upset, it certainly didn't affect his appetite. In short order he consumed a bowl of soup, a large salad, two enormous servings of Helen's lamb stew, four or five dinner rolls, three glasses of milk, and two pieces of homemade banana cream pie.

Ingrid settled for a cup of soup, a black forest ham and brie sandwich on an Italian baguette, and passed on dessert. Difficult to do at Helen's, famous for her homemade delicacies. They both ordered decaf coffee.

"Glad to see you haven't lost your appetite, Billy."

He offered a sheepish grin. "The food's sure good here. Heh, it's three o'clock. Can I buy lunch?"

"Actually I asked you, so it should be my treat. However, I'll accept providing it's my turn next time."

"Okay, Ingrid."

The drive back was more relaxed as they avoided the recent events at Wilton Lake. Billy asked Ingrid to take him to the cabin as he had to pick up his snowmobile. She pulled into his driveway and they both got out.

"Billy, I know it's easy for me to say, but please don't worry about things you have no control over. You can't stop people from talking about what happens. It always seems worse in a small community where everyone knows everyone and what they're doing. But it doesn't make them right. I know you're not responsible for any of this."

"Yeah, but you're the only one."

Ingrid reached up, held Billy's face in both hands, and kissed him, not passionately, more like a sister pecking her brother. "That's nonsense, Billy. I'm not the only one who believes in you."

Bill began to pull away but Ingrid, though considerably smaller, held on with surprising strength. "I'm your friend and believe in you, as do many others. Don't you forget that."

She certainly had a way about her. Bright, blue eyes shone with intensity. They highlighted her fine, attractive features — small, slightly upturned nose and an ever present smile, all framed by her gorgeous, flaxen blond hair. And the voice.

Billy gently removed her hold. "See you, Ingrid."

Chapter 11

THERE WAS A THIN SLIVER of a moon that occasionally peeked through the high cirrus cloud. Fortunately for the killer, it produced little illumination, allowing him to move through the dark night undetected. As usual, his eyes easily picked out the trail. Always dependable, eyes that saw and knew.

It was three-thirty, an ideal time for his visit as most people weren't too alert at this hour. Many of the lake people had returned to the Cities Sunday afternoon but there were a few left.

He was an imposing figure. Despite his muscular frame, he was a graceful skier who moved effortlessly through the woods. Surprisingly the episode Friday night had only fueled his appetite for more. He'd found the experience exhilarating. There'd been a brief moment of remorse, but that had quickly faded.

By Sunday he realized he needed another one. This time he planned to take a little longer, stretch things out, and enjoy the experience even more. He was getting hard just thinking about it.

The large house loomed out of the dark. It was conveniently hidden among huge oaks, maples, and cedars. He'd heard the husband blabbing to everyone that he was leaving Sunday due to a busy Monday in the Cities.

Fortunately for the killer, that left an opening he couldn't ignore.

Chapter 12

SUSAN MICHAEL WAS AS CLOSE TO A SAINT as a human being can be. Considerably younger then her husband, she had nonetheless succeeded in raising his two children after he'd lost his first wife to cancer. Susan who was only nineteen when she married the doctor, he was forty-one, had assumed the role of mother to the twins, aged three, with a maturity far beyond her years.

She was the only mother the twins had known. A lasting love had grown over the years. Susan had developed into as responsible and loving parent as if the children were her own. The twins, in turn, doted on their stepmother and in fact were closer to her than to their father. They'd both married in the last year and Jeannine had become pregnant immediately. The baby was due in two weeks. Susan couldn't have been happier.

The phone rang just before midnight. Susan was jolted awake and reached for the phone clumsily.

"Yes?"

"Susan, it's Phil. Jeannine is going into labor. We're in the car now, on the way to the hospital."

Susan was fully awake instantly. "God, she's two weeks early. Is everything okay?"

"I'm fine, Mom, but the pains are now only ten minutes apart," said Jeannine. "We called Dad. He's on his way over."

"Good. Look, I'll leave here right away. I can be there in two hours."

"Why don't you wait, Susan?" asked Phil. "It's starting to snow here and the report isn't good for the rest of the night. We'd rather you wait till the weather improves and make the trip in daylight. As soon as we know what's happening I can give you a call."

"Well maybe. You know I wanted to be with you when your first arrived."

"We know that, Mom, and we want you here too," said Jeannine. "But a trip in the dark might not be a good idea. We've just arrived at the hospital. Will call you soon with an update, okay?"

"All right. I'll be waiting. Love you." They hung up.

Susan fretted about what to do. Her first grandchild was due and she was eighty miles away. There was the Range Rover, as capable a vehicle as one would want in these conditions and she was a good driver. She went into the bathroom to freshen up.

The phone rang again.

"That was fast," said Susan. "What's happening?"

"It's me," said John. "You're certainly wide awake."

"I'm trying to decide what to do."

"I'm with the kids at the General. It looks like it could be a while. The snowfall is so heavy now, it took me twice the normal time to get here. I'd feel better if you wait till morning."

"You know how much I wanted to be there."

"I understand, Susie dear, but you might not miss anything if you wait. My sense is, this will be a long labor. If you leave around seven, the snow will probably have stopped with the roads cleared by the time you get here. My bet is you'll still be in time to welcome our grandchild into the world."

"Well, all right. I'll have to take something 'cause I'll never get back to sleep."

"Good idea," said John. "If anything happens, you'll hear from us. Otherwise, see you around nine."

"Okay, but don't be surprised if I'm there before that."

He laughed and they hung up.

Susan looked outside. It was clear and so far free from any snow fall. She realized the Cities often had different weather, but still it was tempting.

It was nearly one o'clock, and with only one hour of sleep it would be foolish to venture out right now. Susan took a sleeping pill from the medicine cabinet and divided it in two. That should be more than adequate for four hours sleep. She set the alarm for five-thirty, resigning herself to leaving at dawn.

As she turned off the light, there was a sound from downstairs. Was that a door opening and closing? Susan kept her eyes open for a moment, as if to hear better. All seemed quiet. She closed her eyes. The sleeping pill would kick in soon enough.

Chapter 13

JACK WAS NOT PLEASED when he heard the engines had been sabotaged. Sunday, January 23rd would be a date he wouldn't forget. Reg met him for coffee to go over the notes made during the flight.

"You were pretty cool up there yesterday, Reg. Thanks again for saving both our lives with that fine display of professional flying."

"Thanks. Dead stick landings are no big deal, but when you don't have a decent place to set it down it gets a little hairy. I see you've had a few more agents in to look at the plane."

"Yeah, the specialists arrived early this morning. We've been canvassing people who may have seen someone near your plane while you were coming to get me. It was unattended for only an hour, wasn't it?"

"Yeah, about that."

One of the agents hurried into the office. "Excuse me, Lieutenant, we may have another problem."

"What is it?" asked Jack.

"A Doctor Michael called McCord's a few minutes ago. His wife was supposed to arrive in the Cities by nine o'clock this morning. There's been no answer at the house or her car phone."

"Have Patrolman Watson get on to the State Troopers to check out any accidents between here and the Cities. Get the make of car from the husband. I'll take three agents with me to the lake."

The Michaels had lots forty-six and forty-seven at the southeast end of Wilton Lake. The McCord Trail didn't get any better as they drove south down the east side of the lake. Jack didn't like the feeling he was getting with this.

According to the report from Dr Michael, his wife Susan had been anxious to get to the hospital to see their daughter. She was supposed to have left early this morning.

There'd been a light snow fall at Wilton Lake in the morning and there was some evidence of traffic along the trail. They arrived at the Michael's at nine forty-five. Fresh, virgin snow covered their driveway and the path to the front door. No car had left the Michael's house this morning.

They rang the door bell which echoed through the large house. No sound of any movement inside. They rang again. Jack could sense there was nobody in the house, or at least no one that was awake. If anyone was inside, they were either out for the count or...

The front door was unlocked. The detectives entered and called out for Mrs Michael. No answer. Everything seemed normal on the ground level. There was a winding staircase leading to the second floor. Jack instructed the agents to stay in the foyer while he had a look upstairs.

He was moving quickly but carefully. The first entrance at the top of the stairs had double doors, both of which were closed. He drew his gun, then used the barrel to move the door handle down, opening the door with his foot.

On the bed, spread-eagled and tied to the four posts, was a naked woman. Her eyes were open, showing terror and agony. There were several small marks on her body. She had met a brutal and torturous death. He hurried to the body to check for a pulse. The crime scene was being contaminated but the preservation of life always came first. He had to find out if she was alive.

There was no pulse, and the body was already cold. Jack called down to the agents. "Call the coroner and forensics. We have another homicide."

He couldn't help but look at the exposed body and the marks he'd seen earlier. He realized what had happened. Her body was covered in burn marks, most likely from a cigarette. They were everywhere, more than a hundred. Sick bastard.

The bedroom door closed with a bang that startled Jack. One minute he was transfixed by the ugly scars on the corpse, the next he was instantly alert, gun in hand. He looked around the room. Nothing. He saw the window, open a fraction.

He heard someone running up the stairs. The agent burst into the room. "You okay, Lieutenant?"

"Yeah, I'm fine."

Jack pointed to the open window. "I guess when you guys opened the front door, it made a draft and the bedroom door slammed shut. I'm sure the killer's long gone. She's been dead for several hours."

"Jesus, what kind of monster does something like that?"

"A sick one," said Jack.

They backed out of the bedroom and retreated down the stairs, being careful not to disturb any more evidence than they already had. He knew the woman had suffered. This was similar to the Martin case. Brutal murder of a woman, with possible sexual assault. Nothing appeared disturbed, no sign of a struggle, and no forced entry. The killer must have been known to the victims.

Jack described the crime scene to the other agents who reacted strongly over another senseless killing. The pressure would mount till they found the killer. Find him before he kills again.

One officer took up a position at the back door while the others began a check of the outside. They put up the crime scene tape and secured the area. Jack called the command post to get Dr Michael's phone number in the Cities. How many times had he been the one to deliver news of a tragedy to family members? Too many.

He sat in the cruiser collecting his thoughts.

Jack dialed.

Chapter 14

JEAN MᶜCORD LOVED TO COOK. It was so rewarding, especially on nights like this when Frank and the kids were all at the table. He worked so hard at the store, the family was seldom able to dine as one. However, tonight was such an occasion.

Lisa and Wes were ecstatic. They were having one of their favorite dishes, shepherd's pie, they knew there was a freshly baked apple pie in the oven, and their Dad was home. Bliss. As usual Jean was all ears as the kids excitedly reviewed their day in school. There was some sadness they said, due to the murders at Wilton Lake.

"They had special prayers this morning, Mom," said Lisa, "and Friday, there's going to be a, a comm-oration service."

"That's commemoration, dear," said Jean.

"What's that mean, Daddy?" asked Wes.

"It's paying tribute to those who have passed away, son."

"They didn't pass away, Dad," said Lisa. "They were murdered."

"Yeah, I hear that's what they're saying."

"There's police guys everywhere," said Wes. "They came to the school today. They'll catch the guy right, Daddy?"

"Oh, I'm sure they will, Wes."

Wes always tried so hard to impress Frank, whom he idolized. Lisa was a little aloof and more of a mommy's girl. Jean was thankful they were bright and well behaved. With Frank seldom around it would've been difficult if the children were not obedient. The store kept him so busy, she sometimes wondered if it was worth the long hours he had to put in.

Billy was a hard worker but lacked the skills needed to run the business, resulting in longer days for Frank.

"Can we take the snowmobile out tonight, Daddy?"

"Afraid not, Wes. I have some work to do and it'll be an early start tomorrow. We'll try to get out later in the week."

"Aw, Daddy, just a quick ride, like for twenty minutes?"

"I said no. Can't you understand that."

Wes watched dumbfounded as his father stalked out of the dining room.

Jean broke the ensuing silence. "Who's ready for pie?"

"I am."

"Me too."

"Ice cream, anyone?"

"Yes, please."

"Yes — please!"

"Okay kids, let's clear the table, then we'll have dessert."

Dual shouts of 'yea' as Lisa and Wes helped their mother take away the dishes.

After dessert, Lisa and Wes were excused to their rooms to play computer games. Their bedrooms were at the far end of the bungalow with the kitchen, living room, and den in the middle and the master bedroom at the other end. The kids loved this arrangement as they felt they had their own little private area.

Frank was sitting in the den watching TV. Jean let him be. She knew Frank was stressed this past weekend, with the police in and out of the store and the regular business to attend to. She'd just let him unwind.

The talk at the hospital centered on the Wilton Lake murders. The police had been there today talking to some of the staff. Jean had worked the night shift Sunday and was just leaving when they arrived. The police seemed to be everywhere but, she thought, they're only doing their job. Two murders in three days. Hopefully they would apprehend the person responsible and end these tragedies. She prayed that would be the case.

Chapter 15

JACK ARRIVED AT THE MOTEL before seven Tuesday morning. Sheriff Larsen was joining him along with the forensic expert, David Folk, from St Cloud. They'd review the two cases before the team meeting, set for nine o'clock. Jack had worked closely with David in the past three years and held the brilliant scientist in high regard. The feelings were mutual.

The press had gathered in full force. Newspapers, radio stations, and TV networks all clamored for information. Two killings in a remote and affluent area such as Wilton Lake attracted that kind of attention. Jack handled the questions professionally and carefully. He knew there was a responsibility to keep the press informed while at the same time protecting their own investigation. Ten minutes later he'd reached the command center.

Jack's team had been scouring the area for clues and so far had little to show for their efforts. The two women had been sexually assaulted and brutally murdered. Whoever it was had been very careful. With little to go on, he looked forward to David's input.

Was it a coincidence that a snow fall occurred after each killing? Surely the killer wasn't so controlled that he waited for perfect conditions to cover his tracks.

Note for David. How did he travel to and from the scene? Snowmobile? Vehicle? Walking? Skiing? There certainly was an abundance of snowmobiles and skiers here.

"Ah, the master sleuth at it again." David Folk stood in the doorway to the motel room, removed a wool toque, and ran his fingers through his thick, curly hair which although not wild and unruly, couldn't be considered neat and trim. In the other hand was a well traveled brief case, bulging with files.

"Good morning to you too. That brief case must be older than you."

"It does the job, thank you."

"Breakfast will be ready in a few minutes. Bacon and eggs and all the toast you can eat." Jack often teased David about his eating habits, knowing he maintained a kosher diet at home, but ate everything in sight when out.

"I'm surprised it's not cheese burgers. Only eating burgers twice a day now? What discipline."

There was a knock on the door. "You two at it again?" asked Sven Larsen. The muscular sheriff filled the doorway with his six-three, two hundred and thirty pound frame.

"Good morning, Sven. Come on in," said Jack.

Sven and David exchanged greetings and the three sat down to review their notes.

"This guy is big and strong," began David.

"No doubt it's a guy?" asked Jack.

"None. The similarities strongly indicate one suspect. He's careful, very little evidence so far from the two scenes, and mean. Both killings were not only brutal but sadistic." David removed some photos from his brief case.

"Mrs Martin was repeatedly beaten, long after she died, which shows a dramatic change in the suspect's behavior. This was methodically and carefully planned but then he lost it. He was either in the house before Mrs Martin arrived, or gained access without her knowing. The rape occurred first with few signs of a struggle."

"Her panties were torn, David," said Jack.

"True, but he could've been in a hurry and did that with her offering token resistance. Also, we found nothing under her nails. No skin or hair. I'm not saying she merely submitted, but maybe she was too terrified to put up a fight. If she'd scratched him, we'd have a lot more. We're still looking at hair samples but so far there's only the victim's and her husband's."

"What was your take on him, David?" asked Jack.

"I wasn't there but Sergeant Olsen told me he was genuinely broken up. It was the day before the funeral and his brother was with him. Wally gave Olsen a hard time. Olsen did his best to explain they weren't suspecting his brother of the crime, just eliminating his hair type from the evidence."

"The brother was that way with us. But Olsen did feel the husband was okay?"

David nodded.

"That's our take as well," said Jack.

"The second case is different but there are many similarities. Again he seems to have gained access easily with no signs of a prolonged struggle. He subdued her before tying her arms and feet to the bed posts. Then things got nasty. He raped her first, then proceeded to burn her body with a lit cigarette."

"Those were the marks I saw on her," said Jack, shaking his head in disgust.

"The killer strangled her but left no prints. He was wearing gloves and we're working on the material. Maybe there's a fit with the first murder. It's another example of the anger he shows after the forced intercourse. He's not all there. My concern is, will he become more dangerous with time? I don't want to minimize these two homicides, Jack, but things could get a lot worse."

"Meaning?" asked Jack.

"He's a danger right now to mature women. That could escalate to include practically anyone. No one would be exempt from his tantrums — friends, younger women, maybe girls. He's a planner. Both of these cases indicate they were well thought out and organized. This was not a spur of the moment, isolated incident. This profile shows a sick man whose condition will only worsen without help."

"Any idea of his age, David?" asked Sven.

"I would think he's on the youngish side. He's strong, athletic, and virile. That doesn't preclude an older man, but it's less likely."

"When is he liable to strike again?" asked Jack.

"Hard to say. Could be episodical with frequencies varying on his state of mind. Two murders so close to each other as these were, gives cause for serious concern. It's only a guess as to when he would move again."

"When will you have more for us, David?"

"It's a priority, Jack. As you know it's never slow in our department, but we'll do our best."

"Okay, David. You know the urgency. Time for our team meeting."

The detectives were assembled in the motel room. It was only the fourth day, but already the number of files was massive and the hours spent on the case by the twelve officers were more than most people would work in weeks. They had to find some clues soon before the trail cooled off.

Chapter 16

JIM BRADFORD WAS THE HIGH SCHOOL HERO, captain of the ice hockey team, and president of the student council in his last year. He had a huge thing for Cheryl Dean. She was one year behind him in school and they'd dated for most of the year. Since they worked at McCord's, they managed to see a lot of each other.

The whole weekend had been pretty frustrating for Jim. He'd really hoped Cheryl was finally going to come across and go all the way with him. After all, she'd done everything but. The way she waltzed around the store, flirting with every man in sight, even those two police officers on Saturday, led Jim to believe this weekend was it.

Her blouse was unbuttoned lower than usual. It gave Jim the impression she wanted him as badly as he did her. She had no objection to driving out to one of the deserted lover's lane spots and even initiated the heavy petting session. But then abruptly she stopped. That's far enough she had declared. Jim was furious and they had a bitter argument. He called her a cock-teaser and other assorted slurs. They'd driven home in silence. That was Saturday night. He hadn't talked to her since.

He'd worked a few hours at McCord's Sunday morning, then went out and had several beers with his friends. That was entirely out of character for Jim Bradford. Then on Monday night he'd done the same thing. Tuesday was a rough day in school, with a splitting headache from the serious hangover. He arrived at McCord's at four o'clock for his shift, after being tempted to call in sick.

No sooner had he started work when Mr McCord told him there was a delivery for the Cooper's. He loaded the groceries into the pickup truck and headed out along the McCord Trail to lot number seventeen. He was still a bit angry and experiencing the kind of horniness you sometimes get with a hangover. Thinking about Mrs Cooper didn't help.

In the two years he'd worked at McCord's she'd left an indelible impression. Her style of dress left no doubt about her firm, well proportioned figure, of which she was obviously very proud. Her movements were sultry and smooth, designed to attract attention from the male gender. And Mrs Cooper took advantage of every opportunity to ensure she was noticed. Just asking for it, all the time.

He pulled into the semicircular driveway and stopped at the front door. He took four of the eleven bags of groceries and rang the door bell. When she opened the door, he gasped. It was vintage Mrs Cooper. Her blouse was unbuttoned to a point below her breasts, which strained at the tight fitting garment. Her brassiere must have been flimsy as he could make out the shape of her nipples. The skirt was midi length but it had a slit that ran almost to her crotch. He glimpsed the shapely leg that was clearly visible from ankle to thigh.

"Yes, Jim," the voice said huskily.

He must have been staring for too long. "Uh, I have your groceries, Mrs Cooper."

"So I see. Bring them in, Jim."

She eased back slightly from the doorway but it was impossible not to touch her as he made his way inside. She smiled. He went back for the remaining bags. Stephanie Cooper followed him to and from the kitchen, then closed the front door when he reentered with the last of the groceries. Jim had slipped in and out of his winter boots as he made each trip.

"You have such strong arches, Jim, and an amazing physique."

He was puzzled, but looked at his stockinged feet and understood.

"Care for a soda or a drink?"

God, she was the horniest woman he'd ever seen. He was still so worked up about his topsy-turvy weekend he just wanted to jump her bones right there and then. Would he have time for everything he wanted to do? Wonder where her husband is. "Uh, sure, Mrs Cooper. A soda would be fine, thank you."

"Ice?"

"Yes, please."

She brought the glass of cola and her fingers traced the back of his hand as she set it down. She settled on the far side of the kitchen table and took a sip of what looked like wine.

"I bet all the girls in school are crazy about you, Jim."

"Well, not really, Mrs Cooper. There's lots of other guys you know."

"You're just too humble. I see that girl in the store, what's her name, Cheryl, looking at you as if she wanted you for dessert."

"Yeah, well that's all she does, is look."

"Oh, do I detect a little disappointment there, Jim? Something happen not to your liking, maybe?"

"Nah. Not really."

"I don't think so. There's more to it than your admitting. Want to talk about it? Maybe I could help."

Yeah, you could help all right. I'd like to rip your clothes off and take you right here on the kitchen table. He wondered if he should be so bold and let her know what he really needed right now. To hell with the risk. Christ, she smelled and looked so good. He started to wish he hadn't accepted the drink. This could get out of hand. His head began to pound. He was getting hard and couldn't control it. If he had to stand up now, she would see it for sure.

"You're not talking, Jim. Do I not look like I could help?"

She got up to pour some wine. The way she moved was enough to drive any guy wild. Her tight, round ass rolled around suggestively as she slithered across the room. When she returned, the leg show was on again. She must be twenty years older than he, but that didn't matter. It was beginning to get the better of him, and this wasn't planned.

"You look like your eyes are going to pop out of your head," she said, her mouth softening.

"I don't know what to say, Mrs Cooper. You're, you're really something to look at. You're making me wish I could, you know, be closer to you..." There he said it. He was flushed, hard, and shaking. He'd go through with it, right now.

She seemed stunned by the remark. What the hell. She'd just spent the last fifteen minutes brazenly flirting with him and as soon as he comes out with one suggestive remark, things change. Is she another damn Cheryl?

She sat back and stared at him. "Look, Jim, I don't want you to get the wrong idea. I merely suggested I could help you by listening to you, that's all. You know I'm a married woman, and probably twice your age."

"You sit there dressed like that, come onto me, then tell me you just wanted to talk? Look at this." He stood up and titled his pelvis forward showing his erection. "We're going to get it on, now."

"This has gone far enough. You get out of here."

This was it, he moved toward her. He caught sight of a vehicle coming up the trail, heading this way. What if it's Mr Cooper?

Jim ran to the front of the house, grabbed his boots, and flew out the door. He jumped in the truck and wheeled out of the driveway just as Mr Cooper entered from the other side. Jim gunned the engine and started back along the trail. That was stupid and careless, making a pass at her not knowing where her husband was. He drove away recklessly.

Chapter 17

STEPHANIE COOPER REACHED THE FRONT DOOR just as her husband was getting out of his car.

"What was that all about?" asked Craig Cooper.

"He insulted me. That bastard practically exposed himself and threatened to rape me in our own home. He was like a maniac."

"Hold on, honey. The way you're dressed, I'd like to rape you myself."

"That's okay. You're my husband for chrissake. Craig, I'm not kidding, he scared me."

"How much have you had to drink, Stef?"

"Only a couple of glasses of wine. Craig, I'm telling you, it was bad in there."

"Okay. How bad? Did he touch you or hurt you?"

"No, but he was going to. He was mad as hell and surely would have attacked me if he hadn't seen you coming. I tell you, he had a crazed look about him that really terrified me. Thank God you arrived in time, Craig."

"Wait a minute, you don't think he could be the weirdo who killed Erica and Susan, do you?"

"I, I don't know. Hell it was only the Bradford kid from McCord's. He couldn't be a killer, could he?"

"I doubt it, but you were scared."

"Yeah, but not for my life. I thought he might try to have a go with me, but didn't really think of anything else."

"Guess we should report this. You sure you didn't encourage him, Stef? You're a bit of a flirt you know and right now you look good enough to eat."

"Thanks, honey. I probably was a little coy with him, but nothing serious. What if he is dangerous though? He sure looked like he meant business."

"He certainly tore out of here in a hurry. Why don't I call McCord's and find out more about this lad, see if they've had any problems with him or other incidents similar to this? I don't imagine Frank McCord will be very happy about this — one of his employees making a pass at a customer."

"More than a pass, Craig. I'm sure he would have pulled it out if he hadn't seen your car approaching. Then who knows what he would've done. He's strong enough to have handled me without a problem."

"Was he well equipped, honey?"

"Craig, get serious will you? This could be the guy. I know it seems crazy, a young kid like that, but these murders don't exactly make any sense either. Is that any nuttier than believing that a teenager's involved?"

"Right. Maybe you should call McCord. After all, you could tell him first hand what happened. Let's do this now 'cause if he is dangerous, we've wasted too much time already. I'll be right here, and you know I'm on your side."

"Thanks, honey." They hugged and went to the kitchen to make the call. Craig told her to use the speaker mode so they could both participate. Stephanie dialed the store.

"McCord's, Sally speaking."

"Sally, it's Mrs Cooper. Is Frank there?"

"I think he's in his office, Mrs Cooper. I'll check for you."

They heard the line click over to recorded music, then after a slight pause, Frank answered. "Mrs Cooper, did you get your groceries okay?"

"Yes, but not without a problem, Frank."

"You sound like you're on a speaker phone. Is everything all right?"

"It's Craig Cooper here, Frank. My wife will explain."

"What's going on?"

"It was a terrible experience, Frank. That Jim Bradford tried to rape me. He was getting ready to expose himself when Craig arrived. He was angry and scary."

"What? Are you okay, Mrs Cooper?"

"No, I'm not."

"Is he there now?"

"No, he raced out of here when he saw Craig coming."

"Did he have a run-in with you, Mr Cooper?"

"No. He was pulling out of the driveway as I arrived. I didn't know there'd been a problem."

"Mrs Cooper, I'm very sorry about this. That boy is finished with McCord's as of right now. You're okay are you? I mean, he didn't hurt you."

"No, he didn't get the chance. Frank, maybe this is more serious than an attempted rape. Maybe he's the killer."

"Hmm, hadn't thought of that," said Frank. "I'd call the police for you, but maybe you should."

"All right, I'll do that."

"They're set up at the Wilton Lake Motel."

"I'll call right away."

"We'll take care of this, Mrs Cooper. And again our apologies." He gave her the phone number.

Stephanie hung up and dialed the motel. The operator transferred her to Jack's line.

"Lieutenant Petersen here."

"Lieutenant, my name is Stephanie Cooper. I've just been assaulted in my own home." Stephanie Cooper broke into sobs.

"Are you in any danger now, Mrs Cooper?"

"We're okay now, Lieutenant," said Craig. "This guy tried to rape my wife but drove off when I arrived."

"Does your wife need medical attention?"

"No, she'll be okay. She's upset but he didn't harm her. He was going to but when he saw me coming, he took off."

"How long ago and what's he driving?" asked Jack.

"About fifteen minutes ago. He's driving that blue pickup of his. McCord's will have all the info on the car."

"Why McCord's?"

"He works there part time."

"What's his name?"

"Jim Bradford."

"Mr Cooper, we'll get on this right away. I'll want to talk to both of you a little later, say in an hour or so at your house. Is that all right?"

"That's fine, Lieutenant. And thank you." Craig hung up and Stephanie fell into her husband's arms. The crying started again.

Had she really been alone with a killer?

Chapter 18

JACK LEFT THE MOTEL with instructions for Sergeant Matt Erickson to get full details on the Bradford vehicle, advise all team members of the situation, and to send out an A.P.B. to the State Troopers. Jim Bradford was wanted for attempted assault, possibly attempted rape.

He headed to McCord's with Al Welsh.

"Broad daylight and the husband not away," said Jack. "Doesn't feel right for our guy."

"You're probably right but with a sicko like this, who knows?"

"The guy seems to plan his moves, meticulously. This one appears...spur of the moment."

"Maybe not, Lieutenant. Suppose the husband wasn't expected home this afternoon. If the suspect knew that, this could've been planned. It's daylight, but that wouldn't bother him if he knew the husband was off on a trip."

"We'll know more after we talk to McCord and the Coopers."

They pulled into McCord's parking lot where there were quite a few cars for a Tuesday. Frank McCord met them and suggested they talk in the office.

"This is embarrassing to say the least, Lieutenant," said Frank as they seated themselves in his office. "I gave your Sergeant the information on Jim's truck."

Jack nodded. "What can you tell us about Jim Bradford?"

"He's a nice enough guy. Been working here after school and on weekends for about two years. Never had a problem with him. He does have an eye for the ladies, but don't we all?" Frank offered a knowing smile.

Jack thought it looked more like a leer. "When did you last see him?"

"He came in here about four and I told him we had a delivery for the Coopers. He packed it up and left right away. That was maybe four-fifteen or so."

"Then he was working here today."

"Yeah. Didn't you know?"

"Not till now," said Jack. "So until he got here he wouldn't have known he was going to the Coopers."

"Can't see how he would've. What difference does it make? He went there and promptly made an ass of himself, accosting a good customer. She claims he scared the shit out of her. Acted like he could kill her."

"Has Jim made similar deliveries for you before?" asked Jack.

"Of course, many times. I give him and that part time mechanic, Kyle Ott, a few extra bucks every once in a while. Helps pay for their gas and the service is good for our reputation. Jim won't be getting any more though. He's through working here."

"How long would it normally take to make that trip?"

"Maybe thirty, forty minutes. Why? You suggesting I should've called the Cooper's house when he wasn't back in time? And why are you here questioning me when he's out there on the run, after raping and maybe trying to kill one of my customers?"

"Hold it, Frank. First of all, we have a number of officers looking for Jim. Secondly, we don't know exactly what went on in that house. We just want to get an accurate time frame to help track him down. Let's not lynch this kid before we find out what happened."

"Okay. It hasn't been great around here, losing two lake people already, then one of your own employees screws up like this. People likely to talk about this. Won't help our business."

"This Bradford is the guy who lives with his mother?"

"Yeah. His father skipped out when the kid was five or six. Happened about the time we moved up here."

"Any close friends you know of that he might contact?"

"He's been dating Cheryl Dean for a while now. You met her the first day you were here. Redhead. Nice set of..."

71

"Fine," interrupted Jack. "Is she working today?"

"No. She'll be in tomorrow morning."

"You hear anything about him, call us. Thanks for your time."

Jack and Al left, checked the Cooper's lot number, and pulled away from McCord's.

"What a piece of work that guy is," said Al. "All he seems to care about is his business. Two people dead, another maybe assaulted, and he keeps talking about them as 'his customers,' as if that's all that matters. And his comment about the Dean girl — sorry that just doesn't cut it."

"True, I wasn't that impressed either. In fairness the remark about Dean could be just a guy thing, trying to impress the cops."

Jack called Sergeant Erickson to have him send officers to the Bradford and Dean homes. There was no news on Jim Bradford.

The Cooper house was similar to the Martin's and Michael's, large and expensive. Craig was at the door and invited them inside. He said his wife was shaken from the episode but would talk to them.

Mrs Cooper was wearing a baggy, turtle neck sweater and loose fitting slacks.

"Thanks for seeing us, Mrs Cooper. We won't keep you too long."

She nodded demurely. They reviewed the events of Jim Bradford's visit.

"So you were in the kitchen when he made his advances," said Jack.

"Yes. I'd offered him a soda. I usually do that when I have visitors."

"What did you talk about?"

"He gave me the impression he was having problems with his girl friend, so I asked if I could help with some advice."

"Did he mention his friend's name?" asked Jack.

"Oh, it's Cheryl Dean. I knew that."

"What kind of problems?"

"He never really said. He stood up and was getting ready to expose himself when he saw Craig's car coming down the trail. He looked angry and threatening. Then he took off."

"So he never actually touched you?"

"No, but he scared the living daylights out of me."

"I understand that, Mrs Cooper. Do you wish to press charges?"

"Absolutely," said Stephanie.

"Why don't we think about this, Stef?" asked Craig. "If it turns out Jim just got out of hand and is not the killer, he could end up with a criminal record for a stupid mistake."

"We could bring him in for questioning," said Jack. "If it turns out he has an alibi and wasn't involved in either of our two cases, you don't have to press charges. However, given what you've told us, we have to treat him as a suspect. Will you be staying here for a while?"

"We'll be here for the next two or three weeks. I'm semi-retired so we spend more time up here than most."

"We'll let you know when we find Jim. In the meantime, please be careful."

The Coopers saw them out. On the drive back Jack reflected on the interview.

"Something bothering you, Lieutenant?"

"I don't know if we heard the whole story, but what else is new? It bothers me that a young man would lose it like that, make some kind of sexual advance to a known customer, especially when he was on company business. Is he out of control? More importantly for us, is this the first time?"

They drove back to the motel. It was seven-thirty. No supper at home again tonight. How does Jennifer put up with this? After the last case he'd promised to spend more time with his wife. God only knows she deserves better, always being so patient and understanding. They didn't have any children but had talked recently about getting a dog, or maybe two. He'd met a family during his last case who had a pair of German Shepherds. They were like their kids.

Both he and Jennifer liked large dogs. Maybe he should take home a couple of puppies when this was over. He knew a breeder who provided dogs for the police force.

The news at the motel was not good. There was no sign of Jim Bradford or his truck. His mother couldn't believe this was happening. Jack read the report of the interview with Mrs Bradford. He decided to see her himself after grabbing a quick hamburger.

Chapter 19

JIM BRADFORD WAS CONFUSED and upset. What had possessed him to behave that way? Sure the Cooper woman came on to him, dressed as she was and touching him at every opportunity, but that was hardly enough reason to act the way he had. If Mr Cooper hadn't arrived at that moment, who knows what might have happened?

On the other hand she really deserved it. This had been a different weekend, that's for sure. He'd never been through anything like this — ever. He needed time to think this through before seeing anyone. The timing is rotten. He has a serious falling out with Cheryl because she doesn't come across and then hasn't even called her to apologize. Will people think he's a sex maniac?

Jim had driven straight to Billy McCord's cabin, knowing he'd just started work and would be at the store till late tonight. He parked the pickup behind the garage, out of view from the road.

He started at the sudden movement behind him, turned and saw a young doe standing at the edge of the woods. The fawn had stopped and was looking back over her shoulder. Her black nose and dark eyes contrasted with the light tan face. She was so close he could make out the white circles surrounding the nose and eyes. Her upright ears twitched as she gazed at him. Then too soon, the fawn turned and with tail erect exposing her white flanks and rear, she gracefully bounded into the woods.

He loved all animals and enjoyed the thrill of spotting them in the wild. There was a pang of jealousy at the apparent freedom of the young doe who disappeared as quickly as she came into view. A seemingly unfettered life. However, he realized that was not the case. The deer would spend a lifetime fleeing from predators — humans and other wildlife. The deer, like he, was not free from danger and trouble.

What was happening back in town? Had the Coopers filed a complaint against him and contacted the police? There sure were enough of them around. It might be better if he turned himself in but somehow that didn't seem like the best course of action. He'd take the time to think this through. Mr McCord wouldn't be coming home till ten or eleven, giving him another three or four hours.

Chapter 20

IT WAS EIGHT-THIRTY WHEN JACK AND AL LEFT for Mrs Bradford's. He didn't like the fact that Jim hadn't turned up. True, the young man was in some trouble, but to what extent, certainly hadn't been determined. Why had he fled? Although this scenario had no resemblance to the two homicides at the lake, he'd made a move on Mrs Cooper and his actions could have become violent without the timely arrival of Mr Cooper. How violent?

Mrs Bradford opened the door to her modest bungalow and invited the two officers in. She was upset, having heard that Jim was being sought by the police. A pleasant looking woman, slight of build and in her early forties, she showed deep concern for her son.

"May I offer you anything, officers? Coffee or tea?" asked Mrs Bradford, nervously tugging at her dress.

"We're fine, ma'am, thank you. Now you just relax. We have a few questions for you but we don't know at this point if Jim is in serious trouble," said Jack.

"Why are you looking for my son?"

"He was involved in an incident with Mrs Cooper, who alleges he made advances toward her. So far she hasn't laid any charges. The Coopers are considering that now."

"I don't believe it. Jim has worked at that store for two years and has made more deliveries to those lake people than you can count. Never, never has there been a complaint against my son. They don't have enough to do other than count their money, so now they have to stir up trouble like this. Next you'll be telling me, they think he murdered those other poor souls."

"We don't have a lot to go on, Mrs Bradford, but your son is missing. He didn't return to the store after leaving the Cooper's home. We take it you haven't heard from him."

"No, Jim isn't here and hasn't called."

"We want to review last weekend with you. Will you tell us where your son was for the past three days?" asked Jack.

"What's that got to do with Jim and Mrs Cooper?"

"It may be nothing but we have to look at all the possibilities. There's a complaint against your son and now he's disappeared. We have no choice but to track down his recent activities."

"Are you saying he could have been involved in murder?"

"We won't know that till we find him. You could help us and your son by cooperating with us now," said Al.

"All right."

"Let's start with Friday night," said Jack. "Did Jim come home directly from school?"

"No, he was working at McCord's. He gets a lot of work there on the weekends, that's their busiest time. Fridays he goes right to the store after school, gets a half hour break for supper, then works till closing. He came home about nine-thirty."

"What happened after that, Mrs Bradford?"

"We had a little snack, usually do on Fridays as it's a long day for him. After, he went to his room and did some school work. His light was out before eleven. I was watching a late movie and didn't go to bed till after one."

"So as far as you know, Jim was here all night."

"Absolutely. He's dog tired on Fridays and when he turns the lights off, he's gone till the next morning."

"Could he have left the house without you knowing it?" asked Jack.

"I'm a very light sleeper, officer, and my room is right opposite Jim's. He was in his room all night, believe me."

"What happened Saturday?"

"Jim was up early, about five-thirty. He had to be at McCord's by nine."

"Why did he get up that early?" asked Jack. "That would give him three and a half hours to get ready."

"Jim starts every day with a five mile run to stay in condition. He's captain of the school hockey team you know."

"I didn't," said Jack. "So after his morning workout he went to McCord's?"

"We had breakfast together. Jim eats a lot. He's a big boy and still growing, so it takes a lot of food to keep him going. Not only does he run regularly, he works out with weights."

"Did he work all day Saturday?"

"Yes. He was home around six, then had a quick supper and was out the door to see Cheryl."

"Cheryl?"

"Cheryl Dean. They've been going out for a year now," said Mrs Bradford with a look of disapproval.

"You're not too impressed with this Cheryl?"

"She's okay, I guess. A little too brazen for me. But I'm a mom and Jim's my only son, so maybe I'm too particular. Anyway he was very late coming home Saturday, not unusual when he's out with Cheryl, but also Sunday and Monday nights, which was unusual. As a matter of fact he didn't even run Monday or this morning."

"Do you know where he was Sunday night?"

"He said he was out with some friends — same thing last night. Jim's a good boy officer. On school nights he's always in bed early." Mrs Bradford broke down. "Is my boy in trouble?"

"We don't know that, Mrs Bradford," said Jack. "Did he mention who he was with Sunday night?"

"No, but his best friend, Greg Oakley, brought him home."

"We'd like his address and phone number please."

"Sure. Just a minute." Mrs Bradford went into the kitchen.

"I don't like this, Jack. He's been acting strangely for the entire weekend. Now this."

"Yeah, something's not right with him and he certainly fits the bill. Big and strong and known to the victims. Still, it doesn't necessarily come out as murder."

"Here you are, officer," said Mrs Bradford.

"You said Jim was very late the last two nights, Mrs Bradford. What time did he come home?"

"It was after two in the morning on Sunday. Monday night he was home just after midnight. I know that doesn't sound late, but it's well past his normal time for a school night. He's usually in bed before ten and he's never been that late on a Sunday night."

"Can you be more specific about the time?" asked Jack.

"On Sunday night, it was two-fifteen. They made a lot of noise."

"Who is they?" asked Al.

"Greg was with him. There was a fair amount of mumbling and I guessed Greg was helping Jim. He's not a drinker but he'd had too much that night. On Monday, it was just a couple of minutes after twelve. This time I got up to meet him and we argued about the late hour."

"You've been very helpful, Mrs Bradford. If you hear from your son, please insist that he contact us. It'll make things easier for both of you."

"I will, officer. You'll find out Jim's a good boy."

Jack started the car. "If she's telling the truth, he better be able to account for his time Sunday night. That puts him out of the house at the approximate time Mrs Michael was attacked."

"But at home on Friday," said Al.

"Maybe. It's one thing for her to be alert when waiting for her son to come home, but another scenario if he's already in bed. In the latter case she wouldn't be listening and waiting. He could've slipped out and returned without being heard."

"We going to see Oakley?"

"Yeah, and Dean. We'll broaden the search for Bradford. This could get interesting."

Chapter 21

JIM MUST HAVE FALLEN ASLEEP. The noise startled him. Who'd be coming in here at this hour? He'd decided to spend the night in the store, leaving the pickup back at the cabin. He'd been given a key after his first year in case he had to open up if the McCords were not available. It'd happened only once. Somebody was moving about in the store.

Jim checked his watch. It was past three in the morning. It must be one of the McCords. To his knowledge, no one else had a key. He heard the front door open and close. Whoever it was, had left.

Jim was wide awake now. Maybe the only solution was to leave. Take the pickup and drive south. He'd find some small town and settle down to a new life. Lots of people did that. To hell with Cheryl Dean, she'd get hers someday. Too bad he couldn't be the one.

He freshened up and packed some food for the trip, mostly fruit and drinks. He was keyed up now that he'd made the decision. Where do they keep the money around here? There must be some kind of float, maybe even some extra cash. He started at the cashier's area. There were three long counters set to form a 'U.' Below were a number of shelves and drawers.

It was difficult working in the dark but he couldn't take the chance of turning on any lights. After muddling around he decided to get a flashlight. He cupped his hand over the light and continued looking for the float. He found pencils, paper pads, receipts, staplers, elastic bands, shopping bags in all shapes and sizes, everything but cash.

The three cash registers were all open. Nothing inside. He slammed one of them shut with such force the drawer flew back open and smashed his hand. This infuriated him. Jim wrenched the register off the counter and threw it on the floor. The noise echoed through the empty building. He stopped and listened, as if expecting someone to suddenly appear and react to the disturbance. Nothing happened.

He went back to the office and checked the desk, going through all the drawers, then the filing cabinet. Nothing. There was a safe but he had no idea how to crack a safe. There were crowbars in the store. At this hour no one would hear him trying to pry open the safe.

He went to the hardware section and found just the right tool. He took two. As he picked them up and turned to go back to the office, a car's headlights shone in the front window. He instinctively ducked as the lights swept through the store, then were gone. The car had turned onto the McCord Trail and he watched the tail lights slowly disappear. Jim caught his breath.

He hurried to the back office, shut the door, and turned the lights on. The safe was small and should open easily, but it didn't. After fifteen minutes he realized this was not so simple. He hadn't made any progress and was getting angrier by the minute. Where do you keep your money? He whacked the desk with the crowbar. And again. On the second strike one of the bottom drawers popped open.

Jim looked down, saw that some of the hanging files had separated and there was the top of a metal box tucked in below the folders. A feeling of excitement rose in his stomach. He laid the crowbar on top of the desk and reached down to further separate the files. There it was. It looked like a tackle box, but he knew there was more than lures and leaders in this one.

He lifted the box from the drawer and placed it on the desktop. It was locked. There was a simple looking padlock preventing him from checking out the inside. Coins had rattled when he moved the box, so he was sure this was the petty cash. He grabbed the crowbar and after a couple of violent hits, the padlock snapped in two. Jim opened the box and seeing the money, laughed out loud. There was a wad of ones, fives, tens, and twenties and several rolls of coins. After rifling through the bills, he guessed there was more than five hundred dollars. Enough to get him far away from here.

He went out to the front counter for a shopping bag. He stopped. The office door was open and there was the light, streaming out. Jim ran back and shut the door. He picked up a bag, went back to the office and filled it with the cash, then doused the office light before leaving. Still quiet. Time to pick up some food and take off.

There was yet another set of car lights. What the hell was going on? It was nearly four A.M. and that was the second car he'd seen in an hour. He crouched below the counter and waited. Nothing. After a few minutes he stood again and headed for the door. Despite being in top physical condition, Jim was sweating as if he had just come off the ice at the end of a game.

He had to make this look like a break-in. He and the McCords had the only keys to the store. It was easy as there wasn't any security system needed in Wilton. He took a large rock, broke one of the windows, and reached in to release the latch. That would do it.

The two shopping bags, full of cash and food, were heavier than he'd imagined. Should he carry them all the way back to Mr McCord's where he'd left his truck, or hide them here and pick them up later? He decided it would be quicker if he left them down by the river, then sprint over to the cabin. He should go home for more clothes but could he get in and out without disturbing his Mom? That could be dicey. And maybe the police are there keeping an eye on the house.

Jim moved quickly along the path by the river. It was used by cross-country skiers so there was reasonable footing on the packed snow. Besides, it was a shorter route to the cabin which he should be able to reach in fifteen minutes. A scattered condition of high, wispy clouds allowed the moon to shine through, giving him fair visibility.

It was nearly four-thirty by the time he got to the cabin. Too late to go home for extra clothes. He'd make do with what he was wearing, a set of smart slacks and shirt. They'd be more than suitable for a job interview. Hopefully, that would be tomorrow. He should be able to drive all day, sleep in the car, then be in some small southern town by afternoon.

The cabin was dark and quiet.

He opened the car door carefully.

Chapter 22

JACK HAD SLEPT AT THE MOTEL as they hadn't finished up till after eleven. By the time he completed his notes and phoned Jennifer, it was midnight. He was having breakfast with Sheriff Sven Larsen at seven-thirty. There was still no sign of Jim Bradford.

"You have some questions about this Bradford boy, Jack?" asked Sven.

"Yeah. First Mrs Cooper complained that Jim had made suggestive remarks and was ready to make a move on her. She was saying things like, 'He was going to rape me,' and, 'He was so angry, he terrified me.' But when we asked if she was going to press charges, the husband intervenes and says maybe they should think it over. I'm sure we didn't get the whole story from Mrs Cooper. Anyway, we haven't heard from them yet." Jack signaled for the waitress.

"Then the kid just disappears. We haven't found him or his pickup. So why does he run away? Maybe it's a little embarrassing to face charges of sexual assault on a McCord customer while he's on duty, but enough to skip town? Maybe he has more to hide."

Julie Swenson arrived at the table. She'd been at the Wilton Lake Motel for thirteen years. "You guys ready to order? You may want a normal breakfast Sheriff, but the only thing I've seen the Lieutenant eat so far, is hamburgers."

"Is that a fact? How'd you earn that reputation, Jack?" asked Sven.

Jack took a long swig of coffee and gave Julie a warning look.

"Oh, Sheriff, he has a whole menu of hamburgers. There's singles and doubles, with or without cheese, always lettuce and mayonnaise, some with mushrooms, some with tomatoes, some open-faced with or without gravy, and lately a new wrinkle — mayonnaise and Dijon mustard. And I don't think he's finished yet."

"Heh, this is after I said you make some of the best burgers I've ever had," said Jack. "Is this the thanks I get?"

Jack tried to look downcast. Sven and Julie broke up. So did the next table of seven agents.

"I'll have hot cereal and fresh fruit, Julie," said Sven.

"We have strawberries, bananas, and blueberries this morning, Sheriff. Nice to see someone eating healthy food," said Julie, with a glance at Jack.

"I'll take all three, plus an order of two eggs over easy, crisp bacon, four slices of toast, and a large milk," said Sven.

"So much for our health freak," said Jack, smiling at Julie.

"And for you, Lieutenant?"

"A four egg, cheese omelet, with a side of sausages, bacon, and home fries. Whole wheat toast please."

"Four slices for you too?" asked Julie, with her hands on her hips. It was mock defiance.

"Sure."

Julie turned and left. She had a way of getting on everyone's case but you knew it was just her style. Truth is, she was one big softy who adored her clientele but had the personality to insult them and get away with it. Only don't be rude to Julie. That will bring on a torrent of verbiage that would make locker room talk seem saintly.

"You were suggesting Jim Bradford had other reasons to run, like maybe murder?"

"That's the question, Sven. There're as many reasons to believe he may be the killer, as there are against it. And, we don't have a shred of concrete evidence, it's all circumstantial. Anyway he may have an alibi for the Sunday night. We haven't finished those interviews yet."

"Meaning?"

"His Mother claims Jim was out drinking with some of his buddies, both Sunday and Monday night. At this point we don't know who they were. We have one name but he's out of town right now."

"What about Friday night?"

"She says he went to bed at eleven and didn't leave the house till eight the next morning."

"Not iron clad, Jack, but not bad."

"It'd be okay if his friends say they were with him Sunday night."

"Because you believe the two murders were by the same person. So if Bradford is cleared for Sunday night, he's not responsible for Friday's killing."

"Exactly. We'll know more when David gets back to us, but it has all the appearances of one killer. Now, if Bradford can't account for his time Sunday night, then he could've sneaked out Friday without his Mom hearing. That's still a possibility."

Julie arrived with the mounds of food and made a grand display of setting them on the table. "A feast fit for several kings. Happy dieting boys." She gave each a playful head rub.

"Enjoy, Sven"

"*Varsa god*," said Sven. "So he allegedly terrorizes Mrs Cooper, then takes off. Any other thoughts on him?"

"David says the suspect has a problem. He's big, strong, and was known to the victims. He raped both of them. Jim Bradford fits all of the above, except we don't know if he's mentally unbalanced. But if Mrs Cooper is giving us the straight goods, we don't know what could've happened yesterday afternoon had Mr Cooper not shown up when he did. The rest of the story fits the pattern. He gets into the house, apparently the victims are unaware of any danger, rapes them, then finishes the job."

"So he has the means, the opportunity, but maybe not the motive or the crazies," said Sven.

"Yeah. We'll be talking to Greg Oakley — he was with Jim Sunday night — and to Cheryl Dean. Jim was on a date with her Saturday night. You'd think one of them would've heard from Jim by now. Oakley's his best friend and Cheryl's been his steady for over a year. I'd like you along when we talk to these two. That okay with you?"

"Yeah, that's why I'm here today. Booked it off to help you. Who do we see first?"

"Oakley went to the Cities last night for job interviews and won't be back till tonight or tomorrow. We're meeting Cheryl at McCord's store at nine. She's working there till noon, then her classes start. I also want to talk to the McCords. They knew Jim as well as anyone and could give us an insight into his character. More coffee, Sven?"

"No, lets go. Breakfast's on us today."

"Thanks, Sven. What a deal. We borrow the Brainerd Sheriff and they spring for breakfast."

Jack had a brief visit with the agents, having them concentrate on finding Jim Bradford.

They were at McCord's before nine. Billy and Cheryl were already there. Billy explained that Frank had been in earlier to check on the burglary. He'd be back later in the afternoon.

"What burglary, Billy?" asked Jack.

"Oh, nothing serious. Someone broke in through that window, made a mess in Frank's office and the front desk but didn't get away with much. A few food items and some cash, is all. We'll have the window fixed this afternoon."

"You didn't report this?" asked Sven.

"Frank didn't think he needed to. There wasn't much missing so he didn't want to bother the police. Never had one before."

"Well, it's your call. Is Cheryl here?"

"Yeah, she's in the back. You want to talk to her, Lieutenant?"

"Yeah."

"You can use Frank's office if you like."

"That'd be fine," said Jack.

When Cheryl entered she appeared a little subdued, not as pert and saucy as Jack had encountered last Saturday.

"Still no news about Jim?" asked Cheryl.

"No sign of him. We were hoping he may have been in touch with you," said Jack.

"Not likely after Saturday night."

"What do you mean by that?"

"Let's just say, it wasn't a pleasant evening."

"Let's hear the whole story," said Sven.

"Maybe it's personal and none of your business."

"Miss Dean, we're looking for a young man who may have charges against him for sexual assault and we're in the middle of a murder investigation. You'll help by telling us everything that happened Saturday night between you and Jim, and I mean, everything," said Jack.

"You don't think Jim is responsible for the lake killings, do you?"

"Just start by telling us about Saturday."

"This is crazy. Jim couldn't...well maybe it isn't," said Cheryl. She crossed her legs, placed her hands in her lap, and looked down. "We had a terrible fight Saturday night. Jim called me names, swore at me, and I haven't heard from him since."

"Did he hurt you physically?" asked Jack.

"No, nothing like that. But he was plenty mad."

"Why?"

"He, he wanted me to...to go all the way with him."

"Has he asked you before?"

"Not really."

"Did he have any reason to think you would?"

"I don't know what you mean."

"Tell us exactly what happened, Cheryl. Where you went, what you did."

"We went to the movies, then drove out to Wilton Park. We started to, well you know, play around."

"I think I've seen Wilton Park," said Jack. "It's rather deserted out there, isn't it?"

"Yeah. It's sort of a lover's lane at night."

"Did he tell you he wanted to go out there?"

"Yeah."

"And that was okay with you?"

"Well, we'd been there before. It's no big deal, lots of kids go there. It doesn't mean you'll be screwing."

"So, what's 'playing around,' mean, Cheryl?" asked Sven.

"We were necking and stuff."

"And he got pretty worked up, did he?"

"Yeah. Well there's no way I'm getting in trouble, so I said, 'that's enough.'"

"Then he got mad?"

"He sure did. I've never seen Jim like that. We've been dating for a year now and he's never acted that way. Called me names, swore at me." Cheryl held her head and sobbed.

"But he stopped," said Jack.

Cheryl nodded.

"Then what happened?"

"After a few minutes he started the truck and roared out of the park. He drove me straight home, not saying a word. He just stopped in front of my house and waited for me to get out. Didn't walk me to the door or anything. It was as if I wasn't even there. That was the last time we talked."

"Were you frightened at any time? Did you think he might harm you?"

"I don't think so. When you're going steady with a guy and you're pretty serious about each other, you don't believe he's going to hurt you."

"Thanks for your time, Cheryl. If you hear anything about Jim, get in touch with us right away. Is that understood?"

"Yes, sir."

"That's all for now. Ask Mr McCord to come in please," said Jack. She nodded and left.

"Probably fairly accurate, Jack. What do you think?"

"Maybe colored a little on her side, but no more than one would expect. Even if you believe the two women's versions, so far he hasn't done anything more than suggest he wanted to get into their pants. In

Mrs Cooper's case, I'm not even sure about that. Still, it does leave some doubt about Bradford."

Billy McCord knocked lightly on the door. "You want to see me, Lieutenant?"

"Yes, Billy. You know that Jim Bradford has disappeared after having some trouble with Mrs Cooper yesterday."

"Yeah, I heard. Hard to believe. I always thought Jim was a good kid."

"What can you tell us about him?" asked Jack.

"What do you mean, Lieutenant?"

"Anything about his character."

"I think he's polite and he sure was a good worker. Never late and always on the job. He's been part time with us for over two years. You ask him to do anything, he's always ready and willing."

"Have you ever seen him lose his temper?" asked Sven.

"I don't think so. Not here anyway, but I've seen him lose it in hockey games."

"What do you mean?"

"Well he's a big star with the school hockey team. I go to most of the games and he's taken on a few guys now and then. He never backs away from anybody. Got thrown out of a game last year for fighting. They don't allow that in school hockey you know."

"How has he acted with your female customers?"

"Ah — he's fine. As I said, very polite. We've never had a complaint about Jim, not till now."

"Were you in the store when Jim came in yesterday?" asked Jack.

"Yeah, I think so."

"You were or you weren't, Billy."

"Yes, I was. Sorry, sir. I thought I heard Jim's voice, but he was in and out so quick, I didn't really see him."

"When did you last see Jim?" asked Sven.

"Yesterday, I guess."

"When are you expecting your brother, Billy?"

"He's going to be in later. Don't know exactly when."

"Have him call us when he gets here."

"Okay, Lieutenant. Do you think Jim is the killer?"

"We don't know, but his actions lately aren't helping his cause. Thanks for your help, Billy. We'll let ourselves out."

"Let's go back to the motel and call David," said Jack. "We could use his input on the killings. Something tells me it isn't Bradford, but you never know."

Chapter 23

THE INTERVIEW WITH THE POLICE had upset Billy. There was just too much going on around here. First the two murders, then Jim assaults Mrs Cooper and disappears. Do they think he may be the murderer? He found it hard to remember all these events. To top it all off they get robbed and Frank doesn't seem too concerned.

It was three-thirty, kind of odd for Frank to be this late getting back. Billy puttered around, organizing the shelves, and generally tidying up. They both worked all day on Wednesdays with only two other regular staff as it was normally a quiet day.

Frank finally arrived and in his usual chatty, friendly way, took the time to speak to each of the girls. He always showed interest in their people, not only in connection with their work, but in their personal life as well. The staff liked it. Billy waited for his chance, then told Frank they had to talk, preferably in the office.

"Frank, I'm worried. Everybody's talking about the murders. The police were here again, they're coming back to see you too. Jim Bradford has disappeared. Two women are dead..."

"Whoa. Slow down, Billy. Let's take these one at a time. You say the police were here this morning?"

"Yup. First thing. They wanted to talk to Cheryl Dean, you, and me."

"What did they ask you, Billy?"

"Mostly about Jim Bradford. What did I think of him as a person and a bunch of other things. Oh, they asked about our break-in. Do they think he's the murderer, Frank?"

"I don't know what they think, but obviously Jim is in some kind of trouble. Has he contacted anyone yet?"

"Gee, I don't know. Cheryl said she hadn't talked to him for a while. That's funny, 'cause they're going steady — aren't they?"

"Yeah. Anyway, the minute I see him, he's fired. You can't treat one of our customers like he did."

"What did he do to Mrs Cooper?" asked Billy.

"She claimed he was going to rape her if Craig hadn't shown up. He was awfully mad too, she said. Might've done even more to her."

"What're you saying, Frank?"

"Difficult to know. Young strong guy like that, capable of anything. And you know that a guy with a hard-on uses only half his brain."

"Do you think Jim could have...I mean, be the killer?"

"The word is that both women were raped. It sounds like he was looking to do the same with Mrs Cooper. Now what do you think, Billy?"

"No, not Jim Bradford. He's a nice, young man. I don't understand any of this."

"Didn't you tell me he was the tough guy on the hockey team? You go to all those games don't you?"

"Yeah, I do."

"He got thrown out of a game last year for beating up another player didn't he?"

"Yeah, he was pretty mad that night. And that's not the only time. He's a strong guy and not afraid of anybody." Billy thought about all of this. He was even more upset now.

"Billy, don't let this worry you. It's not your problem, that's why the police are here. Let them do their job and we'll do ours. I see you've been tidying up so why don't you continue with that while I get down to some paper work. You said the basement needs reorganizing. That would be a good project to help take your mind off things. Agreed?"

"Thanks for talking to me, Frank. Sorry I'm such a pain at times."

"Not at all, Billy. You're a great help to me, you know that. Now, let's get to it."

"Oh, don't forget to call the Lieutenant."

David Wickes

Billy left the office and went straight to the basement. He needed time alone now. Time to think. Frank's words helped a bit, but deep down he was still mixed up.

Chapter 24

WHEN CLASSES FINISHED, Ingrid went to the staff room at Wilton High and was immediately struck with the mood and conversation. The lake murders of course were still the main topic, but now the missing Jim Bradford was on everyone's mind as well. Jim, in his senior year, was well thought of by faculty and students.

"Ingrid, Jim Bradford's in your home class isn't he?" asked Muriel Bates, the school principal.

"Yes. On Tuesday he seemed distracted. It wasn't the same Jim Bradford. I just talked to his Mother, who hasn't heard from him since yesterday morning."

"How's she holding up?" asked Janice Bertrand, the guidance counselor.

"Not well. Jim is all she has."

"Do you know the police are looking for him? Seems one of the lake people may be charging him with assault — sexual assault that is," said Edith Quinn, the English teacher.

"Now, Edith, is that a rumor or fact?" asked Ingrid.

"It's more than a rumor. The police *are* looking for him. And has anyone asked Cheryl Dean about Jim?"

"Why Cheryl?" asked Muriel.

"They've been dating for the entire year. You never see one without the other."

"I just met with Cheryl. The police talked to her this morning at McCord's. This has really upset her."

"Frankly, the way he carries on with Cheryl, I'm not the least surprised he's in some trouble," said Edith.

"That's not fair, Edith," said Ingrid. "We don't have enough information to know what's going on. Our main concern should be that Jim is missing. His mother is a single parent, who's beside herself with this whole mess. First the police interview, now her son has disappeared. Let's concentrate on how we can help, instead of spreading rumors."

Edith plucked at her skirt with busy fingers, folding and unfolding a pleat. She turned her gaze to the outside window, obviously not pleased with the mild rebuke.

"Muriel, Mrs Bradford needs some support. I'd like to visit her with Janice. Is that all right with you?" asked Ingrid.

"Certainly. Call me later and let me know how you make out."

Ingrid and Janice left immediately. "Take one car?" asked Ingrid.

"Might as well. You sure put Edith in her place, which she richly deserved."

"Don't like to do that but she was out of line. I know Mrs Bradford will welcome our company. Why don't we have supper with her? We can order something in when we get there."

"I have nothing planned, so it's fine with me."

"What, no heavy date tonight?"

"Maybe later," said Janice with a broad grin. "You know me. Have to have one man every night whether I need it or not."

Ingrid laughed at the half truth. Although opposite in many ways, she'd been close to Janice for several years. They'd met at teachers' college, but Janice had left in the second year to change to professional counseling. Now reunited at Wilton High, they'd become close.

Janice was more vivacious and used her ample figure to advantage when in the company of men. As she slid into the front seat, her coat caught on the door handle and two of the top buttons flew off.

Ingrid broke up. "You're one of the few women I know who's so well endowed, you can bust buttons off a winter coat. And look at you. It's still fastened tightly around your almost invisible waist. Miss hourglass herself."

"Thanks," said Janice. She flashed her dazzling smile which was even more radiant with her full sensuous lips. No wonder Janice always stood out and was pursued by most males. The incident lightened their mood which would change dramatically when they reached Ellen's.

Ellen Bradford was extremely shaken. The recent events had taken their toll and she was on the verge of collapsing.

"I don't know if you've ever met Janice Bertrand, Ellen. She works at Wilton High."

"Pleased to meet you, Mrs Bradford. Sorry it's under these circumstances," said Janice.

Ellen Bradford weakly shook the offered hand. She kept her head down, motioned the two women inside before sitting heavily in one of the living room chairs. A box of Kleenex, now half empty, was on a side table. A waste basket beside the table contained the used tissues.

"All of us share your concern, Ellen," said Ingrid. "We want you to know we're here for you."

Ellen nodded without looking up. The shaking started, accompanied by quiet sobs.

"Jim's a fine young man and we're sure this will be resolved. You must be very proud of your son."

"The police..." Ellen faltered.

"We know they talked to you, Ellen," said Ingrid. "They're only doing their job."

"They suspect something," said Ellen, biting her knuckles.

"After receiving a complaint they have to follow up. That doesn't mean anyone is guilty of anything."

"No, I can sense it. There's more on their minds."

"What do you mean, Ellen?" asked Ingrid.

"They think he's the murderer."

"Oh no. That's just not possible," said Ingrid. "I've known your son for four years. He's not capable of such a thing. Ellen, please don't even trouble yourself with those thoughts. You have enough on your mind as it is."

"They wanted to know where he'd been since Friday. The first murder was Friday night, wasn't it?"

"Mrs Bradford, I don't know your son as well as Ingrid, but I can assure you, Jim is definitely not a murderer. He's a well adjusted young man who has the respect of the entire staff at Wilton High."

"Then why are the police questioning me like this?"

"Since Jim's missing, they need every bit of information to help find him," said Ingrid. "It's not a matter of guilt or innocence at this point. I understand there's not even a formal complaint yet."

"Then why isn't Jim here, if he has nothing to be afraid of?"

"He may simply be scared or embarrassed. Since we don't know what happened, it's difficult to assess. We just don't want you to buy trouble."

"You're both kind to be here."

"Ellen, when did you last eat?"

"I had some coffee this morning."

"We'd like to order in some food and join you for supper. Is that okay with you?" asked Janice.

"I don't know. I don't think I could eat anything."

"We're going to do our best to see that you do," said Ingrid. "Besides, you need your strength. We know a great Chinese takeout service, so you freshen up and we'll do the ordering."

Ellen Bradford managed a few small portions before admitting to complete exhaustion. In the last three nights she'd slept a total of five hours. A sleeping pill would help her get some proper rest tonight.

Chapter 25

JACK AND SVEN RETURNED TO M^cCORD'S when they got the call from Frank. It was after seven. He was on the phone when they arrived, dressed like a G.Q. ad. He waved to them, indicating he'd be a few minutes.

Jack looked around the store. He made a mental note to check out the crafts section. If he stayed over another night, he'd bring Jennifer a gift from the store. No, he'd buy one anyway — pick it up today right after the interview.

Frank greeted the officers in his usual smooth style. Too smooth, thought Jack, almost slick. Jack's mind never stopped. Watching, assessing.

"Good afternoon, Sheriff, Lieutenant. Want to talk in the office?"

They nodded and followed Frank. This time he sat behind his desk, leaving Jack and Sven facing him from the two chairs on the opposite side. The chairs were strategically lower than Frank's. This kind of arrangement went out years ago but apparently still suited Frank McCord.

"You have any news on Jim Bradford, Frank?" asked Jack.

"Not a thing. Minute I see him, he's finished. Can't have that kind of behavior around here."

"Has Mrs Cooper contacted you?" asked Sven.

"No. I'll be calling her today."

"We haven't received a formal complaint yet, so I'm not sure why you'd have to do anything," said Jack.

"The idiot practically rapes one of my customers and I'm going to

99

pretend nothing happened? You guys don't understand how a business like this runs. Service and reputation are everything. Success depends on maintaining a high standard of both."

"I can appreciate that," said Jack. "We're saying there's only one side of the story so far, and Mrs Cooper herself hasn't yet laid a charge. What does that tell you?"

Frank folded his arms. "Then why has Jim run away? His own mother hasn't heard from him. He's been gone for over twenty-four hours so he must feel guilty about something."

"What can you tell us about Jim?" asked Sven. "He's worked here for two years so you must have a good reading on him as a person."

"I'd always thought he was a good worker. At the same time he was a charmer with the women. Several times he needed to be reminded about proper conduct."

"Do you have this documented, Frank?" asked Sven.

"No. We aren't some fancy organization with those kind of records. This is just a small, family business."

"But you had to talk to him more than once about coming on to female customers?"

Frank slowly rubbed his lips before replying. "Yeah. It never got out of hand and none of the women complained to me, so I let it go, till now."

"You've made up your mind without hearing Jim's side?" asked Jack.

"I've seen enough over the years to justify this. Besides, it's none of your business how I run my company."

"Have you ever seen Jim lose his temper?" asked Sven.

"No, but Billy has. Says he's lost it several times at the rink, even got thrown out of a game for fighting last year."

"You seem to have changed your opinion of Jim rather quickly," said Jack.

"Wouldn't you if he'd assaulted one of your customers? He was sort of borderline, then does something like this. That's enough to change anyone's mind."

"If he contacts you, let us know immediately."

"Sure," said Frank.

"Billy said you had a break-in last night."

"Yeah, minor thing."

"Why didn't you report it to us?"

"You guys are busy enough. It didn't seem important enough to get you involved. I'm not concerned."

"Thanks for your time," said Jack. "We'll let ourselves out."

As Jack and Sven passed the crafts section, Jack stopped. "Give me a few minutes, Sven. I want to pick up something for Jennifer."

In no time a woman was at his side. "Hi, I'm Donna. May I help you?"

After a brief explanation of what he was looking for, Donna showed him an attractive, hand painted duck that featured a hard, bristle brush on its back. "Keep this at your front door for guests to clean their boots. It's functional and decorative."

It was perfect for Jennifer. She was a nature lover, particularly fond of ducks. Not a romantic gift, but it's the thought. "Sold," said Jack.

Frank came out while they were at the cash desk.

"Hold it, Donna," he said. "These gentlemen are entitled to the corporate discount. Give him twenty per cent off." He flashed a big grin at Jack, then returned to his office.

"What was that all about?" asked Sven.

"Hard to say. Either goodwill or brown-nosing. Probably the latter."

They returned to the motel headquarters where there was a message waiting for Jack. A Mrs Shirley Davenport had called and wanted to see one of the detectives as soon as possible.

"Who is Mrs Davenport?" asked Jack.

"Betcha Julie will know," said Matt.

"Good idea. Any word on the Oakley kid?"

"Still in the Cities, according to his parents. They know we want to see him."

"Keep on it, Matt. Either he gets here today or we have someone see him in the Cities."

Jack found Julie relaxing over a piece of pie and coffee. Well deserved as she worked most of the day alone and had been here since five-thirty this morning.

"Hello again, good looking."

"Hmpf. You guys never change. Looking for a quick fix, like a double burger? You haven't eaten in what, two hours?"

"No, I'm fine for a while. Julie, do you know Shirley Davenport?" asked Jack.

"Who doesn't? Shirley lives alone, just outside of town. Lost her husband about three years ago. She must be close to eighty now, but sharp as a tack."

"Where does she live?"

"Her property is on the Walleye River, about ten miles west of the main highway."

Chapter 26

INGRID AND JANICE LEFT the Bradford home shortly after eight. They were pleased Ellen had managed some supper, then got to bed at an early hour, hopefully for a sound sleep.

"It must be difficult raising a son on your own, then be faced with something like this," said Ingrid.

"Yes. She really appreciated our company. You're so thoughtful, Ingrid, always helping out. It's only one of the qualities I admire in you, and that voice of yours. If I could sound like that, I'd have to beat them off with a stick."

"Don't you anyway?"

"I wish. Thanks for being my best friend."

"At least of the female gender, Janice." They both laughed. "This has certainly been an upsetting week, even worse with Jim's disappearance. Ellen's not only worried about that, she believes the police think he's a murder suspect."

"We know that's ridiculous," said Janice. "I'm not an analyst or therapist, but my work has broadened my insight into people. If he's that disturbed inside and I didn't see it, maybe I should find another line of work."

"You and me both. He's been in my home class for three of the last four years, and I can't believe he's a deranged killer. Let's hope this gets sorted out quickly."

They pulled into the school parking lot.

"Thanks for coming with me tonight, Janice. Hope you can still make your rendezvous. Anyone I know?"

"I can't tell you right now. It's a little complicated."

"Janice, what's that supposed to mean?"

"I know it doesn't sound very good and I should be able to confide in you. Especially you. I just can't do that right now. You'll have to trust me on this for a while. Please?"

"Of course I trust you. I don't want you hurt, that's all."

"I know. Let's stay in touch with Ellen till Jim turns up."

"Definitely," said Ingrid. "See you tomorrow."

Ingrid couldn't help but reflect on Janice's comment. There were any number of scenarios she could imagine. Was she dating a co-worker which was taboo, a married man, or perhaps even worse, a student? Enough of this. She'd just have to put these thoughts aside and trust her friend's judgement. Still, with affairs of the heart...

Her tiny bungalow was about a mile out of town. It had been built forty years before by a trapper who'd lived alone. He'd passed away last summer and with no family, had willed the home to the town, dictating they were to auction off the property and give the proceeds to the Heart and Stroke Foundation. With a loan from her parents, Ingrid had outbid two others and became the proud owner of her first house.

She was pleased now, but it'd taken three months of cleaning and painting to make the place liveable. It seems the trapper wasn't too fussy about cleanliness or pleasant surroundings. It was isolated but that didn't bother Ingrid. At least until now.

For the first time since the tragic events on Wilton Lake, she entered her house with some trepidation. A chill went through her as she went from room to room, turning on all the lights. It didn't take long, with only four rooms including the bathroom. She then locked the two outside doors. This was crazy. She was going to get a dog tomorrow. There were two good breeders in town, one with Golden Retrievers, the other German Shepherds. Both appealed to her.

Ingrid had grown up with dogs. Her parents always had at least one at home. Most were mongrels, but wonderful pets. When their last dog died two years ago, they decided not to get another. With her Dad's retirement, her parents were going to travel frequently and spend the winters down south. Neither life style suited a dog in their lives.

Ingrid could easily come home at noon to take care of her pet. This was exciting. She wanted to find out how Billy was and who better to tell about her new plans. She put some coffee on and dialed his number. He answered after the first ring.

"Hullo."

"Hi Billy, it's me. How are you?"

"Oh, Ingrid. Hi. I'm okay thanks and you?"

"I'm fine but worried about Jim Bradford. Janice and I saw Ellen Bradford tonight. She's really upset."

"I'll bet. Nobody's seen him since he left the Cooper's. What do you think about this, Ingrid?"

"It's hard to believe he'd act this way. We certainly don't believe he's involved in the murders, do you?"

"Nah," said Billy, "neither do I. And the Mrs Cooper thing. I'm not even sure about that."

"Why do you say that?"

"Well, it's kind of difficult to talk about."

"You can tell me, Billy."

"Well, Mrs Cooper sort of flirts with a lot with men, you know what I mean?"

"I think so. That's not necessarily bad."

"No, I guess not," said Billy. "It's...I think she might have lead him on a bit, Ingrid."

"We won't know till we hear both sides of the story. I tend to favor Jim Bradford, but who knows."

"I just wish we could get back to normal. Something bad is happening every day. It bothers me, Ingrid."

"I can imagine. Let's change the subject. I have some exciting news for you, Billy. I'm going to get a dog, maybe two. Would you like to go to the kennels with me tomorrow and help pick out my new friends?"

"Sure I would. What kind are you thinking about?"

"I'd like a big dog. When I came home tonight, I was actually a little scared. I guess it's all the trouble lately, and living out here alone — well, it just got to me. I need a dog for company and protection."

"There's a German Shepherd breeder here isn't there?"

"Yes, just out of town, on the way to your store. Also, at the other end of town, the Carlings breed Golden Retrievers. I'd like to look at both."

"I could meet you right after school, Ingrid. Is that okay?"

"That should work. Why don't I call you when I'm ready to leave? Will you be at the store?"

"Yeah. I'll bring my truck so I can meet you at the kennel."

"Thanks, Billy. See you tomorrow."

They hung up and the realization of being alone struck her. It had been comforting talking on the phone, but now she felt uneasy. Strange she should feel this way all of a sudden, after having lived here for half a year. What a couple of nasty murders will do to you.

Regardless of the motivation for getting a dog, she would enjoy having one or two around. The way this night was going, it couldn't be too soon.

Chapter 27

JACK CALLED MRS DAVENPORT. Although it was past eight-thirty, she sounded bright and insisted the officers come out to her house tonight. This couldn't wait.

The press had got wind of the Bradford story and were positioned in the reception area of the motel. Many had taken up residence in Wilton as the case was now in its fifth day. Sven and Jack fielded most of the questions before stating they had business to attend to.

"We're going to have to find a better way to get out of here if this keeps up," said Jack.

"Don't like being a TV star, Jack?" Sven grinned.

"Yeah. The Commissioner really appreciates the ratings."

The road along the Walleye River wasn't a lot better than the McCord Trail. The lights were on in Billy's cabin when they drove by. Although they passed a few other homes, it was the only sign of life till they reached Shirley Davenport's. The lengthy driveway had been freshly plowed, as well as the path to the front door. Could she possibly have cleaned away the snow herself?

Jack was impressed immediately when she answered the door. The woman had an excellent posture and friendly manner as she welcomed them to her home. Her appearance was immaculate with just the right amount of makeup, smart clothes, and a full head of perfectly white hair which was neatly coiffed. For a woman of eighty odd years, living alone, she obviously took great pride in herself and her home, which was spotless and handsomely decorated. Her handshake and voice were strong.

Introductions were made and she thanked the officers for coming out so quickly.

"Do you have someone clear your driveway for you, Mrs Davenport?" asked Jack.

"Not at all. I take care of the snow shoveling. It helps keep me in shape. I do prefer the summers as gardening is my favorite, but I don't mind winter. I quite enjoy cross-country skiing, although I don't go as far as I used to. Come on in gentlemen. May I offer you a drink?"

"No thank you, ma'am," said Jack. "You have something to tell us?"

"Yes I do. I thought about it all day, then decided I better call you. Early this morning, I woke up to go to the bathroom. As I returned to bed I saw the tail lights of a truck heading down the road. This was highly unusual because there's nothing past my house but an old, deserted shack. Hasn't been anyone down there for over a year."

"So the truck was going west," said Jack.

"Yes. It turned off the road about where the old shack is and headed for the river. I could see the truck while its lights were on. Then they went out. This got my curiosity, so I picked up the binoculars which I always have handy for the wild life. There's so much to look at here, I never want to miss an opportunity. However, even with the moonlight, I couldn't make out anything."

"About how far away was the truck?"

"Oh, maybe three hundred yards. I can show you from my bedroom window. Once the lights went out I couldn't see the truck anymore."

They went to the bedroom which had two windows facing south and west. The river was clearly in view but that was about it.

"The river is at its widest and deepest here," said Mrs Davenport. "My husband loved to fish and he caught many a fine trout off our own dock. He used to say there's sixty feet of water right here."

"What happened next, Mrs Davenport?"

"Nothing, until maybe five or ten minutes later, I see this skier coming along the road heading back toward town."

"The moon's pretty bright right now, did you have the same visibility last night?" asked Jack.

"Almost as good. Now, why would someone drive out here, leave his truck and ski home? I didn't give it any more thought till this afternoon when I went for my usual cross-country skiing outing. As I passed the shack, I expected to see the truck there, but there was nothing. Then I saw tire tracks in the snow that led out to the river. Did that truck sink through the ice? I stewed over that for hours. It's a terrible thought, but where else could it be?"

"You might have a point. Can you describe the skier?"

"I'm positive it was a man. He was big and moving very fast on his skis. I couldn't make out a face or anything."

"Any idea what model of truck, Mrs Davenport?"

"Not really. But it had an open back. That's all I noticed when I first saw it. Does that help?"

"Anything you can remember might help us."

"That's about it. I'm sorry for not calling sooner, but I just didn't know what to do."

"We understand," said Jack. "Do you remember what time it was?"

"Yes, I looked at the clock when I went back to bed. It was a few minutes to five."

"If you think of anything else, call us right away. We'll have an investigative unit out here tonight to have a look. Thanks for your call, Mrs Davenport. We'll be in touch."

Jack and Sven waited at the end of Mrs Davenport's driveway for the team to arrive. Jack had asked for three investigators and special lighting. He wanted to get on this immediately.

"Do you think it's Bradford's truck, Jack?"

"Yeah, that's a possibility. One that I don't like."

Jennifer's gift would have to wait. This could be a long night. And it was.

The crew arrived and concluded there was a distinct possibility a vehicle had been driven onto the Walleye River where the thickness of the ice was not enough to support it. The ice had also been disturbed to further support the theory. The river, although not too wide, was seventy feet deep. They would have to wait till daylight to search for the truck.

David Wickes

The area was sealed off with crime scene tape. With what they had learned from Mrs Davenport, this didn't look like an accident. Jack and Sven headed back to the motel.

"If it's Bradford's truck, who was the skier and where is Bradford?" asked Sven. "And if Bradford's the skier, who was in the truck, if anybody?"

"Good questions, Sven."

Chapter 28

INGRID SPENT A RESTLESS NIGHT with every sound startling her. The worry over Jim Bradford, and now Janice, kept her awake. What was her best friend up to? Even though she needed more sleep, the morning couldn't have arrived soon enough. After breakfast she called one of the breeders. Chris Eaton worked in a local sporting goods store, raised German Shepherds, and trained dogs. Ingrid knew him from skiing.

"Chris, it's Ingrid Nielsen, how are you?"

"Fine, Ingrid. Just leaving for the store. What can I do for you?"

"I'm looking for a dog, maybe two. Could I see you after work today?"

"Sure. I'll be home around five."

"That's perfect. Do you have any in your kennel now?"

"There's a new litter expected any day and I also have two left over from the last one."

"How old are they?" asked Ingrid.

"Coming up to six months, one of each. The male is a grey. They're considered to be the smartest in the breed."

"Is he grey in color?"

"No, he's black and tan but his head and saddle have tinges of grey and his eyes are much lighter than normal. He's seventy pounds already, going to be a big dog. I was thinking of keeping the female but we could talk about that. You're thinking of two?"

"Maybe. We'll discuss that this afternoon."

"I'm sure popular right now. Seems like there's a run on Shepherds 'cause you're the third caller this week."

"Good for you, Chris. See you at five." They hung up.

This was exciting. Two dogs already six months old would make training much easier. Her upbeat mood lasted until she arrived at the school and entered the staff room. Everyone was discussing the latest police activity.

"What's going on?" asked Ingrid.

"The police have a dredging operation on the Walleye River," said Janice. "It started at dawn. They believe a truck may have gone through the ice just past Mrs Davenport's."

"A truck," said Ingrid. "Was anybody in it?"

"We don't know."

"Good God. And nobody's heard from Jim? Or seen his truck?"

The room was suddenly quiet. The teachers looked at each other.

"Let's stay positive," said Janice. "We have no idea what, if anything, is in that river. Also, Jim Bradford could be anywhere."

"Including at the bottom of the river," said Edith Quinn.

"I believe we'd like to stay positive, Edith," said Ingrid. Her accompanying look was more than enough to silence Edith.

After a brief, awkward silence, Muriel Bates turned to Ingrid. "How did you and Janice make out with Ellen Bradford?"

"She was down but appreciated the opportunity to talk. If she's heard the latest news, it won't be a pleasant day for her. We'll stay in touch."

"I'll call Ellen in an hour or so," said Janice. "If the news has reached her, I'll go over right away."

"Thanks, Janice," said Muriel.

The bell rang. The teachers filed out to their respective classes. The day was long and stressful on both students and staff. Everyone in Wilton was talking about the incident on the Walleye River and Jim Bradford. Janice had been with Ellen till early afternoon when her sister had arrived from the Cities.

Ingrid left the school at three-thirty and went straight to Ellen's. There'd be time to give Janice a break before she met with Billy and Chris.

In addition to Ellen's sister, there were two neighbors and a clergyman there, so Ingrid made her visit a short one. The waiting was unbearable for Jim's mother, who looked far worse than she had the night before. No wonder.

As she drove to the kennel, much of her enthusiasm and excitement had faded with the sorry plight of Ellen Bradford. One could only hope for a happy ending.

Billy who was always early, was waiting for her at the kennel. Ingrid could tell right away how distracted he was. These events were becoming too much for him.

"Hi, Billy," said Ingrid. She wanted to hug him, but could tell it was not the right time.

"Ingrid," said Billy, head down, "when is this going to stop?"

"The whole town feels that way, Billy. We just have to keep hoping."

"I guess so."

She took Billy's arm. "Come and help me choose a dog. Chris says he has two from a previous litter."

Chris Eaton was a calm man in his late forties, whose every move was careful and deliberate. He'd been training and raising dogs as a pastime for fifteen years. "Hi Ingrid, Billy. Come and have a look at these beauties."

The Eatons had eight grown Shepherds, five males and three females, ranging in age from three to nine. They followed Chris's every move, all craving recognition. He had a remarkable way with the animals, displaying a quiet confidence while holding their total attention.

In the midst of the pack were two young, playful Shepherds, constantly nipping and pestering the older dogs. When the three approached, the puppies flew at them. Their energy was boundless. The dogs couldn't make up their minds, going from one person to the next and back again, but they were mainly interested in Ingrid.

It was love at first sight for Ingrid and the two young Shepherds. The male was far more demonstrative but neither dog would leave her alone. "What are their names?"

"Melinda and Bentley. You can change that quite simply if you want to."

"Bentley sounds great but I'm not too keen on Melinda. I've always liked Sasha for a female Shepherd."

"That's easy. Just start calling her Melinda Sasha, then switch to Sasha Melinda, then drop Melinda. It'll take no time at all."

"You going to take both, Ingrid?" asked Billy.

Ingrid was being smothered by the two dogs.

"Looks like that decision's been made for you, Ingrid," said Chris. "I don't think you can leave with just one."

"I do like the idea of two. They'll be company for each other when I'm working."

"Not only that, there'll be less mischief as they can take their energy out on each other," said Chris. "They're house trained and have all their shots. Will they be staying inside when you're home?"

"Definitely."

"Then place an old blanket in your bedroom, one for each of them. They'll quickly adopt that as their bed. When would you like to take them?"

"Why not tonight?"

"That's fine with me. I've got plenty of their kibble so you're welcome to a bag. You can also have a couple of treats. Feed them once in the morning and have lots of water around."

"How much are they, Chris?"

"They're four hundred each, but I'll charge you six hundred for the two, providing you make Bentley available to me for breeding."

"It's a deal."

"I've got a couple of leads for you till you get your own. Just return them when you can."

"Thanks."

"I'm glad they'll have a good home. Let me come and see them once in a while."

"Anytime. I'll probably need some help training them."

Billy helped with the dogs and got them safely in the back of her car. Before Ingrid got in, Bentley had jumped into the front passenger seat.

"He just won't leave you alone."

"Why don't you come back to the house, Billy? I've made a casserole and there's far too much for me. You could help me get the dogs settled."

"Okay, Ingrid."

The minute they entered the house the dogs were off to investigate. They checked every room before returning to the kitchen where Ingrid was preparing supper. Billy had filled a bowl with water and both dogs lapped up a huge quantity.

"Can I take them outside to show 'em your backyard?"

"Sure. I'll have dinner ready soon."

Fifteen minutes later Ingrid and Billy sat down to their meal and the dogs were fast asleep at her feet.

"This has been nice, Ingrid. I even forgot about the trouble around here," said Billy.

"Yes. I saw Ellen Bradford today after school. It was heart breaking to see her so distraught."

The phone rang. "It's for you, Billy."

He just kept saying, 'yes' and 'no,' before hanging up. His face was drained of color.

"Billy, what is it?"

"They found the truck. It's Jim's and he was in it."

Ingrid collapsed. "Oh my God. That poor boy."

"Police say the truck was driven from my place."

"What?"

"Yeah. They said it was parked behind my garage, then driven to the old shack. Somehow it got out on the ice, and sunk through. They found it half an hour ago."

"Why would Jim Bradford's truck be parked at your place?"

Billy shrugged. "Now they want to talk to me."

Ingrid was stunned. Jim Bradford dead and Billy wanted for questioning. What next?

"That's just routine, Billy. There's probably an explanation for his truck being at your place. That'll come out."

"I never saw it there, Ingrid. I don't know what I'll say to the police."

"Just tell them the truth. They'll ask you what you did last night, where you were, what time, things like that."

"But when I don't remember, I don't know what to say. They'll think I'm lying. You know what happens to me. I start to blush and talk quickly."

"Billy, did you have anything to do with this?"

"No, Ingrid, no."

"Then you have nothing to worry about. Other people have trouble remembering, it's not just you. It's only human, particularly when you're under pressure. The police understand that. So if you do slip up and realize it later, just admit it. You'll be fine."

Billy nodded and got up to leave. The dogs jumped in response.

"It's okay guys. Guess I better go, they're waiting for me."

Ingrid walked him to the door, then gave him a hug. For a brief second she thought he would return the gesture but he merely held her shoulders briefly as he moved away.

"I'll be thinking of you, Billy. Everything will be all right."

As she watched him leave, his head down and shoulders sagging, Ingrid wondered. She was not as confident as she let him believe.

Chapter 29

JACK WAS AT THE MOTEL when the news came in. It was six-thirty and he'd just finished the burger special, one of his latest inventions. Two large patties of sirloin beef, generously stuffed with onions, served with a mushroom gravy and fresh Italian bread. A side salad gave the meal a healthy touch. Sven had stayed over night and Jack appreciated his help. He not only liked the big Swede, he respected his talent and welcomed his knowledge of the people and the area.

It was difficult sorting out the emotions on the loss of a seventeen year old. Jim Bradford's behavior in the Cooper house, at least from her side of the story, had marked him as a possible suspect. He had the size and athletic skills to gain access to the homes, perhaps on skis. He was known to the victims through the store. Fits the pattern so far. If he's the killer there wouldn't be any sympathy. If not...

"I want to hear the results of the autopsy, Sven. Could this be suicide?"

"Can't see that, but who the hell knows? Why is someone skiing along that road at five in the morning? That is not a coincidence. Also, if he's a sensible kid like his teachers and the McCords say, I don't see suicide."

"If there is foul play, then the culprit has to be Mrs Davenport's skier."

"Exactly," said Sven. "And is this the same guy responsible for the other killings? Or, is it totally unrelated?"

"Yeah. Could this be Mr Cooper for instance?" asked Jack.

"Wait a minute. Bradford insults the guy's wife — maybe. That's hardly a motive for him to put the kid away."

"Maybe Cooper didn't intend to. Say he ran into Bradford. They

117

quarreled and a fight started. It got out of hand. Cooper killed him accidentally then tried to hide the body. It would have worked had it not been for Mrs Davenport waking up when she did."

"Possible," said Sven, not totally convinced. Neither was Jack. From what they'd heard from McCord's and the school, they doubted Jim Bradford had any enemies. Still, it couldn't be ignored.

"Then there's Dr Michael and Mr Martin. Their wives have been brutally murdered. They hear the story about Bradford and Mrs Cooper, draw their own conclusions, and take matters into their own hands."

"Hmm," said Sven.

"Yeah, neither one seems to fit, right?"

Sven nodded.

"How about Billy McCord?" asked Jack. "The truck was parked at his place, before being driven to the river."

"True. Too bad they lost track of the skier's trail."

Matt Erickson came in. "Lieutenant, we reached Billy McCord. He'll be here in fifteen minutes."

"Where'd you find him?" asked Jack.

"He was at a friend's house, a teacher named Ingrid Nielsen. She happens to be Jim Bradford's home room teacher."

"Interesting. Anything on Oakley?"

"His parents said he'll be back tomorrow."

"Thanks, Matt. Sven, will you start the interview with McCord? I've got to see Mrs Bradford."

"Will do. Not a pleasant task for you. Good luck," said Sven.

He pulled out of the motel parking lot and headed for Wilton. Halfway into town the pain occurred. This time more severe. It was in the same place, the middle of his chest, but different. What the hell is this? Was it just a little anxiety, on his way to visit the victim's mother? This was the first time he'd felt the pain when he wasn't exercising. He pulled over, rubbed his chest, and began breathing slowly.

A few minutes passed and the pain began to abate. For the first time he was concerned. He would definitely call David soon.

118

Jack was met at the door by Ellen Bradford's sister. There were two other women in the living room as well as a priest. He made the visit a short one, offering his condolences to Mrs Bradford, telling her the police would find the person responsible. Jack paid his respects to all and left.

As Jack approached his car, a young woman arrived. She was attractive and strode toward the house purposely, in a graceful, athletic way. She offered a pleasant smile as they neared, but there was a certain sadness in her manner. Obviously a friend of Ellen Bradford's who has come to offer her sympathy.

"Good evening," she said. It was a voice you'd never forget — soft and sexy. Yet today she also sounded somber, yet warm and sincere. She paused. He realized she didn't recognize him, and in a small town, this was rare.

"Ma'am." Jack nodded and extended his hand. "Lieutenant Jack Petersen. I'm with the investigative unit."

"Pleased to meet you. Ingrid Nielsen. I've heard about you of course. In a place like Wilton everyone knows everything that goes on. You're in charge of the murder investigation aren't you?"

"Yes. This whole mess must be difficult for all of you," said Jack.

"Oh, it is. And now Jim Bradford. We were here with Ellen last night and it was bad enough that he was missing, being an only son. This will destroy her."

Her sincerity and genuine concern for Ellen Bradford were evident. Ingrid Nielsen gave the impression of being kind and unselfish. Her soft, kind eyes never wavered as she looked directly at Jack. He felt this was a solid individual and most likely trustworthy. And her voice continued to captivate him.

"Did you know him well?"

"I taught Jim for four years. He was a fine young man, well respected in the school."

"We've heard only good things about him. I understand Billy McCord was with you earlier this evening," said Jack.

"Yes. Lieutenant, he's a little slow mentally, but makes up for it in so

119

many other ways with his drive and street smarts. Not only is he totally honest, he's a caring, thoughtful person."

"I appreciate your comments, Miss Nielsen, but when we're on an investigation, no trace of evidence or information can be ignored. Everyone is suspect until we know they're innocent."

"I suppose that has to be the case. When you're not used to this kind of mayhem, it's hard to cope. This town has never experienced anything like this, Lieutenant. It's more than unnerving."

"Well, we'll want all the help we can get. If you or your friends see or hear anything that you believe may be important to us, we have to know about it. We don't like this any more than you do."

"You'll have cooperation from most of us, Lieutenant. How did Jim die? Was it an accident or..."

"There are several theories right now, but I can't comment on that. Pleasure meeting you, Miss Nielsen."

"Likewise. Hope you find this monster soon."

Jack set off for the motel reflecting on Ingrid Nielsen. An attractive young woman with a warm, caring personality and plenty of smarts. Single too. She'd make a great catch, he thought. Imagine hearing that voice first thing in the morning. Was adamant about Billy McCord. More than a casual interest?

When he got back to the motel, Matt told him Sven was with McCord in the statement room, number 11, which was adjacent to the command center.

Jack knocked before going in. Billy McCord was highly agitated. He barely acknowledged Jack, appearing even more nervous at the sight of another police officer.

"You know Lieutenant Petersen, Billy."

"Y- yes," said Billy. "We met at the store."

"Hi, Billy. What do we have so far, Sven?"

"We've gone over Billy's story, where he was Tuesday night and early Wednesday morning. Home in bed. No witnesses."

"What time did you get home Tuesday night, Billy?" asked Jack.

"About seven. Frank closed up, so I left early."

"And you didn't leave your house that night?"

"N- no. I made supper, watched TV, then went to bed."

"What time was that?" asked Jack.

"Around ten or so. I have to open the store Wednesdays, so I go to bed early."

"You didn't hear anything?"

"No. I got up only once. That was about two in the morning."

"Jim's truck was parked behind your garage that night."

"Yeah, the Sheriff told me."

"But you didn't hear or see the truck."

"No, sir."

"And you didn't hear or see Jim Bradford."

"No, sir. Not that night."

They continued for two hours. Billy Cooper stuck to his story. He didn't appear to be lying...

Chapter 30

THE KILLER WAS RESTLESS again. This was difficult to understand. The headaches were back. The pain would come on slowly, then intensify. He'd heard about people with similar conditions. It seemed the symptoms were usually controlled by drugs. That was not for him. He didn't need help, especially from any kind of substance.

Of course lately the situation had changed and his actions were becoming a little too dangerous. At first it had been just the occasional cat or dog. There were no repercussions from those incidents. A cat or dog goes missing, who cares. It was sort of fun too, watching the little bastards squirm and suffer.

He felt a wave of emotion run though him. Then engulfed by the feelings, the tension mounted, the headache intensified. He realized the only way to overcome the torment was to find another subject. Sometimes he wished it would just pass. No, many times. Like now. He really hoped the pressure would disappear.

He was skiing effortlessly on one of the many trails surrounding the lake. The temperature was well below zero, the night air crisp. There was a quarter moon that provided a trace of light in the cloudless sky.

Ahead was a mile run, most of it up a gentle slope. He would challenge the grade and go all out to drain every last bit of energy from his mind and body. When he reached the top, he was panting and sweating profusely. He began laughing, so hard he doubled over, collapsing in the snow.

The headache was gone, the tension slowly drained away. After several minutes he got up and headed for home. He was at peace for the moment. When would he face the next bout? He had no way of knowing.

The eyes searched the area ahead, the way back home. The eyes were less intense, for now.

Chapter 31

JACK HAD DECIDED TO GO HOME Thursday, regardless of the time. It was too late for supper but at least he'd have some time with Jennifer. There was a fire going and she'd mixed a couple of Brandy Alexanders. They nestled together in front of the fireplace and reviewed the past few days while sipping their favorite cocktail.

"You make the best Alexanders," said Jack.

"You're just saying that because you haven't had one outside of this house for years."

"Well it won't be long before we correct that. When do we leave, three weeks?"

"Actually, it's three weeks and two days..."

"And how many hours?"

"Don't tease me." Jennifer drove her elbow into his chest. "After all, it's only three years since our last holiday, so I don't know why I should be overly excited."

"Yeah, I know. Sorry it takes so long to take care of my favorite person, my best friend, and the love of my life."

She snuggled closer to him. "I know you do your best. It's just seems that every crime in this state has to be solved by you. You're just too good at your job." She kissed him and held on.

Jack stroked her hair and traced the fine features of her beautiful face. "You're too patient with me, too good for me. You deserve more attention." He felt flushed from the Alexander and the fire. It felt good, just being with her.

"How bad is this one?" asked Jennifer.

"It's ugly. All murders are, but this one is really ugly. He's sick. He tortures before he kills."

"Is it the young man who died in the truck?"

"We don't know yet, but somehow I don't see it that way. We'll know in the next day or two when we talk to some of his friends. Heh, enough of this talk, I've got something for you in the car. How about one more Alexander?"

"Is it worth another Alexander?"

"Ah, I don't know about that, but I might look better to you if you have another one."

He gently cupped her face in his strong hands and softly kissed her warm mouth. He loved the touch of her lips. He missed this intimacy and being with her.

"Okay, get of here and get my present before I attack you," said Jennifer, as she playfully pushed him away. "One more Alexander coming up."

Jack retrieved the duck from the car. This was far better than chasing murderers. When he returned, Jennifer had two fresh drinks. He passed her the box and she reacted to the weight.

"What have you got here? It must be made of lead, it's so heavy."

"Not exactly," said Jack.

Jennifer opened the package and peeled away the tissue paper. "Oh, Jack, he's beautiful. What's the brush for? Wait a minute, I know — to clean your boots or whatever. It's adorable."

Jack smiled. "Got it at the local store in Wilton. Thought you'd like the duck."

"I do." She kissed him.

It felt so good, again. "I don't know if I can finish this second drink," said Jack.

"Yes you can, you smooth talker. I haven't had this much fun since Saturday. Now you'll have to wait a few more minutes for the real good stuff."

They laughed and held each other. He wanted it to go on forever. He would not let other thoughts spoil this night. Tomorrow would come soon enough.

Chapter 32

THE PHONE RANG at six-fifteen. Jack picked it up on the fourth ring. "Yes?"

"Lieutenant, sorry about the early hour but there's a Mr Cooper here to see you," said Matt Erickson. "Also Greg Oakley got home late last night. His mother just called to let us know."

"What has Mr Cooper got for us?"

"He says he has to talk to you, nobody else."

"I'll be there in an hour. Have the Oakley kid come in as well." He hung up.

Jennifer was sound asleep. Jack didn't have the heart to wake her and vowed to do his best to make it home again tonight. He needed more of last night. Hopefully Jennifer did as well. He had a quick shower.

Jack left Jennifer a note, poured instant coffee into a travel mug, and headed for Wilton Lake. Why would Cooper talk only to him? He arrived at the motel a little after seven. He was getting good at this trip. There was no press around this morning.

Craig Cooper was in the restaurant and obviously anxious to see Jack. "Can we speak somewhere in private?"

"Yeah, we have a room down here." Jack led the way back to the statement room.

"What is it, Mr Cooper?"

"I want to be sure this will stay between you and me."

"That'll depend on what you have to say. If it's information that's important to our investigation, there's no way."

"The thing is, this is rather sensitive and private."

"Mr Cooper, do you know something that may help our investigation or has anything to do with the recent deaths here?"

126

"Sort of."

"Then you better tell me what you have."

"Well, you know how things are in a small town. Stories get around pretty fast. I heard that maybe this Bradford kid was a possible suspect in the murders because of what happened at our house."

"Go on, Mr Cooper."

"So I talked to Stephanie about that afternoon. It may not be quite the way some folks are thinking. I mean they're saying Bradford tried to rape my wife and lost his temper and who knows what he might have done. Have you heard the same kind of stories, Lieutenant?"

"There's been a lot of talk."

"Maybe it wasn't like that. I got to thinking if the police believed this Bradford kid was capable of violence because of these stories, then I should tell you what really went on."

"And that is?" asked Jack.

"This is kind of difficult, Lieutenant. My wife, Stephanie, sort of acts a little different around men. She doesn't mean anything by it. She flirts a lot, you know what I mean? But it's just her way." Craig Cooper looked down and clasped his hands.

"What happened between Bradford and your wife, Mr Cooper?"

"First of all, you remember how she was dressed when you arrived that night?"

Jack nodded.

"Well she wasn't dressed that way in the afternoon. She was wearing more — more provocative clothes. She'd also been into the wine a bit. In a nutshell, Lieutenant, Stephanie admitted to me that she had come on to the young man. Then after he made a pass at her, she realized she'd gone too far, and was offended. So she got angry and defensive."

"And how did Bradford react?" asked Jack.

"He was upset but really didn't threaten her. Stephanie admitted she had colored her story to you because she was embarrassed by the whole scene. Things just got out of hand."

"Is that why you never pressed charges?"

"Yeah. She feels badly about all this, especially after we heard about the accident. We felt you should know the real story."

"It's good of you to come forward, Mr Cooper. We appreciate it. This won't go any further than our team."

"Thanks, Lieutenant. Guess I better get going."

Jack saw him out. It hadn't been easy for Cooper and Jack admired the man for coming in.

Matt Erickson waved to Jack, indicating Greg Oakley had arrived. One more interview then breakfast.

He was neatly dressed and obviously upset with the news of Jim's death. Matt made the introductions and Jack took him to the statement room.

"He was my best friend, Lieutenant. I came back as soon as I heard."

"We're sorry about that. He certainly was well liked here."

"My Mom and I are going to see Mrs Bradford this morning. Will this take long?"

"Not really. We need a few details about last weekend."

"Last weekend?"

"Were you out with Jim on Sunday night?"

"Yeah, with a few other guys. Why do you want to know about that?"

"There's always a lot of details that we need. What happened Sunday night?"

"Jim called me Sunday afternoon. He didn't sound too happy. Said he wanted to meet me after supper. We met at Ryan's, a sport's bar in town which as usual was packed. Jim was really down. Said he had a huge quarrel with Cheryl Saturday night and hadn't talked to her since. Jerry and Steve arrived and we ended up closing the place. None of us drink that much but Jim had way too many beers." Greg choked up.

"Take your time, Greg. What did you do then?"

"There was only Jim's truck there, so Jerry, who doesn't drink, did the driving. I said I'd get Jim into the house and they left. He was really out of it. He managed to get undressed and into bed, then I left."

"What time was that?" asked Jack.

"It must have been after two, because last call is one o'clock and we had one more beer at closing. By the time we finished that last drink and got to Jim's, it had to be at least an hour."

"And Jim was in bad shape?"

"I've never seen him like that. He couldn't even walk straight."

"I need the names of your two friends and the person who served you at Ryan's."

"Why do you need all this, Lieutenant?"

"It's just a process of elimination, Greg. Nothing for you to worry about."

Jack took the names, learning they were students at Wilton High. He had Elmer Holm and another officer go directly to the school to interview them and the waitress from Ryan's. He wanted their stories to corroborate Greg's version of Sunday night. If they all agreed, it would definitely remove Jim Bradford as a suspect in the Wilton Lake murders. Jack felt that would be the case. He believed Greg Oakley was telling the truth.

It was a good time to call David Folk so he ordered breakfast in the room and dialed David's office.

"David Folk."

It always came out as one word — Davidfolk.

"You just can't slow down, not even to pronounce your own name," said Jack.

"Ah, good morning to you too, Super Sleuth. I have some results for you."

"I was hoping you'd have some news for us, Einstein."

"You should be so lucky. The young man, Bradford, was knocked unconscious by a blow to the back of the head. The coroner states there would've been severe damage to the brain had he not died in the water. Cause of death is drowning. The victim wouldn't have regained consciousness after being hit. The blow was delivered by a strong individual who most certainly was taller than the victim. He was struck with a piece of lead pipe that was found in the car. No prints or identifying marks were found on the weapon."

"Then it wasn't suicide."

"Who said anything about suicide, Jack?"

"Just speculation around here. So the suspect knocked him out," said Jack, "put him in the truck along with the weapon, then drove down river to an area he probably knows was safe. After that he pointed the truck toward the river, put it in drive, and let it move out on the ice till it fell through."

"You don't need help from me, Lieutenant. That's the way we see it. The victim couldn't possibly have driven the truck. No prints. We're checking for other evidence but the water has ruined any chance of finding anything helpful. Unfortunately, once again there's no trace of the other person."

"Why do you say, once again, David? You think there's a connection with the other murders up here?"

"That may be a stretch. The first two definitely point to one killer, but now we have a male victim. What's the motive? There are some ties. No evidence left at the scene, looks like it's a guy, and he's big and strong. You have a witness who saw a skier leave the scene?"

"Yeah. The lady who first reported this."

"The two women were murdered in their homes," said David. "These are isolated properties on the lake, correct?"

"Not totally isolated, but they're on large lots, one or two thousand feet apart."

"And access to these places is rather difficult and restricted, is it not?"

"Yeah," said Jack. "There's a road leading to the lots that's not much better than an old logging trail."

"So, how is this guy getting around? From what you tell me a vehicle might easily be spotted by a neighbor or passerby. But if he travels in the middle of the night, both these murders occurred around midnight or later, he'd be better off moving through the bush on those trails you've been telling me about. That means walking, skiing, or snowmobiling. I can't see walking too far in this cold weather. You'd get there faster on skis or on a snowmobile. Any strong skiers up there, Jack?"

"Only ninety percent of the population."

"But how many fit our description, skimpy as it is at this point, and match the one given by your only witness?"

"You're trying to tie the sexual assault and murder of two women with the killing of a young man. How can these be connected?" asked Jack.

"Ah, that's your department, Dick Tracy. If we come up with some more goodies, we'll let you know. And how is Jennifer?"

"You'll be pleased to know we spent the evening at home last night — alone. I also brought my favorite wife a present."

"I'm proud of you, Jack. Do the same tonight."

"I might do just that," said Jack. "Incidentally, David, do you know a good cardiologist?"

"Of course I do. The B.C.A. has access to the top specialists but you know that. Why are you asking?"

"I'd prefer someone outside of the system."

"Jack, why are you asking? I know you avoid doctors at all costs. You having problems or symptoms?"

"Between you and me?"

"What's going on here, Jack?"

"I want your word on this 'cause it's probably nothing and I don't want Jennifer to worry needlessly."

"You're saying it's probably nothing. I know you wouldn't think of going to a doctor unless it was life or death. Out with it, Jack. What's happening to my favorite detective?"

"I've had a few chest pains, discomfort really. Funny thing is, it only happens when I'm running. They come on early in the run, I slow down for a while, they disappear, and I finish the run pain free. Same thing when swimming. Now it can't be serious when I'm able to complete exercising, right?"

"Probably not, but have it looked at. What's with a few tests anyway?"

"Yeah. Easy for you to say. Just have to find the time."

"Jack, you find the time. Don't fool around with this. And tell your best friend — Jennifer."

"So who do you know?"

"I'll get on it right away. See your own doctor first and by then I'll have a name for you. Make the call today — like now, Jack."

"I haven't time for all of that," said Jack. "Can't you just set it up with the specialist?"

"I'll try."

"Thanks, David. Have to get back to this case."

Given his profession with all the risks, it was incredible that he had trouble getting up enough nerve to visit a doctor.

Chapter 33

INGRID NO LONGER NEEDED an alarm clock. Two excited Shepherds, each weighing more than sixty pounds, leapt on the bed and began smothering her in dog kisses. Time to get up! It was a few minutes after six, close enough to her normal wake-up time.

She threw on a winter coat and boots and went out with her new friends. It was fifteen below. Ingrid was wide awake in no time. The dogs romped, completely oblivious to the sub zero temperature. When their duties were finished, they came immediately Ingrid called and headed for the house. What a great start.

She set out two bowls of kibble then showered and dressed. Bentley and Melinda Sasha followed her every move as she dressed and did her hair. They were fast friends already. After a quick breakfast of hot cereal, Ingrid took the dogs out for another play in the backyard. They had seemingly endless energy, as Ingrid threw snow balls all over the yard with both dogs wildly chasing and digging for the disappearing white missiles.

Back inside she organized their water before saying good-bye. It was difficult leaving them. She hoped the house would be in one piece when she returned.

When Ingrid arrived at Wilton High, the staff room was quiet as everyone reflected on the tragedy. Plans were made to attend the funeral home and extra counselors were on the way to help the students. The funeral was set for Saturday, with the service at eleven o'clock.

The principal had called an assembly in the auditorium where she and a priest made short presentations. The school would be closed for the day and details of the visiting hours at the funeral home and the Saturday morning mass were explained. Counselors would be available at the school for the weekend.

At the request of several students Ingrid stayed on in her classroom and the group spent the rest of the morning consoling each other while reminiscing about Jim Bradford. They adjourned shortly before noon and agreed to meet in the funeral home at two o'clock.

Ingrid went straight home to let the dogs out. They went ballistic when Ingrid entered. Not a thing had been disturbed, other than the old blankets she had laid out for their beds. These had been relocated, she surmised many times, to various areas in the house. One was now on her bed with the other under the kitchen table. They had an hour together playing in the backyard, chasing more snow balls. It eventually wore them down. She hoped they would sleep most of the afternoon.

The break was a welcome one after the stress of the morning. After a quick sandwich, she left for the funeral parlor. It was incredible how the dogs looked at her, as if to say, 'How can you leave us?'

"Be back soon, you loveable creatures," she said, giving each a prolonged hug.

Lang's funeral home was packed. Students and staff from Wilton High made up a large portion of the crowd. Bill Saunders, the pharmacist who employed Ellen Bradford, was there with most of his staff. There would be only a skeleton crew in the drug store for emergencies, otherwise it was closed till Monday. Several other merchants in town had also announced closings for the day of the funeral.

It was a strong showing from the community in support of Ellen, who was deeply moved. She was showing the pain and suffering in having to bury her only son. Ingrid spent several minutes with her before moving on amongst the mourners. She wondered if Ellen had heard a word she'd said, being so overcome with grief.

As Ingrid mingled there was one topic repeated over and over. How could this be happening in their community and what could be done to avoid further tragedies? It was agreed all would have to help the police. A community alert system would be set up. A meeting was organized for

Saturday evening in the town recreation center and everyone agreed to spread the word. They wanted the police represented and Ingrid would make the contact since she'd met the Lieutenant in charge. She presumed the police would be receptive to this kind of support.

The visitation ended at five o'clock and would recommence at seven. The room was still jam packed. Ingrid used the time to go home and tend to her dogs. As she was leaving someone called after her. She turned to see Janice running toward her.

"Ingrid, you'll never believe this," said Janice, slightly out of breath.

"Believe what?" asked Ingrid.

"People are saying the police believe Billy is the prime suspect in the Wilton Lake murders."

Chapter 34

JACK MET WITH SERGEANT TED NORRIS, the profiler. Ted had reviewed the interview tapes, concluding that of all those questioned, only Billy McCord was close to their profile of the killer.

A surveillance team would be set up to watch him, telephone taps put in place, they'd get a warrant for that, and his house searched. They'd need more evidence before the latter, but in the mean time Jack wanted assurance that Billy's every move be monitored. He wasn't to go to the can without someone knowing where he was. If there was any chance he could be the killer, he wasn't to have another opportunity.

"It's not a hundred per cent," said Ted. "Billy may lack the mental instability apparent in the killer. He's obviously a confused young man and has the physical attributes the killer possesses. His behavior with women leaves me with serious doubts. Here's a single guy with no signs of dating or interest in the opposite sex, or in other men for that matter. Apparently he has a platonic relationship with Ingrid Nielsen, and while that's not out of the ordinary, it's strange there isn't a trace of some romantic involvement in his life." Ted looked at his notes.

"The only woman he sees socially, a bright, attractive woman to boot, he has no interest in sexually. Is he asexual? Possibly. No crime there. But it's also a departure from normal behavior, whatever normal is."

"Yeah, I've met the Nielsen woman," said Jack. "Given the rest of his lifestyle, his lack of interest in her makes you wonder."

"At this point there's nothing else to connect him to the murders," said Ted. "David Folk and his team are still going over the evidence but haven't come up with anything to help us. It's skimpy and circumstantial, but that's all we have for now. Do we have enough to go through his cabin?"

"I doubt it," said Jack. "We could slip in on our own, but that might work against us. The evidence wouldn't be admissible in court. We'll leave that for a while. In many ways it's hard to believe he's the guy, but we've been surprised before."

"It puzzles me as well, but you'd be wise to stay on him, Lieutenant. It's not a perfect fit, but it's close enough. We're also setting up more interviews with those that come close to the profile. We're concentrating on Wilton right now."

"Thanks for your time, Ted. I'm off to the funeral home with Sven. When do you see David?"

"First thing tomorrow morning. We're going to put this together with their findings, see what we have. We'll be in touch."

It was a few minutes after eight when Jack met Sven and they left for the funeral home. The visitation would be over at nine. Another storm was brewing, the winds had picked up, and a few flurries were evident. The thought of not making it home tonight was depressing. He and Jennifer finally had managed some quality time together, then this case brings him back to reality. When he's chasing murderers, there's simply not enough time for Jennifer. He must change that, but not until this case is over.

Cars and trucks were parked everywhere. They received a few cool looks from some of the mourners. The word had got out who Jack was and many already knew the Sheriff. The reception was distant to say the least. They joined a line of people waiting to speak to Ellen Bradford. No one spoke to them.

After paying their respects and again assuring Ellen they were doing everything possible to find the person responsible, they moved on. Ellen Bradford was in a daze, and appeared heavily sedated. Tomorrow would be even harder on her.

The McCords with Frank, Jean, and the kids, along with Billy, were talking to Ingrid and Janice. They were on their own, shunned by most.

The word had got out that Billy was a suspect. He appeared nervous and upset. There was a coolness and tension as the officers passed the group. They heard a few muttered comments but chose to ignore them.

What greeted them outside was a total shock. Wilton had undergone a complete transformation. It was like a ghost town, blanketed under a foot of snow with more falling. The wind had increased and viciously whipped the falling snow in circles and eddies, creating mini tornadoes. Drifting was already serious, making driving conditions treacherous.

The crowd slowly made their way from the funeral home. Cheryl Dean's parents had left earlier, and after spending some time with Ellen, Cheryl left to walk home alone. Even in these conditions it would take her only fifteen minutes.

Chapter 35

THE KILLER DROVE SLOWLY along the deserted routes. He'd watched Cheryl leave alone. His truck had been parked in a vacant garage some three blocks away. He knew the route precisely and had plenty of time to get the truck and intercept her.

He'd have to be quick. There wasn't much time available tonight.

The truck's headlights picked up the lone pedestrian a few minutes later. He pulled alongside, rolled down the window, and said, "Cheryl, you better get in. This is not a good night to be out walking."

Cheryl hesitated, then decided to get in the truck. "Guess it is a little cold out there."

She climbed in and they slowly accelerated through the driving snow. The streets were all but impassable. Heavy drifting obscured the very edges of the road but he didn't care. He knew the route he'd take. He could do it blindfolded.

"Heh, there's Maple Street," said Cheryl. "We turn here to go to my house."

"It looks bad. Maybe we'll try the next street."

"They all look the same to me."

The next intersection loomed but the truck showed no sign of slowing down.

"You'll have to take this street."

"I don't think so," he said.

He concentrated on the road and picked out the turn he wanted. It was an old lane that skirted the west end of Wilton Park. His four-wheel vehicle had no trouble churning through the snow drifts. Their trail was quickly obscured by the blowing snow.

"Take me home, please," she said.

"Take off your blouse. Show me your tits."

He saw the look of terror. She moved away, up against the far door. The truck started to skid sideways. She made a move for the door handle. He had to look back to the road and make a hurried correction or they'd end up in the ditch. The truck slowed to a stop. She didn't hesitate, opened the door, and ran.

He doused the lights, and went after her. This would be no problem. He'd catch her easily.

Her footprints were easy to follow. For an instant he saw her shadow ahead in the swirling snow but it quickly disappeared. Just keep following the telltale indentations in the snow. She was faster than he thought. At one point he thought the tracks were fading, indicating he was losing ground. He kept plodding on.

Abruptly the tracks left the lane. He paused and looked around, then saw what she'd done. She'd tried to jump across the ditch before entering the woods and just caught the top edge of a drift. This would make the chase easier. The wind and snow were less severe in the heavily wooded area and her tracks would be clearer. He had to find her soon. They were only half a mile from the main road.

He had to be gaining on her. She couldn't possibly move through this faster than he, yet still there was no sign of her. The visibility was nil. He had only her tracks to go by. How could he have been so stupid? This was getting out of hand.

The wind had picked up to the extent that even in these dense woods you could feel it, hear it, and see it, as the snow whorls flashed wildly by. The trees were whipsawing back and forth in the gale like winds. A few dead branches snapped off, each with a resounding crack, yet barely audible above the storm. The noise was deafening.

Periodically there was a lull, as the winds suddenly abated leaving an eerie stillness in the forest. Just as suddenly another gale would whistle through the trees. The snow stung his eyes and he realized he was becoming disoriented. Where are her tracks heading? She's probably confused and could be going in circles.

There was another lull. He heard something. Had she cried out? He stopped and listened. There it was again. He was sure it was her. The wind whipped up again.

He continued moving, certain he was homing in on his prey.

Chapter 36

JACK WAS JUST FINISHING the burger special when the news hit. The cruiser assigned to tail Billy had lost him when they became mired in a snow drift. The officers immediately called in and two four-wheel drive vehicles hurried to the location. After searching the downtown area and finding no trace of Billy's truck, one of the vehicles was dispatched to his cabin on the Walleye River.

Billy's truck was parked in the garage. There were no lights on in the cabin. The officer noted the truck's engine was cold, indicating it had been there at least half an hour. The stake out was set up for the night.

The phone call came in about the same time.

"Lieutenant Petersen here."

"Lieutenant, this is Clifford Dean. Our daughter, Cheryl, hasn't come home yet and we're worried."

"When did you last see her, Mr Dean?" asked Jack.

"At the funeral home, shortly before nine. Cheryl wanted to visit a little longer with Ellen Bradford, then walk home. That's over an hour ago. We've called everywhere. Nobody's seen her."

"We'll be right over, Mr Dean."

Jack met with six agents in the control room. They had a map of the area on the wall. He pointed out the funeral home and Cheryl's house. "She left here shortly after nine to walk home. The family hasn't heard from her. Matt, assign the quadrants and start a search in these areas. With the shortage of agents we'll join the search after interviewing the Deans. Also have the agents confirm Billy McCord's at home and make sure he stays there till you hear from me. And call the K-9 Unit in Brainerd."

142

They used Sven's four-wheel as the conditions continued to deteriorate.

"Can you believe this? We lose Billy and Cheryl Dean goes missing at the same time. I don't like it, Sven."

"Maybe we should haul this guy in. As your friend David Folk says, there's no such thing as coincidences. If this girl doesn't turn up soon, I say we bring him in for questioning."

"You may be right. Not too much moving around here now."

They passed a fleet of snow plows, which would be out all night. It was difficult just keeping up as the snow fall hadn't lessened. It was forecast to stop at midnight.

Clifford Dean was doing his best to stay calm but his wife Sally was hysterical. They answered the door immediately and let the officers in. Introductions were made.

"We spend all day in a funeral home and now our own daughter is missing. What's going on here?" asked Sally.

"We have three cars looking for Cheryl now, Mrs Dean," said Jack, "but you may be able to help us by answering a few questions."

"I don't want any questions. I want Cheryl."

"We're assigning every officer to this search, Mrs Dean…"

"I don't give a damn," interrupted Sally. "We've had three murders since you arrived and now my daughter is gone. What have you done about that? What have you ever done?" Sally Dean was screaming and crying. Clifford took over. He was a powerfully built man, but he held his wife gently, trying to comfort her.

"Excuse us, officer," said Clifford. "This has been an awful evening. Sally, the best we can do is cooperate with these men. It's not their fault. Come on darling, let's sit in the kitchen and get started."

An hour later they'd called every friend who might have seen or known where Cheryl had gone, as well as the hospital, two restaurants where the kids hung out, the bowling alley, and three of the teachers at Wilton High. No sign of Cheryl. Clifford had succeeded in calming his wife somewhat, but it was going to be a long night. The weather conditions would make the search even more difficult.

"Here's our main number," said Jack. "Call us if you hear anything. We're going to join the search."

"Thanks, Lieutenant," said Clifford. "Please find her."

"We'll be in touch. Good night."

Jack called Matt for an update. No sign of Cheryl. The K-9 Unit was on its way but would be another hour or more, given the conditions. Billy McCord was at home and hadn't moved. Matt gave Jack an area to search and they began tracing the route assigned to them.

It was tedious and time consuming but the search continued. There were now several citizens who had volunteered to help, some on foot, some in vehicles. It was an all out effort. Flashlight beams danced across the wintry landscape. High powered lights used by the police played over the small town in a relentless pursuit of the teenager.

Shortly before two o'clock the K-9 Unit arrived and was immediately dispatched to the Dean house to acquire the girl's scent. They began tracking from the funeral home but after a few blocks the dogs stopped. They scurried around in circles.

"What does this mean?" asked Jack, who had followed the trackers.

"The trail ends here. She probably got into a vehicle. That's the only logical explanation for losing the scent."

"Let's get these dogs to Billy McCord's," said Jack.

Billy presumably was asleep when they arrived as they had to hammer on the door for several minutes before he finally answered.

"Yes, what is it?"

"We'd like to come in for a few minutes, Billy," said Jack.

"Sure. What's this all about?"

He gave all the appearances of having just been wakened. He wore flannelet pajamas, his hair was tousled, and he rubbed the sleep from his eyes.

"We're looking for Cheryl Dean, Billy. When did you last see her?"

"Uh, I guess at the funeral home."

"We want to let these dogs go through your home. Is that all right with you?" asked Jack.

"I, I guess so. Why are you doing that?"

"Cheryl's missing. She hasn't come home yet and nobody's seen her since nine o'clock. That's over five hours now."

"Do you think she's here?" asked Billy.

"We have to check out everyone who was there tonight."

The dogs didn't find any scent in the cabin. The unit went outside to check the garage and Billy's truck. They were back in minutes.

"We've traced the scent to the truck, Lieutenant."

"When was Cheryl in your truck, Billy?" asked Jack.

"She's been in it a few times. I mean, sometimes I drive her home from the store."

"I thought you took your snowmobile to work."

"Yeah, most of the time. But if I have to make a delivery or something, I take my truck. Had it there twice this week."

"When was the last time Cheryl was in your truck?" asked Jack.

"I don't know. Wednesday or Thursday, I think. Frank would be able to tell you."

"And she hasn't been in your truck, or with you, since then."

"No, Lieutenant."

"Where'd you go when you left the funeral home tonight?"

"I came straight home."

"Did anyone see you?"

"I don't know. There weren't too many people out tonight."

"Did you drive directly to your house?" asked Jack.

"Yeah, I think so."

"You did, or you didn't, Billy."

"Well sometimes I go different ways. It depends how I feel."

"Do you know we tried to follow you tonight and lost you?"

"N- no. Why would you follow me?"

"We lost you for over an hour, Billy, and in that time Cheryl Dean went missing. Now we have proof that Cheryl was in your truck and you can't tell us exactly when she was last there."

"I told you. It was Wednesday or Thursday."

"You better get dressed and come with us, Billy."

"Why? Where are we going?"

"To our headquarters. We need some more information from you."

Billy looked down, shuffled his feet, and shook his head. "I haven't done anything wrong, Lieutenant." With that he turned and went back to his bedroom to change.

"What do you think, Jack?" asked Sven.

"I can't help but thinking, he's telling the truth, that he really hasn't committed any crime. But I've been fooled before. Some people are very good liars."

Chapter 37

THE GAGGING SOUND had Ingrid instantly awake. One of the dogs was in trouble. She turned on the bedside light to see Bentley retching.

"Come here, Bentley, come on boy," she said, hurrying to the back door. Fortunately the dog made it outside before vomiting. Sasha, who now responded to her new name, was most interested in the proceedings, following Bentley's every move, and in general being a pest. It was all over in a few minutes and both dogs came rushing back to smother Ingrid in affection.

It was six-thirty, time to get up anyway. Ingrid had planned to get in a run and wanted some play time with the dogs before going to the funeral, scheduled for eleven this morning. By the time she had dressed and stretched, the sun was on the horizon. The storm had passed but not before depositing more than two feet of snow. It took an hour and a half to clear a path from the front door to the garage and then the driveway.

The dogs growled and barked at Ingrid's shovel and tried to catch the flying snow as she worked. It was hilarious and Ingrid's laughter left her gasping for breath from the antics of the dogs and the heavy work. She decided that was enough exercise for this morning. The run would have to wait till tomorrow.

Ingrid was halfway through breakfast when the phone rang.

"Ingrid, it's Janice. Do you know what's happening?"

"I'm afraid to ask."

"I know what you mean. It just gets worse by the minute. Cheryl Dean didn't get home last night and still hasn't been heard from. There's a massive search going on, but so far no results."

"This is a nightmare, Janice."

"That's not all. Billy's being questioned by the police. They picked him up late last night. I'm sorry, Ingrid."

"They're wrong about Billy. There's no way he had anything to do with this."

"I know how you feel and I can't blame you. Billy's special to you, isn't he?"

"Not the way you might think, Janice. He's a fine human being and I have a lot of respect for him, but that's about as far as it goes. I guess that does make me less objective when it comes to Billy."

"Well, you're entitled, Ingrid. Want to meet before the funeral?"

"I'd like to check on Billy first. I'll call you within the hour."

"Sure. I hope you have some good news. Talk to you later."

They hung up and Ingrid tried Billy's home. He answered on the fifth ring.

"Yes?"

"Hi. I heard you've been with the police. Are you okay?"

"It was awful, Ingrid. You've heard about Cheryl?"

"Yes, just a moment ago. Is she still missing?"

"Yeah. The police took me to the motel and kept me there till four this morning."

"I hope I didn't wake you, Billy."

"No, Ingrid. They think I had something to do with Cheryl. I'd never hurt her, or anybody else. You believe that don't you Ingrid?"

"Of course I do, Billy. Would you like to meet before the funeral? Maybe have a bite to eat somewhere?"

"Thanks Ingrid, but I don't think so. I'm going to try to sleep. It's at eleven, isn't it?"

"Yes. I'll see you at the church. Hope you get some rest." They signed off.

Ingrid felt the turmoil Billy was going through. She worried about him but was equally troubled over the series of events that had struck Wilton.

Three murders and a missing teenager. Sasha and Bentley stared at Ingrid, pleading for attention. What a contrast. A pair of loving animals, giving as much if not more in return, compared to some crazed individual who brutally tortures and kills.

When will it end and how will Billy cope? Surely he's not involved. He couldn't be.

Chapter 38

MAX BAIRD GREETED THE THOMSONS, the last of those he'd contacted to arrive. More than sixty of the residents had responded to his call. They were assembled to discuss the week of terror. It was a group of anxious citizens that filled the Baird's recreation room Saturday afternoon, nibbling on petits fours, sipping coffee or tea, and offering ideas on how to protect themselves. Many had attended the funeral service for Jim Bradford earlier in the day.

Conversation ranged from the funeral, how dreadful Ellen Bradford looked, how terrible it must be to bury your only son, Stephanie Cooper's noted absence, the sorry plight of the Dean family still awaiting news about Cheryl, to the killing of two of their neighbors. Julia Baird moved amongst the guests, checking to see all were properly looked after by the catering staff she had hired for the afternoon.

"We have to organize ourselves to provide our own security," said Max, a retired Army Colonel. "For starters, no woman should be left alone until this maniac is caught."

"Are you nuts, Max?" asked Frances Hawkins. "If I don't get Jim out of the house at least once a day, I'll go stark, raving mad." This produced some nervous laughter.

"Do you plan to set up a base camp, Colonel?" asked another neighbor. Continued laughter but more subdued.

The quips had lightened the mood before the group settled into a serious discussion on how to ensure their safety. Some owned or had bought dogs, alarm systems were in place, others had any variety of hand guns, shot guns, or hunting rifles at the ready, but all agreed a meeting with the police would be necessary. A committee was selected to meet with Lieutenant Petersen for advice. Max Baird would be their spokesman.

"Why can't the police provide protection for all of us?" asked Anne Chambers.

"They don't have enough officers to cover all the houses here. They have their hands full as it is, covering this case," said Max.

"I don't see why we should have to take care of ourselves. What're the police here for anyway?" asked the same woman.

"Believe me, they're working night and day on this," said Max.

"Don't give me that, we deserve to..."

"Just leave it," said her husband, Tim. "Max has explained why you won't get protection from the police."

"Oh, has he now. Two women dead already and you guys just don't get it."

"Anne, knock it off."

"I want some action, now, before it's too late."

"That's why we're here, Anne," said Max.

"All you're doing is talking."

"Tim, we'd like to get on with this," said Max.

"Yeah, well she's got a point. You think you're still in the Army and in charge, but you're well past your prime."

"If you're not interested in participating, please feel free to leave."

Tim and Anne looked around the room. No one offered to support their belligerent outburst. Anne lurched from her chair and with some help from Tim made it to the front hall. He wasn't much steadier than she. They gathered their coats and left.

"Let's get back on track," said Al Britain. "I recommend we look into hiring our own security force."

"Good idea," said Max. "I had planned to organize that with the help of the Lieutenant. We'll probably have to hire them from St Cloud or the Cities."

"This maniac kills in the middle of the night. Are these guys going to patrol around our lake day and night trying to spot some nut on the loose?"

"I don't know how they do it but the Lieutenant will be able to explain that. Do we all agree we should contact a private security company?"

"How much is this going to cost us, Max?"

"I don't think that's an issue. Am I wrong?"

A chorus of no's greeted Max's question. Al Britain and Ed Chapman volunteered to go with Max to see Lieutenant Petersen. Max would set up the meeting.

The group began to disperse. The fear was evident. Strange that only half the lake residents attended. Were the others not fazed by the situation, or did they just plan to stay away till the killer was caught?

What no one had taken into account was the second storm that was brewing to the northwest. If they thought last night's snow fall was serious, this was going to make that pale in comparison. Western Canada and the Dakotas were currently in the midst of the worst blizzard and snow accumulation in history. Electrical failures were too numerous to count, airports were closed, and roads impassable with stranded motorists who could not be reached.

More was to come.

Chapter 39

JACK HAD AGREED to attend the meeting Saturday night in the recreation center. They had covered the funeral, checking for any suspicious activity. It was not unusual for killers to attend the funeral of their victims. Five agents had been on hand. Later he went back to the motel to check on the search for Cheryl Dean and tackle some paper work.

He dodged the press with a curt 'no comment' as he headed for the command center. The update was not good. The teenager was still missing and the Commissioner had called. Time to report to higher authorities. That wasn't all. Another serious storm was on its way. The situation was difficult enough without having even more snow to deal with. Sven had wanted to stay for the funeral, but in view of the incoming weather and pressing duties in Brainerd, had decided to leave after breakfast.

"Keep in touch, Jack. We'll do what we can to help."

"Thanks, Sven. Drive carefully."

Jack slipped over to the motel dining room and ordered the latest burger special, a ten ounce patty of sirloin, with cheddar cheese, hot peppers, lettuce, and mayonnaise, all on a toasted multi-grain roll. Julie added a side of home fries.

"I thought it best just to include the fries," said Julie. "Wanted to save you the trouble of having to ask."

"Abuse, all we get here is abuse," said Jack.

Julie responded with her usual 'harumph' and turned on her heels. After the burger, Jack called Jennifer. He'd have to stay over tonight but hopefully get home at a decent hour Sunday. She'd heard the news about the incoming storm. He was looking forward to tomorrow evening, as was she. They both hoped the weather would cooperate. A call for Jack interrupted them.

"Lieutenant, there's a Colonel Baird on the line," said Matt.

"A Colonel. Guess that outranks me," said Jack as he took the call.

"Petersen here."

"Lieutenant this is Colonel Max Baird, one of the lake residents. We want to meet with you as soon as possible. When would it be convenient?"

"What do you want to discuss, Colonel Baird?"

"We want to hire security guards. You probably don't have the manpower to provide 'round the clock protection, which we feel is necessary. No one knows when this maniac could strike again, which means we have to act now. Your expertise and advice would be welcome."

"All right. I'll meet you here at nine tonight." They hung up.

Jack set out for the recreation center. Since the parking lot was full, he left his car at the front door. It was going to be a short visit.

Ingrid met him at the entrance. "Thanks for coming, Lieutenant. I know how busy you must be. Any news on Cheryl?"

"I'm afraid not. The weather is playing havoc with the search and there's more snow on the way."

"Yes, I heard. They've declared a state of emergency in Montana and the Dakotas. Just what you needed." Ingrid's soft smile was there, but her face was etched with concern.

"We'll have to be extra careful. Did you organize this meeting?"

"No," said Ingrid. "My role was to contact you. Are you suggesting the killer may be more likely to strike again in bad weather?"

"We don't know what motivates him, but severe conditions would make it easier for him to move around."

"As if we don't have enough to worry about. Would you like to address the group?"

Jack briefly pointed out the role citizens could play. He cautioned them to be alert, not to be out alone, especially women and children, and to report anything suspicious to the police. He also defined the responsibilities of the police, that they alone would do the investigative work and in no circumstance should anyone try to apprehend this individual.

"The Commissioner has authorized an increase in the force assigned to the case," said Jack. "Any information will be helpful to us. We've set up a twenty-four hour, hot line service. If you see anything suspicious, call this number immediately. The number will be posted in all the town's shops, schools, hospital, bus station, and other public places."

He fielded several questions before leaving. On the trip back to the motel he reflected on the meeting. These were respectable citizens whose lives had been turned upside down by the threat of a crazed killer, not knowing when or where he would attack again. The extra manpower will help, providing it arrives.

The first signs of the storm whipped along the deserted town streets, with flurries being whisked through the night air, creating eddies and strange forms in a seemingly harmless display. It was to be anything but harmless. Wilton, as well as the entire state, was about to experience a disaster unprecedented in winter storms.

Jack returned to the motel. He wanted a meeting with his team to discuss their strategy in view of the imminent weather conditions.

Chapter 40

JAN HIBBARD HAD BEEN COASTING while her husband Ernie was slowly but surely drinking himself into a stupor. Not that that was unusual. But lately, it was happening more frequently and on fewer drinks. Jan, although also prone to the bubbly, managed to retain a reasonable degree of sobriety, at least as compared to Ernie. Tonight, that wasn't saying much.

Following the meeting at the Baird's they'd come home and Ernie promptly filled a pitcher with Gin, a touch of Vermouth, and a little ice. This he stirred gently before pouring the contents into two enormous martini glasses, each having a capacity of six ounces. He left enough room for three large, stuffed olives. He was now on his third while Jan was still on her first. Supper had been postponed as Ernie wanted yet another.

"Imagine the Colonel setting up a local operation to deal with our security. He's a little past that isn't he, Ern?" asked Jan who was lying on her back attempting to balance a cushion with her bare feet and then spin it wildly. It kept falling, much to Ernie's amusement and her consternation. She was trying to master this little game but failing, with her coordination obviously off thanks to the effects of the extra large martini.

"He's got about as much chance as you have of balancing that cushion." He doubled over in laughter.

"Heh, at least I'm trying," said Jan, hit with a similar giggling fit.

"All you're doing's giving me a good look at that cute little ass of yours." More laughter.

"I'm glad you still think it's cute."

"I do," said Ernie. "B'sides, 'salot better than thinking of some stupid killer." Enunciation was clearly becoming a problem.

"Yeah. What makes them think he'll stay around to have another go here? With all the heat on he'd be nuts to try it again. You agree, Ern?"

"I certainly do. He's probably in another state by now. Let's forget all that. I'd rather concentrate on your ass."

"Getting a little horny are you, Ern?"

"I could skip dinner and just feast on you."

"Promises, promises."

"Well let's see about that," said Ernie. He jumped out of his chair but stumbled and fell before getting halfway to Jan.

They broke up in laughter. Ernie was struggling with his pants, trying to get them off while moving toward Jan. She in turn had peeled of her panties and was spread-eagled on the floor, taunting him.

"Hurry up Ern, I can't wait," said Jan.

Ernie made it to Jan on his hands and knees and promptly laid his head between her legs. Jan giggled.

"Heh, Jan, I thought you liked this."

"Oh, I do, Ern but I just remembered that joke Harry told us the other day."

"What was that?"

"The guy who comes home and starts making passionate love to his wife right on the living room floor. He says, 'Ah cherie but you're a little dry tonight.' And she says, 'Move up Henri, you're licking the carpet.'" Another laughing fit ensued.

Gradually they began to focus on their amorous intentions and before long succeeded in having a joyous sexual romp. Well satisfied, Ernie and Jan somehow managed to crawl up on the sofa before collapsing into a besotted nap.

Jan awoke with a start. A log had fallen in the fire place and smacked into the glass doors. The noise which shattered the quiet night, was unnerving. An involuntary shiver, caused by the scare and the fact she was awfully cold, passed through her body. It took several minutes to realize where she was and how she got there. No wonder she was cold, lying there stark naked with no covers.

Jan wrapped herself around Ernie. "Wake up Ern. I just had a terrible fright."

"Huh," mumbled Ernie. "What's going on? Jesus, it's colder than a well digger's ass in here."

"I know. Grab that caftan will you?"

"Huh. Oh, okay." Ernie pulled the caftan over their exposed bodies. As the chills slowly disappeared, Jan sensed the dryness in her mouth, having just awoken from a half drunken stupor.

"I could use a small martini, Ern."

"A hell of an idea. Why don't you put some new logs on the fire while I start up the barbecue? We'll have a couple of steaks and a bottle of wine."

"Ern, it's almost nine o'clock."

"So, what're you doing tomorrow that..."

"What's that?" shouted Jan.

"What's what?"

"Ern, I saw something out there, near the edge of the trees."

Ernie moved over to the window and peered outside. "There's nothing out there."

Jan covered herself in the caftan and joined Ernie. "I swear something moved over there, just to the right of the big oak."

"How can you see anything with all that snow flying around?"

"I'm sure there was something out there."

"Ah, honey, you just woke up, had a little fright, now your imagination is running away on you. I'll mix that martini for us and get started on the steaks. There's nothing to worry about."

"Okay," said Jan. "Guess I'm a little jumpy. Look at that snow. There's even more than last night, if that's possible."

Ernie went to the bar to mix new martinis while Jan continued to stare at the driving snow. She was positive something or somebody had moved near the tree line. Was somebody staring at her? She was certain someone was looking at her. This was crazy.

Ernie came to her side with the drinks. "Tackle this, honey, while I get the barbecue going."

Chapter 41

THE KILLER STOOD MOTIONLESS. He had backed a little further into the woods when the Hibbards came to the window. The husband was starkers while she had donned some kind of blanket to cover her nudity. Must have just missed a little show. They were certainly quite brazen, carrying on like that with the curtains open. Maybe they didn't expect anybody in their backyard at this time of night or they were too drunk to care. He knew the Hibbards drank a lot.

Confident he hadn't been seen, the killer remained, contemplating his next move. The headache was pounding away, making him extremely irritable, in fact irate. *That little Hibbard bitch deserves special treatment.* The husband's presence changed everything — now there would be a risk, but not too much. Then again, it might be better to move on to a safer target.

He was trying to think straight but the pain wouldn't allow him. More exertion was needed so he decided to ski around for a while to sort this out. The trail was easy to find despite the new snow fall.

The headaches were becoming more frequent.

He was moving quickly now, pushing out on each leg as he moved up the incline, a true test of skiing prowess and stamina. Despite the cold, a little sweat was forming. He drove harder. Fifteen minutes later the hill crested. He paused at the top and looked back along the trail. Even in these conditions he could make out the swath cut through the forest. How long had it been there? Perhaps a century.

The headache remained. The eyes darkened. It was not going away tonight. He turned around, coasting back down the slope. No effort required now. The only sound, the soft swish of the skis on the cold snow.

The Hibbard house loomed ahead.

Chapter 42

JACK SHOWED THE COMMITTEE into the meeting room. Max Baird, Al Britain, and Ed Chapman took their seats and Max took over. There was no doubt who was in charge. His bearing and tone of voice gave proof of his military background and rank of Colonel.

"Lieutenant, our group has become more than concerned over the events of the past week. Needless to say we have to find a way to protect ourselves and prevent this maniac from killing again."

Well at least he doesn't beat around the bush. "Obviously our priority as well, Colonel."

"We've decided to hire a Security Force and want your input. Would you recommend some companies — those with proven reputations — that would suit our needs?"

"I'd be pleased to. Most security companies are staffed with ex-police officers so they have the experience and know how. Cam Fletcher runs an outfit called 'Security Plus.' They're one of the best around. Solid, with many references. They have clients on Lake Minnetonka. Large estate lots on the lake not too dissimilar from your situation here. The B.C.A. has worked with them on other projects. They'd be our first choice."

"Would you call them for us?"

"Yeah, I have their number." Jack found the listing, dialed the number, and put the phone on speaker.

Their call was answered on the second ring. "Security Plus."

"Cam Fletcher, please."

"Mr Fletcher isn't available right now. May I have him return your call?"

161

"This is Lieutenant Petersen from the B.C.A. Do you have a number where he can be reached?"

"This is only an answering service, sir, I can't give you that information. But I will take your number and have him call you."

"Tell him this is an urgent matter and have him call as soon as possible. He knows me personally."

"I'll do my best, sir."

Jack gave her two numbers and again stressed the importance of an immediate response. They hung up.

"I'm sure he'll get back to me quickly. In the meantime I trust none of you will try to take matters into your own hands. We're faced with a dangerous individual and you'd be foolish to challenge him. Is that clear?"

"Lieutenant, I'll have you know several of us have a vast amount of military experience and are adequately armed. We're capable of protecting ourselves."

"When did you retire from the Army, Colonel Baird?"

"Admittedly some years ago now, but I maintain a regular exercise routine and am every bit as alert as I was during active service."

"I'm not questioning that, Colonel. However, it's our responsibility to take care of this. Have no doubts, there's a predator here who plans and executes. He's careful and resourceful. This is not a routine exercise, it's a fight for survival. Your help is appreciated. Leave it at that."

"The Lieutenant's right, Max," said Ed. "Let's get some security in place and let the police do their job."

"I agree," said Al. "This stuff's all beyond me. We have to use common sense here and stay alert till they find this nut. I'm all for taking your advice, Lieutenant."

Max Baird sighed and nodded.

"I'll put Cam in touch with you," said Jack. "Leave me your phone numbers. Once you decide, it'll take some time for them to get in place with the weather we're having. I hear it's going to be rough for a while."

"Guess we should be getting back to the wives," said Max.

"Where are they?" asked Jack.

"We left them at my place," said Max. "First step in your rules, Lieutenant — no women left alone. Thanks for your help. We'll wait for the call."

"Be careful — all of you."

Chapter 43

JAN DECIDED TO HAVE A HOT BATH and get some warmth back after waking up on the sofa chilled to the bone. Ernie had taken his martini outside to the barbecue — she'd enjoy hers in the tub.

She slipped into the hot water and felt her skin tingle — heaven. The martini warmed her insides as her body temperature returned to normal. It had been quite a day.

First the funeral, then the meeting at the Baird's which had unsettled her. She couldn't erase the thoughts of a killer on the loose, one who preyed on women. Yet the early evening martinis and sex with Ernie had chased those thoughts away. Just as suddenly they'd returned when she awoke and swore she saw someone in their backyard.

An involuntary shudder went through Jan as she recalled the moment, followed by the sensation that they were being watched. Could there have been somebody out there after all?

Everything was still in the house. Jan heard only the sound of water lapping against the tub whenever she changed position. There was a trace of music coming from the den. She realized that half an hour had passed since Ernie went out to start the barbecue. Where is he?

"Ernie — are you back?"

Surely he should have returned by now.

"Ernie!"

No response. She looked at her unfinished martini. It didn't have any appeal. Jan was feeling a little anxious. More than a little. The water was no longer comfortable and she was cooling off quickly.

"Ernie!"

Still only the muted sound of the stereo.

"Ernie — where are you?"

Nothing. Jan was shaking, not just from the cold. She had to get out of the tub and find out what was happening. She was terrified. The quiet house. No response from Ernie who should have been back by now. If he's teasing her — she'll brain him.

"Ernie — please answer me. This is no time for joking."

No response.

Jan stood up and reached for a towel, slipped and crashed back into the tub, knocking the martini off its perch, the glass breaking as it bounced off the side of the bathtub and into the water. She froze. And listened.

What to do first? The stillness returned as she sat, afraid to move because of the shattered glass, and her growing terror. Why was she thinking that way? If she didn't move, nobody could find her? She had to think straight.

"Ernieeeeee!"

Nothing.

Damn it. Jan eased out of the tub, picked up a towel and slowly began to dry off. She tried to remain as quiet as possible. To be able to hear anyone? What could he be doing? Ernie definitely hadn't come back in, nor was anybody else in the house as far as Jan could tell. Everything was so quiet.

She slipped on a sweater and pair of slacks and went to the top of the stairs. She could see the den and most of the dining room — nothing moving.

"Ernie?"

Still nothing.

"Ernie, if you're down there playing games, I'll crucify you." She felt braver if she talked out loud.

She started down the stairs. The last vestiges of the afternoon drinking had disappeared. She was stone cold sober and frightened. Nothing appeared out of the ordinary, other than the eerie stillness. After a brief stop on the landing she decided to move quickly and hopefully find Ernie.

Jan literally flew down the last half of the stairs, raced to the back door and opened it. She could barely make out Ernie's prone body at the foot of the barbecue, partly covered with the heavy snow.

"Ernie." She ran to him, turned his face upwards — he was alive, but unconscious. He had to be brought into the house, it was twenty below. Jan glanced around the yard. No sign of any danger.

Jan slipped on the snow-covered porch, half stumbling into Ernie. She hooked her arms under his armpits and pulled. Ernie barely moved. This was going to require all her strength as he was out cold and she would be dragging dead weight. He was lying face down away from the door so she'd have to turn him around. She took hold of him again and pulled mightily. This time he moved. She swung him around but just as they started to move across the porch there was a sharp tug and her forward progress was halted.

Ernie's foot had caught the leg of the barbecue stand. It wouldn't budge. Despite the cold, she was sweating from the effort and fear. She freed his foot and managed to work the body over to the back door. There was a small, raised sill in the doorway and she'd have to lift Ernie off the deck to get him inside. Jan tapped his face lightly. "Ernie, can you hear me?"

No response or movement. How was she going to get him over the sill without scratching his back? A sudden gust of wind slammed the door shut. Jan started in terror at the sound. Please don't be locked. She tried the door handle — it moved. With a new rush of energy, she hoisted Ernie and gently as possible eased his inert form into the doorway.

Jan picked up Ernie's legs by the thighs and pushed him into the house. She quickly closed and locked the back door. She had to call 911.

The dark eyes watched as Jan ran to the phone.

Chapter 44

THE KILLER SAW ERNIE HIBBARD go out the back door and lose his footing on the snow-covered deck. He fell backwards and smacked his head against the wooden railing. He had to be out cold as there was no further movement

Jan Hibbard meanwhile had disappeared upstairs — to change? Freshen up?

This was a little complicated. Did he have time to get to Hibbard to make sure he wouldn't be in the way? The pain was lessening. Maybe he should just leave. Tempting though.

He moved out past the tree line and headed for the back of the house. Then he heard the shouting. What the hell was going on? He stopped and waited.

He saw Jan Hibbard on the stair landing, looking around and shouting. The killer retreated to the edge of the forest. This was not going well.

Moments later the back door opened and Mrs Hibbard pulled her husband back into the house. She was obviously going to call for help. He'd never get there before she made the call.

The killer watched for a minute longer, the eyes dark but calming. There'd be more opportunities later. Best to get home. The headache was almost gone. He wouldn't forget Jan Hibbard.

Chapter 45

THE CALL CAME IN at 9:22 P.M. Jack led a unit of four detectives to the Hibbard residence. The four-by-four crunched along the McCord Trail at an agonizingly slow pace. It would take half an hour to reach the Hibbard's.

Four officers on snowmobiles accompanied the K-9 unit. Jack's group arrived minutes later to find one hysterical Mrs Hibbard who claimed someone had been watching them. The killer?

Two medics were on the way, also on snowmobiles. Jack needed more help and the weather was delaying the process. They still had a missing teenager, now more than twenty-four hours, and the search parties were practically at a standstill. Thankfully the K-9 unit had arrived. In a situation like tonight they needed a helicopter, but even that would be grounded with the current conditions.

By the time the medics had arrived, order had been restored. Mr Hibbard had come to, and other than a goose egg on the back of his head plus a hangover from the day's drinking, would undoubtedly survive. Mrs Hibbard however was still in quite a state. Jack took a seat on the sofa with her. She was dressed casually but was certainly stressed.

"As I told the other officer, Lieutenant, there was someone out there tonight. I'm sure I saw him and I could *feel* him looking at us. I know that seems crazy, but it's true."

"Can you describe the person, Mrs Hibbard?"

"That's difficult. It was dark and with the blowing snow — well I really couldn't tell if it was a man or a woman. It felt like a man but I guess that sounds silly. Maybe the whole thing does. Do you ever get the feeling you're being watched or stared at? Well, I had that sense."

"I understand," said Jack. "Where did you see this person?"

Jan pointed to the area. "Right over there, at the tree line. It's only twenty or thirty feet from that back window. One of your officers went out there earlier. He said there was no sign that anybody had been there, but with these conditions, any trace would have been erased."

"Mr Hibbard, are you all right now?" asked Jack.

"Yeah, I'll be okay. They gave me something for the headache. Guess I need some sleep."

"We'll leave an officer with you for the night but he'll have to leave first thing tomorrow. Will that work for you, Mrs Hibbard?"

"Thanks, Lieutenant, we'd appreciate that."

Jack returned to the motel. The night was unsettling. If the killer had been there, would they have been able to stop him? There were several messages waiting for him. The Deans, Cam Fletcher, Jennifer, and David Folk. He called home first.

"How's the most important woman in my life?"

"If you mean me, I'm fine," said Jennifer. "Since it's after eleven, I guess you're staying at your favorite motel again."

"Yeah, but it's not just the late hour, it's all that white stuff. Imagine you're getting it too."

"We sure are. Isn't it incredible?"

"It doesn't look good. It's even worse, given the situation here. We had to call off the search for the young girl and it's going to be more difficult to keep everyone safe from this lunatic."

"No breaks yet?"

"Not a thing. I'm sure going to miss you tonight."

"Me too. There's a nice fire going but it's just not the same without you."

"Saturday night and no heavy date," said Jack. "What a waste of two talented lovers."

"I just read that one of the ways you can tell somebody's age is to find out what they do on Saturday nights. What does that say about us, Jack?"

"We'll just have to change that, and quickly. You're much too desirable to leave alone on Saturday night, or any other night for that matter."

"Thanks, you smooth talking fox," said Jennifer. "But there you are, in downtown Wilton and I'm here on my own."

"Why don't you join me for a night in a strange motel room? I'm available."

"I'm sure you are, Jack. But what would we do with all those little darlings who keep knocking on your door all night?"

"Have you been to Wilton yet?"

"Just kidding. Any chance you'll be home tomorrow night? We can watch the Super Bowl together and tackle anything else you think you could handle."

"I won't get to sleep tonight if you keep talking that way," said Jack. "Let's hope for a break in the weather and the work load here. I'll need both to make it back. Keep your fingers crossed. Sorry but have to make a few more calls before it's too late. Love you — talk to you soon."

"I love you too — take care."

Jack called the Deans. They had no news. Mrs Dean had been sedated and thankfully was getting some rest. They realized a change in the weather was needed to reinstate the search. Jack said he'd be in touch if anything broke.

His next call was to Cam Fletcher. Jack explained the situation and gave him Max Baird's number. Yes, Cam could handle the job but didn't know when they'd be able to get to Wilton Lake. He'd call Baird first thing in the morning.

David Folk answered on the first ring.

"Hi, David. How's America's number one football fan? Can't sleep in anticipation of the big game huh?"

"That doesn't even come close to warranting a response. Why are you calling me at this hour?"

"You won't believe this, but it's not about work."

"Finally a set of priorities that make sense," said David. "I guess you want the name of a cardiologist. How close am I?"

"Ah, you're always ahead of me."

"Have you discussed this with Jennifer?"

"Not yet."

"Not yet, he says. As if you're about to. Jack, she's your wife and best friend. There's no choice here. Also she'll castrate me if it comes out that I set you up with the appointment knowing she was in the dark about this."

"All right already, to quote a friend of mine. I'll tell her as soon as I get home."

"And that will be when?" asked David.

"When my dog sled arrives. Come on, David, what's the news?"

"Dr David Breckenridge will see you Wednesday, February 2nd, at ten-thirty. He's the top guy in the state and we're lucky to get him this quickly. He happens to be married to a cousin on my mother's side so we had a little influence. Make sure you get there — he's booked into the next millennium."

"Thanks, David, I'll do my best."

"No, Jack, that's not good enough. You will be there, period. Deal?"

"Okay. You're on."

"I take it things are not going well in Wilton."

"You could say that."

"I just did," said David. "We're still looking at some areas — maybe you'll get some goodies soon."

"We could use the help."

David gave him the doctor's address and phone number before hanging up.

Jack checked into the command center — no news. Once in his room, he looked outside before getting into bed. The snow was up to the window sill and the wind was howling. How bad can this get?

Chapter 46

INGRID AWOKE and stared at the calendar. She didn't have to be reminded — January 30th. One year ago today, her fiancé had been killed at the mill. They were to have married last summer. She'd been unable to get over the loss and still had no interest in dating. Her work, vigorous exercise, and Billy occupied most of her time. It was uncomplicated being with Billy, purely a platonic relationship, but one she treasured. He was good company and needed someone — especially lately. Now there was another part of her life — Sasha and Bentley.

It was 'Super Sunday' today but that held little interest for Ingrid with all the other distractions. She'd go to Rick's grave before calling Billy.

The dogs were ready to go out. Ingrid bundled up and joined them in the backyard. They played with great abandon — so full of life, as Rick had been. Why did they take Rick away? The tears flowed as she numbly watched her new friends cavort. Their playful action not bringing the usual joy.

She didn't know how much time had passed, just sitting on the back door step in a trance, watching the dogs. It must have been a while as she began to feel the cold. Ingrid stood and the dogs came quickly. The three reentered the house. She wiped snow from both dogs before sitting down and giving each a prolonged hug. God she needed the comfort of their love.

The phone interrupted her thoughts. She let the answering machine take the call. After feeding the dogs and a light breakfast she listened to her message.

"Hi, Ingrid. It's Janice. Just a quick call to see how you're doing. I know what today means to you. If you'd like company or just a phone visit, please call. You know I'm here for you. Love you. Bye."

Such a good friend. She'd call her later. One look at the roads and she realized driving was out of the question. The trip to the grave site would have to be made on skis. Luckily she knew the route well as the visibility was near zero in blowing snow. Never had she seen such accumulations. There was hardly any sign of life as Ingrid made her way. There was no vehicular traffic and only a few pedestrians had ventured out to brave the conditions.

Ingrid left her skis at the entrance to the cemetery and shuffled through the drifting snow to Rick's grave. She dug through the snow, more than three feet now, and placed the single rose at the base of the head stone. She knelt, prayed, and sobbed. "I miss you, Rick."

Her skis were still standing in the snow drift but her poles had fallen and already were half buried in the heavy snow. The reports warned about the severity of this storm with Montana and the Dakotas literally paralyzed. She quickly moved out to return home.

At the first intersection another skier passed directly in front of Ingrid. He hadn't seen her, so restricted was the visibility. Just a sudden blur as the skiers crossed at ninety degrees. A quick glance over her shoulder and the skier was gone. It had to be a man, judging from the size and speed. A strong skier.

It was eleven o'clock when Ingrid arrived back home. The phone was ringing. By the time she'd removed her boots and extricated herself from Sasha and Bentley, it was too late to get the call. The answering machine indicated it was Billy. She called him right away.

"Hullo."

"Hi, Billy, it's me. How are you?"

"Okay thanks, Ingrid. I was thinking about you 'cause I know what today is. Are you all right?"

"It's nice of you to ask, Billy. You're right, it's not a great time for me, but I'll be fine. What's happening with you?"

"Nothing new, Ingrid. They still haven't found Cheryl so I'm going to help in the search this afternoon, if they don't cancel it. Frank too. He's going to have Betty take care of the store — doesn't think we'll be busy with this storm. If there isn't a search, I'm going to help plow the parking lot."

"That could take all day at this rate."

"Yeah, but I guess we have to try. Sometime this afternoon I'm taking the kids for a while — tobogganing or something. Want to join us?"

"You're such a good uncle the way you spend time with those kids. You probably see more of them than their father does."

"Well Frank is awfully busy with the store and all, Ingrid."

"Yeah. Anyway it sounds like fun. Call me when you're ready."

"It'll be around two or so by the time I get done. The kids want to see your dogs."

"That's fine."

"Of course, if the police do have the search, I'll want to join them, Ingrid."

"So will I. Just let me know one way or the other. And thanks for the call, Billy."

After they hung up Ingrid couldn't help but wonder why the police even considered Billy as a suspect in the recent murders. She would trust him with her life.

Chapter 47

THE WIND WOKE JACK. The motel wasn't the most solid structure and the building creaked and groaned from the gale force winds. It was after eight, an unusually late hour for him to be in bed. Several nights with only four hours sleep will do that. He had a quick shower before visiting the command center.

"It's like time has stopped, Lieutenant," said Matt Erickson. "Practically every highway has been closed, emergency vehicles only, and there are power outages all over the state. The National Guard is on full alert as well as the military. The Governor has declared a state of emergency."

"I could hear and feel the storm. Any news here."

"Nothing is moving so its still a no go on the Dean search. The snow is forecast to stop by noon but the wind is causing havoc out there — serious drifts over all the roads. It's a sea of white, Lieutenant. Beautiful, but it's making our job more difficult. Snowmobiles, skis, or snow shoes are the only means of getting around."

"Call a team meeting for nine-thirty. I'm going to have a quick breakfast before I make some calls."

"10-4, Lieutenant. The fourth estate is anxious to talk to you."

"I'll bet. Can't they concentrate on this storm?"

"Murders make better news, I guess."

Jack grunted but did meet with the press before breakfast. The number of reporters hadn't increased, only because the storm had restricted travel in the state. The case still attracted a lot of attention. Thirty minutes later he managed to free himself and get to the coffee shop.

Julie was hustling about with breakfast orders. "How did you get here so early, beautiful?" asked Jack.

"Early he says. Here you are too late for breakfast and too early for lunch. I've been here since five-thirty, boss man, just waiting for you."

Several snickers around the room. "Any eggs left?" asked Jack.

"The state may be closed but the Wilton Lake Motel is prepared to take care of you and your team, Lieutenant. What'll you have?"

"The usual, Julie."

"The usual, he says. From a guy who has twelve different hamburger specials and hasn't had the same breakfast more than once." More snickers.

"Aw, Julie, give me a break. Just a few eggs like only you can arrange. Add some meat, your choice, and a stack of pancakes. Make that a small stack."

"No toast or juice this morning?"

"Okay. A large orange juice and four slices of whole wheat please."

"Lieutenant, how do you manage to keep a reasonably trim figure?"

"Chasing beautiful women like you, Julie."

"Men. You're all the same."

Matt signaled Jack. "Lieutenant, call for you."

He took it in the command center. "Petersen here."

"Jack, it's Cam Fletcher. How're you doing?"

"Fine, Cam. Did you get to the Colonel?"

"Yeah, talked to him this morning. He seems a little stuffy but certainly knows what he wants."

"Are you taking the job?"

"We've agreed, just a few details to work out when I meet them. Only problem right now is getting there. We have the personnel but we can't move. It could be another day from what I hear. How bad is it up there?"

"Not good. All the highways are closed. We can use your help with this one, Cam. We just don't have enough agents to cover the area."

"Sounds like a great spot other than this nut case. How much have you got on him?"

"Not a lot. David Folk's on the case but so far we're drawing a blank."

"You sure it's one guy?" asked Cam.

"It looks that way. The profiler picked out one suspect here but it doesn't feel right. We've been watching him."

"We'll do all we can, Jack. The moment we're mobile we'll let you know. Look forward to seeing you again."

"Same here. Bye." Jack went back to the coffee shop.

"Good timing, sir. Just off the griddle."

"Thanks, Julie." Jack polished off his breakfast and took a cup of coffee to the meeting.

They discussed strategies to be used given the present weather. Extra snowmobiles had been obtained from the local dealer and some had been donated by citizens. The K-9 unit would be able to work the search for the Dean girl but volunteers and other help would have to wait for better conditions.

The news about Security Plus received a mixed reaction. Private companies often didn't have the full endorsement of B.C.A. agents. Jack assured them Fletcher was one of the best in the business.

The team assigned to Billy had nothing unusual to report. "Seems like a model citizen."

"Don't let up," said Jack. "We're going to set up some patrols for the lake properties till Fletcher's group arrives. These conditions make it easier for this creep so we'll have to use lots of lights. Teams of two snowmobiles, both with head lamps and extra spot lights. I want it to look like Christmas out there."

The meeting continued for another half hour. They'd reconvene tomorrow morning unless something broke.

As they left the room, Jack was called to the phone.

"Petersen here."

"Good morning, pig. Do you really..."

Jack was waving frantically, mouthing the words, 'get on this,' motioning to call display.

...think you can stop me?"

The voice was disguised, the message disjointed — had to be male.

"What do you mean, stop you?" asked Jack.

"From the next one — soon." Click. He heard the caller sign off.

"What'd you get?" asked Jack. He ran across the room. "Any kind of trace?"

"Nah. We don't have the gear to locate a number that quickly."

"Order that right now, Matt. I don't want to miss him if he calls again."

Every agent in the room was galvanized into action. "We've got a caller. The creep was on the phone."

"Play it back, play it back." All incoming calls were taped.

They replayed the call. Everyone was still as the voice invaded the room.

"Good morning, pig. Do you really think you can stop me?" Jack's voice, then -

"From the next one — soon." Click.

"He's recorded that, then slowed the tape down. Have Forensics work on that for us. We'll have his real voice in no time."

"Get this off to David Folk, now," said Jack.

"How, Lieutenant?"

"What do you mean how?"

Matt pointed outside. "Remember what's happening out there?"

In the excitement of the moment they were all focused on the call. The outside world had temporarily been forgotten.

"Dammit," said Jack. "Of course. We're stuck here. How the hell do we get this to a lab?"

Nobody moved or said anything. The wind battered the motel. Windows rattled and the entire building shook.

"Call David and play him the tape," said Jack. "Maybe he can work from that. Do they need the original for analysis?"

"Don't know," said Matt.

"Call him and find out," said Jack. "Get all the agents back in here."

Jack had a blown-up map of the area displayed on one wall. Circled in red were the Martin and Michael houses, scenes of the first two murders, as well as the Walleye River where they'd found Jim Bradford. Outlined in blue was the last place Cheryl Dean had been seen, including a grid of the search area.

"He threatens to move again, soon. We'll double the patrols on Wilton Lake. Have we got the manpower for that?"

"For a day or so, Lieutenant," said Matt. "We'll have to lengthen the shifts, cut back on rest time until we get some help. More agents are scheduled in, but who knows when they'll get here. Hopefully before these guys wear out."

"The Hibbards are here on Lot 22. She claims there was someone in her backyard last night. Who knows? Anybody that moves out there is to be stopped and questioned. Do all of you have walkie talkies?"

A chorus of "Yeah, Lieutenant."

"Make sure they're working. This guy is strong and probably armed so we don't want any one-on-one situations. Matt, set up the routes and times for the patrols. Check in with each other frequently."

They went over the details. There would be nonstop patrols until further notice. No Super Bowl party here. With the Vikes out it took away some of the pain of missing the big game. There was a bigger 'game' here with much more at stake. Find the low life. Pray for a let up in the weather to allow more troops to get here. They were going to need all the help they could get.

Chapter 48

INGRID THREW YET ANOTHER SNOWBALL. The dogs flew after it, then furiously dug in the snow where it had disappeared. She marveled at their strength as they plowed through the deep snow, only six months old yet amazingly strong. They were a great source of comfort and incredible companions.

Billy and the kids would be arriving in an hour so Ingrid went back in the house to prepare some snacks. They were going to Wilton Park for some tobogganing or skiing, depending on the conditions. The police had advised that the search was postponed till tomorrow morning.

She called Janice who answered immediately.

"Hi, Janice. How are you?"

"Fine thanks, Ingrid. How's it going?"

"Pretty well thanks. I appreciated your call. I'm going out a little later with Billy and the McCord kids. Care to join us?"

"Sounds like fun, but actually I have a date."

"Is this the Mister Mysterious I'm not to know about?"

"Yeah. I just can't bring myself to discuss it with you. I know I should."

"I don't want you hurt, Janice, that's all. The fact that you can't talk about it only means something's not right."

A long pause.

"Janice, I'm your friend and you mean a lot to me. Why don't you tell me?"

"He's married, Ingrid."

Longer pause.

"Well, it's not my worst fear realized, but pretty close," said Ingrid. "I guess I don't have to tell you there's no future in such a relationship."

"True."

"I don't even want to know who he is. How do I help you stop it, Janice?"

"I don't know."

"You could start by canceling today's date and joining us."

"I wish it was that simple, Ingrid."

"Meaning?"

"I'm in love with him."

"Oh, God almighty. And I suppose he's in love with you. No way."

"Why not?"

"Do you talk about the wife and kids?"

"Ingrid, lay off."

"Does he have kids?"

"Ingrid!"

"Well, does he? And is that the problem? Poor man, isn't appreciated at home, but can't leave his wife because of the kids. So he carries on with you, the love of his life — for now. And if he ever leaves her to marry you, who will his next lover be?"

"I understand why you're upset..."

"Upset? The more I think about it, the angrier I become. Oh, Janice. I'm sorry, but I'm not. You know what I mean?"

"I guess so."

"These relationships never work out," said Ingrid. "Well maybe that's not totally accurate, but the odds are certainly not favorable."

"I understand all of that, Ingrid, but things happen. You can't just turn off those feelings. It's not that simple."

"How can I help?"

"I'll think about it. At least now you know. We'll have to talk."

"Why not start today? Come out with us this afternoon then you and I can get together for supper — alone."

"Not today, Ingrid. But I'll meet you early in the week. Is that okay?"

"It's not my first choice but I suppose it's a start."

"Thanks. I know you care. See you tomorrow."

The dogs ran to the front door, barking and growling. "Billy's here. If you change your mind, we'll be at Wilton Park."

"Bye, Ingrid." They hung up.

Ingrid ran to the door to let Billy and the kids in. The dogs, not being familiar with children, were slightly puzzled at the sight of Lisa and Wes. The kids however were fearless, dying to touch them. Sasha was immediately receptive while Bentley remained a little standoffish, but not for long. Soon all four were cavorting all over the house. Billy had been recognized but ignored, the kids were far too much fun.

Ingrid set out the snacks and everyone dug in while they planned the afternoon.

"Will you toboggan with us, Auntie Ingrid?" asked Lisa.

"Of course I will. As long as we can see far enough. What was it like coming over, Billy?"

"Still very bad. I didn't bring the truck. We were able to fit three on the snowmobile but I don't think it'll take four of us, Ingrid."

"That's okay, I'll ski over. It's not that far."

"Can the dogs come?" asked Wes.

"Not this time, Wes. When they're a little older and we have the truck with us we could manage, but I'm afraid not today."

"Can we come back later?"

"Sure. If it's all right with your parents, you can stay for supper."

"Can we, Uncle Billy? Can we?"

"I'll call your Mom and ask her." Billy made the call. Jean had no problem as long as the kids were home early. It was Sunday.

The afternoon was a huge success. Billy took very seriously the responsibility of looking after the kids. He monitored all the toboggan runs carefully. They in turn adored their uncle. Conditions continued to worsen so they decided to get back earlier than planned. That was okay with Lisa and Wes — there were dogs to play with.

They had an early supper and too soon for Lisa and Wes, it was time to go. Ingrid promised they could come back anytime.

"Billy, be careful on the way home."

"Don't worry, Ingrid, I know all these routes like the back of my hand. Good night and thanks." Hugs for the dogs and kids.

The company and outing had helped pass the day. The news about Janice lingered. Ingrid took the dogs out. Now that it was dark, the dogs disappeared from view in an instant. She could hear them, knew they were close by. They barked and squealed as they romped in the snow, always coming back to check with Ingrid.

She felt the cold stab through her. When will this storm let up? Wilton was in for a long night of serious weather. It was a good night to stay put.

Not everyone in Wilton felt that way.

Chapter 49

NANCY BRITAIN LOVED A GOOD TIME and the Super Bowl bash was in full swing. Their hosts, the Chapmans, knew how to throw a party. They had set up a pool with the Rams' and Titans' logos and pictures of prominent stars — Eddie George and Kurt Warner. This, of course, was NFC country so the majority were pulling for the Rams. But not Nancy. The gorgeous blonde from Tennessee was cheering loudly for her Titans while enduring the good natured catcalls of her friends and neighbors.

Only sixteen of the thirty odd invited had been able to attend, weather being the main factor in keeping people away. Those who had arrived came by snowmobile except immediate neighbors who had walked over.

The men were totally absorbed with the game while the women, with the exception of Nancy, paid little attention. They were more interested in just visiting. Of course the main topic was the threat facing their community and the meeting yesterday at the Baird's. Most were pleased that a private security firm had been contacted and would be in place as soon as the weather allowed.

Nancy, meanwhile, was in the thick of things with the husbands. And she knew her football, as much or more than a lot of the men.

"The Rams will kill them."

"You haven't seen Eddie George run," said Nancy.

"He'd run really good if he were after you, Nancy."

Nancy smiled and accepted the compliment gracefully. The guys loved having her near. She was a good sport and certainly an eyeful. At half time Nancy joined the other wives.

"Nancy, you sure are outnumbered over there. How's your team doing?"

"They're coasting a bit. They'll come back in the second half. Julia, we thought Max did a fine job in organizing that meeting and getting some security organized. Congratulations."

"Thanks, Nancy. We've been discussing that. It's the waiting that's getting us, what with this awful weather."

"Well it's also mobilized the police. You can see their snowmobiles cruising up and down the McCord Trail. That has to bring some comfort."

"We'll all be better off when they catch the killer," said June Chapman. "I don't know about you but I'm having trouble sleeping at night."

"Me too," said Julia. "Even during the day I'm worried. Always starting at any strange noise. It's crazy."

"We're going back to the Cities as soon as possible," said Frances Hawkins. "If this weather hadn't hit, we'd have been out of here yesterday. We're leaving the moment it clears and not coming back until this maniac is caught."

"Can't blame you," said Nancy. "But I don't think he'll try anything now with all these policemen around. Once we get our Security Force in place, we can all breathe a little easier."

"Second half starting, Nancy," her husband Al called out. "We need you here 'cause you're the only female and the only Titans fan we have to needle."

"Better join them, Nancy," said June. "Their egos need you."

"Do you need any help with the meal, June?"

"No thanks, Nancy. There's plenty of us and we know you enjoy the game. Go to it and give those guys the business."

Nancy braced herself with another glass of punch which was pretty heavily laced so she was being careful. Enough to have fun but still capable of taking in the game. The Titans played a strong second half and almost succeeded in tying the game in the waning seconds, falling short by only a few yards. Nancy did have the winning score in the Chapman pool which brought a chorus of boos from the men, cheers from the women.

A delicious looking buffet had been set up and everyone was anxious to get at it. Nancy excused herself to go to the washroom. She was feeling the effects of the last glass of punch. The clock in the front hall read nine o'clock. Rusty, their eleven year old Golden Retriever had been in the house now for five hours. Time to let him out. Her coat and boots were in the front closet. They lived just two lots over — it would take her only a few minutes.

The conditions were worse than she'd remembered. She braced herself against the strong wind, barely able to move forward. God, is this a good idea? Well Rusty needed her. She had trouble keeping her eyes open as the wind and snow whipped at her face. She could actually feel tiny snow particles smacking against her eyeballs. They hurt. Nancy put her head down and strode forward.

Halfway to their house she saw a snowmobile on the trail. Probably one of the police patrols. It was encouraging to see them covering the area. For some reason the headlight was off.

The vehicle neared and slowed to a stop. As Nancy approached, she could make out only one snowmobile. She thought that was odd. Didn't the police always travel in pairs?

Chapter 50

JACK WAS GETTING READY to join Elmer Holm on patrol. With the shortage of agents he wanted to pitch in till reinforcements arrived. He tried to reach Jennifer before leaving, but got the answering machine. He remembered she'd said the neighbors were having her over for dinner. He left a message saying he would call back around eleven.

The darkness and limited visibility from the blowing snow promised poor conditions for their patrols. They'd established an emergency route between the motel and the McCord Trail with the trip taking about fifteen minutes. The occasional snow blower could be seen as residents tried to keep their driveways open. It was a losing battle so far. The town's snow plows were working around the clock in an attempt to clear the main thoroughfares. Also a near impossible task.

Jack and Elmer strapped on the head gear with emergency lamps and ear phones. They checked in on the frequency in use. Nothing untoward happening. Elmer gunned the engine as they picked up the trail. He was a new agent with three years on the force.

"Is this northern Minnesota or Siberia?" asked Elmer. "I've seen a lot of winter storms, but never anything close to this."

"Likewise," said Jack. "The timing couldn't be worse for us. Was that call for real?"

"He's at a disadvantage too, Lieutenant. He doesn't know if he's going to run into one of us."

"True. But he knows where he's going. We don't."

The noise crackled in their headsets. Their lights played over the area.

Visibility was poor but it wasn't zero. The snowmobile had a strong headlight plus an extra spot light mounted on the dash. Ten minutes along the trail they picked up a light heading toward them. Radio contact confirmed it was one of the patrols. They stopped and conferred briefly before continuing. Nothing moving.

One snowmobile was positioned on the lake with five others working the trail. Each vehicle covered twelve lots, thus overlapping a couple of properties at the end of their runs. Since McCord's was close to the lake properties, they'd asked for the use of the store for breaks. Frank had agreed to have a staff member on hand to serve hot drinks and snacks. The men could take brief rests to warm up and be only ten minutes from the start of the patrol route. The machines bobbed along the trail while the agents kept their eyes peeled for any sign of activity.

The ear phones continually crackled, sometimes with talk between agents or just static. It was tiresome work but necessary given the caller's threat. Goggles protected their eyes, but didn't ease the strain of staring into the blinding snow.

"You're still puzzled about Billy McCord, aren't you, Lieutenant?"

"Yeah. We've had three interviews with him. Nothing conclusive has come out. It's too close a match to drop the tail on him, but something tells me we might not have the right guy."

"He's a bit weird isn't he?"

"I wouldn't say he's weird," said Jack. "He's different. And although slow, he's not stupid. Could he be fooling all of us? If he has, this is one hell of an actor. Always insisting on his innocence. Would never hurt a flea. Yet strong as an ox and living a rather secluded life. Loners always concern me."

"Is he mixed up about women?"

"He doesn't appear to be interested in women but that isn't a crime. Nor does it mean he'd want to abuse them. He might just be shy or lack confidence. On the other hand..."

"All vehicles, get over to Lot 31, now. We have a missing person."

Elmer did a one-eighty and raced down the trail.

"Petersen here. Give us some details."

"Lieutenant, it's Al Welsh. I'm just leaving the motel. A Mr Chapman called saying one of the wives at his party has disappeared. He's hosting a Super Bowl party and one of the wives suddenly wasn't there anymore."

"How the hell does somebody just disappear?"

"When the game was over, they'd set out a buffet dinner. The woman, Nancy Britain, apparently went to the can and never came back. They were all milling around the spread when someone said, 'Hey, where's Nancy?' A couple of the guys went to the Britain house — they live two lots over at number 33. Nobody there, just the family dog."

"Are they sure she's not in either house?" asked Jack. "Maybe she passed out in a bedroom or something."

"Chapman claims they've looked everywhere. Jim and Ed are there already. They say the people are frantic. There won't be any welcoming committee for you."

"How many agents have you got coming?"

"We had four crews taking power naps. They're on the way and we've left one team with Matt. The K-9 unit's also helping. We'll be there in twenty minutes."

"10-4. See you there," said Jack.

"This is going to be an ugly scene," said Elmer.

"Maybe not as ugly as what's happened to Mrs Britain. Let's hope she's okay."

Jack called Matt at the command center. "Matt, I want you to take a look at the map of the lake area. Do you see anything around Lot 31 that might help us?"

"Just a second, Lieutenant. There's one of those logging trails that intersects with the McCord Trail just south of Lot 32. It heads easterly then bends around to continue northeast. It goes for miles, all the way back to Wilton. Crosses over a few county side roads. Other than that, solid brush."

"Matt, get two snowmobiles on that trail right away. We're on our way to the Chapman's. Any other reports?"

"Nothing serious."

They signed off.

When Jack arrived at the Chapman's some semblance of order had been restored but there was still a hostile group facing them. The fact that most had been drinking didn't help, although the incident had sobered the group considerably. Several comments and questions were heard as soon as they entered the house.

"Lieutenant, what have you got going so far?" asked Max Baird, who was front and center.

"We'll ask the questions, Colonel. I want to talk to the host and the husband of the missing woman."

Max was momentarily caught off guard but Jack had clearly established who was in charge. The Colonel began to make another point but was cut off.

"Mr Britain and Mr Chapman, please," said Jack.

They stepped forward. Jack offered his sympathies to Al Britain and suggested they reconstruct the events up to the disappearance of his wife.

"Have both houses been thoroughly searched?"

"Yes, Lieutenant. Nancy isn't in either," said Ed.

"Lieutenant, her coat and boots are gone," said Al. "Nancy left here and never made it to our house. What could have happened? You have patrols out there don't you? What the hell were they doing? What're they doing now?"

"We're searching the area between the two houses and along the logging trail. What about Lot 32? Who lives there?"

"That's the Richardson's. They're not here this time of year."

"Do any of you look after their place? Have a key to the house?"

"We do, Lieutenant," said Ed.

"Let's have a look there. What about the other side, Lot 30?"

"It's vacant. They're going to build this spring."

"What condition was your wife in when she left?" asked Jack.

"What do you mean?" asked Al. "Was she drunk or something? What kind of a question is that?"

"Al, I think the Lieutenant has to know anything we can give him," said Ed. "The most important thing is to find Nancy as quickly as possible."

"Yeah I guess. She had a few drinks, but Nancy was basically okay, didn't you think so, Ed?"

"Feeling mellow, that's about it," said Ed.

"Was she disturbed about anything? Any recent problems?"

"Not at all," said Al. "She was the life of the party and had no problems. Dammit, Lieutenant, what's going to happen here? This won't find Nancy."

"We need a description of your wife, plus the coat she would have worn. We'll do an all out search. You can also help. We'll lay out a grid for you in the immediate area. Stay in pairs, don't leave anyone alone, especially the women. Any men that join the search ensure your wife remains in a group here."

"That madman's got her, hasn't he, Lieutenant?" asked Al.

"We don't know that. She may have fallen, lost her way. In this weather it's very easy to become disoriented. Let's get on with the search. Mrs Chapman, here's the phone number of Sergeant Erickson at our headquarters. If you hear anything, call him. All the agents are in contact with the office."

Two agents remained to organize those who would assist in the search. Jack left with Elmer.

"We're going up that logging trail, Elmer. Are we okay for gas?"

"We'll be fine, Lieutenant."

Jack was frustrated. With this storm, the chances of finding Mrs Britain were grim. He strapped on the head gear.

"Let's get at it," said Jack.

Chapter 51

THE KILLER FELT FREE to roam. With the battering from the storm everything was in turmoil. The police investigation was hampered and they'd called off the search for the Dean girl.

It was dark now but he knew all the trails. He had really just wanted an outing but the headaches had returned. The snowmobile easily handled the drifts. Winds must be in the forty mile an hour range. He enjoyed these conditions. Nothing was too severe for him. Bring it on. He laughed out loud. But he was angry.

The lights from one of the houses glared in the blizzard. They weren't sharp but they were there, an eerie glow in the night and snow. Not the only lights. He could see a single light moving on the lake. A lone snowmobile cruising along the shore line. Then another light, coming along the McCord Trail.

He'd stopped at the edge of the tree line and shut down his machine. He'd wait this out to determine what was happening. There was plenty of time. Since it was only eight o'clock there was still another nine or ten hours of darkness. He studied the pattern over the next hour. There was obviously some kind of patrol. He had timed the coming and going of the snowmobiles. Fairly regular.

Maybe he should come back in the early morning. Surely there wouldn't be as many out at that hour. He was parked near the trail, only fifty feet away, when he saw a flash of light from the Chapman house. The front door had opened and in that brief instant he was able to make out the form of a single person leaving the house. He was sure it was a woman.

He eased the machine down to the trail. There wasn't a patrol due for another five minutes. Her head was down and her walk a little unsteady. She looked up and saw him but kept coming.

When she was alongside, he reacted instantly. His fist caught her on the chin, knocking her backwards, half unconscious. He tied her arms behind her back, hoisted her onto his machine, and took off, back up the logging trail. It was awkward balancing her inert form but he managed. He raced along the path.

She started to revive. He clamped one hand over her mouth. "Don't try anything. Don't move and you'll be all right. Understand?"

No response. She struggled against him. He moved his arm around her neck, applying a choking hold. "Stop moving or I'll break your neck." All movement stopped.

After ten minutes he pulled over. He took out a blindfold and covered her eyes. Just as quickly he took off again. The stranglehold remained. It took the better part of an hour to reach his destination. They hadn't met another vehicle or person. He drove around to the back of the house. Nothing could be seen other than snow.

He easily hoisted her onto his back, carried her into the house, down a narrow stairway to the basement, and into a small room. There was a single cot at one end of the room and a small bathroom.

He locked the door when he left.

Chapter 52

INGRID LEARNED that classes were canceled but there'd be an assembly to organize volunteers to help in the community. Hardly a surprise. The storm showed no sign of letting up. When she let the dogs out in the morning, they had to negotiate a six foot drift that blanketed her back porch. The winds continued to howl although the reports said the snow fall had lessened. It was difficult to sort out what was new snow as opposed to blowing snow from previous accumulations.

Time to call Janice. The phone rang five times before she answered.

"Good morning. Did I get you out of bed?" asked Ingrid.

"Hi, Ingrid. Yeah, sort of. I was up around six, but decided to lie down for a while. What time is it now?"

"Nearly eight. That was some little nap."

"Yeah. I'm glad you called. Are you going to the school this morning to volunteer?"

"Of course," said Ingrid. "There'll be lots to do. We're lucky there's been no power failures. They're happening all over the state with lines down everywhere."

"We're in for more according to what I heard earlier this morning. And, Ingrid, what are people doing if they're sick and need hospital care? I hear they're looking for volunteers to get to the elderly as well. It just doesn't end."

"I imagine that'll be on the agenda when we get to the school. I'd like to see you anyway, Janice."

"I know. I'm relieved that you know about my...situation. It's time we talked."

"I'm glad you feel that way," said Ingrid. "Then we'll meet at the school?"

"Great. I'll see you there in an hour or so."

The turn out at Wilton High was impressive with the entire staff and most of the student body attending to volunteer their help. The news of Nancy Britain's disappearance was yet another blow. The police had nothing to report on either missing person, Cheryl Dean or Nancy.

They assembled in the auditorium where Muriel Bates addressed the group.

"Thank you for coming in today. It shows the spirit of our school and the willingness to band together to help each other during this crisis. We have several organizations with us to outline areas where help is needed. Each is set up around the room. Please visit them and see where you fit in. Classes are temporarily postponed until the weather improves and our help is no longer needed. Again, thank you for attending."

The group dispersed, eager to get involved in the different projects. Getting meals and medical aid to the elderly was a priority. Medical emergencies presented a serious problem. There were only so many doctors, nurses, and snowmobiles. Downtown services and businesses needed help to assist the community. Snow shoveling was a major priority.

Ingrid and Janice took on transportation duties — moving volunteers to kitchens where meals were being prepared for the needy, then delivering the meals. It was exhausting and time consuming. Since many of the streets were impassable even for snowmobiles, careful routing had to be planned just to get the meals delivered. They would take six at a time in heated containers and drop them at preselected houses. The next challenge was getting to the front door as often severe drifting blocked the path. It was yet another chore for the snow removal teams.

The town was responding to the emergency in an all out effort by young and old alike. Ingrid had been fortunate to be able to fit in a fast trip home to let the dogs out. It was after five before Ingrid and Janice were able to stop for a snack. They huddled in a corner to devour delicious home made chili, fresh Italian bread, and hot chocolate.

"What can you tell me about your secret affair, Janice?"

"Ah, Ingrid, never one to beat around the bush. Just get straight to the heart of the matter." Janice held her friend's hand and smiled.

"Sorry. I didn't mean to be so abrupt. You know I really care."

"I know you do," said Janice. "Believe me, I couldn't have this conversation with anybody else. It's not going to be easy."

"Where would you like to start?"

"I suppose you'd be more interested in finding a way to help me end the relationship."

"For your sake, Janice, and the others involved. Do they have kids?"

"Yes," said Janice. She held her head. "I know it's wrong. I've been thinking of nothing else lately."

"I won't insult you with a discussion on the moral issues here. I just want to see you out of this. What can I do to help?"

"You're already helping by just being here for me and getting me to talk it through. You're the only one who knows. I'm sure...he hasn't discussed this with anyone."

"Do you want to tell me who it is?" asked Ingrid.

Long pause. "Not yet. I don't know why, but just not yet. I suppose that sounds silly."

Ingrid looked at her friend, feeling for her, yet wanting to grab her by the shoulders and shake some sense into her.

"You are thinking about ending this," said Ingrid. "Otherwise we wouldn't be having this conversation."

"Yes. I'd even thought the best thing to do is to leave Wilton. Start a new life somewhere. Would you come with me?"

"Can't say I haven't thought the same thing," said Ingrid. "Especially on a day like yesterday."

"I'm sorry, Ingrid. Here I am burdening you with my problem. That's not very fair of me."

"That's okay." Ingrid reached out and held Janice. They were both on the verge of tears. "We'll work this out."

"Thanks again, Ingrid. Could I stay with you tonight? I'm getting nervous about what's going on here."

"It'd be comforting for me too. You may be assaulted by two playful puppies early in the morning."

"Great. Let's get back to work."

The storm was gradually breaking up and conditions were forecast to improve.

Finally one piece of good news for Wilton.

Chapter 53

JACK AWOKE at seven-thirty. He'd managed three hours sleep. The rest of the team had been equally deprived as the search for Mrs Britain was maintained throughout the night. The only good news was the turn in the weather. The snow had stopped and the winds abated. Cleanup in town was well underway and life would soon be back to normal.

Normal? Not with a serial killer at large. The search for Cheryl Dean and Nancy Britain would continue. The all out alert for the killer would intensify with the addition of another ten agents due to arrive today. Cam Fletcher's team was to arrive in Wilton by noon.

Jack called Jennifer before she left for work. The phone rang till the answering machine cut in. Midway through the message Jennifer interrupted to say, "Hang on, I'm here." The message finished.

"Hi, Hon," said Jack. "Did I get you at a bad moment?"

"I'm dripping wet from the shower but I thought it might be you."

"I'm glad I caught you. You look terrific."

"Thanks. Do I get to see you tonight?"

"It's looking a lot better here," said Jack. "That's as in the weather at least. The case though, is not."

"Not another murder?"

"Don't know yet. We have another missing person which doesn't look good."

"I'm sorry, Jack. Any help on the way?"

"Yeah. We're expecting more B.C.A. agents and Security Plus today. Barring an emergency, I'll be home tonight. For one thing I have an appointment in the Cities tomorrow morning and for another, I really want to see you."

"You're going to the Cities in the middle of a murder investigation, Jack? I don't believe it. What's so important?"

"I'll let you know tonight. It's no big deal. I'll be back in Wilton by one or so."

"Well, I'll be delighted to have you here. I'll prepare your favorite."

"That's you and you don't need any special preparation. I like you just the way you are."

"Right now that's half dried and shivering," said Jennifer. "Will you make it in time for dinner?"

"That's the plan. Can't wait to see you. Love you."

"I love you too, Jack. Till later."

Jack cleaned up and headed for the coffee shop. He joined Matt and Al at a table. Julie, as usual, was on the job.

"What a wonderful sight first thing in the morning," said Jack. "How are you, Julie?"

"I rush to get here and what do I get? Sarcasm from a married man. Let me see. What's the Lieutenant going to inhale for breakfast this morning?"

"The Irish breakfast looks good to me, Julie."

"How you ever managed to talk our cook into preparing Irish breakfasts is beyond me. But, okay you've got it. And, how will you have the eggs?"

"Soft poached, please."

"At least we got a break in the weather, Lieutenant," said Matt. "That'll make it easier to track this creep."

"Just being able to get more agents is a relief. Any news from the patrols?"

"Afraid not," said Al. "I just finished and we didn't find any clues, let alone a body. Let's hope she's still alive."

"I understand Fletcher is coming up today," said Matt. "How much will he help us, Lieutenant?"

"They're a good outfit that'll take some of the pressure off us. Cam has a lot of experience and knows how to manage men. I'll be meeting with him around noon. Anything from David on the phone call tape?"

"Nothing so far," said Al. "I'll call him before the team meeting."

"Okay," said Jack. "We've moved that back to ten o'clock this morning, due to the late patrols. Has anyone talked to the Deans this morning?"

"I'll get on that," said Matt. "We'll resume the search today?"

"Yeah. Both of them — Britain and Dean. We've got to find this guy soon."

"You cooling off on Billy McCord, Lieutenant?"

"Maybe a little. What did they have to say about last night?"

"He volunteered yesterday for snow clearing," said Matt. "Report is, he seemed tireless, worked about fourteen hours straight."

"Always in sight of one of us?"

"Afraid not, Lieutenant. It got really hectic out there as the crews were on the go constantly. Our surveillance was there most of the time but we also had to spell off the patrols. We're really short staffed. The tail will be back on him later this morning."

"We were that short of agents we lost him? For how long?"

"Hard to say, Lieutenant. But he was always in a group, never alone."

"How do you know that?" asked Jack. "If we can lose of track of him, why couldn't others, especially those not involved in surveillance?"

Silence.

"It was difficult, Lieutenant. We needed the men. With a woman missing, we had other priorities and had to make a call. As I said, it's not like we left him alone."

"He may not seem to fit but he's still under suspicion. When do you get somebody back on him?"

"We'll have someone on it by ten."

"See that it doesn't happen again."

"10-4, Lieutenant."

Jack grabbed a cup of coffee to take to the meeting. The arrival of ten new agents and Cam Fletcher's group was welcome news to the team. The

Dean and Britain searches were allocated. The need to flush out the killer was given top priority.

David Folk had sent the report on the tape, confirming what had been suspected. There was a mixture of three different voices used — male and female. More work was underway to isolate each voice.

The meeting ended just as Cam Fletcher arrived. There was no mistaking him. Two hundred and forty pounds of muscle evenly distributed over a six foot, two inch body wasn't all — Cam sported a head of bright red hair complemented by a full moustache and half beard. All this with a perpetual grin, which was either friendly or a threatening sneer.

"Good to see you, Jack." Jack's hand disappeared in Cam's large paw.

"Likewise, Cam. You seem as fit as ever."

"Try to stay that way. Fill me in, will you."

Jack briefed him on the three murders, and the two missing women, Cheryl Dean and Nancy Britain.

"The killings occurred in the early morning hours," said Jack. "But the latest events with the missing women are different. Both happened around nine o'clock but under different conditions. Saturday and Sunday nights had us in the middle of the storm."

"So he gets bolder in bad conditions. Feels he can't be caught because the weather's so bad?"

"David Folk knows he's unbalanced, but doesn't know what triggers the attacks. There isn't any pattern to the timing. All the victims have been women except the Bradford kid. That's out of the mold."

"Was it done to throw you off?" asked Cam. "Here he's playing his deadly game so he switches targets. Disrupts the pattern."

"Or did Bradford stumble onto something?" asked Jack. "Maybe he surprised the killer. He did disappear early in the morning. That's the time our guy is out and about."

"And you say there's been no sign of forcible entry. The guy just knocks on the door and they let him in?"

"We don't know how he gets in but it appears he's known to the victims. No signs of a struggle. He surprised both of them."

"Forensics has nothing for you?" asked Cam. "He's got to leave something behind. Foot prints, hair...something."

"So far, not a thing," said Jack. "And everything outside has been erased with the wind and snow."

"Phone call, Lieutenant," said Matt. "I think it's him. Just hold it. We can trace the location in seconds."

Jack waited then took the call. "Petersen here."

"Hey, pig, going away tomorrow? Too bad."

"Why is that? You want to arrange a meeting?"

"I might take the day off — or I might not. You won't get me anyway." Click.

"Pay phone — in Wilton. Go."

Jack was out the door with Al Welsh, into his Jeep. Two other agents took a snowmobile. Two more on patrol were contacted and directed into Wilton.

The highway was passable but not completely cleared. Al had the siren going. Three minutes later Matt called.

"Welsh."

"Len's Hardware, Main and Church. The phone booth's on the corner, right beside the store. We've got Len outside looking right now."

"Thanks, Matt. We'll be there in a few minutes." He hung up.

"That's just past the first traffic light, Al."

"How do you know that?"

"The funeral home is one block over on Main. Move this thing."

Seven minutes after the call they'd arrived at Len's. The phone booth was empty. "Secure this area, Al. Nobody's to go in that phone booth. Call Matt and have him get forensics over here."

Len was alert and eager to help the police.

"Did you see anyone in that phone booth in the last ten to fifteen minutes?"

"Yeah. There was a woman in there about that time. I happened to be at the door and saw her talking on the phone."

"Can you describe her?" asked Jack.

"Of course. It was Jill Reed. She came into the store right after. Needed some batteries."

"How long ago was that?"

"Same time you're talking about, maybe ten, fifteen minutes ago."

"After her, did you see anyone else?" asked Jack.

"I thought I saw a guy walk by, shortly after that. I was busy with Jill, so didn't pay too much attention. But I'm quite sure I caught a glimpse of some guy walking toward the booth."

"Did you see him use the phone?"

"No, can't say I did."

"Did you see him before that, or anyone else in the area?"

"Nope, don't believe I did," said Len. "But you know something, maybe Mrs Reed saw him. See, she was in here only a few minutes, got her batteries and left. That was about the time you're talking about. Am I right?"

"Could be. Did Mrs Reed mention where she was going?"

"No, but probably home. I'll get her number for you. There's a phone book right here."

"We'd like to use your phone, Len."

"Of course. It's right here, on the counter."

They dialed the number. There was no answer.

"We'd like her address as well, please," said Jack.

"Here you are. Do you think the murderer used that phone this morning?"

"We don't know that, Len. If you remember anything else, call this number — anytime."

"Will do, officer."

"Thanks for your help, Len."

The other agents had arrived. Jack told them to secure the area till forensics had been through the phone booth. "Let's get going, Al."

They were at the Reed house within minutes. An elderly man answered the door.

"Mr Reed? Is Mrs Reed home?"

"I'm not Mr Reed and Mrs Reed is not here. Who are you?"

"I'm Lieutenant Petersen, this is Sergeant Welsh. Does Mrs Reed live here?"

"She does."

"What's your name, sir?"

"Fowler."

"And what's your relationship to Mrs Reed?" asked Jack.

"She's my daughter."

"This is urgent, Mr Fowler. When are you expecting your daughter?"

"Not for a while."

"Have you any idea when she'll be back?" asked Jack.

"Yes."

"When is that, Mr Fowler?"

"In an hour or so."

"Do you know where she is now?"

"Yes."

"Do you have the number where she can be reached?"

Fowler nodded. "Is my daughter in some kind of trouble?"

"No, sir. We just need to talk to her."

"I see."

"Now, do you have that number please?"

"Yes."

Nobody moved.

"We'd like the number, Mr Fowler."

"Why didn't you say so?"

Fowler retreated into the house. Al smiled at Jack. "Gotta be specific, Lieutenant."

"If he was fifty years younger, I'd brain him."

Fowler returned with the phone number. "It's the Regan's."

"Thanks, Mr Fowler. You have nothing to worry about."

They retreated to the Jeep and made the call.

"Hello."

"Is Jill Reed there please?" asked Jack.

"Yes. Who's calling?"

"This is Lieutenant Petersen. It's urgent."

"All right. One moment please."

They heard muffled voices before Jill Reed came to the phone.

"This is Jill Reed. What's happening?"

"Lieutenant Petersen, here Mrs Reed. We understand you were in Len's Hardware store earlier. We need to see you immediately."

"I'm at 146 Cornwall Avenue. That's one block north of Main."

"We'll be right over."

A few minutes later they arrived at the Cornwall address and were admitted into Mrs Regan's house. Introductions were made.

"You may use the den if you wish to talk to Jill alone, officer."

"Thank you, we will."

"Mrs Reed, earlier this morning you made a phone call outside Len's Hardware, then spent some time in his store. Is that correct?"

"Yes. I called my father to see if he was okay. I'd been out since seven and like to keep in touch with him."

"And then you made a purchase in the hardware store and left."

"Correct. Where is this leading, officer?"

"As you left the store we believe there might have been someone at the same pay phone you had used. Do you remember that?"

"Yes. I was going to cross the street so I looked both ways, and it was then I saw a man in the phone booth."

"What can you tell us about him?"

"He was big, just about filled the whole booth. Tall too. He had a ski mask on that covered most of his face."

"Did you see his face?" asked Jack.

"Not really, just a glimpse. He was turned about three-quarters away from me."

"Do you remember his clothing?"

"Yes. A dark blue parka and pants. The ski mask was blue and white."

"We'd like you to come to our headquarters and work with an artist to create a computer image of what you saw."

"Are you the officers in charge of that murder investigation?"

"Yes. Anything you can give us may be helpful."

"Did I see the murderer?"

"We don't know that, Mrs Reed. Would you come with us now? We'll take you home as soon as you're finished."

"Of course. I'd like to call my father."

"You can do that from the cruiser."

Jack instructed the other agents to start combing the area. They'd send more agents over immediately. "Ask every store owner and clerk if they've seen the man described. As soon as we get a composite we'll circulate it all over town."

Thirty minutes later they had a sketch of the mystery caller — the man that could be their killer. Jack was excited. This could be there first break. The composites were distributed quickly to businesses and public places. Included was the hot line number. He called a late afternoon meeting. Mrs Reed, who had been quite impressed with the entire process, was driven home.

Jack and Al sat with the profiler, studying the composite.

"His size fits, Lieutenant. Too bad he was wearing that mask. She was only guessing about the nose but the bone structure around the eyes helps a bit."

"Could it be Billy McCord?" asked Jack.

"It doesn't rule him out, but it's not a confirmation either."

"She gave us a good description of the clothing. There's probably a lot of parkas like that around here but it's something we can work with."

"Maybe we should look at McCord's closet, Lieutenant."

"Heh, where was McCord at the time of the call?"

"I'll check it out for you," said Al. "He was supposed to start work at eight o'clock."

"Find out what time he arrived and see if he stayed in the store till now. Also what he was wearing — especially his coat. See if it matches Mrs Reed's description."

Shortly before noon the new agents began to arrive. Jack briefed them on the case while Matt handed out their assignments. They'd interview anyone fitting the description obtained from Mrs Reed. If the person seemed to fit, they were to be brought to the motel where Jack and the profiler would continue the questioning. Calls to the hot line were increasing. The press were anxious with the new activity. Jack had no comment.

The Commissioner called. At least Jack had some encouraging news. It would help his request for more agents.

Chapter 54

JACK HAD AGREED to a meeting with Cam and Colonel Baird. Cam Fletcher's team had assembled by three o'clock. John Tanner was the senior guard, having been with Cam for eight years after serving fifteen years with the B.C.A. He was partnered with the newcomer, Rob Mullen, a brash youngster who knew it all. Despite his arrogance, Cam saw in him a solid person who with maturity could develop into a top- notch guard. John was charged with the responsibility of keeping him in line.

The second team of Will Stevens and Ross Clarkson were proven veterans with more than twenty years of policing and security work between them. It was a well rounded unit.

They had two Jeep Cherokees fully equipped with flood and spot lights, semiautomatic rifles, a shot gun, other assorted weaponry, four snowmobiles, and two German Shepherd dogs. A helicopter in the Cities was available if needed.

Max Baird arrived with Al Britain and Ed Chapman. Al looked like a beaten man. The sunken eyes showed the lack of sleep and his hollow cheeks were evidence of the strain he was under. The furrowed brow told of the pain of not knowing the fate of his wife.

Jack offered his condolences, assuring him of their all out effort in searching for Mrs Britain. Introductions were made and Cam briefed them on his company's equipment and resources. Using the map in the command center they presented the plan of surveillance, using the vehicles and dogs. They'd need schedules indicating which homes were presently occupied, by whom, and for what period of time.

The patrols would start immediately, running from dusk to dawn, approximately twelve hours. The McCords had again offered the use of their store. The guards had time to make a circuit before dark to better acquaint them with the area. Ed and Al would join in to help familiarize them with the territory. Their first shift would be a little longer than twelve hours.

Jack updated Colonel Baird's group on their investigation. He handed out copies of the composite obtained earlier in the day, explaining how it was being distributed in the community. He told them of the hot line and the addition of ten new agents.

Jack welcomed the assistance but reminded them to be cautious. The B.C.A. agents and the security guards were the only ones to challenge any suspicious persons. The group dispersed shortly after three which would give them about an hour and a half of daylight for their initial reconnaissance of the lake.

Jack returned to the command center where Matt told him the hot line had been ringing off the wall. The usual collection of calls ranging from confessions to useful tips were recorded. Still no word about Cheryl Dean or Nancy Britain. There were numerous sightings of men in blue parkas with blue and white ski masks. None led to an actual apprehension for questioning.

"Phone call, Lieutenant."

"Petersen here."

"Ah, my favorite sleuth. How goes it?" asked David Folk.

"Could be worse. We could have absolutely nothing. But now, with the help of one master forensic scientist, the case might be blown wide open."

"Well I don't know about that, but I do have some tidbits for you."

"Fire away," said Jack. "And I believe in your terminology, 'tidbits' does augur well for us."

"With the help of our audio and voice wizards we have a reconstructed tape of your mystery caller. Now all you have to do, Jack, is find a match. Good luck. Additionally we have some fibers from the first two murder scenes that appear to match."

"I'll look forward to the tape," said Jack. "Now what's with the fibers?"

"We found some on the frying pan. Most likely from gloves. I also noticed a resemblance to fibers from the body of the second victim. We're having them analyzed. It's possible we may be able to pick up some prints as well, but that's not guaranteed. I'll keep you posted."

"What will it tell us about the gloves?"

"We'll be able to give you a good description of them," said David. "There's a good chance the evidence will prove that one person was responsible for both murders."

"That won't surprise me. Anything else, David?"

"Yes. You will be at Dr Breckenridge's office tomorrow morning?"

"You can count on it."

"And Jennifer has been informed?"

"I've already indicated I'm going to the Cities, which of course shocked her. She wanted to know what could possibly take me away from an investigation, even for a few hours. I promised to tell her tonight."

"You're going home tonight?" asked David.

"In a couple of hours, if all is well."

"Congratulations."

"Get back in your cage, David. We need all the help you can provide."

"Do I grunt before saying goodbye?"

"Goodbye, David."

"Good night, Lieutenant."

Jack met with Matt to review the current activities. The hot line calls continued at a brisk pace. Nothing solid yet. The trail for Dean and Britain was cold. The tape and evidence David had gathered would help.

It was six-thirty when Jack left. He'd make it home for dinner.

The press were nowhere in sight as he left the motel.

Chapter 55

INGRID WAS EXHAUSTED by the time she finished her last delivery. It was seven-thirty. Life was slowly returning to normal in Wilton. As school wouldn't reopen till Wednesday, Ingrid and Janice had continued with their volunteer work. Janice was already at the center when Ingrid came in.

"Last night was wonderful," said Janice. "Do you mind if I stay with you again tonight?"

"Of course not," said Ingrid. "Let's pick up something for dinner."

"I want to get a couple of things from my place, so I'll do that on the way over. Anything you'd prefer?"

"Surprise me," said Ingrid. "I'm off to see my dogs. See you when you get there."

Most of the town's streets had been plowed. Towering snow banks flanked the streets, occasionally covering parked cars that hadn't been removed in time. Driveways were being cleared, with entire families pitching in.

Ingrid had spent little time on her own driveway, clearing a primitive path from her garage to the street which was just enough to allow her 4 Runner out. She'd finish the job tomorrow after school. Two excited dogs greeted her at the door. It was so comforting. Whether she was gone for a few minutes or several hours, the welcome always had the same enthusiasm.

The phone rang. It was Billy.

"Hi, Ingrid. How are you?"

"Fine, Billy. You must be dead beat. I hear you were on snow removal for the past two days and nights."

"Yeah. It wasn't too bad. Do you need help with your driveway?"

"It is a mess but you've already done more than your share in this town."

"That's okay. I'll be over right after school tomorrow, how's that?"

"That'd be great. Plan to stay for dinner. Janice is staying over tonight, and maybe tomorrow as well."

"Will that be okay?" asked Billy.

"Of course. See you tomorrow afternoon." They hung up.

Janice arrived soon after with buckets of Chinese food. "Didn't think we should cook tonight. It's been a long day."

"Great idea," said Ingrid. "I happen to have a delicious white Chardonnay in the fridge, which I'm sure you'll appreciate."

"I'm not much of a wine drinker but I'll bow to your expertise."

They managed to polish off all five portions and the bottle of wine. Two tired women were now well sated. After cleaning up they lingered over some coffee while going over Janice's plight again. It was only ten o'clock but the effect of the last two days, culminated by the meal and wine, had taken its toll. They gratefully retired for the night, falling asleep in minutes.

At two o'clock Ingrid was awoken by the barking and growling. Both dogs flew at her bedroom window. She'd never seen Bentley in such a state. His hackles were raised as he continued to growl and stare at the window. It faced the backyard and with only open fields behind, there was no need for curtains.

Janice came running into the room. "What's going on?"

"I don't know. Occasionally they wake up at night and make a minor fuss, but never like this."

"Look, what's that?" asked Janice.

"I don't see anything."

"Over there, to the right, heading for the woods. Isn't that a skier?"

The dogs were highly agitated. The barking and growling continued.

"Maybe it is," said Ingrid. There was something moving, or was there? With a solid overcast and poor visibility it was difficult to know for sure. Both women continued to stare at the frozen outside. A peaceful night — disturbed by an intruder? Or just imaginations stirred by the late hour, the recent events?

Certainly the dogs were upset. There must have been something out there. They shivered at the thought.

Ingrid took the flashlight from her bedside table and played its powerful beam across the backyard. Nothing could be seen. She moved the beam back and forth over the yard and the open fields. Then they saw the tracks.

The light caught the defined trail in the snow. There was no doubt. They could see two distinct parallel grooves carved neatly in the snow. A trail leading up to the window and away. A trail that could only have been made by cross-country skis.

Chapter 56

THE KILLER MOVED STEADILY across the field. The dark night limited visibility which gave him complete cover. He felt safe.

He skied around the house to the window at the back — her bedroom. As he neared the window, he heard the commotion. Puppies barking. They'd be no problem. Then he saw the bedroom door open and another person enter the room. Two women approached the window.

He turned to ski away quickly, reached the corner of the house, and headed across the field. He was confident they wouldn't see him. Best to get away though. He reached the forest, found the trail, and picked up his pace. The isolated cabin was only minutes away on the other side of the woods.

The woman would be there. He'd decide what to do when he got there. It would depend on the pain. That was beginning to abate.

Why did the Nielsen woman have a guest with her? That was unusual. And who was it? Two people plus the dogs presented too many problems. He'd research this before returning. But he would return.

Chapter 57

BILLY SLUMPED into the chair. He started a fresh pot of coffee for the guards, cleaned up the few dishes left from the last shift, and sat down. He was exhausted. It was five o'clock in the morning and he'd hardly stopped for the last two days. Thankfully the storm was over. Between the volunteer work in Wilton and his regular duties at the store there'd been little rest. And now they were staying open all night for the security guards.

He and Frank had taken turns keeping the store open during the night. As soon as Frank arrived this morning Billy was heading home for some badly needed sleep. Just a couple of more hours.

A blast of frigid, arctic air accompanied the entrance of John Tanner and Rob Mullen. The thermometer read twenty-five below and the severe conditions were clearly evident from the action of the two security guards. They stomped their feet and wrung their hands as they entered.

"Colder than a witch's tit," said Rob.

"At least," said John.

"Did ya find the coffee this morning, Billy Boy?" asked Rob. The sneer accented the scar that ran down the side of his forehead. It started at his hairline and ended at the top of his ear. 'Scarface,' as Billy referred to him, had been like this from the beginning. One day he might go too far with his insults.

"Cut it out, Rob," said John. "Thanks again for your hospitality, Billy. It makes this a lot easier for us."

John was the opposite of Rob. Although Billy had only met him earlier in the evening, he had come to respect the senior guard for his manners and consideration. It was nice to be noticed and appreciated. He had the deepest, dark blue eyes Billy had ever seen. Billy thought of him as 'Old Blue Eyes.'

He poured two mugs of coffee and carefully placed them on the counter. John nodded thanks while Rob stared and sneered. Billy ignored him.

"Would you like a sandwich or anything?" asked Billy.

"If ya have to make it, do ya have the directions written down somewhere?" asked Rob. Again the sneer.

John whacked him on the shoulder. "No more of that."

Billy glared at him. Highly unusual for Billy, who was always courteous to customers or visitors to the store. His eyes didn't leave 'Scarface.' The message was clear. Enough is enough.

John broke the silence. "What about some of that delicious black forest ham on a bagel, Billy?"

He slowly withdrew his gaze and looked at John. "Sure. Mustard and lettuce?"

"Perfect."

Billy moved away to prepare the sandwich. The fatigue was getting to him. He needed a break. He served the sandwich and moved away on the pretext of having to tend to other business. The risk of staying near 'Scarface' was not worth it.

The men finished their snack and braced themselves for another patrol. John approached Billy. "My apologies on behalf of Rob. He doesn't mean to be rude or ungrateful. It's been a long night. Thanks again."

The morning stretched out, dawn broke, and the first employees started to arrive. There was a brief rush of customers who hadn't been able to get in due to the storm. It was nearly ten o'clock before Billy realized Frank hadn't shown up. He was supposed to have relieved Billy at eight.

Billy went to the office to phone his brother. Jean answered the phone.

"Hi, Jean. It's Billy. Is Frank there please?"

"Hi, Billy. I think he is. And Billy, I've been meaning to call you. Lisa and Wes haven't stopped talking about the outing with you and Ingrid. And the dogs. They want to go back to Ingrid's as soon as possible."

"I thought they had fun."

"I'm trying to talk Frank into getting a dog but he won't budge. It would be great for the kids. He says I'll have to quit work first and he doesn't think we can afford that right now."

"Maybe I'll take them over there again this weekend. I'd have to check with Ingrid though."

"Right. Well, I'll get Frank for you."

He could hear the muffled responses before Frank reached the phone.

"Good morning, Billy."

"Frank, it's ten o'clock."

"Yeah, I know that."

"You're supposed to be here at eight." Billy was too tired to care that he was challenging Frank.

"I didn't sleep well last night."

"I haven't slept for twenty-four hours, Frank. You should've been here by now."

"Don't get upset, Billy. I'll be there soon."

"I am upset. You're just taking this like nothing's wrong. Well it is wrong."

Over the years there had been spats between them, a few resulting in an actual fight. Billy was stronger but Frank was smarter and quicker. They usually ended in a draw.

"All right, Billy. You're overtired so I understand. I'll leave right away."

Billy puttered around for the next hour until Frank arrived. It was easy to see his brother had not slept — the baggy, sunken eyes were obvious proof.

"I'll open tomorrow morning, Frank. See you."

Chapter 58

INGRID AND JANICE eventually went back to bed but both had trouble sleeping. The dogs as usual were up at six and although it was too soon for the women, they had no choice. When it was light, Ingrid and Janice went outside to have a look at the tracks left earlier in the morning. They were clearly made by skis. With no wind or fresh snow they were still well defined.

They decided to call the police. At the time of the incident they'd been uncertain about what to do. Now there was no doubt.

Ingrid dialed the number Jack Petersen had given her.

"B.C.A. Sergeant Erickson here."

"May I speak to Lieutenant Petersen please."

"He's not here. May I help you?"

"When do you expect him?"

"This afternoon. Who's calling please?"

"This is Ingrid Nielsen. We want to report an incident."

"You can give me the details, ma'am."

Ingrid went over the story.

"You and your friend saw these tracks this morning?"

"Yes. The dogs have disturbed some of them but most are still intact."

"We'll send two agents out to your place right away. Please stay clear of your backyard till we get there."

"I have to leave within the hour," said Ingrid. "Will you have someone here before then?"

"Yes, in the next fifteen minutes. Thanks for your call ma'am."

Matt arrived shortly with a forensic specialist. The dogs reacted predictably with Bentley taking the lead role as protector. Despite their youth and short time with Ingrid, they had established that this was their home and their job was to guard it and Ingrid.

Matt Erickson introduced himself and Special Agent Al Welsh. "That's a handsome pair of Shepherds you have there ma'am," said Matt.

"Thank you," said Ingrid. "This is my friend Janice Bertrand, who was with me last night."

"If you'd show Al where those tracks are he can get started. I have some questions for both of you which won't take too long. I believe you have to get to work soon."

"Whoever it was came right up to my bedroom window. If you go out the kitchen door, you'll see the tracks to your right."

Al said he'd get right at it while Matt joined the women at the kitchen table.

"You said the dogs woke you up at one-thirty?" asked Matt.

"Yes. They were at the window, barking like mad."

"And you went to the window?"

"It took me a second to realize what was going on. By then Janice had come into my room and we both went to have a look."

"Is that when you saw the skier?"

"Not right away. It was a few minutes before Janice saw what she thought was a skier."

"Where was he then, ma'am?"

"In the open field," said Janice. "At first I wasn't sure what I had seen, but it looked like someone on skis. Then Ingrid got her flashlight and we picked out the ski trail near the window."

"Can you describe the skier?" asked Matt.

"I'm afraid not," said Janice. "He was just too far away and the visibility wasn't that great last night."

"You said, 'he.' Are you sure it was a man?"

"No, I just assumed."

"You were able to confirm this from the ski trail you saw this morning, Miss Nielsen?"

"Yes, we saw the trail leading to the woods. It certainly fits with what Janice thought she saw."

"Do you know of anyone who might want to harm you, Miss Nielsen?"

"N — no. Not at all."

"And you, Miss Bertrand?"

"Not to my knowledge. Besides I only decided to stay here yesterday. Nobody would have known I was here."

Nobody spoke. Ingrid lowered her head and nervously rubbed her hands together.

"Well," said Ingrid, "that's not entirely...oh but it doesn't matter."

"What were you going to say Miss Nielsen?" asked Matt.

"It's really not important."

"Excuse me ma'am but you never know what's important or not. Please continue."

"One person did know Janice was coming over but he's a good friend of mine. Besides, he hardly knows Janice."

"Who's that?" asked Janice.

"Billy called last night just before you got here. It's nothing."

"Would that be Billy McCord, ma'am?"

"Yes. But it's absurd to even consider that he was here last night. I hear you have him under surveillance. In my view that's totally unnecessary." Ingrid sat up straight and glared at Matt.

"I appreciate your views ma'am, but we have to follow every lead. Do you know Billy McCord, Miss Bertrand?"

"Can't say I know him well but we've met a few times, mostly with Ingrid."

"Has there ever been any incident involving you and McCord?" asked Matt.

"Hold on, Sergeant," said Ingrid. "I find this preposterous. First you're assuming this person came here last night looking for Janice, not me.

Now you're trying to dig out something between Billy and Janice. I can tell you he has absolutely nothing against Janice, nor if he had, would he threaten or harm her."

"If that's true, you or McCord has nothing to worry about. Miss Bertrand?"

"He's just doing his job, Ingrid. No, Sergeant I've never had a problem with Billy McCord."

"Could there be anyone else who knew you were coming here?"

"Not unless somebody heard us in the center," said Janice. "There were a lot of volunteers there."

"Miss Nielsen, have you noticed anyone following you lately?"

"No."

"Are you planning to stay over again, Miss Bertrand?"

"I really hadn't thought about it."

"It might be a good idea. Since you've had one unusual visit, Miss Nielsen, you'd be better off if there were two of you here."

"You think we could handle some lunatic?" asked Ingrid.

"It's far less likely he'd try anything with two people plus your two dogs. His attacks so far have been on women alone."

"We'll certainly think about that," said Ingrid. "I'm sorry for my remarks about Billy. I just get sensitive when it comes to him. He's misunderstood."

"I understand ma'am. Thanks for calling us. If you think of anything else, let us know. We should be out of here shortly."

"We have to get going, Sergeant. May I lock up?"

"Yeah. The rest of our work will be outside."

"I'll have to let the dogs out before I go."

"Please take them around to the other side until we've finished our work."

"Will do."

Nobody noticed the pickup as it cruised down the street.

The driver however, took in every detail of the activities at Ingrid's house.

Chapter 59

JACK MADE IT HOME in time for dinner. Jennifer had prepared a rack of lamb, their favorite. It was after the meal when Jack went into the details of his chest pains. "I guess it's best to have a doctor's opinion. David's arranged an appointment for me."

"Absolutely," said Jennifer. "Who did David recommend?"

"Doctor Breckenridge at the General. Says he's the best in the state. I see him at ten tomorrow, then it's back to Wilton."

"Thank you for finally telling me. Don't keep things like that from me, okay?" She leaned against him and kissed him hard. "That's for us to share."

"Yeah, I know."

"Yeah, you know," said Jennifer. "You macho son of a gun." She ruffled his hair and smiled. Jack loved it.

"I'll keep you up to date, I promise."

"How's Wilton going? Any progress at all?"

"Some, but nothing great yet."

"I don't want to seem selfish but are we going to be able to get away this month?"

"Let's hope so, for everybody's sake."

"That was an insensitive thought," said Jennifer. "I'm sorry."

"I know you care more about stopping the insanity and saving lives. I also know you can't wait to get me alone on that Caribbean island."

"You should be so lucky."

"I've been thinking about getting a dog," said Jack. "Maybe two."

"I'd love to have a dog but how could we handle that with both of us working. It's just not fair to the animal."

"That's why we should get two. They'd be good company for each other."

"I suppose," said Jennifer. "Let's think about it. Would you care for your favorite cocktail before we retire?"

"So you can take advantage of me?"

"Of course." She leaned over and kissed him. "You relax while I clean up the dishes."

"One more kiss," said Jack.

"Dishes first." She playfully pushed him away. "There'll be time to play after."

Indeed there was. They both wished the night would never end. Could they really be going on a trip this month? It seemed too good to be true. Was it time to get a desk job? Jack had been thinking about that a lot lately.

Jennifer had to leave first but they did have breakfast together.

"Don't forget to call me after your appointment. I don't want to jinx us, but will I see you here again tonight?"

"Two nights in a row," said Jack. "Can you handle that?"

"I can, Jack. How about you?"

"I'll give it a hell of a try."

They laughed and hugged.

Two hours later Jack was at the General. He liked Breckenridge immediately. The young doctor had a direct, no nonsense approach. It was easy to tell why he was considered the top man in his field. His thorough physical examination showed Jack to be in good shape.

"I'm going to order some blood work plus a stress test. If we can reproduce the pain while you're under surveillance, it will be helpful. We'll evaluate the results and see you again."

"Can this wait for a couple of weeks?" asked Jack.

"David warned me that you might have other priorities. This is not to be taken lightly, Lieutenant. I want you on these tests immediately — that means this week."

"I see."

"If you wait a few minutes I'll have my secretary make the appointments."

Fifteen minutes later Jack was on his way to Wilton. The blood work could be done in Wilton but a twelve hour fast was required. The stress test was scheduled for early Friday morning at the General. Dr Breckenridge would supervise.

What if he couldn't make it Friday? Breckenridge had been quite insistent. He called Jennifer at the law office where she worked as a legal secretary.

"Brewster and Brewster."

"Mrs Petersen please."

"Is that you, Lieutenant?"

"Yes, Joan."

"Hi. Your lovely wife told me you'd be calling today. How are you?"

"I'm fine thank you."

"I'll put you right through. Nice talking to you."

Jennifer came on the line. "Jack. How did it go?"

"Fine. He's a good guy who seems to know his stuff. I have some tests set up but he gave me a clean bill of health otherwise."

"What kind of tests?"

"Blood work and a stress test. The first is easy, just have to fast for twelve hours, but I have to go back to the Cities for the stress test. That'll cost me another full morning."

"Jack, this'll have to be a priority."

"Tell that to the maniac up here who insists on brutalizing innocent people."

"Isn't Matt Erickson with you in Wilton?"

"Yeah."

"And you said he's one of the best."

"You're right," said Jack. "It'll work out."

"Thanks for the call, Jack. Will I see you tonight?"

"Hopefully. Got another call. Talk to you later." He switched over to the incoming call.

"Petersen here."

"Good morning, Lieutenant," said Matt. "Just came back from Ingrid Nielsen's house. She had an intruder last night."

"Did she see him?"

"Not really. He skied up to her bedroom window — we saw the tracks this morning — but the dogs woke up Miss Nielsen and an overnight guest, and he moved away. By the time they got to the window he was gone. They're sure they saw somebody."

"Who was the guest?"

"A Janice Bertrand. She works at Wilton High. We had forensics over — hopefully they'll come up with something to help us."

"Where was McCord?"

"At the store all night. They're staying open for Cam's guards. Can't see how he could have left there and got back unnoticed."

"Anything else?" asked Jack.

"Searches are still on but nothing's turned up."

"See you in half an hour." They hung up.

Jack took the exit off #25 that lead to Wilton. The roads were snow covered but plowed. He reflected on the case. Mrs Hibbard claimed she saw someone in her backyard. Her husband was with her. Nothing happened. If the killer was there, did he change his mind because she wasn't alone?

Somebody skied up to Nielsen's bedroom window. She and a guest woke up, the intruder left. Same scenario. He found out she had company so he left? Is he becoming more cautious or was he always careful?

And now the phone calls. Doesn't that suggest he's more brazen? Daring us to catch him? Well, he will be caught.

When Jack arrived at the motel, he ordered lunch before going to the command center. "What's the burger special today, Julie?"

"Does it really matter, Lieutenant? I mean, it's not like you're going to order anything else."

"I'd just like to know, Julie. I might order two instead of one."

"That wouldn't surprise me. It's a ten ounce sirloin burger, your idea, with Monterey Jack, lettuce, mayonnaise, and onions, all on a large kaiser. Soup or juice is included, along with home fries and dessert."

"I'll be back in half an hour, Julie. Hold one of those for me will you?"

"Yes, sir."

He reviewed the calls on the hot line, checked his messages, and told Matt to set up an evening meeting with the team.

"Any news from David Folk?"

"Not today, Lieutenant. I'd like to go over the Nielsen interview."

"Let's do it over lunch."

Jack's burger special arrived.

Matt had a salad. "Miss breakfast, Lieutenant?"

"Or hasn't he eaten for three days?" asked Julie.

Jack grunted, waved her away, and indicated to Matt to get on with it.

Matt went over Ingrid and Janice's story.

"Do you think they really saw someone?" asked Jack.

"Who knows? The marks from the skis were real, Lieutenant. And the tracks did go all the way from her property to the woods. They traced them well into the woods before the tracks ran into one of those logging trails the skiers use. At that point the trail was lost. There were just too many grooves to isolate our skier."

"Was he after Nielsen or Bertrand?"

"Good question. We don't know but the odds favor Nielsen. Only a couple of people would have known about the Bertrand woman staying over."

"Only a couple we know of," said Jack. "What if he had spotted her going there? And what about McCord?"

"He was in the store all night. Our guy claims there's no way he left. Admittedly he said there were times when McCord was out of sight. He'd go back to the office or down to the basement. He certainly never left the store by the front door."

"Is there an exit from the basement?"

Matt stared at him. "I don't know, Lieutenant."

"Find out, Matt."

Matt nodded, made a note.

"What response has there been from the composites?" asked Jack.

"As expected, many calls. They've produced interviews, some of which you'll want to look at. The problem is sorting through the crank calls and as usual there's been a few confessions."

"If only it was that easy."

Jack spent the rest of the afternoon going over the interviews of men who came closest to the profile and physical description. He selected four who warranted further investigation. Prior to the evening meeting he met with the agents who had interviewed the four. All had decent alibis but these were being checked now.

The evening meeting wasn't over till ten-thirty but Jack decided to go home. He preferred to be with Jennifer. At least he'd have most of the night with her.

Chapter 60

ROB MULLEN WAS STILL FUMING. That half-witted moron staring at him, trying to threaten him. Who the hell did he think he was? They finished their shift at six-thirty, dug into a hearty breakfast at the motel, and Rob was in bed shortly after. He was up before three. Six hours of sleep was enough for him.

As he went through his vigorous exercise routine, he always traveled with his weights, the image of Billy McCord wouldn't leave him. John had kept saying how nice a person Billy was but that didn't get through to him. Nobody stared at him like that and got away with it.

Darkness came early this time of year so they were back on patrol before six o'clock. The cold didn't bother him. It was twenty below, headed for a low of thirty before morning. The gear that Cam provided was more than adequate for the conditions. Special under garments kept moisture away from the body so you didn't need cumbersome, heavy jackets to stay warm. They also had goggles, affording excellent visibility as well as protection from the elements. Cam Fletcher didn't stint on equipment for his troops.

The snowmobiles whipped along the McCord Trail, their powerful lights sweeping the snow-covered terrain. The twelve hour shifts were taxing on the guards with the severe temperatures adding to the stress. Yet these men were in top physical condition, finely tuned to cope with the rigorous work.

For the most part they maintained silence on their radios keeping the channel open for emergencies. Their call signs were Boxcar one and two. However, periodically there was the odd gibe or remark, particularly when they met on the trail. Tonight Rob was not communicating at all. His thoughts were still on Billy McCord. John had tried to calm him down but to no avail. Heaven help anyone who got in his way tonight.

They'd set up a grid for the patrols that changed constantly. There'd be no way to predict where or when their vehicles would be at any given moment. With the time it took to cover all the houses they had to ensure the killer could not chart their route and give him enough time to stage an attack. The average time any home would be without surveillance was fifteen minutes, but sometimes that would be five minutes, or twenty minutes, there was no pattern.

They'd been on duty more than eight hours when the call came in. It was two-twenty. "Center here. Lone skier spotted near Lot nine — Wilson's house. Do you know it?"

"Boxcar two here. We're three lots away. Be right there."

"Boxcar one — your position?"

"We're at the other end. Lot forty."

"Continue your normal patrol till we know what's happening."

"You sure?"

"There're four B.C.A. agents on the way. We'll be okay."

"10-4."

"Let's go down there, John," said Rob. He was itching for action.

"We'll stay put."

"The hell with that. I'm off to Lot nine." Rob gunned the snowmobile and raced down the trail. Nobody was telling him to stay away. He could take this guy by himself if he had to.

The snow sprayed wildly as he pushed the vehicle to its limit. There was a tight bend coming up. He knew this entire route, could do it blindfolded. With the speed he was going now...Christ, the sharp turn came up sooner than he expected. He throttled back and careened around the corner. The snowmobile went up on one ski, then slammed back on the hard packed snow. The jolt shook him but undaunted he poured on the power again.

The trail was too rough for this speed with the machine and operator taking a vicious pounding. He didn't care. He hunkered down behind the wind screen and plunged ahead recklessly. He hit a huge drift which skewed the machine off the trail. It just missed a large tree and skimmed over another drift, before coming to rest up against a hedge. Rob selected reverse, spun around back to the trail, and headed off at high speed again.

As he flew by the intersection of one of the logging trails he had a hunch. If the creep was in the area and saw all this activity, he'd probably decide to take off. Lot thirty was just ahead. If he'd been spotted around Lot nine, he'd work his way through the woods to here where it would be safe to come out on the logging trail. Lot nine was about four miles away.

The trail ran easterly away from the lake. He drove about a mile down the trail and maneuvered the snowmobile into the edge of the woods. He was alive with the prospect of running the killer down, which would help take out his earlier frustrations.

The trail had a slight uphill grade, approximately half a mile long, which then leveled off. He took a position just past the crest. The skier would be tired after skiing up the hill.

Half an hour went by, then an hour. Had he made a serious mistake? Where was the rest of the team? In the heat of the moment he had selfishly taken off on his own. Not only was that reckless, he had abandoned his partner. The solution to all this would be for him to apprehend the killer. That would save him.

Three-thirty. Still nothing. Then he saw it. There was a lone figure, slowly coming up the slight grade. The goggles helped. He looked away, then back at the spot where he was sure there'd been somebody moving. At first, nothing. Then, there it was. Look slightly away from the object, he'd been taught. It was weird, but it worked.

It was a skier. He was sure now. The figure moved rhythmically from side to side as he worked his way up the slope. It was strenuous exercise taking its toll on the skier. He knew that, had planned on it.

He removed his hand gun from its holster and took the safety off. At twenty-eight he'd never killed anyone, never had to. But he knew he could do it if necessary. Hopefully he wouldn't have to. Once he had him cuffed, he'd call the others.

Thirty yards and closing. Rob was sweating, despite the cold. His heart was pounding. This was proving more difficult than he thought. He steeled himself. This had to be done.

The skier's head was down, his pace had quickened. Rob bounded onto the trail, gun in hand. "Stop, right now."

The head popped up but he didn't stop. He was closing faster than Rob had anticipated.

"Stop."

The skier plowed straight ahead, bowling him over. The gun flew out of his hand. Rob was flat on his back and stunned while the skier was still upright and getting out of his skis.

He saw the ski pole aimed at his head and rolled frantically to his side. The first thrust just missed. He rolled away, avoiding the ski pole as the attacker swung wildly.

Rob looked frantically for his gun. The killer's ski boot smashed into his back. Rob tried to grab his leg. He was met with a vicious blow to the head.

Rob Mullen blacked out.

Chapter 61

THE PHONE RANG at four-thirty. Jack picked it up on the second ring.

"Lieutenant, we've had another sighting. One of the security guards was badly beaten."

"Jesus. Who's the guard?"

"Rob Mullen, the young guy."

"Is he okay?"

"I think so. He's been taken to the hospital for X-rays."

"Anything on the visual?"

"Not much. An elderly couple was sure they saw a figure on the lake. We sent four agents over to join the security guards. None of our men saw him."

"I'll be there within the hour. How's Cam taking this?"

"None too pleased. You won't like the details."

"See you soon."

Jennifer half woke up. "Trouble?"

"Yeah. You go back to sleep. I'll call you later."

Jack dressed and was out the door in minutes. He was used to snow but had never seen this much. His headlights picked up huge snow drifts framing the highway. The road crews as usual had done a remarkable job considering the storm had ended just last Monday. He'd make good time this morning. Very little traffic at five o'clock.

At five-twenty he entered the motel. Even the press was there. They didn't miss much. Jack begged off till he could get briefed on the latest.

Next was Julie. "Are you trying to set a record, coming in earlier and earlier?"

"Couldn't sleep so thought I should come in for some abuse. Thanks for not disappointing me, Lieutenant."

Jack put his arm around her as they walked down the hall toward the command center. "What's my favorite girl got for breakfast?"

"Talk like that'll get you nowhere. But I do have something special in mind for you guys, despite your sass."

She shook free and waltzed proudly off to the kitchen. The command center was buzzing.

"Morning, Lieutenant," said Matt. "See you ran into Julie. Imagine, she gets wind of the trouble and gets herself and the cook over here to take care of us. Quite a woman."

Jack smiled thinking of his talk with Julie and her feigned excuse of not sleeping. "Yeah, quite a woman."

"Cam's here. He's anxious to talk to you."

"Anything on the killer, I mean — anything?"

"Forensics are still at the scene. They're using sulphur prints 'cause the skier had stopped. We'll have some news later."

"I want to see the report from the couple," said Jack. "What's their name?"

"Wayne and Judy Wilson."

"You said they're elderly. How old?"

"I've got that right here. He's sixty-eight, she's sixty-four."

"These days, that's not elderly, Matt. You better be careful."

Matt grinned and nodded. "Cam's in the interview room."

John Tanner was with Cam. Both men were grim faced as they tackled the paper work.

"Morning Cam, John. Sorry about Mullen."

"Thanks, Jack," said Cam. "Let's hope there's no serious damage. John's been kicking himself."

"What happened?"

John went over the events. "I've been working on this guy for a year now. He's brash and impulsive but deep down a good guy. I thought we were getting somewhere. He has so much going but his temper keeps getting the better of him. If only I'd been able to get through to him sooner..."

"So he went looking for the prowler on his own?" asked Jack.

"Yeah," said John. "When we got the call, I told him we had to stay on our patrol. Who the hell knew what was going to happen? He goosed his machine and was gone. I never caught up to him."

"Did anyone try to reach him on the radio?"

"He'd turned it off."

"Who found him?" asked Jack.

"I did," said John. "The guy had left him lying in the middle of the trail. There was some blood."

"What did he do to him?"

"Beat him up pretty badly. He was still unconscious when I got there. He took Rob's hand gun."

"Now why would he do that?" asked Jack. "That doesn't add up with what we know about this guy so far."

"What do you mean, Jack?" asked Cam.

"He hasn't used any weapon for any of the killings so far."

"How does he kill?"

"Sorry, can't say at this point," said Jack. "Anyway, the gun thing doesn't fit."

Matt came in. "Mullen's going to be okay. He took a nasty blow to the head, resulting in a concussion. He won't be working for a while."

"I'm going over to see him, Jack."

"Tell your guys to be careful, Cam."

Chapter 62

INGRID HAD SPENT THE LAST TWO DAYS in a fog. It was comforting having Janice stay over with a killer on the loose and the intruder's visit the other night. Was it the killer? Even with the dogs it was disconcerting, to say the least.

The discussions with Janice about leaving Wilton had escalated. Was it realistic? After all, this'd been her home for most of her life. But this last year with the loss of Rick, things hadn't been the same. Maybe a change would be wise.

It certainly seemed like a good fit for Janice. But was that really the answer? If she was just running away, that wouldn't solve the problem. That would have to be resolved before leaving. Then a change of scenery might be more in keeping.

After classes, Ingrid had gone straight home since she hadn't been back at lunch. The dogs had been inside for more than eight hours and were more than anxious to be let out. They seemed more agitated than usual and literally flew out the back door.

She could sense something wasn't right. And what was that smell? She turned and saw that her bedroom door was closed. That was strange, she always left it open as the dogs' beds were there. As she neared the door, the odor was stronger. Ingrid had never smelled anything like it before.

The bedroom door was heavily scored with claw marks from the dogs. Why? This had never happened. The putrescent stench was now overpowering. She was about to open the door but hesitated. Should she get the dogs first? Or call someone? There definitely was something wrong.

An involuntary shudder racked her body as she backed away from the door. What was in there? The dogs had returned and were pawing at the back door. Someone had been in her home.

Enough of this, she had to find out. Ingrid strode back to the door and opened it slightly to take a peek. The stench hit her first, but she was even more affected by what she saw. She collapsed against the door frame, screamed, and slammed the door. She'd never witnessed a more gruesome sight.

Lying on the bed with her head at a grotesque angle, was Cheryl Dean. Her tongue was protruding through badly swollen lips. Even more upsetting were the open eyes, showing fear, pain, and the vacant stare of death.

She made it to the telephone and dialed 911. The emergency operator said an ambulance and the police would be there momentarily.

The call was patched through to the police. "Are you sure the person is dead ma'am?"

"The smell is awful and she has no color at all."

"Don't touch anything. We'll be right there."

Ingrid let the dogs in. They raced to the bedroom door immediately.

"No," said Ingrid. "No. Come here."

She coaxed the dogs away from the door. They hesitated but came to her. She tried to pour herself a glass of water but her hand shook so much, the water spilled over and she dropped the glass. It shattered with shards of glass skittering over the kitchen tile. Stunned, Ingrid fell into a chair and broke down. Bentley and Sasha came to her side, staring at her with inquisitive looks.

The door bell rang, jolting Ingrid out of her trance.

Jack Petersen was at the door with another agent. An ambulance was pulling into the driveway.

"You'll be all right now, Miss Nielsen," said Jack. "This is Special Agent Al Welsh. He'll be examining the scene. Where's the body?"

Ingrid pointed to the door. "In my bedroom." Her normal throaty, soft tones were missing.

"Would you please secure the dogs. We don't want anything disturbed."

More agents arrived. They were the same team that had taken prints of the ski tracks.

Ingrid took the dogs to the den where Janice had stayed. "I'll stay with them till you're finished."

"Did you go right into your bedroom?" asked Jack.

"No. I opened the door, took one look, and closed it."

"I'll want to talk to you a little latter if you're up to it."

Ingrid nodded and joined the dogs in the den. The moment she closed the door the tears started again. Why would anyone place a dead body in her home? Maybe the Lieutenant would have some answers. She sat in a daze, too much in shock to think straight.

It seemed like hours had passed before she heard the knock on the door. Actually only fifteen minutes had elapsed.

"This won't take long," said Jack. "You said your bedroom door was closed when you came home. I take it that's not normal."

"No, I always leave it open. How did someone get in there and close the door, yet keep the dogs away?"

"Your bedroom window has been jimmied open. They could've distracted the dogs at the back door, then entered your bedroom and closed the door before the dogs got back."

"How would they have time to do that?" asked Ingrid.

"They'd jimmy the window first, leave it open a crack, then get the dogs to the back door. That'd give them time to slip in the open window and close the door before the dogs got back."

"Really?"

"Could be," said Jack. "The other possibility is, whoever this was, knew your dogs. They could enter the house without the dogs' interference, then simply close off the bedroom and bring the body in."

"But you said they broke in through the window."

"That could've been done to mislead us. Can you think of anybody that the dogs might allow in the house?"

"The only men would be Chris Eaton and Billy McCord," said Ingrid.

"To consider either would be absurd." Once again Ingrid found herself defensive about Billy.

"No one else?" asked Jack, making notes.

"Well the dogs are young. I don't know how they'd react to a stranger. Maybe anyone could come in when I'm not here. If I'm home, they certainly are protective. In any case it's definitely not Billy, regardless of what you might think."

There was no reaction from Jack. Ingrid pulled at the sleeves of her sweater. She liked the Lieutenant but didn't appreciate his work or what he had to do, like suspecting everyone, including Billy.

"What time did you leave for work this morning?"

"A little after eight."

"And you came home at four this afternoon?"

"Yes."

"Is that your normal routine?" asked Jack.

"It was before I had the dogs. But now I try to come home at noon to let them out. I didn't make it today."

"Tell me what you did when you arrived."

Ingrid went over the entire episode. Even talking about it upset her. The shaking started again.

"You then made your call."

She nodded. Ingrid reached for a Kleenex. "Would you like coffee or a soda, Lieutenant?"

"Thank you, no. The coroner will be here shortly to remove the body. One more thing, Miss Nielsen. We'd like to move you to a safe area."

"Why?"

"You had an intruder here the other night and now this. It'd be in your interest to leave here for a while."

"That's difficult with the dogs here. Where would they go?"

"I'm sure you could make temporary arrangements," said Jack.

"I want to think about this."

"There's something else. Whoever was here left a note for you. We're going to provide around the clock protection for you, starting now."

"Why?"

Jack handed her the note, sealed in a plastic envelope.

Ingrid stared at the words. They had the eerie look of a kidnapper's note — a variety of letters taken from newspapers or magazines.

"You could be next."

Chapter 63

JACK FELT FOR THE NIELSEN WOMAN. There should be a happy future in store but now her life was in danger.

He called Matt to bring him up to date. "We'll need an agent at the Nielsen home to start 'round the clock protection until further notice. Set up a meeting in an hour with Ted to go over all the interviews. I'm on my way to the Dean's. Matt, have forensics transport the body to St Paul and advise David Folk." They hung up.

"How do you figure this, Al? He kills this young girl, then a week later takes her body to the Nielsen home. Is he taunting us again?"

"Maybe he figures he's too smart to get caught. Proves it by delivering one of his victims here in broad daylight."

"And now he says she's next," said Jack. "How sick is this guy?"

"If David's right, he could be getting worse. It certainly looks that way."

Jack shook his head. He dialed the Dean's.

"Hello," said Mrs Dean.

"Mrs Dean, this is Lieutenant Petersen. Is Mr Dean home?"

"Yes he is. Do you have news about Cheryl?"

"We'll be there in a few minutes," said Jack.

Jack had alerted Matt to contact the Dean's priest and send him to their house. He arrived just as Jack and Al were leaving. Not a word was said by either on the trip back to the motel.

The press corps, which had dwindled but was still well represented, were at their usual place at the motel. The latest incident had sparked renewed interest in the Wilton story. Jack had only a few minutes to spare but he did confirm the Dean homicide, providing no further details.

Ted Norris was waiting for Jack. He had three new names on their suspect list.

"Let's see them."

"Bill Sherman, Kyle Ott, and Hal Ledyard. All three have a strong physical resemblance but two are married."

"Why does that rule them out?"

"It'd be difficult to be out in the middle of the night without your wife knowing," said Ted. "Surely she'd get a little suspicious."

"Yeah, if the wife wasn't in on it."

"How sick is that?"

"I've seen worse," said Jack. "I want to look at all three. Who's the single guy?"

"Kyle Ott. 35, six-one, 200 pounds. He works part time at Sam's Garage. He isn't very reliable according to the owner, Sam Gage. Rents a room with...the Lofton's."

"Have Holm and Adams question Gage and the Loftons."

"He's also had odd jobs with others in town, like the McCords. Runs errands for them, stuff like that."

"Get the names of all the others," said Jack. "What about the other two?"

"Bill Sherman, 56, six feet, 180 pounds. Married, no kids. He's the janitor at Wilton High. According to Muriel Bates, the principal, he's very reliable. He's quiet, keeps to himself. His wife, Ruth, is a nurse at the Wilton General."

"Is she on shift work?" asked Jack.

"Yeah. Let's see, she works nights, eleven to seven."

"And his hours?"

Ted checked his notes. "Six to one-thirty."

"Isn't that convenient? Have them questioned as well. The third guy?"

"Hal Ledyard, 51, six feet, 210 pounds. Wife, Millie, two grown sons — both live in the Cities. He's big and mean enough with a serious drinking problem. Works for Mann's Construction. According to the owner, Jessie Barr, he's on the job most of the time. At quitting time he's off to Silver Heights, a local bar, where he drinks himself into a stupor most nights.

He's usually gone by eight or nine and goes home to bed."

"How does he stay married?"

"Geoff, the bartender at Silver Heights, says his wife has wanted to leave for years, but just can't get around to it. Rumor is he belts her the odd time."

"He sounds like a gem," said Jack. "What does Millie do?"

"No job but she's into a lot of volunteer work. The hospital, library, old folks home — she keeps busy."

"Have Geoff, the bartender, and his wife interviewed. It's six, time for the team meeting. See if you can set up all those people tonight."

"Don't forget the McCords, Lieutenant."

"McCords — plural?"

"Yeah, Billy and Frank."

"Good point," said Jack. "I've been thinking only Billy. Frank fits the profile as well."

"Except in his case there appears to be a solid marriage. Jean would know if he was leaving the house in the middle of the night and she certainly isn't the type to be in on something like this."

"Have the agents talk to her anyway," said Jack. "Time for the meeting. I have a quick call to make — be there in a few minutes."

He dialed home. "Hi, Honey," said Jennifer.

"This call display is going too far," said Jack. "Next they'll be showing pictures."

"That could be scary."

"How are things?" asked Jack.

"Fine, but I guess a call at this hour means no supper with my favorite lover."

"Hmm — that suggests there may be others."

"Yes, there's Jack Monday, Jack Tuesday, Jack..."

"Okay, okay. You're right about tonight. We've had a bit of a break and it's going to be busy around here. I won't see you till tomorrow."

"Don't you have your tests tomorrow morning?"

"Yeah. I'll go straight from here."

"Do you want me there?" asked Jennifer.

"Of course I do but it's only a couple of stress tests. I'll have to get right back here anyway. Things are heating up."

"Are you getting close?"

"Not close, but there's progress."

"Top secret?" asked Jennifer.

Jack chuckled. "For now, beautiful. Talk to you later." They blew each other kisses. After twenty years it still felt good — intimate and fun. Once this case was over and the tests were complete, he'd ask for a desk job.

The team meeting was over by seven. The mood was more up-beat. The loss of Cheryl Dean was upsetting but at least they had four or five solid suspects. The hot line was paying off even though too many of the calls were bogus. Assignments were handed out including Sergeants Elmer Holm and Dan Adams who were selected for the interviews, starting with the seven people on Jack's list. They'd have a second go with the suspects later.

Jack found time to have a quick burger before he got back to work.

"How would you like it today 'Numero Uno'?" asked Julie.

"Lettuce, mayo, Dijon mustard, and a few hot peppers."

"Two patties?"

"One only thanks, Julie."

"Finally cutting back are we?"

"Any decaf brewed?"

"For you, of course."

They smiled at each other.

Chapter 64

AGENTS HOLM AND ADAMS found Muriel Bates working late. "Thanks for talking to us, Mrs Bates. This is Sergeant Dan Adams. We have a few questions about one of your employees — Bill Sherman."

"I'm not actually his employer, but he does report to me. I'm surprised you have an interest in Bill but I'll be pleased to help anyway."

"How long have you known Mr Sherman?" asked Elmer.

"Since he started working at the school, more than twenty years now."

"He must be a good employee," said Dan.

"Oh, he is. Bill's a little quiet perhaps and he doesn't mingle with the kids too much."

"Any kind of temper?"

"He can be a little cranky now and then but who isn't?"

"His wife works nights, yet he starts when she finishes. Does that strike you as odd?"

"Not really. Bill told me long ago that Ruth could get any shift she wanted but they like their afternoons together, and she enjoys night work. The arrangement works for both of them. They're always on the go with various outdoor activities — skiing in the winter, gardening in the summer — you name it."

"Have you noticed any change in Mr Sherman lately?" asked Elmer.

"No, can't say I have. He's concerned like the rest of us with what's going on. The school's been hit hard with the loss of Jim and Cheryl. You don't lose two youngsters without a serious impact on students and faculty. We've had extra crisis counselors brought in to help."

"Did Sherman work today?"

"Yes. In fact I talked to him just as he was leaving."

"What time was that?" asked Elmer.

"Before two o'clock. His usual time."

"I think that's all. Dan, do you have anything else?"

"No, that's fine with me."

"Thanks for your time, Mrs Bates."

"Anytime, Sergeant. This is about the murders, isn't it?"

"There's a lot of detail in an investigation," said Elmer.

"We all hope you catch him soon."

She saw them out. Next call was the hospital. They found a supervisor who told them Ruth Sherman would be taking a break soon. They could meet in the coffee shop if that was satisfactory.

"We'd prefer some privacy if that can be arranged," said Elmer.

"There's an office on this floor that's not used at night. I'll take you there."

It was small with a single desk, two chairs, and a filing cabinet. "This'll be fine," said Elmer.

"Nurse Sherman will be along in ten minutes or so."

Fifteen minutes later Ruth Sherman came into the room. She had an air of confidence about her. Introductions were made. Elmer was surprised at the strength of her handshake.

"You have my curiosity aroused, Sergeant," said Ruth Sherman. She leaned forward with her elbows on the table, her hands forming a steeple, looking directly at Elmer.

"We have only a few questions for you, Mrs Sherman," said Elmer. "How long have you been married?"

"Twenty-eight glorious years."

"Have you noticed any changes in your husband lately?" asked Dan.

"That's a funny question. Maybe you should tell me what this is all about."

"We're following up several leads, ma'am. There just routine questions."

"Leads? For what? You're here investigating the local murders, aren't you?"

"Yes."

"What the hell has that to do with me or Bill?" She sat back with her hands on her hips.

"Probably nothing," said Elmer. "We have to question many people — you never know when we'll find something useful. Your cooperation will be much appreciated."

"You're a sweet talker, Sergeant. All right, what do you want to know?"

"Your husband's moods recently — anything unusual?"

"Not really. He's definitely down about the two students from Wilton High. Bill may not be too sociable but he cares about people and the students over there. This has hurt him more than you'd know."

"Your routines have been normal lately?" asked Dan.

"Yup. I get up around two and we usually have some outing planned for the afternoon. We're outdoor types."

"What happened today?"

"I got up a little late, around three. We went skiing and then I had to come in early 'cause we're short staffed tonight."

Elmer and Dan indicated that was enough and thanked her for her cooperation.

"Why is this guy on our list?" asked Elmer. "From what we got from these two he looks clean to me."

"Yeah, but in the first interview Sherman was quite hostile. That, along with his size and their work schedules, made us take a second look."

"In terms of a suspect, he may not be a 'discard' yet, but he's close."

"Agreed," said Dan.

"Who's next?"

"Sam Gage. He owns the garage where Kyle Ott works. They said he'd see us at his place." Sam Gage lived alone in a small bungalow on the edge of town. It was modest and surprisingly neat, considering the man himself.

Sam Gage looked as if he'd just left his garage. There were no frills about this man. Cancer treatment had permanently damaged his vocal cords, giving his voice a pronounced rasp. His rough hands spoke to his demanding physical work. Town people held him in high regard — one who gave reliable and honest service.

"What can I do for you?" asked Sam. He made the agents feel at ease immediately. This guy was a straight shooter.

"We have some questions about one of your employees, a Kyle Ott," said Elmer.

"That's going to be tricky, fellas. Don't know too much about him. Can I get you coffee or anything?" The gravelly tone of his voice held their attention.

"No thanks. How long has he worked for you, Mr Gage?" asked Elmer.

"Call me Sam, guys. Never could get used to Mr Gage. Kyle started with us about two years ago as a part-timer. Still is, for a couple of reasons."

"And what are they?"

"First off I didn't need another mechanic full time. I already had two good ones, plus myself. Second, don't know if I'd want Kyle full time."

"Explain that please," said Elmer.

"Don't get me wrong here, he's a helluva mechanic and a nice enough guy. And he's as smart as they come. But he's just not that reliable."

"He doesn't show up when he's supposed to?" asked Dan.

"Yeah, like that. So if he can't make it in when he's part time, what would it be like if he was full time? Yet he finds work at other places in town as well."

"Why do you keep him on?" asked Elmer.

"'Cause he doesn't miss work that often and he's a good worker. Can't say he's ever screwed up a car on me. Besides, he's a likeable sort, though he keeps to himself most of the time."

"Does he have any friends or any social life?"

"I hear he's dated a few times. Small town, you know, Wilton. Things like that sort of get around, if you know what I mean."

"Yeah, we do, Sam," said Elmer. "Do you know any of the women he's dated?"

"No, but it'd be easy to find out."

"We'd appreciate that. Could you give us his work schedule for the last three weeks?"

"Sure. I've got all that stuff at the garage. It isn't too fancy but my records are right up to date and they sure are accurate. I've always run my business that way. Sort of a thing with me I guess."

"We'd like to see those records tonight. Would you mind?" asked Elmer.

"Not at all. Be pleased to help you guys."

"Did Kyle work today?"

"No. He's booked in for tomorrow and Saturday. Gets busy then."

It was fascinating listening to Sam Gage. The timber of the voice and his down to earth sincerity were endearing. His information had Elmer and Dan's interest piqued. They went to the garage and in no time had Kyle Ott's work schedule for the past three weeks.

"Thanks, Mr Gage, er Sam," said Elmer. "Much appreciated."

"Anytime. Good luck with finding this animal."

Al and Shirley Lofton owned the house where Kyle Ott rented a basement apartment. A phone call revealed that Ott was not in at the moment and yes, the police could talk to them. They welcomed the agents into their home.

"We have some questions about your tenant, Kyle Ott," said Elmer.

"Oh, Kyle is a nice young man," said Shirley.

"How long has he been with you?"

"Coming up to two years now, I think. He's a lovely, quiet man. Always pays his rent right on time."

"Do you see much of him?" asked Dan.

"Not really," said Shirley. "He has his own entrance at the back of the house, leads right into the basement. We fixed it up a few years ago so we could take boarders. Helps with the bills, you know. There's a nice bed sitting room with a bathroom including shower and tub. I'd show it to you but I think that would be invading his privacy."

"Does Kyle have his meals with you?"

"No. He prefers to eat out so we made a special deal for him to exclude meals. He seemed like a dependable sort who would stay for a while. It's worked well for us 'cause he's still with us."

"Where did he come from?" asked Elmer.

"We don't have any idea," said Shirley. "Truth is we don't know too much about him. He seems to like his privacy. When he pays the rent he visits for a little and he's always cordial. That's about the only time we see him. When we do run into each other, he stops to chat but never for long. He always seems to be on the go."

"Does he ever have friends over?"

"Like girls, Sergeant?"

"Anyone," said Elmer.

"None that I know of. Al, have you ever seen Kyle with anybody at the house?" Her voice had risen and she turned toward her husband.

"Nope," said Al.

"And he's never disturbed us, Sergeant."

"Does he keep regular hours?"

"That's hard to answer. Al's a little hard of hearing and I'm a real sound sleeper. We get to bed pretty early now 'cause we're early risers. You'll find us at the breakfast table by seven every morning. So we wouldn't know what time Kyle gets in at night. Sometimes we see him leaving for work in the mornings, but not always."

"Does he own skis or a snowmobile?"

"Of course, Sergeant, he has both. Most people here do."

"Did you see Kyle today?" asked Dan.

"Well, I don't think he went to work, at least I didn't see him leave this morning. Did you, Al?"

"What?"

"Did you see Kyle leave here today?"

"Yup."

"When was that, Al?" asked Elmer.

"Afternoon."

"What time?"

"Early," said Al.

"Like one or two?"

"Yup."

"Did he take his skis or snowmobile?" asked Dan.

"His snowmobile," said Al.

That was probably as long a reply as you would get from Al.

"What time did he come back?"

"Don't know."

Elmer looked at Dan. "Is that enough for you?"

Dan nodded.

"Thanks for talking to us," said Elmer.

It was ten-thirty when they reached Jessie Barr, Hal Ledyard's employer. They had just completed the introductions and he was still standing in the doorway of his apartment.

"This'd better be good," said Jessie. "I've been up since five and it's well past my sack time." He stood only five-eight but packed 180 pounds of muscle on his stocky frame. There wasn't an ounce of fat on him. He stared at the detectives with his hands on his hips.

Dan Adams was no slouch either. "Mr Barr, we're investigating a multiple murder case. If we have to deprive you of some of your beauty sleep to help us, we will." The two glared at each other.

"Let's get on with it," said Barr. He reluctantly let them in. They sat in the living room which was handsomely furnished. If there was anyone else in the apartment, Barr didn't let on, but the decor spoke to a woman's touch.

"How long has Hal Ledyard worked for you?" asked Elmer.

"Christ, your guys already asked me about him."

"How long, Mr Barr?"

"Twelve, thirteen years."

"What's he like?" asked Dan.

"He's a nasty one, but a real hard worker. Although he drinks a lot he always shows up for work and we've never had an accident with Hal."

"What's his attitude toward women?"

"I dunno. Kinda mean I guess. I hear he doesn't treat Millie very well. There's a lot of talk about that here. Small town, you know, so word gets around."

"Does he play around?" asked Elmer.

"How would I know?"

"Small town, you said."

"I hear stuff," said Jessie.

"Like what?"

"He goes to the Cities every once in a while when he stays sober long enough. He likes the hookers."

"Any incidents or fights with your other workers?" asked Dan.

"Nah. Hal minds his own business. Since he's kinda ornery most guys give him a wide berth."

"And he doesn't miss any work days?"

"You could count 'em on one hand."

"Did he work today?"

"Yeah, till three. We had to quit when we ran out of material at the site, so I let the guys go early."

"Thanks, Mr Barr. You think of anything, call us right away."

"Yeah. Good night." He showed them out.

Elmer raised his eyebrows. Dan smiled.

Geoff Saunders wasn't overjoyed at being questioned at the end of his shift but he was willing to offer his help.

"We understand Hal Ledyard is a regular at your bar."

"A regular? He's a fixture."

"How long have you known him?" asked Dan.

"I came here about three years ago. Started tending bar at the Heights right away. Hal's been coming in practically every night of the week since I've been here."

"You always on the night shift?"

"Mostly," said Geoff. "Take days occasionally. You guys are looking for the killer, right?"

Elmer and Dan nodded.

"Then why Hal? I know he's got a bit of a mean streak but I find it hard to believe he could be a killer."

"Why do you say that?" asked Elmer.

"You know bartenders. We're amateur psychologists. He's here so often I've come to understand him pretty well."

"If we give you some dates over the past three weeks, could you confirm when Hal was in your bar and for how long?"

"I think so," said Geoff. "His routine is so regular, I should be able to do that."

"Tell us about it."

"He comes in every day about five or six, working days that is. He doesn't always get drunk but he never leaves sober either. Sometimes he'll eat a little supper at the bar. He's gone around eight or nine at the latest. Hal seems to know he's got to get to work the next day so he leaves early enough to sleep it off. At least, that's how I figure it."

"What about weekends?" asked Dan.

"Ah, that I don't know. He's come in the odd Saturday, but it's rare. And Sundays — never. Monday through Friday, like clockwork."

They went over the dates when the crimes occurred. Geoff was not sure about a couple of the dates and since one murder was on a Sunday, he had no way of knowing where Hal was.

"And, today?" asked Elmer.

"He came in right on time, a little after five."

"Thanks for your help, Geoff."

Elmer and Dan updated their files on the suspects. Each categorized as either 'discard,' 'active,' or 'extremely active.' A full report would be given to Lieutenant Petersen who with their recommendations would classify each suspect.

It was after twelve and they still had to see Jean McCord, Millie Ledyard, and Kyle Ott's other employers as well as the women he had dated. They'd start first thing in the morning.

Chapter 65

WHEN JACK FINISHED AT MIDNIGHT, he checked in with the command center. It seemed Matt was always there. There was nothing new on Mrs Britain. "Matt, see if Sven Larsen can come over tomorrow. I'd like to go over the suspects with him. He may be able to help us."

Jack went to his room and called Jennifer.

"Sorry it's so late, honey, but wanted to call for a quick hello."

"It's okay. I'm just turning in and I'm glad you called. How did it go?"

"We're further ahead than we were this morning."

"You don't sound overly excited," said Jennifer.

"I'm just bagged but it does look encouraging. Hope to see you tomorrow."

"As I do. What time are your tests?"

"First one's at eight. I should be done around ten or so. I'll call you on my way back here."

"Good luck. You're not worried about this, are you?"

"Strange but I'm looking forward to it. He's a great doctor. David chose well."

"I miss you. Big surprise if you come home tomorrow night."

"What's that?" asked Jack.

"You have to be here to find out." Jennifer chuckled.

"Gotcha. I'll be there. Love you." They hung up.

He had to be up at five to make it to the Cities by eight. Although he needed the sleep, the images of the suspects wouldn't leave him. Billy, Ott, and Ledyard all looked possible. Billy, a little slow, but in many ways quite clever. Hates women because he's frustrated? Ott. New suspect.

A loner. Above average intelligence — brilliant? Unknown past — look into that. Has the freedom of movement but considered to be likeable and a nice guy. Ledyard. Is he sober long enough to plan and execute the crimes? Frank McCord. Take a closer look at him? He's bright enough, big enough, and doesn't possess the most charming persona. Yet, how could he get away so often without Jean knowing? Sherman. The least likely of the five. Still he does have the freedom of movement. Does he have any motive?

Five suspects. Is the killer one of them? None of them have a decent alibi for today. Still have to check out both McCords about that.

Jack left Wilton at five-thirty just as Julie was arriving.

"Skipping breakfast, Lieutenant?"

"No time this morning. I'll be back to catch your lunch special."

"Coffee to go?"

"I'll pass, thanks."

Dr Breckenridge had arranged to have the blood work done right after the stress test so Jack had been on water only since eight last night. He might just stop at his favorite burger place in St Cloud on the way back. Pete's would be an ideal place to break a fourteen hour fast. How long had it been since he'd devoured one of Pete's finest? His mouth watered just thinking about it.

Traffic had been light but as he neared the Cities it started to build, even at this early hour.

The stress test went smoothly. Breckenridge was impressed with Jack's stamina but he was puzzled that despite getting his heart rate up to 190 there was no pain. The doctor said he would book a Thallium test for early next week.

"What's that?" asked Jack.

"It's another stress test. When we get to your maximum level, we inject a dye into your blood stream. Diagnostic pictures are then taken to evaluate your arteries."

"Next week might be difficult for me, Doctor."

"Well this could wait, but not for long. I want you tested within two weeks. Call my office Monday morning for the results of your blood work and a date for the next test."

Jack was clear of the Cities in fifteen minutes. He called Jennifer.

"Brewster & Brewster."

"Hi, Joan. Is my lovely wife there?"

"She certainly is, Lieutenant. How are you today?"

"Great, thank you."

"Good. I'll pass you through."

"Hi."

"Good morning. How are things at B & B?"

"Same old, same old," said Jennifer. "What happened?"

"Test was okay. Ran the treadmill into the ground. Couldn't reproduce the pain which puzzled Breckenridge. He's ordering a Thallium test in a couple of weeks."

"I've heard of that. It's a more definitive test."

"Clever girl. We'll have the blood results Monday."

"Good timing. We'll have everything done before we leave."

"Yeah," said Jack.

"I recognize that tone of voice, Lieutenant. It says — assuming we catch this maniac in Wilton."

"We're getting somewhere. What's for dinner?"

"You." They laughed.

"Call you later. Love you."

"And I you," said Jennifer. They hung up.

He checked in with Matt. Rob Mullen was off the critical list but it would be several hours before he was conscious. They were relieved but also anxious to get a description of his attacker. Sven Larsen was on his way.

Jack had time to stop at Pete's. The special featured a generous portion of top sirloin smothered in Pete's home made sauce. Recipe — top secret.

It was only eleven. Plenty of time for two of Pete's finest.

Chapter 66

ELMER AND DAN ARRIVED at the hospital at seven-thirty. Jean McCord was starting at eight and had agreed to meet the two agents before her shift. They were shown to an administrative area where an office was made available. Jean sat primly in one of the chairs. You could have put two of her in the chair. Despite her size she had a firm handshake and strong posture. This was a woman of strength and character.

"Thank you for seeing us, Mrs McCord," said Elmer. "Your husband runs the store with Billy's help. That must involve long hours."

"Yes it does. And Frank shoulders most of the load because Billy...well Billy, God bless him, just can't handle some of the responsibilities of running a business. He does all he can but it's a limited role."

"Does the pressure affect Frank?" asked Elmer.

"From time to time. The kids and I would like to see more of him but we understand. One day the business will be able to afford a manger, giving Frank more time at home."

"His time away from home is all work related?" asked Elmer.

"That's a personal question, Sergeant," said Jean. She sat up even more erect and challenged Elmer.

"Please excuse us, ma'am," said Dan. "Sometimes we have to get into matters that aren't too pleasant. It's the nature of this business. Investigating murders leaves us no choice."

Jean brushed away a lock of hair. Her gaze fell to the table and she didn't speak for several seconds. Slowly she raised her head. Some of the spunk had gone and there was a sadness in her eyes. "Frank has ways of dealing with the stress...private ways."

"Please elaborate, Mrs McCord," said Elmer.

"He tends to spend time alone, outdoors mostly. He'll take long hikes or go skiing for hours. It's just his way to unwind."

"So you can tell when he's under pressure."

"Of course. We've been married twelve years, Sergeant. I know my husband."

"Have you noticed any change in Frank in the last two or three weeks?" asked Elmer.

"Wait a minute, Sergeant. You mean since the killings started?"

"Yes."

"Are you suggesting my husband is a suspect in these murders?"

"We're looking at everybody, Mrs McCord. It doesn't mean they're all suspects."

"I assumed you were really interested in Billy. That's what the talk is. I thought you wanted to know more about me and Frank to learn about Billy. This...this doesn't appear that way at all."

"Don't take this personally, Mrs McCord," said Elmer. "We never know when we're going to pick up a clue. This murderer has to be found before there's another killing. I'm sure you understand that."

"Of course I do. But I don't know how you could think of Frank as a killer."

"We're not suggesting he is," said Dan. "Your husband's actions or habits may tell us something about people he interacts with. It all has to be looked at."

Jean McCord hesitated. "Frank has seemed more tense than usual lately. He's been out on his own more frequently. Yes, there's been a change but I'm sure he'll come out of it. We're all affected by this. Perhaps Frank more than others, what with losing two long standing customers. Those customers were friends as well. And the two teenagers who worked for Frank. Well that indeed was too much. He's known them for years."

Her strength and resolve had returned. Jean McCord believed in her husband.

"Where was your husband yesterday?"

The defiant look was back. "He had to go to the Cities, Sergeant. He was back home about five-thirty."

"I think that's all for now, Mrs McCord. Thanks again."

"Find this monster, Sergeant. We all want you to find him soon."

Elmer and Dan met Millie Ledyard at the local library, one of her volunteer jobs. There was a lunch room for the employees which wasn't occupied. Millie was in her late forties but unfortunately looked ten years older. Life hadn't been too kind to her.

"You want to talk about Hal?" she asked.

Elmer and Dan nodded.

"Is this to do with all the murders around here?"

"Yes," said Dan.

"Well I can hardly blame you for thinking Hal might be involved. He comes off as a mean son of a bitch, doesn't he?"

"Maybe we should go back a bit, ma'am," said Elmer.

"But he's only mean on the outside," said Millie, as if she hadn't heard a word. "You've probably heard that he beats me. Rubbish. He's a pussy cat at home. He fools a lot of people with his gruff exterior but it's all show. Mind you he's strong enough to do some damage if he wanted to, but mostly it's just talk."

"We'd like to go over a few dates with you, check on where your husband was. Is that all right with you?"

"Of course."

Millie couldn't say with certainty where her husband was on any of the dates mentioned, including the afternoon when Cheryl Dean's body was left in the Nielsen house. As far as she knew he was in bed during the nights in question, but they have separate bedrooms so that couldn't be confirmed. She was asleep and he could have left the house on any of the nights without her knowing. And yesterday afternoon — they'd have to check with Jessie about that. Millie never went near their work sites.

Elmer and Dan returned to the motel and completed their reports. Jack was expected back around noon and they knew he was anxious to look at the interviews.

Chapter 67

JACK PULLED INTO THE MOTEL shortly before one. The moment he entered the motel he was challenged by an irate Frank McCord.

"What the hell's going on, Lieutenant?" He stalked toward Jack who stood his ground. They were eye to eye.

"What's your problem, Mr McCord?"

"Your men have been badgering my wife. Who do you think you are?"

"There's a serial killer loose here and we'll do everything in our power to stop him. If that means talking to your wife, we'll do it." Jack continued to stare him down.

Fortunately for everyone, Sven Larsen chose that moment to walk in the front door. "Someone trying to interfere with your investigation, Lieutenant?"

Jack hadn't moved. He had McCord locked in his sights. One more comment and Jack would take matters into his own hands. The press had appeared, taking in every word.

"Frank, I'd like to talk to you," said Sven. The Sheriff wedged his large frame between the two and eased Frank out of the way. "The Lieutenant's got a job to do here, Frank. We need all the help and cooperation we can get from the fine citizens of this town and that includes you. Now maybe you've got a business of your own to run?"

Frank didn't like it but backed down. "I know Jean can handle herself so I'll leave it. See you, Sheriff." He stalked out.

"Anybody in my territory not want to cooperate with your team, Jack, we'll deal with them. You've got enough on your plate. And I don't want to read about this anywhere." The sheriff was looking directly at the gathered reporters.

"Good to see you, Sven," said Jack. "Have you had lunch?"

"Yeah, let's get at it. You want me to look at some of your suspects?"

Matt handed him the reports from Agents Holm and Adams. They took them to the statement room.

"Thanks for coming over, Sven. Good timing too."

"Yeah. Frank McCord's not all bad, Jack. He's just a little testy at times."

"Maybe he's not all good either," said Jack.

"Hmm. Is he really on your suspect list?"

Jack reviewed the events of the last few days — the phone calls, the physical description of the caller who had to be the killer, and the spate of interviews. "Here's the list of our active suspects as well as interviews of those connected with them."

Jack got caught up with the recent interviews while Sven looked at the reports on the suspects.

"I know only two of these personally, Billy and Frank. I can't see either being involved but have to admit you may have a case with Billy."

"And the other three?"

"I like Bill Sherman the least as a suspect. I do like Ott and Ledyard. We'll run all three on our system. If anything comes up, I'll send it over right away."

"The initial interviews with these guys produced identical alibis," said Jack. "They all were at home in bed. Billy and Ott have no one to corroborate their stories. Jean McCord admits Frank does take off alone. Millie Ledyard says she'd never know 'cause they have separate bedrooms, and Sherman's wife works nights."

"What about the Dean girl? Wasn't her body moved during the day?"

"Yeah. We're going to have another talk with all five suspects. None of them have been accounted for in these reports."

Al Welsh came to their table. "Lieutenant, we just picked up this note." He held a plastic evidence bag which contained a large, plain brown envelope with a label — 'Deliver to Lieutenant Jack Petersen.'

"The guy who owns Jim's Variety Store says a customer found this in their magazine rack," said Al.

"How many people handled it?"

"Just the customer and Jim."

The envelope was flat and not of a size to indicate anything suspicious, like a letter bomb. They took it to the command center, opened it, and took out the contents with a pair of tweezers. It was a single piece of paper with a message that had been produced on a computer printer. Some of the words were in bold type.

"To the head pig — Lieutenant Petersen."

So you've been talking to people. I hear you have a list of suspects. Congratulations.

How many do you have?

Whatever the number — it's not **enough**!

Why not? You want to know — **pig**?

First there's another body for you to find.

Do you know who it is? Of course you don't — because even I don't know yet.

But I will — soon.

Now, what's wrong with your list?

Why isn't it complete?

Because I'm not on it!

"Al, get this dusted for prints, then fax it to David Folk. Get Jim and his customer printed as well so we can eliminate them. Matt, here's the classification of our suspects. Sherman and Frank McCord are 'active.' Billy McCord, Ott, and Ledyard are 'extremely active.' I want around the clock surveillance on these five, starting immediately."

"We'll need more agents, Lieutenant," said Matt.

"I'll talk to the Commissioner," said Jack. "How many computers with printers are in the area, Sven?"

"About a hundred, maybe more."

"Find out what make of printer this is, then check everyone that matches. We'll start with the five suspects. Also check the ink, printing, and paper. Maybe we'll get lucky with something special."

"So you don't believe him when he says he's not on your list?" asked Sven. The grin was wide.

"Yeah, of course," said Jack.

"He's playing with you, Jack."

"I know. He's cool isn't he? Is he on the list or not? I'm sure he wouldn't use his own computer for this note. He's evil but he's not stupid."

"Everybody gets careless, Jack."

"Yeah. Let's hope he starts making mistakes and soon."

"Lieutenant, David Folk on the phone."

"David, I've been expecting your call but not that quick."

"On what, Sherlock?"

"The letter, of course."

"I heard there was a fax for me. Sorry I haven't got to that yet but I do have something for you. We have some fibers from Miss Dean's coat which we believe came from a car seat. You'll want to check that out. Send us some samples from your suspects' vehicles, both of the material and any foreign fibers you find. If we identify the car there'll probably be fibers from her coat on the seat. That would help you."

"We'll get that done right away. Thanks, David."

Jack had Al Welsh get search warrants to examine the suspects' cars. "We need it done tonight."

Jack called Jennifer. No dinner at home tonight, in fact he wouldn't make it home at all.

Not with the killer threatening to move again.

Chapter 68

THE KILLER WAS FURIOUS. Too many police around plus this stupid security company. If all their guards are as easy to take as the one he leveled the other night, maybe he shouldn't care.

Why wouldn't the headaches leave him? Here it was only seven-thirty in the evening and he was being tortured again. He'd only wanted to frustrate the Lieutenant with his latest threat but now he might have to find a release. The one truth in the message was he didn't know who he would choose. And was he on the Lieutenant's list? That would be for them to find out.

He had to keep thinking clearly. The planning and execution must be perfect. He had to be ready. Since he didn't know when the next headache would come he had several plans he could call on. But he didn't feel prepared tonight.

Not like two weeks ago. Only two weeks? He'd heard the Martin woman might come up alone so he'd prepared his entrance in case he needed it. Was the headache that night real or imaginary? And on Sunday? Did he have to experience the pain or was the need for a victim all that mattered? Was he losing it? He didn't believe that could happen. He must always be in control.

He moved along the trail without paying any attention to where he was. Yet there was her house again. Nobody was home, at least it appeared that way. Maybe he should take care of the dogs. That would make the next visit simpler. He left the woods and started to ski across the open field leading to her house. Just then the back door opened and someone came out with the two dogs. It wasn't her though, it was...a cop! Had to be. Why had he been alone in her house with all the lights off?

He didn't like this. What if the dogs picked up his scent? Without hesitation he returned to the woods, skiing back to the main trail he knew so well. Minutes later he thought he saw a lone skier up ahead.

He slowly closed on the figure.

Chapter 69

DR JILL INGALL LOVED FRIDAYS, especially this one. She lived for weekends and didn't get many off. Divorced three years ago, she was now having the time of her life. At thirty-six she was in no hurry to remarry.

She felt the stress drain from her body as she moved fluidly over the groomed trail. After two straight weeks on the ward, the next three days off were going to be a treat. The feeling in the pit of her stomach was similar to that when one drops quickly in an elevator. Exciting.

Tonight was dinner with two fellow doctors. Richard and Trent were both single, decent young men, but neither held any romantic interest for Jill. It was Trent's birthday so she'd accepted the invitation to join the celebration.

"It's the last time I'll see the thirties," Trent had said. "You have to be there, not just because you're interesting, but you're also great to look at."

Trent always threw compliments her way and she knew he was sincere. He was great for the ego but that was it. She felt a little taller, even more attractive than Trent said she was.

She checked the time. Seven-thirty. She was late! The dinner was planned for eight o'clock. Time to turn around and get home to change. Skiing always exhilarated her. Her nose prickled as the clear, cold air rushed in. The smell was clean and pure.

Saturday she was off to the Cities for a weekend with Morris, her current beau. He was a successful architect and their relationship was ideal. He too was divorced, not ready to settle down again, so they were enjoying a carefree, loving time together. No pressure from either to take it any further. Her heart sang as she thought of all the good things in her life. As stressful as her practice sometimes was, she loved her work and was proud of her accomplishments.

She caught a glimpse of a shadow down the trail. Was it another skier? At this distance it was hard to tell. It was unusual to find skiers on this trail in the evening but during the day, especially on the weekends, it was packed

It was deserted out here. An involuntary shiver worked its way through her body. The stories around town about a mass murderer were unnerving. There were a few side trails that led off the main trail. At the end of the woods there was a stretch of open fields backing onto a few houses. Maybe she should take one in case. A strong skier, she could outdistance most, even men.

Was the lone figure coming toward her? It appeared that way. It had taken on the shape of a good sized skier, probably a man. He was definitely moving in her direction. Jill felt a dryness in her throat. Could this be trouble? They were totally isolated out here.

What were her options? Turn around and ski like hell. But it was too far, over a mile before she'd reach the road that bordered this trail on the west side. She could try to make it to one of the turn-offs before they met. If one of them came up soon, she should be able to reach the fields and houses before he caught up to her. It was a stretch of only two or three hundred yards.

On the other hand there may be nothing to worry about. After all she knew many skiers here. There were hundreds of them who weren't dangerous. The uncomfortable feeling wouldn't leave her. It would take only one bad one.

Where is that turn-off? One has to be coming up soon. She hadn't passed any yet and there were two or three for sure. The two skiers were getting closer. There was a turn-off! She handled the turn easily, then poured on the speed — just in case.

He'd been thirty yards or so from the intersection when she made the turn. She'd check in a minute to see if he followed her. If not she could relax and get back to thinking of dinner and the weekend. Her stride was okay but lacked her normal energy and speed. The side trail was not as well groomed and there were a few turns which slowed her pace.

She had to look back. She was a little tired and there was no point going all out if it wasn't necessary. She slowed to be able to turn around and look back along the path. He had turned with her. He was also closing fast!

Jill's heart was pounding. She had to get to the open fields. Another two hundred yards at least. She willed her legs to power her forward. Keep it smooth. Her poles dug at the snow. She thought she heard him. There was no way she could chance trying to take another look. Were those lights ahead? Through the trees? She sensed they were nearing the edge of the woods. There were houses and people out there. They would help her.

There was one more turn to negotiate. She hit the turn at maximum speed, didn't lose any momentum as she managed it perfectly. The opening was just ahead. Jill felt a second wind. Her legs seemed stronger. The adrenalin lift carried her forward, faster than she believed was possible.

She was clear of the woods. All the houses had lights on. She set her sights on the nearest home and somehow found even more energy. She wanted to scream for help, never having been this terrified. There was a slight downward incline and her speed increased. It felt good. She knew she would make it at this rate.

Her left ski caught a rut and almost upended her. In a panic she forced the other ski hard into the snow to regain her balance, then tried the same with her left leg. Jill Ingall cartwheeled forward, falling hard on the packed snow.

Get up and go she willed herself. She scrambled to stand up and get out of there. One of her skis was jammed in the snow and wouldn't move. She yanked at the ski. It didn't move.

Jill looked back. The night was perfectly still. There was no skier, only the line of trees forming the edge of the woods. He had vanished. Relieved, but still terrified, she worked her ski loose and struggled to get back on her feet.

The figure at the edge of the woods started to move.

Chapter 70

IT WAS EIGHT-THIRTY when Jack took the call.

"Petersen here."

"Lieutenant, this is Doctor Trent Davis. We're at the Gardenview Restaurant waiting for Dr Ingall. We've been calling her for the last half hour, getting only answering machines on her cell and home phones. This is not like her. We're concerned."

"Could she be on the way or in the shower?" asked Jack.

"Jill's never late. She would've called if there was a problem."

"When did you last see or talk to her?"

"She left the hospital a little after five. Said she was going to ski for a while, then would meet us here for dinner."

"Any idea where she'd go?"

"Yes," said Trent. "She has a favorite route which we know well. It's deserted out there and I asked her if she'd be okay alone. Jill said nobody's out there at night."

"Where is it?"

"The trail starts at Wilton Park. You'll need a snowmobile."

"Meet us at the park in ten minutes," said Jack. "We'll want you to show us the way. Give us her phone numbers please."

"We'll be there," said Trent. He gave Jack the numbers.

Jack ordered four snowmobiles with eight agents for the search. He and Al would monitor activities from the park.

They tried Jill's phones but each time they reached an answering machine. Her message was warm and full of humor. This was a person enjoying life. They hoped she still was.

Trent and Richard were pacing back and forth in the parking area. They hurried over to meet the officers.

"Lieutenant, I'm Trent Davis. This is Richard Ogilvie. I told her not to ski this trail alone." The words came in a rush.

"Hold on, Dr Davis," said Jack. "We don't know if any harm has come to Dr Ingall."

"There's her car," said Trent. "She definitely came here to ski. She's out there somewhere. She just came off fourteen straight days and was looking forward to this dinner." Trent was breaking up. Richard held his friend, trying to calm him.

"Do both of you know the route Dr Ingall would take?" asked Jack.

"I've been with her several times, Lieutenant," said Richard. "The trail runs west for about four miles. It ends at the Town Line road."

"So it's straight out and back?"

"Yes, other than a few smaller trails that lead south to some open fields and Willow Avenue."

The four snowmobiles arrived. "All right, let's get going. Richard, you ride with Agent Holm in the lead vehicle. Trent, you go with Agent Williams. You can split up to check the smaller trails, but always stay in pairs."

The four snowmobiles took off. They would be in radio contact with each other and Jack.

"Doesn't Ingrid Nielsen live on Willow Avenue, Lieutenant?" asked Al.

"Yeah. How often does our killer ski that trail and was he out there tonight? We have to find this guy, Al."

"Have you talked to the Commissioner lately?"

"He's to call me this evening," said Jack. "We need another twenty agents up here. With surveillance and protection duties, we're running out of people."

"Is there more than one killer, Lieutenant?"

"I doubt it. The killings fit the same MO with the exception of the Bradford kid."

"Lieutenant, Holm here."

"Go ahead, Elmer."

"We've reached the end with no sign of anybody. We're going to take a look at those side trails."

"10-4."

"We've got five guys, including Billy McCord. He had a rough time from Mullen the other night," said Al.

"Yeah, I heard about that. I can't see Billy taking off from the store. He was the only one there and he knew the other guards could be coming by at anytime for a break. That scene doesn't fit."

"According to John, he gave Mullen a look that could kill."

"From the way Mullen was taunting him, it's no wonder," said Jack. "In any case the skier was seen by an elderly couple around their house. Do you think Billy would stage something like that just to punch out Mullen? He'd have to be nuts to take a chance like that."

Al looked at Jack. "Yeah?"

"I'm not saying he couldn't be the guy..."

"Lieutenant, Holm here."

"Go," said Jack.

"No sign of Dr Ingall, Lieutenant. We've been down the three trails. We'll have to start looking off the trail."

"We'll be here."

Ten minutes passed before they had another call.

"Petersen."

"Lieutenant, good news," said Matt. "We just had a call from Dr Ingall. She's okay but has quite a story to tell. She's at the Wagner's house on Willow Avenue. Do you want to pick her up?"

"Yeah, we'll get right over there. Thanks, Matt. Call Elmer with the news and have them secure the area."

"That's not all, Lieutenant. Rob Mullen is awake and the doctor said we could talk to him. Ted's on his way to the hospital now."

"Good news. See you soon." They took the address, pulled out of the parking lot, and were at the house in five minutes. Bill Wagner let the officers in.

"I'm Lieutenant Petersen. This is Special Agent Welsh."

"We have one shaken lady in there, Lieutenant," said Bill.

They took Dr Ingall's story. She, unfortunately, was unable to provide a description of her pursuer, only that he was a big man.

"You did see him following you on the side trail?" asked Jack.

"Definitely. I turned to look back after a hundred yards or so. I was so scared I had to know if he'd followed me."

"Did you see him again?"

"No," said Jill. "I couldn't take the chance of turning around 'cause he was closing on me. I kept going till I was well out into the field. I fell about halfway across and my ski jammed in the snow. I panicked and took another look. Luckily for me he must have stopped when I got in the open and gave up."

"Have you received any threats lately Dr Ingall?"

"No."

"Have you noticed anyone following you?"

"No, Lieutenant. Nothing like that."

"You're sure he was chasing you?"

"Yes," said Jill. "I took this side trail that goes nowhere, unless you live here or in this area. He turned after me and was closing fast. If he lived here why didn't he continue? He obviously changed his mind."

"Excuse me, Dr Ingall. May I use your phone, Mr Wagner?"

"Of course, there's one in the kitchen."

"Erickson here."

"Matt, get two agents out here with the sulphur kit. Send them to the Wagner's house on Willow Avenue."

"Right away, Lieutenant." They signed off.

"Dr Ingall we need to know where this trail comes out of the woods. If this guy stopped there before retreating, we could get some valuable information."

"Sure. After that I'd like to get going."

"We'll take you back to your car as soon as we're finished."

Two agents arrived with the kit and were taken to the area. The sooner the work could be completed, the better chance they had of obtaining some useful prints. There was a clear set of tracks showing where the second skier had stopped and turned around. They needed this to get any kind of meaningful print.

Jack watched the procedure. The sulphur was melted at the site, the most time consuming part of the process. Fortunately it wasn't snowing. Otherwise, they'd have to cover the burner while they liquified the sulphur.

Once it was in a liquid form, they poured the sulphur onto the tracks. It hardened instantly to produce a set of prints. Hopefully they'd match those taken the other night when Mullen was attacked or those at the Nielsen house.

After taking Dr Ingall to the parking lot, they returned to the motel. Matt said the Commissioner wanted him to call right away. Jack dialed his number.

"Jack, what the hell's going on up there? I hear you had another close call tonight."

"Yes, sir. We've got five suspects now, all under full surveillance. There's not enough to bring anyone in. We're getting closer but we're short of agents."

"Jack, I've just finished talking to the Governor. He wants this over — quickly. How many agents do you need?"

"At least twenty. We also need authorization for two helicopters. Will you clear that with Brainerd?"

"We'll have the agents to you tomorrow and I'll have the helicopters arranged. Get him, Jack. I don't have to tell you what this means. We're looking bad. The press is bad. It has to stop."

They signed off and Jack headed for the meeting. The mood was tense. The agents were frustrated and upset. The news of more agents helped. They'd be able to monitor the existing suspects and keep up with the investigative work.

Al Welsh burst into the meeting room. "Lieutenant, we've got a match."

"With the skis?" asked Jack.

"Yeah. Come and look at this."

The agents crowded into the evidence room. The impressions clearly showed two nicks on the skis. It was as clear as a finger print.

"Here on the right ski approximately where the bindings are, there's a groove about two inches long running at a forty-five degree angle. That was taken tonight. Look at the impressions of the ski taken last Tuesday at Neilsen's and Thursday when Mullen was attacked. Identical."

Excited murmurs by the agents.

Al took them to another set. "As well, the left ski has a similar mark running down the middle of the ski just forward of the bindings. Again a perfect match to Tuesday's and Thursday's."

"I want the skis of those five guys examined right away," said Jack. The agents took their assignments and left.

Jack grabbed a cup of coffee. He was too geared up to eat. A call to Jennifer confirmed the all too familiar news. They were too close for him to be anywhere but in Wilton tonight. He was headed for the command center when Ted arrived.

"Got some goodies for you, Lieutenant."

"Let's go." They went back to the statement room.

"Mullen suffered a concussion and will be off duty for a while but he's going to be okay. He was able to describe his attacker. He said he's big and fast. That could eliminate Ledyard and Sherman."

"Why?"

"He thought this guy moved like a younger man. He also believes it wasn't Billy. He figures the guy was leaner and that's not all — he had some hair showing. He swears it was blond, real blond."

"Do any of our suspects have blond hair?" asked Jack.

"You bet. Kyle Ott."

Jack bolted from the room to find Matt. "Who have we got on Ott?"

Matt checked the board. "Riley was assigned to Ott but last we heard he hadn't found him. We've added three more agents to assist in the search."

"Call him."

Matt got through to Riley and handed the phone to Jack.

"Where's Ott?"

"I went to Gage's as soon as I got the assignment, Lieutenant. He didn't show up for work. I checked with the Loftons and they hadn't seen him since this morning. His snowmobile and skis are missing. There's four of us looking for him but so far nothing."

"We're adding the K-9 unit. Keep on it."

Chapter 71

NANCY BRITAIN OPENED HER EYES. How long had she been asleep this time? She was losing all track of time.

The room was small and dark. The one window had been boarded up on the outside and there wasn't a single crack to allow daylight in or to be able to see out. She'd been fed periodically. It was difficult trying to figure out the time interval between meals, if you could call them meals.

The bed was at the far end of the room, facing the lone door. There was a bathroom without a window. She hadn't seen her captor or heard him speak.

She had a vague recollection of the night she was taken. One minute he'd been sitting on his snowmobile, the next thing his fist had smashed into her face. She'd been blindfolded, taken into the house, and downstairs to this small room. It wasn't the Four Seasons but it was warm.

Earlier she'd received written instructions on how her food would be delivered. When he knocked on the door she was to lie face down on the bed with her eyes closed. To disobey would result in severe punishment. No conversation was allowed.

He'd open the door and place a tray inside the room. Only after hearing the dead bolt secured was she allowed to get up and retrieve the food. The same procedure was used in reverse when she was finished eating. She was to place the tray by the door exactly where he'd left it, knock on the door, and return to the bed, face down with her eyes closed. Absolutely no exceptions to the instructions would be tolerated.

The food was served on paper plates with plastic utensils. Initially she found it difficult to get anything down. Her anxiety left a knot in her stomach with no hint of an appetite. Her mind raced, unable to concentrate. She paced around the room like a caged animal. Keep moving or go nuts.

She exercised constantly, doing push-ups, sit-ups, stretches, and anything to keep herself occupied and physically fresh. Eventually she began to eat. The exercise had helped create the need for food. Was it the fourth or fifth meal, two or three days? She'd find a way to keep herself together.

Why had she left the party alone? What an idiotic thing to do. And who could this be? A chill went through her as she thought of the recent killings. Well she wouldn't give up without one hell of a struggle. The exercise routine would be increased daily. More push-ups, sit-ups, more of every kind of strenuous activity possible given the surroundings. There wasn't much to work with but she stayed creative. The bed and single chair provided a couple of useful tools.

She kept developing new ideas on how to work out with what she was given. It helped keep her mind occupied as well. She clung to the thought that Al would find her. Anything to give her hope.

Ten more sit-ups. And another ten.

He really wouldn't harm her. If he'd wanted to, he would have acted by now. Surely...

Ten more push-ups.

Panic gripped her again. She pounded the floor till her knuckles bled. Don't be too long. Please hurry.

There was a knock on the door.

Chapter 72

SILVER HEIGHTS WAS QUIET, not unusual for a Saturday morning at eleven o'clock. Only two customers sat at the bar with another two at a table. Cam Fletcher and Al Britain had arranged to meet at Al's request. Neither was impressed with what was going on in Wilton.

"Nothing about my wife for five days now," said Al. "How long do we let this nonsense go on?"

"I'm not impressed either, Mr Britain, but I don't know how much more can be done. I've known Jack Petersen for a long time. He's one of the best there is."

"He may well be but someone out there is making our lives a living hell. I want the bastard and soon. I'm willing to finance some faster action."

"Just what did you have in mind, Mr Britain?"

"Make it Al, will you?"

"Fine. Al, it is."

"I understand the police have a list of suspects. Something like three or four names."

"That's what I've heard," said Cam.

"What if we conducted our own private investigation with these suspects?"

"We're not supposed to get involved in that side of the operation."

"We're not supposed to get killed or have our wives go missing either. So I don't really care who's supposed to do what or why. It's time we put a little pressure on these guys. We could start with Billy McCord. He's always been kind of weird in my book."

"What's your, uh, proposal, Al?"

"You find my wife or her killer, there's twenty thousand in it for you — cash."

"That's awfully tempting," said Cam.

"My wife is missing. I want her back, Cam. If she's still alive, we've got to find her before it's too late. That probably means finding him first. This investigation isn't moving fast enough for me."

"I'll have to think about it," said Cam.

"No. I want an answer, now. And action, now. Twenty thousand, cash. I'll give you five thousand today."

Cam stirred his drink slowly. He'd hardly touched his rum and coke. He moved the ice cubes around. "What exactly do you have in mind?"

"I say we talk to each of these suspects. Use a little persuasion to see if you can get them to talk. You must know how to do that."

"That's kind of risky. I could lose my license over this."

"I need help. I can't just stand by and wait for Nancy to show up. I have to know where she is. You can understand that."

"Yeah." Cam downed his drink. "Yeah."

"Billy McCord's at the store. I saw him when I came over here this morning. He should be there till five or so. Why not start with him?"

"Billy McCord. Big guy."

"You're bigger and definitely smarter."

"He's got a tail on him," said Cam.

"You'll figure something out. That's your business. The cash is in my car. Do we have a deal?"

"This is real tempting," said Cam. "That's a lot of cash for a guy like me but I can't give you an answer today. Sorry but that's the way it has to be."

"I'll give you twenty-four hours," said Al. "You will think about it?"

"Yeah."

Al went to the bar and paid for the drinks.

Geoff had the early shift today. He watched the two leave. Bartenders didn't miss much.

Chapter 73

INGRID AND JANICE entered Chapman's funeral home shortly after ten o'clock. Two young people buried in less than a week. Both murdered. How much more could the town of Wilton take?

A group of citizens was meeting with Lieutenant Petersen today. Some wanted the National Guard brought in. Others suggested a mandatory curfew for everyone. Drastic measures indeed but steps that might be necessary to stop these senseless killings.

Ingrid couldn't help but think of Rick every time she attended a funeral. Was it time to leave Wilton? Maybe she should join Janice and start a new life elsewhere. And now this note from the killer, threatening her. With the 24 hour police protection she'd felt safe, yet it was a constant reminder of the danger.

When she saw Cheryl's parents, a sob caught her throat. A feeling of emptiness engulfed her. How true the sentiment...parents should never have to bury their children. The room was packed but she couldn't see Billy. That was unusual as he always showed up to offer his support. Cheryl had worked at McCord's for at least two years, yet neither Billy nor Frank was here. Well the service didn't start till eleven. There was still time.

Ingrid was still feeling the effects of yesterday's ordeal. The image of Cheryl's distorted body and face wouldn't leave her. Janice had arrived just as the police were leaving. She too had been devastated with the discovery.

They made their way through the salon to talk to the Deans. The casket was closed.

"From what you told me I'm relieved someone had enough sense to close the casket," said Janice. "The poor thing."

They offered their condolences to the Deans. Ingrid couldn't rid herself of Cheryl's image or of thoughts of Rick. She was putting on a brave front. They were moving amongst the crowd when Ingrid felt someone take her arm. She turned to see it was Muriel Bates.

"Hello, Ingrid, Janice. That must have been a terrible ordeal for you last night. I'm sorry."

"Thank you, Muriel. It's the Deans I feel for."

"Yes. First Ellen Bradford, now the Deans. It's just too much, Ingrid."

"I know. To lose your only son or daughter is far more than a parent should endure. And the students are having difficulty coping with this."

"The counselors are staying on at the school," said Muriel. "Do we have enough to handle the students, Janice?"

"We could use more help, Muriel. We're going to the school today to be available for students. Dealing with this second tragedy so soon after Jim's death will be even more stressful."

"I'll join you as soon as I can," said Muriel. "I've been asked to attend the meeting with Lieutenant Petersen. Parents are irate. We've been swamped with calls demanding action."

People were still coming in.

"I can't understand why Billy isn't here," said Ingrid.

"Yes. Cheryl worked with the McCords didn't she?"

Ingrid nodded. "I'd have thought Frank would be here as well."

"That doesn't surprise me," said Janice.

"What?" asked Ingrid.

The funeral director announced they'd be leaving for the church. The crowd began to disperse toward the exits. She stared at Janice who had turned to leave.

Ingrid fell into step beside her. "What did you mean by that?"

Janice kept looking straight ahead as they inched forward.

"Nothing," she said.

Chapter 74

JACK WAS IMPATIENT. They'd checked the skis belonging to Billy McCord and Sherman. No match. Ledyard's skis were badly scored and also didn't fit. Agents were due in soon with reports on Frank McCord's and Kyle Ott's. Still no news about Ott.

"Lieutenant, why don't you have Julie fix up a burger?" asked Matt. "The guys won't get here any faster with you wearing out your shoe leather."

"It's close. I can feel it. Do we have extra guys on Ott?"

"Yeah, but still no luck. Do you think he's the killer?"

Jack shrugged. "He certainly could be the guy who went after Mullen and Dr Ingall. The skis could clinch that. He was also at the Nielsen place."

Matt took a call and handed the phone to Jack. "It's David Folk."

"How did it go with Breckenridge?"

"David, we're getting somewhere here. I don't have time to talk about Breckenridge."

"All right already. What about some new evidence, Sherlock? Do you have time for that?"

"Have you been holding out on me, David?"

"Just got this in. We have some hair samples from the second murder scene — that's Mrs Michael right?"

"Yeah, yeah."

"Because that took place in their bedroom, I wanted another look at the evidence. There's all kinds of hair samples from the rest of their house, but the bedroom — how many visitors do you have there? We came up with two hair types that didn't belong to the doctor or his wife.

One probably female, one unknown."

"How can you tell?" asked Jack.

"The first samples were dark brown, nine inches in length and curly. The hair had been permed and colored. That suggests it was from a woman, although not conclusively. The second samples were shorter, two to three inches, and natural. They were blond. Most likely from a male. Your killer is male. I'd check the Michael's cleaning lady. Odds are she has medium length, brown hair, that's curly. Who owns the other sample? That could be interesting."

"Thanks, David. Send that sample up here please."

"Consider it on the way."

"Sorry about the earlier remarks," said Jack. "Breckenridge is a great guy. I'll have some results Monday."

"Good luck with both," said David. "Best to Jennifer. Meanwhile, back to my cage."

They hung up.

"Matt, we need Ott picked up — now. Get everyone on it. Folk has hair samples from the Michael's bedroom. They're blond."

"Helicopters, Lieutenant?"

"Yeah. Have one start at the area where Dr Ingall was followed. I think he's been there before, checking on the Nielsen woman. Let everyone in town know we're after this guy."

"We've got more reports from the interviews here, Lieutenant," said Ted. "Some with a couple of women he dated."

"Let's get at that right away."

They pored over the notes. Nothing was helping. There were five women in all and he'd dated only one more than once. "Let's talk to Myrna Johnson again. She claims they dated six or seven times."

The center was alive with tension and excitement. The helicopters were airborne. They still had about three hours of daylight. The center could communicate with every agent, the K-9 unit, and the helicopters. The hot line was ringing. In the next hour Kyle Ott was 'seen' in several parts of Wilton. All were checked — no sign of him. The word was out. Agents were canvassing businesses and homes. The Lofton house was being closely watched. Another hour passed.

"Lieutenant, there's a Sam Gage on the phone."

"Petersen here."

"Lieutenant, I've got a guy here you should talk to."

"What is it?"

"He remembers something Ott told him a long time ago. It might help. It might not, but thought I should call."

"Put him on."

"Hi, Lieutenant, it's Wilf. I've known Kyle since he's worked here. He never talked much, but when he first started he did tell me his folks owned a place out of town. Real nice place he said. They gave it to him when they passed away."

"Do you know where it is?"

"No, but there is something unusual about it. See, he told me there's a lake right in his backyard and though there's a lot of lakes around here, there might be only one shaped like his."

"And what is that, Wilf?"

"It's almost a perfect heart. The cabin faces the point of the heart and he could see the outline of the lake from the back porch. Like I said — a perfect heart."

"Did he tell you where it was?"

"Only that it was about fifteen minutes from town."

"In which direction?" asked Jack.

"Sorry, I don't know."

"You've been a big help, Wilf. We'll get back to you later. Thank Mr Gage for me will you."

"Will do, but he prefers to be called Sam."

"Then thank Sam. See you."

"Get the choppers on the line." Jack went for the map and notes from his flight with Reg. He spread them on a table. One more hour of daylight.

Jack gave the details of the lake to the two pilots. "It's about fifteen minutes out of town. Start at the north 'cause there's no small lakes south of town."

The pilots agreed to start their search from the middle of town and work east and west on the north side. The background noise from the airborne choppers invaded the command center. The rush of air and whirring of their engines were constant reminders of the airborne units closing in on their suspect.

A half hour went by. Jack was becoming more restless by the minute. "They've got only thirty or forty minutes left before dark."

"We've deployed most of our units north of the town in case he's up there," said Matt.

"Yeah," said Jack. "We've almost got him. Come on guys, where's that lake?"

Ted Norris came back in the room. "Lieutenant, there's a group of people at reception who say they have an appointment with you."

"Jesus that's right. Is it five-thirty already?"

"Yeah."

"Ted, hold them off for a while. I can't leave here now."

"Will do, Lieutenant."

The minutes seemed to fly by. Darkness was setting in. Nobody spoke. The radio squawked into life. Everyone perked up.

"Lieutenant, I think we have it."

"Where are you? What's it like?"

"Oh yeah, it definitely fits your description. The cabin sits right at the point of the heart. We're about five miles north of Wilton. There's a road here, Town Line, that runs north. Take the third concession road and go east. The cabin's just north of that road. It's the...fourth cabin from the Town Line."

"Is anyone there?"

"Looks like it. There's lights on and a snowmobile out front. We're down to twenty feet now."

"Be careful," said Jack. "We'll have agents there shortly."

"There's somebody coming out the front door now — he's got a rifle."

The sound of increased power echoed through the center.

"Are you guys all right?" asked Jack.

"Yeah, we're okay. Any idea if he's alone, Lieutenant?"

"We don't know. He may have a hostage in there. Keep out of firing range."

"No problem. We'll just hover here till you arrive."

"We're on the way."

Jack and Elmer Holm raced out of the room and headed for the parking lot. As they ran through the reception area six startled citizens watched.

"Emergency, folks," said Jack. "The sergeant in charge will brief you."

Elmer drove while Jack tuned the radio into the choppers' frequency.

"Bears one and two, this is Petersen, over."

"Read you, Lieutenant. He's back inside. It's pitch black out here but we've got our lights on the cabin."

Elmer wheeled onto the highway heading for Wilton. Jack was navigating. They picked up Town Line in a couple of minutes. "Take Town Line north to Concession Road number three. That'll be about five miles."

"Lieutenant, he's moving! Took the snowmobile and is heading due east. Lot of brush coming up."

"Can you stay on him?"

"Yeah, we've got him lit up like a Roman candle. Might be tougher when he reaches the brush."

Jack had all units on the same frequency. They were converging on the area. The helicopters continued to track the fugitive.

"He's reached the woods. There's a trail here, we can see him easily. He's really moving. Still going east."

Jack and Elmer had reached Concession Road three. They turned east. "How far is the cabin?"

"Fourth one over."

"Lieutenant, he's turned off the trail. It's dense in there. Now he's doused his head light. We could lose him here."

"Have you still got him?"

"Yeah, we get a glimpse now and then. Oh, Christ."

"What is it? What's happened?"

"He's hit a tree. Just a second. Okay, I've got it now. The snowmobile is a mess. What's left of it is on its side. He must be under the machine 'cause nothing's moving, Lieutenant."

"Can you get anywhere near him?"

"No, it's too dense. I can see the wreck but no body."

Jack checked the other units.

"Lieutenant, it's Sergeant Adams, we can see the chopper's lights. We're getting close."

"Anyone else in the area?"

"Not yet, but we're only a few minutes ahead of Hampster three."

"Roger. Bears, are you sure he didn't get out of that crash?" asked Jack.

"We haven't seen anything move, Lieutenant. We're right over the snowmobile now. It's bad."

"How far off the trail is he?"

"Maybe fifty yards. We've got one of your units in sight."

"We're near the scene now, Lieutenant," said Adams.

"Wait for Hampster three. I want four of you going in there."

"10-4, Lieutenant."

"Still quiet, Bears?"

"I can see part of him now, Lieutenant. His legs are visible but that's all."

"Williams is here now, Lieutenant," said Adams.

"Go and take a look but be careful. This guy's dangerous."

They'd arrived at the cabin and found the front door unlocked. They drew their weapons and entered. Jack had his radio with him.

"Lieutenant, Adams here. We've found him. He's dead."

"Do you have an I.D.?"

"Yeah. It's Kyle Ott all right. Williams had interviewed him."

"Adams, get the coroner up there. Have the body sent to St Paul, we'll want an autopsy. Secure the area and complete your reports."

"10-4, Lieutenant."

Jack and Elmer moved through the cabin. Facing the kitchen was a den with a TV. There was a hallway, one full bathroom off that and at the end, a bedroom. Nobody on the ground floor. They went down to the basement. It was small and unfinished but there was one door. It was dead-bolted from the outside.

"Is anyone in here?" asked Jack.

Silence.

He knocked on the door. "Anyone there?"

"Who — who is it?"

"It's the police. Are you all right?"

"Really? It's Nancy Britain. I'm okay."

Jack and Elmer had their weapons trained on the door. He released the dead bolt and carefully opened the door. Nancy Britain was cowering on the bed. They quickly swept the room, saw the bathroom, and moved down the wall.

"Is it empty?" asked Jack, mouthing the words.

"There's no one here," said Nancy. She buried her head in her hands and sobbed.

They checked the bathroom before consoling Nancy. "You're going to be fine now," said Jack.

"Oh thank you. I can't believe you're here. Where is he?"

"He's dead. Let's call your husband. Would you like some help?"

"No, I'm fine thanks. I worked out every day and he fed me often enough. By the way, what is today?"

"It's Saturday, February 5th."

"God, it's been only six days. Seemed longer than that."

Nancy called her husband while Jack and Elmer looked around. On the kitchen counter there was a large envelope addressed to Jack. He opened it carefully.

Lieutenant Petersen:

If you're reading this, then it's over. I'll be dead 'cause you're not getting me alive.

I knew you were getting close and I couldn't take the chance of not telling you the truth.

You'll probably find the Britain woman. Too bad I didn't find time for her. She stayed in the room where my parents used to keep me. Only there was no bathroom in those days. I built that after they left. They're in the bottom of 'Heart Lake.'

I'm responsible for the two women on the lake but I DID NOT do the kids. They had no interest for me. You've got yourself another killer.

"What is it, Lieutenant?"

Jack handed the letter to Elmer.

"Jesus."

Chapter 75

JACK CALLED MATT to organize a team meeting. "Ott left a letter. If he's telling the truth, we have a second killer."

"How's that, Lieutenant?"

Jack gave him the details. "We'll be back in fifteen minutes. We have Mrs Britain with us."

"Yeah. Her husband's here already. That interview with Ott's girl friend, what's her name — Johnson. You want that canceled now?"

"No," said Jack. "We need all the info we can get on this guy. Maybe she can account for his time when the other murders occurred, then we'll know he wasn't kidding."

When they arrived at the motel, a relieved husband was anxiously waiting. He and Nancy fell into each others arms. The press were just as anxious. Jack briefly updated them, begging off as there was work to do, but promised more later.

"Great work, Lieutenant," said Al. "I was afraid I'd never see her again."

"Glad we found her. Your wife's a remarkable woman, Mr Britain. We need to talk to her if she's up to it."

"What do you say, honey?"

"Sure. Can we do it over some hot food?"

"Of course. Julie will find you something."

Jack had Ted interview Mrs Britain while he called David Folk.

"Did you get him?"

"Yeah, he's dead. And we found Mrs Britain who'd been locked up in his cabin."

"That's the woman who went missing from the Super Bowl party?"

"Exactly. However, it may not be over. The killer left a note."

"There might be a second killer?" asked David.

"How in the hell did you know that?"

"I didn't but the Bradford case bothered me. It didn't fit at all. What did your killer say?"

"His name was Ott, David. Says he had nothing to do with either Bradford or Dean."

"And you want to know if he's telling the truth or putting you on?"

"Yeah."

"I tend to think you have another sick puppy up there, Jack."

"Ott's been playing games for weeks, David. You sure he's still not messing with us?"

"It just doesn't fit, Jack. Take the Bradford case. Where's the possible motive? This guy went after women. Why would he want to kill a young man?"

"Maybe Bradford learned something about Ott. He threatened to go to the police."

"Fine. Only Bradford was running away from you at the time, was he not?"

"Maybe," said Jack.

"Jack, he makes a pass at one of the women...who was it?"

"Mrs Cooper."

"Yes, Mrs Cooper. Then he disappears, doesn't contact anyone. This occurred late afternoon didn't it?"

"Around four."

"So you find him in his truck. The lady on the river sees the truck at five in the morning, or something like that. What's he been doing for more than twelve hours? And wasn't his truck parked at Billy McCord's?"

"Yeah, we traced it back to his driveway."

"And hadn't the kid ransacked McCord's for some cash and food?"

"Yup."

"Now, Jack, do you see Ott and Bradford?"

"No."

"Then there's the Dean girl. I do admit that sounds more like Ott. But why deny both? If he had nothing to do with Bradford, I suggest it's the same for Dean."

"But the Dean case was so similar" said Jack. "Taking the body to Nielsen's house fits him perfectly."

"Even you can figure that out."

"I know but it's not the solution I want. There's another monster here and he knew what Ott was doing. So he started his own rampage and made the Dean crime seem a copy of Ott's work."

"He may be more dangerous because he doesn't know how sick he is. His targets will be unpredictable. I believe your stay in Wilton is not over, Jack."

"Time to go over the files. We still have four suspects."

"Your people seem to like one of the McCords as the most likely."

"Yeah. I have my own thoughts."

"And they are?"

"They both fit the profile. Billy's a loner, seems mixed up, and certainly is free to move around. It's easy to dislike Frank. He's slick and likes to put people down but that doesn't make him a murderer. So it's a toss up."

"Good hunting, Jack. We'll revisit the Dean and Bradford cases. The Dean autopsy is on my desk now. Say hello to my favorite girl."

"Thanks, David. Talk to you soon." They hung up.

The wall clock said eight-thirty. He dialed his home number.

"Guess things heated up," said Jennifer.

"Yeah. We caught the first guy but there's some complications."

"What do you mean, the first guy? There's another one up there?"

"Possibly. He left a note saying he had nothing to do with the last two killings."

"How bad does it get, Jack?"

"Bad enough that I have to stand you up again. The minute this is over, I'm applying for that desk job. You'll have to put up with me every night."

"I'll do my best to handle that," said Jennifer. "Guess it's the Wilton Hilton for you tonight."

"When we're finished, I'll bring you up here. It's really charming."

"I'm sure it is, particularly without the monsters."

"Exactly. David Folk says hello."

"Hello, David back."

"I'll call you tomorrow," said Jack. "Love you."

"Two weeks today we leave and I'll have you all to myself. I can't wait. Love you too." Blown kisses before they hung up.

Jack would talk to the Commissioner after the team meeting. He knew the press were waiting for him. They'd been lucky so far in that there'd been no leaks and he wanted to keep it that way, particularly with this new development. The team was stunned by the news that there might be a second killer. The mood was one of relief and frustration. The consensus was one of the McCords. Ledyard and Sherman were downgraded to 'active' with Frank and Billy listed as 'extremely active.'

"Bradford's death was sometime between midnight and five in the morning, Wednesday, January 26th," said Jack. "Cheryl Dean wasn't seen after nine o'clock, Friday night, January 28th. Her body was taken to the Nielsen house Thursday, February 3rd, between eight and four in the afternoon. We'll go over these dates with each suspect. Let's put the heat on all of them."

They went over the files from the funerals and visitations at the funeral home. Agents who'd been assigned to cover both events dug out their notes. They had bugged the caskets in the hope of picking up a confession. Jack felt it was a bizarre practice but they knew confessions had been heard before by people 'talking' to the dead.

New surveillance teams were organized to track the four suspects. They couldn't afford another killing. There'd been too many already.

Chapter 76

INGRID COULDN'T BELIEVE IT. After the funeral they'd gone to a reception at the community center. They were back in Ingrid's house when Janice admitted to her affair with Frank McCord.

"How could you? You know those kids. You know Jean."

Janice was crying. "I never thought it would go this far."

Ingrid slammed the kitchen table. The dogs started. They nor Janice had never seen Ingrid this upset. "That's not good enough. And of all men to pick — Frank McCord. He makes a pass at any woman he thinks may be available."

"I didn't — *pick* him. It just...happened."

"Then just stop it. When I think of Billy being such a good uncle with those darling kids, and of Jean who's a saint, I can't understand it. I'm not in the least surprised to find that Frank is being unfaithful. I've never had a very good opinion of him. But to learn that my best friend is his playmate...Christ!"

"You make it sound so sordid."

"And it isn't?" Ingrid glared at her.

"I love him."

Ingrid sighed and got up to let the dogs out. She donned her coat and boots and went with them. She had to calm down. It wouldn't help to berate her friend this way. It was frustrating but she had to find a way to help. She watched her pets in the snow. Who said, 'it's a dog's life?' There's many moments when that seems ideal. Certainly less complicated.

Ingrid returned with the dogs. Janice hadn't moved.

"Would you like some coffee?"

Janice nodded.

"Maybe a bottle of wine would be better."

"I feel so bad," said Janice.

Ingrid put an arm around her friend. "It's never too late to change."

"I'd decided to call it off. It's getting around to actually doing it. Anyway, he's coming over tonight. I'm going to tell him then."

"Will he be a problem?"

"I hope not. He does have mood swings but I don't think he's violent, if that's what you mean."

Ingrid shrugged. "Coffee or wine?"

"Neither thanks. Maybe I'll come back for the wine later if the offer's still open. I'll probably need it then."

"You make sure you come back. That's not an offer. It's an order."

"Thanks, Ingrid."

They hugged and Janice left. It was five-thirty. Ingrid was uneasy about the coming evening. Maybe she should call Billy. He'd made it to the funeral after all. Frank had not. He claimed one of them had to be at the store and Frank had insisted.

She called the store. Billy answered.

"Hi, it's me. You have a minute?"

"Oh, Ingrid. Yeah. How are you?"

"Okay. Would you like to come over for supper?"

"Uh, yeah, but..."

"What is it, Billy?"

"Jean has to work till eight tonight 'cause they're short of staff and Frank asked me to take the kids out for supper."

"Why?"

"The afternoon sitter has to leave at six and Frank's got a lot of work to do."

"I'll bet he has."

"What, Ingrid?"

"It's nothing, Billy."

"I was just getting ready to leave."

"Why don't you bring them here? I'll make some pasta."

"They'd love that, Ingrid. They think we're going for hamburgers. This'll be a great surprise."

"See you when you get here."

Ingrid began preparing dinner. She had to talk to Billy, alone. How to break it to him?

Lisa and Wes jumped out of Billy's truck and ran to the door. They couldn't wait to see the dogs. "Hi, Auntie Ingrid." They took time to give her a hug, all the while itching to get at Sasha and Bentley. The dogs were equally curious and excited. Billy followed and they waved to each other.

"Can we play outside for a while?"

"Sure," said Ingrid. "But stay in the backyard, okay?"

"Yeah. Let's go."

Ingrid led them to the kitchen where all four bounded out the back door. She turned on the outdoor lights and watched the kids. Billy was beside her.

"The kids are so excited about this, Ingrid. Thanks a lot."

"They mean a lot to you, don't they, Billy?"

"Yeah, I guess. They're family you know."

"Billy, there's something I have to tell you. It's not going to be easy."

"Oh?"

"Your brother is having an affair with my best friend!" She just blurted it out, not knowing how to soften the blow.

Billy stared at the floor. "I know."

"You know?"

"Yeah, for a while now, but I don't know what to do."

"They're meeting tonight."

"Frank and Janice?"

"Yes."

"I didn't know that but I guess it's not a surprise."

"She's going to call it off, Billy. Do you think she'll have a problem with Frank?"

"What do you mean?"

"Would he...become violent?"

"Gee, I don't think so. He's got a temper but...hurt a woman?"

They stared out the window. The kids and dogs were running amok with carefree abandon, unaware of the marital problems.

"I'll figure out something," said Billy.

His tone of voice held a quiet resolve which she found alarming. It was almost as if the words had been spoken by someone else. Ingrid looked at Billy. He hadn't moved. The silence was disturbing.

"Time for the kids to come in," said Billy. He opened the door and called. All four came charging in. Ingrid put the water on to boil. The sauce was simmering, she just had to cook the pasta.

Lisa and Wes carried the conversation through dinner. The pasta was delicious. The dogs were cool. Could they stay over? Can they take the dogs home to show Mom and Dad? When could they come back? It kept the mood upbeat.

It was just past eight when Billy called Jean to let her know where they were. "Should I bring them home now, Jean?" Billy nodded and hung up. "We gotta go soon."

Everybody helped clean up despite Ingrid's protests. The kids hugged the dogs goodbye and thanked Ingrid for a great supper.

"Don't worry, Ingrid. I'll take care of everything." Billy herded the kids off to his truck.

Ingrid watched them go. She'd never seen Billy like this. He was like a stranger. Could she have been wrong about Billy? After all these years it seemed out of the question. How could she possibly have not seen this side of him? It's more likely he's just upset. That has to be the case.

Ingrid decided to concentrate on Janice's problem. She debated whether to call the police.

Maybe the Lieutenant should know about this.

Chapter 77

JACK WAS REVIEWING THE EVIDENCE against Kyle Ott. Strands of his hair had been sent to David Folk, which he fully expected to match David's sample from the Michael's house. Ott'd confessed to the Martin and Michael murders but denied involvement with Bradford and Dean. Was he putting us on?

He called David.

"David Folk."

"Shouldn't that be two words, like David, pause, Folk, not Davidfolk?"

"Do you have any other brilliant observations, Monsieur Poirot, or is that the extent of your criticism for today?"

"I want to discuss Ott."

"I can well imagine. You're pondering his note. Is he telling the God's truth, or is it a game?"

"Exactly. I'm sure the hair sample will match, which puts him in the Michael's bedroom. Since he's confessed to the two lake killings anyway, that's a wrap. Then there's the sulphur prints taken at three different sites which matched his skis."

"Which sites are you referring to?" asked David.

"February 1st outside Ingrid Nielsen's home, February 3rd when he attacked Rob Mullen, and February 4th pursuing Dr Ingall."

"Run those one at a time."

"He was at Nielsen's house in the middle of the night. We have to assume she was an intended victim but when he found another person there he decided to leave. The night he ran into Mullen he'd been seen by the Wilsons near the lake. It was late, so he was on the prowl again.

And Dr Ingall believes he was after her but she managed to get away. All three fit his pattern of looking for victims."

"Perhaps."

"Let's say he was after Nielsen," said Jack. "Two days after his visit, Cheryl Dean's body is deposited in her house. The person responsible, presumably her killer, leaves a note claiming she's next."

"Ergo, one would conclude it had to be Ott. He stalked her, now leaves a note. Could be."

"If that scenario is correct, David, then he lied to us in the note about Dean. If he lied about Dean then he lied about Bradford. That means the case is solved."

"Then the interviews you're conducting with the four suspects and your new surveillance teams are just to keep your agents occupied so they won't get into trouble?"

"Something tells me he wasn't lying. Besides it's too risky not to follow up."

"Jack, there could very well be a second killer for all the reasons we've discussed. The Nielsen issue could be just another smoke screen. The second killer takes the opportunity to emulate the first just to confuse you."

"Yeah. Anything on the car seats?"

"Not yet," said David.

"We've got the heat on the suspects but we need more. Can we have that tonight?"

"Maybe. We're close. I have the feeling you like a particular suspect. Who's your first choice, Sherlock?"

"I don't like Sherman and Ledyard. Billy McCord seemed to fit the lake murders but these last two? I like him less there than I did with the first cases. He's a mystery, David. I'm meeting with Ted to review the Bradford and Dean killings and both McCords. Meanwhile, all four suspects will remain under surveillance."

"You don't have much to go on with Bradford but this evidence on the Dean case might do it for you."

"Thanks, David. In the next hour would help."

"We'll do our best." They hung up.

He asked Ted to bring in the files on the Bradford and Dean cases along with all the interviews. Eight-thirty. Time to call the kitchen.

"Julie speaking. What can I get ya?"

"What're you doing here at this hour?" asked Jack.

"Waiting for you to order your supper so I can go home. What'll it be?"

"What's the special?"

"Lieutenant, you know very well it's an enormous burger prepared anyway you desire."

"I'll have two, both your choice, gorgeous."

"I happen to have a sauce we've been working on just for you. I'll serve them open faced with a gang of home fries. The side salad will provide some healthy nourishment. Promise you'll eat it all?"

"Of course."

"And to drink?" asked Julie.

"Just a second. Ted, have you eaten?"

"Yeah, I'm okay."

"Care for coffee?"

Ted nodded.

"A pot of coffee please. And, Julie, as soon as it's done, get out of here will you?"

"See you tomorrow, boss man."

Jack hung up and chuckled. "Julie's something else isn't she?"

"She's working as many hours as we are. What a woman."

Ted briefed Jack on the Britain interview. Unfortunately there was little to help with the new investigations. She wasn't wearing a watch and with no view of the outside, passage of time became impossible to monitor. Having lost all track of time she only knew he had fed her, probably two or three times a day. She could not confirm actual dates or times when Ott was in the cabin or away.

They pored over the files, concentrating on the McCords. Both had alibis the day the Dean corpse was moved to Nielsen's house. Billy had been at the store, most of the day. Frank was in the Cities, according to Jean.

"Let's lean on him. Find out who he has to corroborate that trip."

"The other two guys also had opportunity, Lieutenant. Ledyard and Sherman both had uncorroborated alibis for those hours."

"True, but Ledyard was home in bed the night Bradford was killed. Geoff, the bartender, said he left the bar after nine and his wife claimed he was fast asleep by ten, too drunk to get out of bed in the middle of the night. I believe we're looking for one killer, which would rule him out. Besides, the night Cheryl went missing Ledyard was definitely at home. She was abducted a little after nine and he was already in bed."

There was a knock on the door. Dinner had arrived.

"All you guys need is some candles and wine."

"Only if you'd join us, Julie."

"The offers are always from married guys like you. Why don't you get some singles up here, Lieutenant?"

"Can't find anyone good enough for you, Julie."

She plunked the tray down, gave the typical Julie glare, turned on her heel, and left the room.

They smiled. The entire team had come to respect Julie and recognize her hard work and big heart. A tough exterior but a softie inside.

"And what about Sherman?" asked Ted.

"We've only his word for the night Bradford was put away but when Cheryl went missing he was with his wife. They were watching a movie at home before she left for work. I tend to believe her. That leaves the McCords."

"Well, Billy was missing for a couple of hours that night," said Ted.

"Yeah. We also had him in here for questioning. I thought at the time, if he's lying, he's one hell of an actor. And Frank claims he was just off on his own in the storm, thinking."

"It's too close to call, Lieutenant. They both fit the profile. Neither has an iron clad alibi for either killing."

"David has some evidence for us — we're looking for a match of fibers left in a car or picked up from the seat. Maybe we'll get lucky."

"We know she had been in Billy's truck. The K-9 unit picked that up and he admitted it."

"Yeah, but he has vinyl seat coverings. David confirms there were fibers left on her coat picked up from some foreign material. The seats in Frank's truck are cloth. What if there's a match?"

"And what if there isn't? She could've been in other cars."

Matt was at the door. "Both guys are moving, Lieutenant."

"What're they using?"

"Frank left the store on his snowmobile. Billy's in his truck. He left the Nielsen house with the two McCord kids. Looks like he's headed to Frank's house."

"Have them stay close."

"10-4, Lieutenant."

It was going to be a long night.

Chapter 78

FRANK WAS PLEASED he'd taken the snowmobile. It would give him a ready-made excuse for Jean if he arrived home later than expected. He just had to travel the trails for a while to unwind.

He was looking forward to his date with Janice. The experience usually rid him of the pressure he felt — practically every day recently. He'd ride around a bit, no need to rush this. She'd be waiting, as always. It was peaceful at this time of night with only the occasional skier or snowmobile out.

He left the trail and cut through a wooded area that backed onto Janice's apartment building. It afforded a convenient place for his snowmobile where he could park, sight unseen. Janice had given him a key to the back entrance thus avoiding the risk of running into anyone. He knew too many people in Wilton and wouldn't want to be seen here at this late hour.

He shunned the elevator to use the fire exit stairs. Janice's apartment was on the fourth floor, conveniently located at the rear of the building. A quick peek revealed the hallway was deserted. Frank knocked on her door. Janice invited him in but seemed rather cool.

He tossed his coat on a chair. "What's up, Jan?"

"We have to talk, Frank"

"Yeah, well let's have a drink first."

"I don't think so."

"You don't think so. We have to talk. What the hell's going on?"

"I've been thinking about this for a long time now, Frank. You and me, it just isn't right. I don't want you to be upset."

"What's there to be upset about?"

"Well, it's about your family, Frank."

"They're okay, Jan. I take good care of Jean and the kids."

"Dammit, Frank, that's ridiculous and you know it."

"I was only kidding. Look, did you have a bad day or something?"

"Let's not make light of this."

"You mean a lot to me, Jan. With all I go through, it wouldn't be possible without you."

"This isn't right and you know it."

"Things might change."

"No, Frank, they won't. We have to stop seeing each other." The tears started. Janice reached for a Kleenex.

Frank moved to the bar, picked up a wine glass, and turned to face Janice. "Red or white?"

"Neither, Frank. It's over for us and I'd like you to leave." She couldn't stop trembling.

He glared at her. The veins on his forehead stood out and there was a sudden crack. The wine glass shattered. Pieces fell to the floor and he hurled the rest of the glass at the wall. He didn't seem to notice that his hand was bleeding.

This only strengthened Janice's resolve. "Get to the kitchen sink, Frank, you've cut yourself."

He looked at his hand. There was a small piece of glass imbedded in his forefinger. Reluctantly he followed Janice to the kitchen where she ran cold water on the cuts. Frank picked out the sliver of glass. More blood flowed.

"You'll need stitches for that, Frank. You should go to the hospital now."

"To hell with any..."

The intercom buzzed.

"You expecting anyone?"

"No," said Janice.

"Don't answer it."

"Frank, take this towel and leave. I'm going to answer that call."

"No, you're not. I'm not through with you yet." He pushed her against the wall and grabbed her face with his injured hand. Blood flowed from the wound, down her neck, soaking her blouse. He squeezed so hard more blood spurted from his hand. Janice's face was contorted from the vicious hold.

"Frank, let go. You're hurting me."

"I'm hurting you? And what're you doing? All of a sudden you want to throw me out."

"It isn't like that. Please stop, Frank."

There was a loud knock on the door. They both froze.

"Let go of me!"

The knocking continued.

"Tell them to go away," said Frank. His eyes were glazed.

Janice raked his hand with her nails, tearing at the open wound. Frank flinched, releasing his grip. She ran to the door and yanked it open.

Billy McCord walked into the apartment.

"What the hell are you doing here?" asked Frank

"What happened to your hand?"

"Nothing, just a small cut."

"I want you to leave with me, Frank."

"And how'd you know I was here?"

"Your snowmobile is parked where it always is when you come here."

"What're you, a detective or something?"

"I should've done something a long time ago," said Billy.

"You pretending you've known about us for a while?"

"I'm not as smart as you but I knew about this. You're leaving, Frank. We're going…to see Jean."

Frank stared at Janice. "First you, now my own brother. You two in cahoots about this?"

Billy, who seemed embarrassed, lowered his head and stared at the floor.

Frank was on Billy before his brother had a chance. The first blow to the solar plexus doubled him over. The next caught him high on the forehead. Billy fell to the floor.

Frank took one menacing look at Janice before leaving.

He slammed the door, reached the rear exit, and flew down the stairs.

Chapter 79

JACK, AL, AND TED WERE HUDDLED in the statement room reviewing the recent interviews with the McCords. Agents had met Frank at the store shortly after eight when he was in the process of closing up. He didn't like being detained but had no choice. Billy McCord, who'd just dropped the kids off at Jean's, was more cooperative. The latest report had Frank entering an apartment building. The tenant list was being checked. Billy McCord seemed headed in the same direction.

"Frank doesn't have a decent alibi for either of the nights the teenagers were murdered," said Al. "Same goes for the afternoon Dean's body was moved."

"Does his story fit with Jean's?" asked Jack.

"Most of it. The night Bradford got it he was out late but back home just after midnight. Jean was asleep, so not wanting to disturb her, he bunked out in the den. That part is corroborated by Jean who found him there the following morning. There's only his word on when he got home."

"And the night of the Dean case?"

"Claimed he was at the funeral home for the visitation but left at eight. Took Jean home then went to the store. He had a lot of paper work to catch up on and it was after eleven when he finished. Jean was sleeping by the time he got back. Again it's only his word." Al checked his notes.

"The day the body was moved, he drove to the Cities. He met with three of his suppliers and was back in Wilton by five. He gave us the names but said you couldn't reach them on a Saturday night."

"Did he have any of their home information?" asked Ted.

"No. He got quite upset when we asked him. Claimed he knows them only through business and how in the hell could we expect him to know their home phone numbers."

"Ted, have Matt get on this right away. Check the business info first. If they have a security system there'll be home contacts. What have you got on Billy?"

"Much the same. Home both nights but nobody to verify it. Body moving day he was at the store. He did take an hour off to ride around on his snowmobile. Said he just wanted to unwind."

"Are we discarding Sherman and Ledyard, Lieutenant?" asked Ted.

"Who do you like, Al?"

"It has to be one of the McCords."

"Ted?"

"I agree. There's more on Billy but that doesn't rule out Frank. Why not set them up with Jason? You never know what'll happen when a guy takes a polygraph test."

"We don't have enough to bring them in, so it'll have to be voluntary," said Al.

"It's worth a try," said Jack. "Jason's good at reading people and getting information that's more valuable than the test itself."

"Like what, Lieutenant?" asked Al.

"He's able to read a person through their body language and speech pattern. If it appears they're lying, he'll go for an inculpatory statement, which of course is admissible in court. Jason has the suspect sit in a chair that's fixed to the floor, but his chair will be on castors allowing him to move right in on the guy."

"I know the technique," said Ted. "The polygraph technician will say things like, 'We know you didn't mean to do it — you'll feel a lot better if you tell us about it,' stuff like that. Gets right in his face."

"It might be difficult tonight," said Jack, "so let's approach them tomorrow in the store."

The phone rang. "Lieutenant, McCord's moving again," said Matt.

"Which McCord?"

"Frank. They said he was in a real hurry."

"Who did he visit in there?"

"We just got that info. Billy McCord went into the same building and we took a chance sending one of the agents in with him. Apparently Billy didn't recognize the tail. He got off at the fourth floor, went to the apartment of a Miss Janice Bertrand. There was some shouting, then Frank came flying out of the apartment. Didn't even notice our agent who was still in the hallway."

"I know her," said Jack. "She and Ingrid Nielsen are close friends."

"Frank's on his snowmobile heading back to the same trail he used before. We've got three different snowmobiles monitoring him."

"Keep on him," said Jack. "What about Billy?"

"He's still in the Bertrand apartment."

"Thanks, Matt."

The three officers looked at each other.

"Janice Bertrand, she's quite the number," said Jack.

"You think Billy's doing something there?" asked Al.

"I can't see that, but suppose Frank's marriage isn't as solid as we thought."

"But he's gone and Billy's still there. She's not cozy with both brothers is she?" asked Al.

Jack shrugged. "What's the connection and why were they arguing?"

A light snow had started to fall. With the overcast conditions the helicopters would be grounded. That would hamper the surveillance.

It was ten o'clock but the night was only beginning.

Chapter 80

CAM WENT TO THE MOTEL. With the news about Mrs Britain and a possible second killer, he'd set up a meeting with Jack. Finding Mrs Britain was welcome news. Not only was she alive, it removed the burden of deciding what to do with Al's offer.

It wasn't like him to accept money that way but the amount of cash involved in the offer had made him think twice. It was over which was a relief.

Jack joined him in the command center to brief him on the changes, starting with Ott's note. "It's a possibility we can't ignore. We've got both McCords under surveillance."

"If Ott's telling the truth I don't see this second guy as a threat to the lake people," said Cam. "He seems to have a different agenda. I'll talk to them first but maybe they don't need us anymore."

"Let them make the decision. But if this guy's nuts enough to kill two teenagers, then move a body in the middle of the day, who knows what he might do? Before they decide make those facts known to them."

"Many of them are at the Britain's celebrating her return so I'll go over there right now. Meanwhile, our guys are still on patrol."

"Remind them to stay alert, Cam. We've still got a dangerous situation here."

"I understand."

"Let us know if you're staying on."

"Will do, Jack." He took the four-by-four to the Britain's.

Al greeted Cam at the door. "I want to apologize for the other day, Cam. I put you in an awkward situation. Needless to say, this is a far better solution."

"Amen. How is Mrs Britain?"

"Amazingly well. Come and see for yourself."

It was a happy but subdued group that was gathered at the Britain's. Cam offered his best wishes before asking for a meeting.

"You're probably aware of the latest news. Kyle Ott, the man who abducted Mrs Britain, is dead. He confessed to the murders of Mrs Martin and Mrs Michael but denied having anything to do with the teenagers, Bradford and Dean. If this is true, there's still a threat to the community."

"But if he's putting us on and was involved in all the killings, there's no further danger," said Ed Chapman.

"Correct," said Cam.

"However, if he didn't kill the teenagers," said Max Baird, "there's another killer on the loose."

"Who doesn't appear to have any interest in us, Colonel," said Ed.

"How can you say that?" asked Max. "Do we know how he chooses his victims? Just because his first two are youngsters, what does that tell us?"

"What do you think, Cam?" asked Al.

"If there's a second killer we don't know yet who it is or what his motives might be. It'd only be a guess."

"I say we keep Fletcher's group here till this is resolved," said Max. "There's still a risk and we could use the protection."

"We've had enough problems here," said Al. "I for one want them to stay."

"The police would take the same position," said Cam.

The group agreed.

"We'll maintain the same patrols," said Cam. "Alert your neighbors to exercise caution until we have the killer in custody."

Once again the lake residents faced the sobering realization that life was not back to normal.

Chapter 81

JANICE DIDN'T KNOW WHAT TO DO. Call the police? How could she explain the evening? Billy had collapsed on the sofa and was staring into space. Ingrid was the only one she could talk to. She dialed her number.

"Hi, Ingrid. It's awful here."

"What happened, Janice?"

Janice went through the evening's events.

"How's Billy?"

"I don't know. He's not saying anything. I'm worried."

"Janice, it's Billy. He won't hurt you."

"I don't know, Ingrid."

"Well call the police then."

"I don't want to do that either."

"Janice, you have to do something."

"I'm afraid to, Ingrid."

"Listen, if you're that worried go downstairs to the lobby. I'll come over right away and we'll take care of this together."

"I'd like that."

"I'll see you in ten minutes." They hung up.

She turned to find Billy standing behind her. Janice didn't like the look in his eyes.

"I'm going to need your help."

"What do you mean?"

Billy swayed, almost lost his balance, before lurching back onto the sofa. He just sat there shaking his head.

Janice backed up against the wall, her legs were trembling. She had to find a way to leave. This was scary and she had no idea what Bill was going to do.

"I'll be okay in a minute, Janice. I'd like a glass of water."

This was her chance. Just get to the lobby and wait for Ingrid. He was between her and the door but didn't look alert. She moved toward the front door.

"The kitchen's the other way, Janice."

She froze. Should she run for it? Surely in his condition he couldn't catch her.

"Just a glass of water, Janice."

She hesitated, then turned to the kitchen. Why was she so frightened? Maybe she should have called the police.

Janice filled a glass with water. She stared at the blood stains left from Frank's cut. What an evening this had turned out to be. The tears rolled down her face. Somehow she took the glass of water into the living room. Billy hadn't moved.

He took the glass.

"Billy, I'm sorry about Frank and me."

"Yeah."

He sipped the water. What was going on in his head? He was bigger than Frank, probably more powerful. She rubbed her cheek, remembering the force of Frank's hold earlier. She knew Billy doted on the children. What were his thoughts about her? Was he just mentally slow, or was there some other imbalance? He was an enigma.

"I didn't want to hurt anyone, Billy."

"But you did."

"I'm sorry."

"You're...sorry."

The look in his eyes was terrifying. She couldn't believe Billy McCord was capable of being this angry.

"Billy, it takes two, you know." Janice wanted desperately to leave. She looked at the door.

"Don't think about it, Janice. I need something from you."

"What do you want, Billy?" She tried to speak calmly but it didn't work. Janice buried her head in her hands and sobbed.

"Just give me the keys to your snowmobile."

"What?"

"It's the blue Arctic Cat out back, isn't it?"

"Y — yes."

"Where are the keys?"

"Hanging beside the phone in the kitchen."

"Get them."

Janice retrieved the keys and brought them to Billy. Could he really be leaving? Is this all he wanted?

He took the keys and studied Janice. The buzzer sounded.

"I'll see you later." Billy turned and let himself out.

Janice stood there, stunned. The buzzer sounded again. She went to the intercom.

"Yes?"

"It's me. Are you all right?"

"Come up please, Ingrid."

Chapter 82

IT WAS AFTER ELEVEN when Jack received the news from Matt. Billy had left the Bertrand apartment and taken a snowmobile, yet he'd arrived in his truck.

"Elmer and I are going to Bertrand's apartment to find out what went on," said Jack. "How many snowmobiles do we have over there?"

"There's three out on the trail with Frank and one tailing Billy," said Matt.

"Get two more on Billy and use the same technique. Make it look like they're just out there for a Saturday night cruise, but stay on both of them."

Jack checked in with Matt and told him they were going to the apartment. "David Folk will be sending me some new evidence, Matt. Let me know as soon as you hear from him."

"Will do, Lieutenant."

They arrived at Janice's apartment fifteen minutes later. Ingrid opened the door.

"Lieutenant, what are you doing here?"

"Miss Nielsen, this is Special Agent Holm. May we come in?"

"Uh...sure. Janice, the police are here."

Janice came out of the kitchen. She was still wearing the bloodstained blouse.

"Good evening Miss Bertrand, this is Special Agent Holm. We'd like to talk to you about tonight."

She didn't move.

"Janice, I think it's time to bring this out," said Ingrid. "Let's sit down."

Janice still didn't move.

"We understand Frank and Billy McCord were here earlier," said Jack. "We need to know what went on."

"This is a private matter, Lieutenant, and I don't think it's any of your business."

"What you don't realize is they're both under suspicion of murder. This is our business."

"What do you mean...murder?" asked Ingrid.

"Just what the Lieutenant said and we don't have a lot of time," said Elmer. "Now tell us what happened here."

Both women were shocked. Ingrid led Janice to the sofa. "You better start, Janice."

Janice went through the night's events, interrupted by her sobbing.

"Has Frank ever mistreated you physically?"

"No."

"Never?"

"I said, no."

"You said you were terrified. He was hurting you. If he hadn't been interrupted, how far would he have gone?" asked Jack.

"He was upset. We've been...dating for some time. I'd just told him we were through. He would've cooled off, I'm sure."

"But he was ready to take it out on Billy, wasn't he? He was still angry."

"He loved me. He wouldn't hurt me." Janice looked at Ingrid as if to ask for confirmation.

"Why did Billy come here?"

"I can answer that, Lieutenant," said Ingrid. "Billy had supper at my place tonight and I told him about Frank and Janice."

"You...what," said Janice.

"I was just trying to help, Janice. I was worried. If Frank became violent Billy might help. And he did."

"Billy scared me more than Frank," said Janice.

"What do you mean by that?" asked Jack.

Janice broke down again. "Oh, he was just different, and I was upset."

"Back to Frank and Billy," said Elmer. "One of them is a dangerous killer. Where do you think they were going?"

"I have no idea," said Janice. "But if one of them is a killer, it's certainly not Frank."

"Frank threatened you and he's not dangerous?"

"I told you. He was upset."

"Why were you afraid of Billy?" asked Elmer.

"He seemed distracted, sort of out of it and then he just asked for the keys to my snowmobile. But then he became angry, said he'd be back. That frightened me. Why would he want to come back here, unless it was to hurt me?"

Elmer looked at Jack.

"Miss Nielsen, you believe Billy came here mainly to protect Miss Bertrand?"

Ingrid looked down and fussed with her watch. It was several seconds before she replied. "I've never liked Frank McCord. He's a womanizer, but murder, I don't know. I'm not qualified to understand killers."

"I was asking about Billy, Miss Nielsen," said Jack.

Again a nervous pause.

"Miss Nielsen?"

"I know you all blame Billy but I just can't believe he could kill anyone."

"But you're not telling us everything," said Jack.

Ingrid sighed. "I have to admit he was different tonight. When we discussed Frank's affair with Janice he reacted in a way I've never seen. It bothered me. Still, I can't believe I could be wrong about someone who has been a friend for so many years."

"What was he wearing, Miss Bertrand?"

Janice frowned. "Just normal clothing, a winter jacket."

"He didn't have snowmobile gear with him," said Jack.

"No. Why is that important, Lieutenant?"

"You're going out in this weather on a snowmobile, it's twenty-five below — wouldn't you want to be dressed properly?"

The women looked at the officers.

"He's on a mission," said Jack. "He didn't stop to think about what he was wearing. He didn't care. Just left and took your snowmobile."

Chapter 83

HE CRUISED SLOWLY along the trail. Tiny snow flakes danced through the beam of his headlight. Winter nights like this were magical for him but it was little consolation tonight.

He had no sense of the cold, as if impervious to the elements. Troubles dominated his thoughts. Where was he going from here? He needed time to sort it out.

It'd all started so innocently. He'd been captivated by Cheryl Dean. She became an obsession for him. Then he watched in frustration as that Bradford kid romanced her, right in front of him. Every time they were together in the store, you could see the chemistry between them. She flirted openly with him. How far had their relationship gone? He could only guess.

Then Bradford tried to make out with Mrs Cooper. Not only that, he ransacked the store. That did it. With the lake killer around it seemed like a good opportunity to take care of him. Maybe the police would blame the other guy.

Cheryl was different. He'd wanted her for so long, it was like a dream come true, even if she did resist. The memories flooded back. Maybe he should go back to Janice's apartment.

He felt the need for speed. He opened the throttle and accelerated rapidly. The machine bore into the night at an ever increasing speed.

Another snowmobile materialized as he rounded a curve at too great a speed. They nearly collided. He maintained his speed, cutting into the dark void. There'd been two figures on the snowmobile — both male? There was always an occasional snowmobiler on this trail but at this late hour on a Saturday night it was usually a single or a guy with a girl. The police usually traveled in pairs. Could they be out here and if so why?

They'd found Ott who was responsible for the killings. The word was that he'd been killed in a snowmobile accident and nobody got to him before he died. The entire town was talking about it, relieved that the case was closed. But was it? Why had the police questioned him tonight? Would they think there was more than one killer?

He didn't want to think about these issues. The fact is, he didn't know what to think. He caromed around another turn and started up a gentle rise in the trail. He had the throttle wide open but he wasn't moving fast enough. He willed it to speed up. The hill was winning. He had coaxed the maximum speed out of the machine.

He couldn't continue his life this way. The thoughts and memories were taunting him. How was it going to end?

He reached the top of the hill and with the level terrain the machine began to accelerate again. Soon he was hurtling along the trail, feeling better now that he was going faster, as if the increased speed would help solve his dilemma. The tree line rushed by, snow flew wildly, and the machine bucked violently. Despite his size, the turbulent ride had him bouncing. He held on and eventually slowed down.

It was time to leave Wilton. It was beyond him to understand the events of the last two weeks. Hopefully they'd eventually fade from his memory.

He was excited with the prospects of a new life. After all he deserved it. He'd worked hard all his adult years. And he had plenty of money saved that nobody knew about. It'd been wise to start salting cash away.

He headed for town. It wouldn't be long now.

Chapter 84

JACK AND ELMER RETURNED TO THE MOTEL to check on the surveillance teams. The McCords were being monitored. Both were driving erratically.

"Matt, anything from David?" asked Jack.

"Not yet, Lieutenant."

Jack thought of calling home but it was past one in the morning. He decided not to and headed for the restaurant. No one was there, but the motel staff, mainly Julie, ensured there was always a selection of sandwiches available in the fridge, as well as soups and other assorted snacks that could be cooked in the microwave. They knew the police were on twenty-four hour duty and needed this service.

Al and Ted joined him.

"What's the master chef making tonight?" asked Al.

"My favorite late night food. Sardines on toast."

"Ugh," said Ted.

"Don't knock it. Sardines on well done toast with malt vinegar and pepper make one tasty snack. Anyone interested?"

"I've just eaten thanks, Lieutenant," said Ted. "I'll settle for coffee."

"Same for me," said Al. "But I'm going to have a piece of Julie's blueberry pie. Hear she made it today."

They sat at one of the tables, set by Julie.

Jack was the last to sit down. "That Julie thinks of everything doesn't she? Let's get her a gift when we're finished here."

"Good idea, Lieutenant," said Al. "You think it's soon, don't you?"

Jack nodded.

"Have you ever had one like this, Lieutenant?" asked Al. "I mean, you've got two solid suspects here."

"Not this long into a case. Let's go over those files again. Maybe we'll find something."

When they entered the command center, Matt was just getting off the phone. "We've traced two guys from those companies McCord met with in the Cities."

"The day Dean's body was moved?" asked Al.

"Yeah," said Matt. "They did see McCord that day. The last guy wasn't too happy about being called this late."

"What time were the appointments?" asked Jack.

"First was at eleven-thirty. It was over by noon. The second was from twelve-fifteen to one o'clock."

"They must have been right beside each other."

"Yeah, they're in the same complex," said Matt. "We haven't been able to find the other company. McCord had given us three names."

"Suppose there's no third company and he had only two appointments," said Jack. "He would've left the Cities at one and had time to get back here to move the body before Nielsen got home."

"Or the third meeting might've been his first of the day, still giving him enough time. He did say he was gone all day."

"But if he did have a meeting after one o'clock there'd be no way he could've moved the body," said Ted.

"We can't find anything on that last company," said Matt. "Maybe it doesn't exist."

"Stay on it, Matt."

They laid out the files of all the interviews. Jack had diagramed the events chronologically on a large wall chart. The three agents went over the material. They'd been on the job since seven this morning, more than eighteen hours now. The fact remained, it could be either McCord.

"Why don't we bring Frank in, Lieutenant?" asked Al. "He did assault the Bertrand woman and Billy. At least we'd have one in here for a day, might get a polygraph test out of him."

Jack looked at the chart. "Maybe you're right. We keep the tail on Billy and see what we get from Frank. Is Jason Wills, the polygraph tech, here?"

"Yeah, he's my roomie," said Ted. "He hit the sack earlier."

"Matt, get on the horn to the guys tailing Frank McCord. I want to talk to one of them."

"10-4, Lieutenant."

Seconds later the lights went out, plunging the entire motel into darkness. Assorted curses were heard as the agents scrambled for flashlights and candles.

"Al, check with the night manager about this black out. They must have an emergency generator or something to get some power on here."

"Will do, Lieutenant."

Jack worked his way to Matt and the radios. "Are the lines still open, Matt?"

"Yeah, so far."

"Who do you have tailing Frank?"

"Adams, Williams, and Munford."

"Get Adams for me will you?" Jack knew Adams was a seasoned veteran. He'd be best suited for the job at hand.

"I've got Adams for you, Lieutenant."

Jack took the call. "Dan, are you on Frank McCord?"

"Yeah, Lieutenant. We just passed him off to another unit a few minutes ago."

"What about Billy McCord?"

"Last I heard he was on the same trail but a couple of miles from here."

"We're going to bring Frank in on an assault charge. I want you to handle that."

"Okay, Lieutenant."

"Make sure all three of your units are on hand when you confront him. One of those guys is a killer and could possibly be armed."

"10-4, Lieutenant."

"How's the visibility out there?"

"Not bad. There's only small flurries so far. Let's hope it stays that way or stops."

"Call in as soon as you've made contact. Alert the others that we have a power failure here. We'll let you know when it's restored." They signed off.

Jack looked outside. Light snow continued and there wasn't a light to be seen. He knew there'd been considerable damage during the storm last week with several electrical failures. With these severe temperatures one could only hope power would be back on soon.

Chapter 85

SPECIAL AGENT DAN ADAMS wheeled his snowmobile around and headed back to find Frank McCord. His partner, Chris Talbot, was in only his second year with the B.C.A. but had four years policing in the Cities with the municipal force. Despite his youth and inexperience, he showed a maturity and good sense beyond his years.

Adams briefed the other two units on the new mission.

Talbot had heard the conversation between his partner and Petersen. "How do you think McCord will react to this, Dan?"

"Hard to tell. I've met him twice in interviews and he doesn't seem that bad a guy. He's a little brusque, tries to be superior. Don't know if he's a killer but as the Lieutenant says, it has to be one of these guys."

"I saw him only once. I wouldn't want to take him on alone," said Chris.

"He's big and strong all right but he doesn't have the training we have."

Their earphones crackled into life.

"Hampster One this is Hampster Three."

"Come in, Three."

"We haven't seen McCord for several minutes now. He was headed back to town, then the last time we passed him, he turned around and slowed down."

"What's your position, Three?"

"Maybe a quarter mile north of the second concession road. You want us to go back after him?"

David Wickes

"Negative. We'll wait for Hampster Two before we overtake him. We're just crossing that road now so we'll have you in sight soon."

A few minutes later the first two units had hooked up. The agents waved at each other with Hampster Three executing a one-eighty and settling in behind Adams' vehicle.

"Hampster Two, this is Hampster One. Are you reading this?"

"Hampster Two here. Yeah we got it all. We're about a mile south of you. See you in a few minutes."

The first two vehicles accelerated to close in on Frank. The powerful machines skimmed over the trail which was remarkably smooth. The strong headlights shone through the tiny snow flakes, invading the dark night.

The six agents were geared up. They knew the assignment was critical and dangerous. It'd been a long two weeks and now it was nearing the end. In the middle of the night at twenty-five below zero, two brothers were on some kind of mission. One was a killer. Which one?

The radios were quiet. They'd covered a couple of miles and still no sign of Frank. They should've overtaken him by now. Adams was concerned.

"Three, didn't you say he had slowed down?"

"He had when we passed him. We should've overtaken him by now."

Both units increased their speed to the maximum. They flew over the trail. Hampster Two, who was well back, wouldn't catch up at this speed. Adams let them know.

Minutes passed, the trail was deserted. Ten minutes later there was still no sign of Frank McCord. He'd disappeared. They were at the point where the trail ended, leading out onto a small lake.

Adams pulled off to the side and was joined by Williams. "He was never up this far. We must have covered seven or eight miles by now."

"Dan, he must've left the trail. We'd definitely have seen him by now."

Dan nodded and called Dean Munford who still hadn't caught up to them. "Hampster Two, what's your position?"

"Still going north but haven't seen you or McCord. This is new territory for us."

"We've lost him. He's not on the trail. We'll have to double back and see if there's a side route he could've taken. We should meet you shortly."

"10-4."

Dan called Petersen. He wasn't going to be happy.

"Lieutenant, Adams here. We've temporarily lost McCord."

"What about Williams and Munford?"

"Williams had seen McCord turn around and head north again. That's when we joined up and went after him. We took the trail until it ended at a small lake. No sign of McCord. Munford was south of us. We've turned south again, looking for a spot where he could've turned off."

"Are there any side trails up there?"

"Not that we've seen, Lieutenant."

"How long would it take you to get back to town?"

"A good ten to fifteen minutes on the trail, but if you had to go through the brush, much longer."

"Any idea where Billy is?"

"Last we heard they were closer to town, that's south of where we are now. Maybe ten minutes away."

"Lieutenant, this is Hampster Four. Billy's just turned south and he's really moving."

Chapter 86

JACK WAS AT THE WALL MAP. Fortunately, power had been restored. The locations of the McCords were marked as accurately as the information would allow. They'd posted agents at Frank's house in the event he decided to go home and the Bertrand apartment was also covered.

Units were positioned on the outskirts of Wilton, monitoring the areas where the snowmobilers would probably return. The fact that Frank McCord had slipped the surveillance produced a nervousness at the command center. Had he realized there was a tail on him or had he merely chosen a route known to him but not obvious to the agents?

"The sooner we get these guys with our polygraph tech the better, Lieutenant," said Al.

"Yeah. But there's no point in hauling them in tonight. They may have been drinking and they're definitely psyched up. Matt, any word from David Folk?"

"Not a thing, Lieutenant."

It was nearly two in the morning but the center was alive with activity. They could sense the case was winding down. Monitor the McCords till morning, then bring them in. The radio lines to the agents were open and on speakers. The static and crackle invaded the room.

"Center, Hampster Four here."

"Go ahead, Four."

"Billy McCord has just left the trail. He's turned westward and is heading for town."

"When will he get to Wilton?" asked Jack.

"Maybe twenty minutes, Lieutenant. He must be in a hell of a hurry 'cause he's still going all out, close to seventy right now."

"Does he know you're tailing him?"

"I doubt it. He never looks back."

"Stay on him."

"10-4, Lieutenant."

"Hampster One, this is Center, do you read?"

"Center, this is One. Go ahead."

"Where's Frank McCord?"

"Still no contact, Lieutenant. We know approximately where he left the trail but that's it. It's like he disappeared into the brush. We haven't found any side trails off the main one."

"The west end of Wilton is covered so bring your unit back into town. Check in when you arrive."

The Center heard Hampster One instruct Two and Three to join him. More waiting.

Jack needed a snack to tide him over but didn't want to leave. As if he had read Jack's mind, Matt explained that one of the agents called from the restaurant to say that Julie had just arrived.

"That's unbelievable," said Jack. "How does she know when we need her?"

"You hungry again, Lieutenant?" asked Matt.

"I haven't had a bite for five or six hours."

That brought a chorus of guffaws and laughs from the agents. Jack ignored them and called Julie. "Where's the evening burger special?"

"First of all it isn't evening and secondly I've just arrived, you ingrate."

"Surprise me with one of your specials, darling."

"You want a burger at two o'clock in the morning?"

"There isn't any time of day when you can't enjoy a good burger and yours are first rate."

"Oh stop it. One special coming up. I suppose you want it delivered."

"That would be greatly appreciated. When can I expect it?"

"Soon, if you let me off this phone."

Jack smiled and hung up. Once again Julie was going out of her way to serve the troops. The exchange helped lighten the mood but didn't detract from the focus. A suspected killer roaming the night. Who is it and what's his agenda?

"Center, we have a visual on a snowmobile. He's in Willow Park, heading east onto a trail."

"Do you have an I.D.?"

"Yeah, it's Frank McCord. He's the guy with the red Yamaha isn't he?"

"That's him. What's he doing?"

"Just cruising, very slowly."

Jack looked at the blowup of Wilton. McCord was heading onto the trail that ran by the back of Ingrid Neilsen's house. "He could be headed for the Neilsen place. Do we have anyone over there?"

No response from the snowmobilers.

"Hampster Four, where's Billy?"

"We just lost him, Lieutenant. He left the trail, right into the brush."

"We could've used the choppers for this. What's the weather doing out there now?"

"Starting to clear, Lieutenant."

"Call the Bears, Matt. See if they can get airborne. Hampster Four, stay where you are, we're trying to get the choppers up."

"10-4, Lieutenant."

The room was silent again. It was as if they didn't want to make any noise. The phone rang. "Lieutenant, it's David Folk."

"David, what have you got?"

"A couple of morsels for you, Jack."

"Like what?"

"We found semen on Dean. We're running DNA testing now."

"Jesus, that'll do it."

"We've also checked the fibers on her coat."

"And?" asked Jack.

Jack listened while David explained the findings. He was nodding furiously.

Jack hung up and turned to Al Welsh. "Let's go."

"Where are you going, Lieutenant?" asked Matt.

Jack was already out of the room. He almost collided with Julie, who had his special on a tray.

"Lieutenant, I've got your burger."

"Later, sweetheart."

Chapter 87

INGRID HAD STAYED WITH JANICE, who mercifully had fallen asleep after taking a sedative. It was already two o'clock and Ingrid wanted to go home to take her dogs out.

"We don't want you going back there alone," said Agent Daley, who with another agent had remained in Janice's apartment.

"They can't stay inside all night."

"All right, I'll go with you. But I want you to pick up whatever you need and come back here for the night. We haven't got enough men to cover two places."

They drove through the deserted streets in Daley's cruiser. Wilton seemed so peaceful with the town tucked in for the night. It was anything but for those chasing a suspected killer.

The dogs were all over Ingrid as soon as they entered. Bentley remained aloof as he checked out the B.C.A. agent.

"I'll take the dogs out while you get your things organized."

"Okay. They'll stay in the backyard with you." She showed Daley to the back door.

Ingrid went into her bedroom and laid out a change of clothes. The house was eerily quiet. In the middle of the night, quiet always seemed accentuated. Like now. Ghostly still. She'd heard the dogs yelping as they ran out of the house. Now all was silent. It was unnerving. She felt some movement behind her and wheeled around. Nothing but the vacant house.

She moved quickly out of the bedroom, found nothing out of the ordinary in the kitchen or den, and went to the bathroom to pack toiletries. With a policeman and the dogs outside, there was nothing to worry about. Still, the events of the past evening wouldn't leave her. It was hard to believe Billy or Frank was involved in the killings but the police were confident that one was the murderer. And from what Janice said, both were acting strangely last night.

She filled two vanity cases with assorted cosmetics. It would have been easier to have Janice stay with her but once the sedative had taken effect she wouldn't wake up for several hours. The back door opened and she knew the dogs would frantically search the house till they found her.

Ingrid picked up her cosmetic bags and turned off the bathroom light. Where were the dogs?

"Agent Daley?"

"No, Ingrid, it's not Agent Daley."

Chapter 88

HE MANEUVERED THE SNOWMOBILE carefully. The snow had stopped and the cloud condition was now scattered. Bright moonlight peeked through, creating shadows of the tall, bare trees, casting them across the snow-covered landscape. They were as clear and well defined as those produced by sunlight, yet it was two-thirty in the morning.

How long had he been cruising around these woods? Hours. He thought he knew what must be done but wasn't sure. Why was it so confusing? Something was controlling him and he didn't know how to stop it.

He entered the house through the back door. His brother was already there.

Ingrid was stunned. "Billy, Frank. What's going on here?"

"I'm here to help Frank. There won't be any more problems."

"What the hell are you talking about?" asked Frank.

"I'm sorry, Frank, but I mean it. You have to listen to me."

"I have to listen to you? I've been protecting you for years and now *you're* going to help *me*?"

"I think you know what this is all about."

"Billy, I want you to relax and think about this. You're the one with a problem. Haven't I always been there for you?"

"Don't try to mix me up, Frank. You need help and I'm going to see that you get it. It's not too late."

Frank inched forward. "Billy, it's me you're talking to. When did I ever do anything to you?"

"Don't come any closer." Billy drew a gun and leveled it at Frank. "I want you to come outside with me. Everything will be all right."

"You're nuts."

"Don't say that." Billy's angry voice startled Ingrid.

Billy shifted his feet — seemed embarrassed. Then in a softer voice. "The police are here. They'll help us."

"Help us? You have lost it. What do you think they're going to do? They don't know anything about you and me."

"I'll tell them," said Billy. "I can explain it all."

"What're you doing with a gun?" asked Ingrid.

"I had to make sure this time and I wasn't going to take any chances."

"Will you two stop it? Please."

"Billy's lost it, Ingrid. You have to talk some sense into him. This is dangerous."

"Ingrid, it's not that way. Frank has...some problems. I have to save him."

"Save him from what?"

"This is nonsense, Ingrid. Billy's not in control right now. Give me the gun, Billy, and we'll discuss this sensibly."

"No, Frank. Don't try and talk me out of this. I've known about you for a long time. Now it's over."

"What do you mean by this, Billy?" asked Ingrid. "You certainly don't need a gun to talk to Frank."

"Yes I do."

"Why, for God's sake?"

"He's killed some people."

"Knock it off, Billy. You're the killer, not me."

"And, Ingrid, you know about Janice."

"Billy, just give me the gun. Everything will be all right."

"Don't move, Frank. Just don't move."

"One of you is a murderer?" Ingrid looked frantically from Frank to Billy.

"Don't listen to him, Ingrid," said Frank. "If we leave, he'll shoot me then come back for you."

"I'd never hurt you, Ingrid. But Frank is not well, we have..."

He never finished the sentence. Frank flew at him, knocking the gun out of his hand. Billy's head struck the baseboard, stunning him. Frank pummeled his brother.

"Stop it Frank."

Frank leaned back, still astride Billy. "I had to make sure we were safe, Ingrid."

"I'll get the police."

"Let's wait a minute. Everything will be okay now. Just want to catch my breath."

Ingrid watched as Frank rolled to a sitting position.

He stared at the gun in his lap.

Chapter 89

INGRID WAS TERRIFIED. Which brother was telling the truth? She was afraid to move but knew she had to think fast. The dogs were yelping at the back door.

"I have to let my dogs in, Frank."

"Not just now."

"What's happened to Agent Daley? He was with the dogs."

"You've never liked me, have you Ingrid?"

"That's not true, Frank."

"That's not true, Frank. Who do you think you're kidding?"

Ingrid couldn't speak. She tried to swallow but there was no saliva.

"You were always so fond of Billy but now you're not sure. Maybe he's a killer. What would you think then? Maybe you'd find time for me."

"I couldn't do that."

"I thought so."

"It's not what you think. It's because I respect your marriage."

"Oh, so that's it. A moralist. I can see through you, Ingrid. You've got a fine body, and that voice of yours...I bet you're really something."

She didn't want to listen to this but she had to keep him talking. Surely the police would get here soon.

"Did you kill those kids?"

"You asking Billy or me?" He leered at her — continued to play with the gun.

Billy stirred. Frank looked at his brother. The dogs were now scratching the back door.

"Well, it's time for me to get out of here."

"You don't look too well, Frank. I could get some help for you."

"Could you now."

Silence again. Ingrid decided she'd have to act soon. Frank was unsteady. There was a glazed look in his eyes. Could she make a run for it?

A rush of cold air swept the house.

"Drop it, Frank," said Jack. "We have three guns on you."

Frank looked up to see Jack and two agents. He brought the gun up quickly. The sound of gunfire was deafening. A bullet caught Frank in the left eye, toppling him backwards. He died instantly.

Frank had got off one round. Jack stumbled forward, clutching his stomach, then went down. Within seconds the house was full of agents.

"Get an ambulance," said Al.

Chapter 90

JENNIFER WAS IN THE WAITING ROOM of the Minneapolis General. One of the police helicopters had transported Jack and medical aides to the Cities' major hospital. Sven had picked up Jennifer in the second chopper on the way to the Cities. David Folk had arrived first and witnessed the trauma team take over. Jack was in the operating room in minutes.

They'd acted quickly given Jack's condition. Facilities at the Wilton Hospital were inadequate to handle gunshot wounds and the doctors had said the first hour was critical, the 'golden hour' as it's called. Two circumstances worked in Jack's favor. The Sheriff's helicopters were still in Wilton and they'd succeeded in getting Jack to the General in time. The leading B.C.A. surgeon, Dr Solursh, was available and he headed the operating team along with two other surgeons.

Jack was still in surgery. The bullet from Frank McCord's gun had caught him in the stomach. Jennifer wanted to know all the details of what had transpired at the McCord house. She was going on nervous energy and had to occupy her thoughts.

"We were close, Jack knew that," said Al. "Then David Folk called to confirm what Jack had believed for some time. They finally had the proof to nail Frank."

"And what was that?" asked Jennifer.

"When David discovered fibers on Cheryl's coat, he narrowed them down to those from a car or truck seat. Jack had our forensic team go over Frank's truck. They struck gold. Not only did the fibers from the seat match but they found fibers from her coat in the truck."

"That only proves she'd been in his truck," said Jennifer, "but not necessarily on the day she was killed."

"That's true, but they also found traces of Cheryl's blood there. Apparently she nicked her hand getting out of the truck leaving stains on the side panel of the door. There was a small tear in her coat pocket caused by the door frame. A tiny fragment of her coat was lodged in the door. That meant she had tried to get out of his truck in a hurry. They were sure Cheryl had tried to escape."

"So it had to be Frank."

"We still didn't know but there was a DNA report coming that would clinch it. When Frank fired at Jack, we didn't need the DNA."

A nurse entered the room and Jennifer started.

"Anything we can get for you?" she asked.

"Jennifer?" asked Sven.

"No thanks. Do you have any information for us?"

The nurse shrugged apologetically. "Sorry, not yet."

"He's in good shape, Jennifer," said Sven. "And he's tough. He'll come through."

"Thank God he received a clean bill of health from Breckenridge."

"What was that?" asked Sven.

"I guess he didn't tell you. Jack had been experiencing chest pains for a while so he went through a series of stress tests recently. Dr Breckenridge was the cardiologist who ran the tests and concluded there were no heart problems. They determined the pains were muscular."

"He took those tests in the middle of this case?"

Jennifer nodded. "They've been operating for what...three hours now? How long can it take?"

Jennifer was strong but the strain was showing.

"Let me see if I can find one of our doctor friends," said Al. He left and found Jill Ingall in the coffee shop. She'd heard about Jack and had come to offer her support.

"How are things up there?" asked Jill.

"Jennifer could use a professional opinion."

"Absolutely."

When they arrived, Jennifer wasn't in the waiting room. Sven explained she'd just gone to freshen up and would be back in a few minutes.

"Thanks for staying around."

"I owe a lot to the Lieutenant," said Jill.

"Jennifer's getting more concerned because it's been more than three hours since he went in and still no word."

"That's not unusual for this type of surgery."

When Jennifer returned, Al introduced her to Dr Ingall.

Jill gave her a hug and they sat together. "Are you holding up okay?"

"Sort of. In his eighteen years on the force this is the first time he's been shot, so I guess we've been lucky. It doesn't make this any easier."

"No, once is too often," said Jill. "I can't comment on how the surgery is going but don't want you to be alarmed by the length of time. A bullet can do a lot of internal damage which will entail considerable repair work, but not necessarily be more critical or life threatening. There certainly is a risk factor involved in any surgical procedure but he's in very good hands. Dr Solursh is one of the best in the state, if not the nation."

A nurse came in and went directly to Jennifer. "Mrs Petersen, Dr Solursh will see you now."

Jennifer stood but her legs were rubbery. She willed herself to cross the room and head for the surgeon's office.

Chapter 91

HE DIDN'T RECOGNIZE the surroundings. There was an IV in one arm and something else connected to the other. He was alone. There were more gadgets and monitors than he'd ever seen. He knew it was a hospital and this was probably the Intensive Care Unit.

The memory of the incident at the McCord house flooded back. The deafening sounds of gun fire, the smell of cordite, and the sharp pain before he blacked out. When he heard the door open he turned his head.

The nurse smiled. "And how is our favorite patient today?"

"Where am I?"

"Sorry, that's my question."

"Huh?"

"Do you know your name?"

"Yes."

"What is it, please?"

Jack looked at her blankly. She was serious. "Jack Petersen."

"What day is it?"

"Sunday?"

"Good guess. Actually it's Tuesday. Do you know where you are?"

"Some place I'd rather not be."

"Well at least you have a sense of humor. That's good. You're in the I. C. U. in the Minneapolis General and there's some people anxious to talk to you. Welcome back, Lieutenant."

The nurse looked at several dials, took his blood pressure and temperature, and recorded the information on a clip board. "You're doing fine. See you."

Time seemed to stand still. He felt powerless, unable to move off the bed. He could hear people moving and talking outside the room.

Jennifer appeared to glide to his bedside. She reached down to kiss him, then placed her face gently to his. Not a word was said. He felt her warm tears. They remained in a soft embrace, neither wanting to let go.

Several minutes passed before Jennifer sat up. She held his face in her hands and bravely smiled. "Don't you ever do this again."

"I'll try not to," said Lieutenant Jack Petersen.